One Wish

Linda Lael Miller

One Wish

WHEELER
PUBLISHING, INC.
ROCKLAND, MA

★ AN AMERICAN COMPANY ★

Published in Large Print by arrangement with Pocket Books, a division of Simon & Schuster, Inc., in the United States and Canada.

Wheeler Large Print Book Series.

Set in 16 pt Plantin.

Library of Congress Cataloging-in-Publication Data

Miller, Linda Lael
   One wish/ Linda Lael Miller.
     p. (large print) cm.(Wheeler large print book series)
   ISBN 1-56895-878-1 (hardcover)
   1. Children of the rich—Fiction. 2. Ranch life—Fiction. 3. Drifters—Fiction. 4. Large type books.
I. Title. II. Series

[PS3563.I41373O54 2000]
813'.54—dc21   00-039917
                                                  CIP

For Mary Ann
cousin, sister and friend
with love

Jubilee, Washington Territory

April 1874

He lay still and silent on the dusty, rough board floor of his private refuge, a ramshackle tree house high in the leafy branches of an old oak. Every bruise and scratch on his small body throbbed in time with the thud of his heart. Below, Jubilee Creek rushed past, swollen with melted snow, muddy and contentious— and no damn place for a girl.

There she was, all the same, be-ruffled and be-ribboned, picking her dainty way along the steep, rocky bank, and murmuring to a doll in clothes fancier than any his ma could ever hope to wear. The girl was eight or so, by his reckoning—he was eleven himself and had no interest in the doings of females, as a general rule, but this one had invaded his territory, and might well discover his hideout. He held his breath, waiting for her to pass.

As if to spite him, she sat down on a fallen birch log, only a few feet away, and propped the doll beside her. A sort of desperate exasperation rose within him; he willed her to go on about her business. Instead, she peered intently at the water, then kicked off her small, glimmering shoes, stood up and, gathering the doll close, waded straight into the roiling, splinter-spiked scallops of shallow

1

water at the edge of the creek. She moved as purposefully as Moses leading the children of Israel toward the Red Sea.

A shout of irritated alarm charged up into his throat. Even a girl should be able to see that the water was too high, too swift, too angry for such foolery. *Come back*, he commanded silently, but of course she only went farther out, holding the doll in one arm and raising her skirts with the other hand.

He growled a swear word and hoisted himself onto his bare feet. "Get out of there!" he yelled, spitting the words one by one like the seeds of some bitter fruit. "Are you stupid or something?"

She looked up at the sound of his voice, and he saw by her expression that she was only baffled, not scared, like any sensible person would have been. Just that small motion of her blond, ringleted head was enough to throw her off balance; she slipped and went under.

He cursed again, climbed down the tree with knee-skinning haste, and bounded into the cold waters of the creek. The girl floated downstream, her petticoats brimming around her upturned bottom like the petals of a water lily.

He splashed after her, an action contrary to his thoughts, which were anything but charitable. She was too dumb to live, he reflected, shivering as he fought the icy currents to reach her.

Somehow, he got to her, managed to curve an arm around her middle and drag her upright. Her head broke the surface. She

2

sputtered and choked, her thick lashes beaded with water, her wide eyes gray as a storm-brewed sky, and kept a death grip on the doll, as though it might somehow save her.

Hell-nation.

Renewing his resolve, he began fighting his way toward shore, numb to the center of his bones, praying to a God he had never believed in that he could hold on, reach solid ground before they both drowned. The effort required nearly all his considerable strength, but he managed it, after the fight of his young life, and lay breathless and spent in the mud, still grasping the girl.

She sat up and regarded him solemnly, blue with cold, wet to the skin, and apparently heedless of the fact that she'd nearly gotten them both killed. "I've muddied my dress," she said. "My *best* dress." She held out the doll. "And just *look* at poor Delilah!"

He stared at the girl in furious amazement. "I figured you must be touched in the head," he grumbled, scrambling up off the cold ground, "and I was right. If my pa sees I got my clothes wet, I'll get whupped for sure. Come to that, I'll probably die of the pneumonia before he can lay a hand on me!"

She had the gall to smile at him, and that was when he realized who she was. It only made him madder, that she was the only child of the wealthiest, most powerful rancher in that part of the territory. As such, she should have had better sense or, leastways, somebody to look out for her.

3

"Since you saved my life," Charity Barnham announced with a queenly sniff, "I hereby grant you permission to kiss me."

He made a face.

She looked indignant, on top of being bedraggled, filthy and wet clear through. "Very well, then," she said stiffly, "you may have three wishes, if you won't take a kiss. Tell me your name."

"Luke," he answered, without intending to speak at all. "Luke Shardlow. And I don't need nothin' from you."

She sighed in a long-suffering fashion. "One wish, then. But if you read fairy tales, you'd know that you are fully entitled to *three.*"

"All right," he agreed. "I wish you'd go back to your big ranch house and leave me be."

She got to her feet with no help from him. "Do you go to school in Jubilee?" she asked, as though he hadn't just made his feelings plain enough for a field rock to understand.

"Do you?" he countered, knowing full well that she was getting her teaching on the Barnham ranch, from some eastern woman who never went into town. Somebody was always offering up an opinion on old Jonah's keeping his daughter out of school. Most folks figured he thought his girl was too good to mix with the children of farmers and miners and store-keepers, though that theory didn't make much sense to Luke. He had reason to know Jonah Barnham was a generous man.

"No," she answered sadly. "It's just Delilah and me."

He felt a stab of sympathy for her, but it was quickly gone. She had a big house, a father who loved her, fine clothes and plenty of food. While he didn't begrudge her any of those things, neither did he think she needed pity from the likes of him. "You're not missing much," he said, by way of consolation. Between the old man's drunken rages and his own inability to sit still for long periods, he didn't spend much time in the schoolhouse himself. What he knew about reading and the like, he'd learned from his ma. Numbers came easily to him; it was as if he'd always understood how they fit together, and they made a certain mysterious music in his head. "What were you doing in that water, anyhow?"

She looked at him with an irritating expression of impatience. "I thought I saw a magic frog," she said. "If I saved him, he might have granted me some wishes."

There she went again, yammering about wishes. "You risked your life—and mine—for a magic frog?" he scoffed, gazing ruefully down at his woolen pants, which were already shrinking from his dousing in the creek. Oh, yes indeed, his pa was going to throttle him. "If there's something you want, why don't you just ask your rich daddy to buy it for you?"

Charity set her jaw for a moment, plainly annoyed by the question. He figured she didn't have any right to be annoyed, given the circumstances, and stared her down.

"That's all you know, Luke Shardlow," she said, moving past him, up the slippery, crumbling bank. "There are lots of things in this world that a person can want, that aren't bought with money."

He was often hungry, the clothes he was wearing were the only decent ones he had, and he wanted plenty—pretty dresses for his ma and a spotted pony for himself, a hunting rifle, shiny boots bought just for him, not rummaged from the poor box over at the mission school. All of which, contrary to Miss Charity Barnham's ideas, could be had for a price.

"Like what?" he called after her.

"Like a mother," she answered, from the top of the bank.

"That's what you want?" he asked. He thought of the store his own mother set by church and God, for all the good it seemed to do her. "Why don't you just pray for one, then?"

"Don't you think I've tried that?" Charity retorted. Dripping and shivering, she made a proud and pitiful sight, standing there at the top of the hill. He wondered if she'd catch it for spoiling her dress, and decided it was more likely she'd be fussed over, kissed and coddled, wrapped up in a blanket, given something warm and sweet to drink. The images stirred an ache, deep down, and he quelled it instantly. Such comforts were for girls and little sissy-boys. Him, he'd just be grateful to get by without another beating.

"You want me to see you home or something?" he asked, as an afterthought.

"No need," Charity answered, assessing him with those strange, stormy eyes of hers for a long moment. "My pony cart is just beyond those trees, up there on the road. Do you want that for your wish? My pony cart?"

He didn't give a damn for the cart, but the pony was another matter. It was all he could do not to scramble up the hill after her, unhitch the animal, and ride it home. Where, of course, his father would take it from him and swap it for a couple of jugs of corn liquor before the sun went down.

"I reckon I'll just bide my time," he said, knowing some of the sadness he felt was leaking past the grin he'd stuck to his face like a bill on a brick wall. "Get that wish of mine some other time. You won't forget, will you?"

"No," Charity said. "I won't forget."

But of course she would, and so would he. Until the time came to remember.

1

August 1889...

Charity Barnham lay facedown and spread-eagle in the tree house, staring through a crack in the floor. Only a minute or so before, she'd been alone with her misery, but the whinny of a horse and a disturbance in the thick brush of the hillside had put an end to that. The rider reined in directly beneath her, swung down from the saddle and spoke soothingly to his black and white pinto gelding.

When the intruder swept off his hat and set it carelessly in a crook of the tree—one of the footholds Charity had used to climb to her leafy sanctuary—she saw that his hair was fair, the color of late-summer honey, and long enough to brush the collar of his black canvas coat.

Her heart skimmed over a few beats. She knew every man who worked on the Double B, her father's ranch, and most of the population of Jubilee as well. This man didn't fall into either category, which meant he was a drifter at best, and an outlaw at worst. Either way, she didn't relish the prospect of an encounter.

She hoped he hadn't noticed Taffeta, her black mare, grazing in the little meadow at the top of the hill.

The stranger whistled softly through his teeth as he began unsaddling his horse. His

9

motions were easy and deliberate; it was almost as if he knew she was there, as if he were teasing her by taking his time.

He tossed the saddle aside, slipped the bridle off over the gelding's head, and watched for a moment or two as the animal made its way down the bank to drink thirstily from the creek. Then, to her profound perturbation, the man proceeded to set up camp. Just far enough from the tree for safety, he made a circle of stones, then got busy gathering dry sticks and branches for firewood. From his saddlebags, he took what looked like a length of fishing line.

She tensed, ready to flee the minute he disappeared around the bend in the creek. He didn't look like a greenhorn; surely he knew that the gelding would have scared off any trout that might be passing by; if he wanted to catch anything, he'd have to go downstream to the swimming hole, where the water was wider and calmer.

The pinto, thirst assuaged, moved off into the sweet grass to nibble.

The man, shedding his long coat and thus revealing a Colt .45 riding low on his left hip, strode to the creekbank, hunkered down there to dig a mess of earthworms from the wet ground with the blade of a hunting knife, then tucked the squirming handful into the pocket of his vest.

She let out a long, slow breath. Now he would leave, and she could scramble down from the tree, find Taffeta, and be away before the stranger ever noticed her.

Instead, as if to thwart her, he walked out onto a log, fallen across the creek during the last big windstorm, baited a hook, and cast his line.

She muttered something unladylike and calculated her chances of making it down the trunk and up the hillside without catching his attention. Impossible, she decided. He was only about twenty yards away, and he looked agile, able to close the distance between them as fleetly as a grizzly on all fours. On the other hand, she reflected, he might be a perfectly decent fellow, just a weary traveler, going innocently about his business.

The .45 and the ease with which he wore it belied that idea, though. The pistol, heavy as it was, might have been a part of his anatomy. He could be a lawman, she concluded, her mind racing, but it was just as likely that he was a gunslinger, a claim jumper or a bounty hunter. Such men were not, of course, to be trifled with.

It was about then that he pulled in the first fish.

She sighed in exasperation. At this rate, she would be imprisoned in this dratted tree until the man broke camp and moved on. Taffeta would wander home, riderless, and within minutes the whole ranch would be in an uproar. Her father was bound to turn the countryside upside down and inside out, looking for her, thinking she'd taken a spill riding or even gotten herself kidnapped. He was protective where she was concerned.

The gunslinger—by now she had decided for

sure that this man was trouble—having put the flailing trout out of its misery with a quick motion of his knife, rebaited the hook and cast the line again. The whole process was repeated four times before he brought his catch back to the edge of the stream, where he left it in the cold water, secured by a twig. The pinto, by this time, had wandered some distance away, but Charity didn't waste a moment hoping the man would go after it; he simply whistled, and the beast raised its head from the grass, flicked its ears, and ambled back toward camp.

Beneath her indignation, her impatience, and an overwhelming sense of caution, she felt a swell of resentment. There was about this man an elegance of motion, an elegance of *thought*, that said he commanded singular powers. Instinctively, Charity knew that things came to him—not just horses and trout, but people and even events—because he summoned them. This insight both intrigued and unnerved her, for she was of an independent nature, strong in her own right, yet here was someone who surely made her match. A worthy adversary.

While the sun moved behind the tips of the trees on the western horizon, the man made his fire, fetched a small, scorched fry pan from his gear, and began cooking the trout. The scent rose through the branches of the tree, teasing her rumbling stomach.

At home, Peony, the family cook, would be setting out supper. Fried chicken, peas from the kitchen garden, mashed potatoes, gravy. Charity emitted a small groan and rested her forehead on her now-folded arms. How long had she been cowering in this tree? One hour? Two?

When she raised her head, the stranger was looking directly at her—though of course he couldn't have seen her, for it was the height of summer and the tree was thick with leaves. His eyes were blue-green, his grin was audacious, and she felt a sweet, tightening sensation, deep within, just looking straight into his face that way.

"I reckon you ought to come down now," he said. "Because after I eat my supper, I plan to bathe in that stream yonder."

Her eyes widened, and she swallowed. After a few moments spent collecting herself, she got to her feet and shinnied down the tree trunk, nearly stepping on his hat, which still rested in the lowest crook of the branches. Covered with dust and cobwebs, she shook out her divided skirt and brushed busily at her blouse. Her light blond hair was coming loose from the many pins and combs required to restrain it, and she supposed her face was splotched with dirt into the bargain. She was twenty-three years old, well past the age for such foolishness; she'd just been caught lurking in a tree house, and her pride was nettled.

She saw no point in asking how the man had known she was there, though she wondered mightily. She had, until then, fancied herself to be capable of great stealth, like an Indian medicine woman or a hunter. Now she would have to reassess that perception, and that was irritating.

The stranger pulled his supper from the fire and set it aside with an expert motion of one hand, rose from his haunches, and sauntered toward her. He moved, as she had noticed before, with a disturbing, animal-like grace. She was at once drawn to this man and frightened enough to turn on one heel and run like a startled deer. Only the formidable power of her own will kept her from making a scrabbling dash up the hillside.

Stopping a few feet from where she stood, head tilted slightly to one side, hands resting on his hips, he regarded her with a look of insolent amusement. "Well," he said, as though that single word were a complete thought all in itself. "Were you planning to pass the night in that tree?"

She met his gaze squarely, even though her heart was thundering against her ribs. "If necessary," she admitted.

He laughed and the sound found its way into her very soul and echoed there. "You don't need to be afraid of me, Miss Barnham. Or are you somebody's missus by now?" He folded his arms and studied her thoughtfully.

She was fresh out of patience and under every inch of her skin, renegade nerves ran riot. "How do you know my name, sir?" she demanded.

He flashed that wicked grin again. There was an arrogance in him that should have been insufferable but instead made him even more attractive. "I couldn't have forgotten you," he said with a nod toward the chattering stream. "After all, I nearly drowned, hauling you out of that water."

"Luke Shardlow," she breathed, amazed. And that time, she took a step back, resisting the odd power he seemed to have over her.

The aqua-colored eyes narrowed slightly, and some of the easy geniality was gone from his manner. "I see the Shardlow name is still poison around here, just like it always was."

She felt a pang at that, though she couldn't have identified the emotion behind it. The name *was* accursed, after all—Luke's father had gone to prison and later hanged for the murder of his wife, and his elder brother, Vance, was wanted for a whole string of vicious robberies. Luke himself had left Jubilee—nobody seemed to know where he'd gone—after old Trigg Shardlow's trial, when he was around fifteen.

"I-I'd better be getting on home," she said.

"I'm not about to hurt you," Shardlow said, with a note of mingled sorrow and disgust in his voice. Then, without another word, he turned his back on her and walked away, toward the campfire. The gelding was snuffling at the fish cooling in the frying pan, and Luke growled a command that sent the animal skittering backward.

She didn't move. "I never thanked you properly for saving my life," she said clearly.

Luke turned, looked at her over one shoulder.

15

The grin, though tenuous, was back, and he inclined his head slightly in acknowledgment of her words.

"Did you get a beating?" she asked, wondering even as she spoke why she was lingering. It was like passing a finger back and forth through a candle flame, daring the fire to burn her, talking to a Shardlow. Suppose he was an outlaw, like his brother?

"Pardon?" he picked up the frying pan, assessed the contents for horse damage, and apparently found nothing amiss.

"That day when I fell into the stream. You said your pa was going to whip you for ruining your clothes."

"You didn't fall," Luke pointed out, the affable defender of truth. "You *waded* in, after a frog prince or something." He paused and shook his head at the memory, then answered her question. "No, I came out of that one with my hide intact. The old man was off someplace, I guess. Otherwise occupied." He glanced toward the brilliant, fading sun. "You'd better get on home, Miss Barnham. They'll be looking for you."

She nodded, turned and started up the hillside.

Sitting cross-legged on the ground, a few feet from the fire, Luke ate his supper and watched the dying sunlight flicker on the surface of the stream. Although he had his demons, like everybody else, he was used to solitude and at peace with his past, turbulent though it was.

16

His reflective mood had, in fact, nothing to do with the frustration and shame of being old Trigg's younger son; no, he was thinking about Charity. How much she had—and hadn't—changed in fifteen years. The spark in her slate gray eyes that said she was on comfortable terms with her own spirit and the world around her. The proud, graceful way she carried herself. She was tall and, though slender, womanly in a way it would behoove him not to consider too carefully or too long. Feminine she most definitely was, but there was nothing fragile about her.

He chuckled, remembering her bristly discomfiture at being stuck up in the branches of that venerable oak. He'd noticed her right away, of course, for he'd taken refuge in the same place many times, as a boy. And in the interim, hard experience had taught him not to make camp underneath any tree without making damn sure he knew what was up there. Once, he'd been jumped by a cougar, and lost a good horse and a strip of hide off his back in the ensuing dispute. On another occasion, a man he was tracking had laid for him in the same way, and he'd almost lost that scrap, too. He had scars to show for the lesson.

His meal finished, he ferreted a bar of soap wrapped in cheesecloth from his saddlebags and headed toward the creek. Reaching the water's edge, he unstrapped his gunbelt and laid it carefully on a flat rock he'd long since chosen for the purpose. Then he kicked off both boots and tested his fast-moving bath with a toe.

He drew in a harsh breath at the chill, but he'd been on the trail for the better part of a week, and figured he probably smelled like his horse, which left him with little choice in the matter. The home place, though private, was nothing but a pile of rotted timber and cobwebs now—he'd already been by there. He could have gone to Jubilee's one rooming house for a decent bed and a hot bath, he supposed, but the return of Luke Shardlow, after all these years, was bound to draw attention. He wanted time to get his bearings before he made his presence known.

So he got out of his clothes and flung himself, blue-lipped and cursing, into the biting cold of the water. It was, given some of the thoughts he'd been having about Charity Barnham, a good decision, however painful. After a lot of splashing and sputtering, and another fit of swearing, he came out again, clean. Or at least reasonably so.

He kept a spare set of clothes rolled up in his blanket, and hastened into them, dancing there in the sweet summer grass like a one-legged man on a bed of hot coals. It was a good quarter of an hour before his teeth quit chattering, but the bath had left him feeling a certain exhilaration. If he'd been anywhere else, he'd have been ready for a night of drinking, card-playing and woman-chasing, but this was Jubilee. Here, more than any other place on earth, he needed to keep his wits sharp—to watch and listen and, at the same time, give the impression that he was in town purely to raise hell.

That last part shouldn't be so difficult, given the family reputation.

After donning the gunbelt again, he whistled a summons to the pinto, called Shiloh, and staked the animal on a lead long enough to reach the stream bank. He started to make his bed in the grass, as twilight fell, then changed his mind and climbed up into the tree.

The platform of old weathered boards was much as he remembered it, except that Charity's scent lingered there, with the green smell of the leaves and the odors of pitch and dust. She'd apparently swept with a branch or something, for the place had a tidy look about it. In her haste to depart, she'd left behind the stub of a candle and a battered book. *Grimm's Fairy Tales.*

He smiled, thumbing the pages. Miss Barnham, it would seem, was still looking for a magic frog. Fancy that, after all these years.

He spread the bed roll carefully, stretched out with a sigh, and slept.

Charity had been right in thinking she would be late for supper—the dishes had been cleared and her father and Mrs. Quincy—Blaise—the attractive widow he planned to marry come the fall, were lingering over coffee. Aaron, Blaise's ten-year-old son, had already been sent to bed.

Thankfully, neither Jonah nor his intended wife remarked upon Charity's late arrival and hasty slapdash ablutions; they were too caught up in each other for that. Jonah stood and drew back his daughter's chair, and Mrs. Quincy favored her with a bright smile. Peony, who had already made her opinions of folks who couldn't be bothered to get themselves home to supper known in the kitchen, when Charity arrived, carried in a plate of lukewarm food, still grumbling, and plunked it down in front of her.

Never graced with a delicate appetite, Charity began to eat almost before the aging cook had drawn her hand back. "Who owns the old Shardlow place?" she asked.

Jonah's expression turned solemn. He was a powerfully built man, in his mid-fifties, with brown eyes and plenty of gray in his dark, still-thick hair, and Blaise was envied, far and wide, for his devoted affections. "Still in the family, I suppose," he answered. "If there's any family left, that is."

"Oh, there is," she replied, between bites. "Luke is back—I saw him tonight."

Jonah had been raising a china coffee cup to his mouth, but at his daughter's words he set it down again—slowly and with a care vastly out of proportion to the demands of the task. "Where?" he asked simply.

"By the creek." She reached for a biscuit, sighed because it was cold, and buttered it lavishly. "He's camped there."

Blaise, pleasantly solid, reasonably intelligent, despite her sometimes flighty ways, and possessed of a head of gleaming chestnut hair, always neatly and rather elegantly coiled at her nape, paled slightly. "Charity, you didn't—?"

"Speak to him?" she finished cheerfully. "Well, I didn't intend to, but as it happened, I wasn't given an alternative. I was up in that oak tree, and he rode in and started making camp beneath it. I couldn't very well stay there all night."

Though of course she might have done exactly that, if Luke hadn't guessed that she was there. She saw no need to go into excessive detail, however.

Jonah leaned slightly forward in his chair. He could look as stern as a hellfire and brimstone preacher when he wanted to, though in truth he was the kindest of men. His deep voice rumbled, low and charged with contained energy, like thunder gathering force on a not-so-distant horizon. "From what I know of that boy, you'd have been better off to wait him out."

"What were you doing in a tree?" inquired Mrs. Quincy. Dear Blaise, she was generous and sweet, but so besotted with Jonah that she tended to miss things, and chime in when the conversation had already moved on without her.

Jonah patted Blaise's elegant hand, but his gaze had not left Charity's face since she spoke. "What happened?" he demanded. "What did he say? Did he lay a hand to you?"

She pushed her plate away. "Nothing happened," she answered evenly. She wasn't surprised by her father's reaction—the Shardlows were notorious for miles around, after all—but it disturbed her all the same. If Jonah, a

21

fair-minded man, would ask such questions, then Luke had been right in calling the Shardlow name poison. It seemed unjust, to judge a man purely by the deeds of his family.

She wondered what her father would say if he knew Luke had once saved her life.

Jonah's jaw tightened visibly, then relaxed again. "I'd better ride over there and find out what he wants," he said, with grim resolve.

Blaise made a small, fussy sound and began to fan herself, even though the dining room was almost cool enough for the fireplace to be lit. "Good heavens, Jonah, you mustn't. He may be an outlaw. Suppose he shoots you?" Her first husband, Malcolm, had been killed in a hunting accident and she was understandably sensitive where guns were concerned.

"If he was of a mind to shoot anybody," Jonah pointed out reasonably, patting Blaise again and keeping Charity pinned to her chair with his level gaze, "I reckon we'd know it by now. I'll talk to him in the morning."

"I'd best go look in on Aaron," Blaise said, rising distractedly.

Jonah stood as well, and did not sit down again until she had left the room. "What," he asked, echoing the widow Quincy's earlier inquiry, "were you doing in a tree?"

She sighed. There was no point in lying to Jonah, he'd learned to read her face a long time before. "I needed to get away," she said softly. "To hide, if you will. I just couldn't deal with—with things."

22

"Things?" Jonah raised his thick eyebrows quizzically.

"I wanted to think," she said, faltering. To weep in despair, though she wasn't about to admit that. To make frantic, impossible plans to escape before Raoul returned from Texas with several hundred head of longhorns to add to the large herd already ranging from one end of his grandfather's ranch to the other. They made a sort of reverse dowry, those cattle.

She lifted her chin a notch. She would stay, for the Double B was in her blood, an extension of her very soul, but she did not want to marry the man her father had chosen for her, and she'd made no secret of the fact. Jonah, fearing that she would someday find herself alone, with neither husband nor brother, uncle nor father to look after her, had sworn to leave his holdings in the care of a flock of city lawyers if she refused Raoul's suit. She didn't care about the money, of which there was a great deal, but without the ranch sprawling around her in all directions, she wasn't sure she would even be able to breathe. And she didn't trust the lawyers to hold the land.

"I do not love Raoul," she said carefully.

Jonah closed his eyes for a moment. "Your mother and I were married because our fathers were partners, back east." His tone was at once gentle and intractable. "Together, we built this ranch. We had you. And two people never loved each other more than Rianna and I did." He paused, struggling with old emotions. "Raoul is a good man, Charity. Surely you don't hold his—well, the circumstances of his birth—against him?"

Raoul Montego was thirty years old, with a mane of dark hair and eyes that were nearly black. His father, Jubilee's version of the Prodigal Son, had never married his beautiful Mexican mother, Maria, and in the end, had abandoned them both. Raoul's grandfather, owner of the second largest ranch in that part of the territory, had learned of their existence by accident, and sent for them when Raoul was twelve. The young woman who had carried him in her body had soon perished of a fever, yearning for her homeland and calling out for the man who had betrayed her. Raoul, bitter and proud, had remained, but he had taken Maria's surname, not his grandfather's.

"You know," Jonah persisted quietly, "how much Raoul cares for you?"

The words had the power to wound. This time, it was Charity who closed her eyes. "He deserves a woman who loves him in return. Please, Papa. For the last time—don't make me do this. Let me wait for the right man."

Jonah blinked away a sudden sheen of tears. "Raoul," he said at length, his voice hoarse, "*is* the right man. This time next year—maybe much sooner—you will see that." He paused again, then went on. "Raoul will be back any day. In a month, he will be your husband and a half interest in the Double B will pass to you. I'm asking you, as your father, to trust in my judgment and stop tormenting yourself this way."

She clamped her teeth down hard over her lower lip. Then she spoke just once more. "If I were a man, instead of a woman," she said, "I would not have to pay for my birthright with my body. It would be mine as a matter of course!"

Had Jonah Barnham been of another sort, she felt sure he would have slapped her. As it was, he simply sank back into his chair with a broken sigh, and she bolted from her chair, headed for the large archway that opened onto the entry hall. By the time she reached her upstairs bedroom, with its expansive view of the land and the mountains beyond, she was nearly sick with frustration.

For a time, she paced, too agitated to be still. Then, when some of her emotion was spent, she sat down on the edge of her bed and kicked off her slippers. Her soiled riding boots had been left, at Peony's insistence, on the small porch off the kitchen.

She went to her desk, a delicate thing that had traveled, despite its fragility, across the rolling seas from England and then over the rails and trails to Jubilee and finally to the ranch, where her father had presented it to her on the occasion of her sixteenth birthday. She cherished the piece, not only for its beauty and its sentimental value, but because to her it symbolized the singular strength of womanhood. Though finely made, and certainly beautiful, it was also useful, and formed to endure.

From a drawer, she took a pen and her leather-bound journal. Ink at the ready, she turned to a fresh page and began to write—not about Raoul, or her seemingly insurmountable differences with Jonah, the patron saint of all mules and blast-proof tree stumps, but about Luke Shardlow.

The dream sent him hurtling upward into wakefulness, and he had already drawn and cocked the .45 before the stars came into focus, silver speckles of light among the dark leaves of the oak. A sweat colder than creek water covered him like a liquid skin, and his heart thundered so loudly that, for a few breathless moments, he could not come to grips with the fact that he was twenty-six, not fourteen. That the screech he'd heard in his sleep was not his mother's, but merely the cry of an owl.

"Shit," he muttered, and sat up to ease the pistol back into its holster. Here he'd gone to all the trouble to freeze his ass off in the creek, and he'd sweated through the only clean clothes he had left. For the hundredth time, or maybe the thousandth, he told himself he was going to have to stop living like this. Get himself a wife, and that ranch he'd been saving for ever since he'd earned his first nickel mucking out stalls in a livery stable.

He looked down at the fire and saw that it was only embers, but he felt chilled, as though it were January instead of mid-August, so he made his way out of the tree and built the fire up again. Then, using the small pot he carried in his bed roll and some of his precious and

26

rapidly dwindling store of coffee, he brewed himself some midnight comfort.

Nickering, Shiloh ambled over and nuzzled him hard between the shoulder blades, nearly sending him sprawling into the small, crackling blaze. He laughed. "Get away, horse," he said. But he was grateful even for the presence of the pinto, because the shadow of the nightmare was still with him.

He stared into the fire, making no effort to push the memories from his head; it never worked. The best thing was just to face up to them, to endure. He'd stayed sane, since that final, horrible night, not by turning away from pain, but by enduring it, embracing it, outlasting it—in much the same way he would have broken a horse to ride. He just stayed with it until it was done.

By his second mug of coffee, he was wide awake and his clothes were beginning to dry, though he still felt clammy. The pictures and sounds unrolled before his mind's eye, as vivid as if it were all happening again.

Trigg had come home drunk that night— nothing unusual in that. He'd climbed up into the loft—how much easier it would have been for everyone if he'd fallen from that ladder and broken his neck—got a sleeping Luke by the hair, and hurled him some seven feet to the cabin floor.

Bellowing, he'd come after him, the old man had, stinking of moonshine and stale sweat and plain hate. "Bastard!" he'd screamed, kicking at Luke. "You ain't mine, you little bas-

27

tard. Your whorin' mother made you in some alley."

Luke had started to his feet—he hadn't been scared, just madder than hell—and Trigg had laid him out flat with one massive fist.

He'd heard her sobbing then, pleading, trying to get between her husband and her son. Vance, Luke's half-brother, older by some five years, had been away that night. He'd missed the whole ugly incident.

Luke had gotten up, somehow, and Trigg had come at him again, shoving his wife out of the way with brutal force. She'd fallen, struck her head against the fender of the stove, and lay unmoving on the dirt floor. Trigg, suddenly docile, had crouched beside her, prodding, pleading. She hadn't moved.

Trigg had shaken her, harder and harder, but that time Luke didn't try to intercede. He knew, had known from the moment his father laid hands to her and sent her hurtling away from him, that this was the time, the night he had dreaded for as long as he could remember. She was gone.

He hadn't wept—in a way, he'd been happy for her. Life had always been too difficult and illusive for Marietta Shardlow. Too painful.

Trigg, on the other hand, had bellowed with grief, gathered her up into his arms, carried her small, inert frame out through the gaping cabin door, into the first faltering light of a new day. Luke had tried to rise, but passed out cold before he ever gained his feet.

When he'd awakened, Vance was back from his travels, sitting at the table, watching him.

Luke lay curled into a ball, hurting everywhere, seething with silent, helpless, murderous rage. "He killed her," he said, after a long, long time. "He *killed* her."

Vance got up, crossed the narrow space between them, and leaned down to speak slowly and clearly. "You just imagined that, boy. Your ma, she was a delicate type. She just couldn't take this hard life we got here. Climbed up into the hayloft and flung herself down, that's what she did. You hear me, boy? That's what she did."

Luke had nodded. "I hear you," he said. But when Marshal Asa McCallum arrived a few hours later, to put the questions the law required, he spoke up. "She never jumped from nothin'," he'd said. "My pa murdered her." And then he'd recounted the whole incident, moment by moment.

McCallum had believed him, put a sobbing, half-drunk Trigg under arrest, and hauled him off to town, where he'd locked him up in the cellar of the general store, that being the closest thing the town had to a jail back in those days.

Trigg had come to Marietta's funeral, a few days later, handcuffed and under guard, blubbering and carrying on something fierce. He didn't know how he'd go on without his dear, precious wife, he'd wailed.

It rained that day, Luke recalled, rained long and hard. Turned the churchyard to mud and washed away any tears the other mourners might have shed.

Now, he held Trigg's features clearly in mind. *You son-of-a-bitch,* he told the image silently, *you better hope I don't go to hell when I die, because if I do, the devil's only going to be* half *your problem.*

2

$\mathcal{T}$he churchyard was still, except for the first tentative strains of birdsong, the breeze fresh, the grass damp with dew. Leaving Taffeta untethered in the road, Charity slipped between the whitewashed rails of the fence, carrying a bouquet of yellow roses in a fold of her skirt. As she approached her mother's well-tended resting place, with its impressive pink marble monument, she was less surprised than she might have been to catch a glimpse of Luke Shardlow. He stood a fair distance away, hat-in-hand, beside a grave marked only by a wooden cross.

She had gathered a dozen blossoms from the garden at the ranch—roses had been her mother's favorites—and she laid six at the base of Rianna's tombstone, said a brief prayer, and then turned resolutely toward Luke. The grass grew deeper as she approached him, the graves humbler and closer together.

"Mornin'," he said, with an inclination of his head.

She bent to lay the six remaining roses beneath the marker and straightened again before replying. "Good morning."

Luke was wearing his long black coat and, beneath it, the ominous Colt. From an inside breast pocket, he produced the small volume of fairy tales she had left in the tree house. "You forgot this," he said.

Their fingers brushed together as she accepted the book, and her response was so sudden, so visceral, so intense, that it took her breath away. For a long moment, she could not speak.

"It is yours, isn't it?" Luke asked. His eyes were amazing; neither green nor blue, but some uncanny blend of the two.

"Yes," Charity said, awkwardly and at length.

His smile was slow, and sort of tilted. He looked down at the flowers resting on the untended grave. "Thanks. My ma's buried here. She never had much that was pretty when she was living."

Charity felt a brief and almost overwhelming sadness for the woman resting in this shady and seemingly forgotten corner of the church-yard. It was as if, even now, in death, she was set apart from everyone else, and somehow excluded. "What was her name? Her given name, I mean?"

Luke's pleasant expression didn't alter as he looked down at the grave. "Marietta," he replied.

"Was she beautiful?" It was a ridiculous question, and she did not know why she'd asked it. She knew very little about Marietta Shardlow: that her life had been difficult, that she had died by the hand of her own husband.

He met Charity's gaze easily. "She was to me. But she was fragile."

Charity had an image of a delicate wildflower, meant to thrive in a grassy meadow but sown instead upon hard, stony ground. Never able to take root. "So was my mother," she said thoughtfully, indicating the grave she'd just left with a gesture of one hand. "She died when I was six."

"Do you remember her?"

She nodded, smiling wistfully.

Luke sighed, and his forehead creased into a frown that was gone as quickly as it had appeared. "Mostly, I can't bring Ma's face to mind, but I remember that she liked to laugh. Even though things were the way they were, she was always smiling and singing."

The revelation amazed Charity, given the way Mrs. Shardlow's life had ended. Everybody knew the family had been desperately poor, depending mostly on the church for food and clothing. Each year, when hogs and cattle were butchered for meat on the Double B, Jonah had made sure a share found its way to the Shardlow place, though he'd fancied that no one knew. It was good to hear that Marietta Shardlow had laughed and sung, as well as cried.

"I didn't see your horse," Charity said, and immediately felt foolish. She seldom tried to impress people, but for some reason she wanted Luke Shardlow to see her in a flattering light.

He gestured toward the trees at the edge of the cemetery. "He's back there, pulling up the grass," he said, with the flash of a grin.

Only then did it occur to Charity to wonder if Luke was trying to keep his presence in

33

Jubilee a secret. He'd taken care to leave his horse out of sight, and though the farmers and ranchers had already put in half a day's work, the townspeople were just beginning to stir in their beds. "Will you be staying in Jubilee long?" she asked.

His expression altered so slightly that she almost didn't notice. "Long enough," he answered, without emotion. "I have some business here."

She nodded, well aware that she was blushing. She wanted to ask so many questions—where he'd been since his mother's murder, what he'd been doing, whether or not there was a woman somewhere, waiting for him to return.

Probably, she thought ruefully, there were women from Canada to Mexico, watching the road and hoping.

"You make a habit of turning up in grave-yards at the crack of dawn?" he asked good-naturedly, and she was grateful to him for breaking the strange, awkward silence that had descended a few moments before, while she was doing her wondering.

She shook her head, smiling. "I always wake up early," she said, "and I like to go straight to the flower garden to cut bouquets for the house. The roses looked and smelled so especially fine this morning that I decided to bring some along. I go right by here to get to the mission school anyway."

"You're a schoolmarm?" he looked and sounded surprised, and Charity wasn't sure whether to be flattered or offended.

She laughed, as much from nervousness as amusement. What was happening to her? She felt shaky, and so warm that she pressed the back of one hand to her forehead. "No. I just help out with the little ones sometimes. With their reading and spelling, mostly."

"I didn't think school was in session at this time of year," Luke observed. He seemed in no particular hurry to end the conversation, and the fact pleased Charity in unaccountable ways.

She explained that the students at the mission were mostly Indian children who came and went as the spirit moved them. Some were sick, some were orphaned, all were wary of whites. That they accepted Charity as easily as they did Father Elias, the Jesuit priest, was to her a matter of secret pride.

Luke replaced his hat as Charity finished speaking. "I could see you back to your horse," he offered.

"That won't be necessary," she answered. "Thank you, Mr. Shardlow, for returning my book."

"I'd be honored, Miss Barnham, if you'd call me Luke," he said, with that quicksilver grin. The brim of the hat cast a shadow over his face, but the golden spikes of a new beard glittered in the sun.

She felt lightheaded, and despised herself for a simpering fool. She had never been the sort to tremble and blush under the attentions of a man, no matter how charming, and she did not know how to cope with this new facet

35

of her nature. "Then you must address me as Charity," she replied.

He tugged at the brim of his hat. "I'd be proud," he said, and then he turned and walked away with a stride that would have been a swagger, had he been anyone else.

Watching him go, Charity asked herself why he might have returned to Jubilee, a place that must surely hold terrible memories for him. She wasn't at all sure she wanted to know the answer.

When Luke went back to his camp beside the creek—he'd stowed his belongings in the tree house—he felt agitated and restless. These were new emotions for him, for he had trained himself over the years to be calm, to measure his thoughts and his actions in precise proportions. Meeting up with Charity Barnham again had upset his equilibrium in a way that was unsettling but not entirely disagreeable.

Methodically, whistling softly through his teeth, he gathered his possessions, which were already bundled into his bed roll, mounted the pinto again, and set out for the home place. He'd gotten his bearings, settled his plans. And although he'd taken care not to be seen by too many people, he knew a few early-risers had gotten a glimpse of him, headed for the churchyard. He'd set the stage and now it was time for the performance to begin.

Reaching the tumble-down cabin that had once been a halfway decent homestead, thanks

36

mostly to his mother's efforts, he walked around the perimeter, assessing the damage, taunting the memories, the private specters, daring them to get too close.

The roof of the little house had fallen in, and the place was probably full of mice and other objectionable critters, but it was in better condition than he'd first thought. The barn was completely gone, and his mother's cherished fruit trees were in dire need of pruning.

He was compiling a mental list of the tools and supplies he would require when the sound of an approaching rig came to his ears. He turned and watched as a middle-aged man— none other than Jonah Barnham, in fact— drove out of a copse of birch trees. So, he thought, with a half-grin, the old man knew about his encounter with Charity, down by the creek. Like as not, he'd come to warn him off.

Old Jonah hadn't got where he was by being slow-witted.

Luke had shed his coat and hat, but the Colt was in place on his hip. He saw Barnham's gaze go to the .45 as he drew the buckboard to a stop with a low word to the horses, a fine pair of sorrels, and a long draw on the reins.

"Mr. Barnham," Luke said flatly, by way of a greeting.

"Luke," Barnham affirmed, with a slight nod. He wound the reins around the brake lever and climbed down from the box with the ease of a much younger man. He put out his hand, and Luke accepted it.

"Place looks pretty run-down," Jonah said,

when they'd shaken hands. "If you're thinking of selling, I hope you'll give me the opportunity to make an offer."

The Shardlow homestead bordered the Double B, and although it was his way to leave folks to their own business, Jonah had never made a secret of the fact that he coveted the place. It was a half-section, with timber and a good spring and plenty of grassland. Although Luke meant to move on when his business was complete and set himself up somewhere else, Montana or Colorado or maybe even Mexico, he wanted to give the impression that he'd come back to make his home right under the sanctimonious noses of Jubilee's upright citizens.

It might be the only way to draw Vance out without raising his suspicions.

"I figured I'd stay on awhile," he said.

Jonah looked regretful. "You're planning on settling around here then."

"Maybe."

"I understand you met up with my daughter yesterday, down by the creek."

"Yes, sir," Luke replied, without a trace of deference. "I did indeed. She's a beauty—like to take my breath right away."

Jonah showed none of the instinctive caution that other men did when they spoke to Luke. "She's engaged to be married," he said plainly. "The wedding is in a month. With all due respect, I'll be obliged if you kept your distance."

Luke knew his countenance revealed nothing

of the emotional flash-flood the news of Charity's forthcoming marriage had unleashed within him. "I'm not sure," he said, "but I think I ought to be insulted."

Jonah's look was devoid of good humor. "We both know young girls can develop foolish attachments to men like you."

"'Young girls'?" Luke echoed. "I can understand why you wouldn't have noticed, but Charity's become a woman. A smart one, I think, despite her propensity for hiding out in trees."

A flush moved up Jonah's neck and throbbed around his muttonchop whiskers. His brown eyes had a fiery light in them. "Just leave her alone."

"I think you're giving me a mite too much credit for charm, Jonah. Charity and I have spoken once or twice, that's all. I'm not about to start serenading under her window of a night."

"You don't need charm, men like you. A lot of otherwise intelligent women are drawn to your sort."

"That's the second time you've used the phrase 'men like you.' What exactly do you mean by that, Jonah? Why don't you just say it straight out? I'm a Shardlow, second cousin to Lucifer himself. Isn't that what you really mean?"

Jonah had the good grace to look chagrined. "Your old man was as worthless as anybody I've ever heard of, but you can't help that you were born to him, and I truly don't hold your name against you. But Charity is—well, she's *confused* about things right now. I don't want you complicating matters."

"You still haven't explained why you think I'd choose to do that."

"I have tried to be tactful," Jonah stated patiently. "You're obviously a drifter—hell, for all I know, you have a price on your head. You wear that .45 the way most men wear their elbows or their kneecaps, and there's a look in your eye that says you might indeed be kin to the devil. So I'll ask you again, in the plainest words I can, to stay clear of my daughter."

Luke said nothing. He hadn't planned to pursue Charity, but she was still an unmarried woman, and to his way of thinking, he had as much right to talk to her as anybody else did.

"What do you want here?" Jonah blurted, apparently unable to contain the question. It was clear that he had tried. "I'll pay you top dollar for this land and you know it. And whether it's fair or not, folks around Jubilee will remember what your pa did, what he *was*, and they'll hold it against you. It just doesn't make sense, your coming back here to stay."

"Even Cain wanted a home," Luke said. "Now, if you'll excuse me, I've got to go to town and buy some tools and lumber."

Jonah tried to stare him down for a few moments. His eyes were narrowed, but there was a dark gleam of respect in them all the same.

"If you're even thinking about turning this place around, you've got more gumption than your pa showed in his whole miserable life. But folks are folks and they won't make you welcome. You'd do better to move on."

Luke forbore from saying that he might take a wife before he went, and carry her away with him, because he owed Barnham for past kindnesses. Furthermore, he liked the man. "That would be a little too much like running for my taste," he said.

Barnham heaved another sigh, this one gustier than the last. Although there was no physical resemblance, Luke could see how Charity came by her grit and brains. "Damn and blast it," he muttered.

"Your daughter must have gotten her good looks from her mother," Luke said, and old Jonah laughed in spite of himself.

"You send word to the Double B when you come to your senses and decide to sell this place. A man could do a lot with a good stake like I'm willing to put up."

"He could indeed. If he were somebody else besides me."

"Hell," Jonah said. "I'm going home before I run clean out of patience."

Luke smiled. "That sounds like a good idea to me," he replied, but he was almost sorry when Jonah climbed back into his wagon and drove away. He'd enjoyed the exchange.

It was hot that day, so he left his coat behind when he mounted up and rode off toward Jubilee. As he covered the short distance between the homestead and town, he considered the discovery that Miss Charity Barnham was going to be married in just a month's time. He hadn't seen her since she was a little girl, and she'd damned near got him drowned the first time they'd met. No telling what she might do now that she was all grown up.

The reasons to avoid her just kept on coming. She came from the best family in town, he from the worst. While she might be having "foolish notions" where her impending marriage was concerned, most likely her future husband wasn't. If he was worth a damn, he wouldn't cotton to Luke or anyone else taking an interest in his bride, and jealousy could make a man do idiotic things, especially if a little whiskey entered into the equation. His past, and the Shardlow name, would follow him from this place, and he had no right to taint a woman with that curse.

Any or all these factors should have turned his thoughts aside from Charity—he was not a sentimental man, and he knew a bad bet when he saw one—but her image was still with him when he reached the outskirts of Jubilee.

His arrival generated a rash of swishing window curtains, and a few people were so bold as to stop whatever they were doing and stare at him. Tipping his hat and smiling cordially, like a ringmaster squiring in a circus train, he rode straight to the livery stable, where he bought a used wagon and a couple of run-down horses. There was a small mill in town, and he stopped there to order and pay for the lumber he would need to make the cabin livable.

Except for the proprietor, the general store seemed deserted when he stepped over the threshold, though he was aware that there were hidden observers. It amazed him that people knew who he was—he'd been a scared, gawky fifteen-year-old when he left Jubilee— but of course that was the way of small towns. Those who had gotten a glimpse of him earlier in the day, when he'd paid a visit to his ma's grave, had had plenty of time to confer with their neighbors, speculate on his business in their fine community and decide upon his identity.

He would do nothing to correct the impression that he was up to no good. It served his purpose well, their linking him with his mean, worthless father, and he meant to live up to the family reputation as best he could. His only regret was that Charity would by necessity see him in the same sorry light as the others did.

Reaching the general store, he bought a wagonload of food, tools and household goods, volunteering nothing. The storekeeper, a squirrely little man with a mustache that seemed heavy enough to topple him over frontwards, made no effort to draw him out.

When he'd secured his purchases in the wagon, he left everything unattended and strolled across the street to the Chief Joseph Saloon. The name was an insult to a remarkable man, in Luke's opinion. It was still the

43

only bar in town, too, though in his pa's day, it had been known as Dixie's Garter.

He had an understandable aversion to the effects of alcohol, and disliked its taste heartily, but tossed back a double shot at the bar, assessed a poker game going on at a table in the back, and bought two bottles of rye whiskey to take with him when he left. He wanted folks to say they'd seen one of the Shardlow boys that day, that he was no better than he should be, wearing a big-iron on one hip and spending good money on rotgut hooch. Just like his pa before him.

He made his way to the wagon—it was no surprise that no one had dared to touch it, and that restraint said something about the prudence of the common folk, too—he tucked the whiskey carefully in amongst the bags of flour and sugar and pinto beans and then swung up into the box. The gelding was tethered to the back of the rig, and trotted obediently along behind when he released the brake lever and whistled the nags into slow, bumbling motion.

Back at the homestead, he put the pitiful team to pasture in the tall grass, and set the pinto free to wander down to the spring. Then he set to work clearing the fallen roof out of the cabin, a task that took the rest of the day.

At nightfall, Luke fetched water from the spring, filling two of his new wooden buckets. One he would use for cooking and drinking, the other for washing up. He'd bought a good-sized copper tub at the general store— a topic of discussion at more than one supper

44

table that night, he would have bet—but he was too worn out to carry and heat enough water to fill it.

After building a fire, he made himself a decent hash of eggs and canned meat, along with a pot of coffee. Some people complained that the stuff kept them awake of a night, but nothing ever interfered with Luke's sleep. He had a gift for dropping into it like a stone into deep water, and rising to the surface in the space of a heartbeat. Old Trigg had taught him that last part, and the skill had saved his hide on more than one occasion.

Looking up at the stars and sipping his strong brew, Luke let his thoughts stray back to Charity Barnham. He recalled how she'd laid those yellow roses down at the base of his mother's grave marker, and looked him square in the eyes afterward. She was a beautiful woman, that went without saying, but there was much more to her than that. A man could spend a whole lifetime learning her secrets, one by one, and still find out only half of what there was to know. Although she was old enough to be considered a spinster in some circles, she wasn't hankering to throw a rope around the first man who passed by, that was clear from what Jonah had said. Whoever her prospective bridegroom was, she had her doubts about hitching up with him.

Luke sighed. There was no place for Charity in his plans, and yet he could not deny that she intrigued him mightily. His interest in her wouldn't matter in the end, of course; she'd soon despise him, and so would the rest of the town, because by the time he was done, Trigg Shardlow would look like a saint by comparison.

A week had passed since Charity's last meeting with Luke Shardlow, and she'd thought of him practically every moment of that time. She'd even gone to the creek once, to the place where he'd camped, and sat tossing stones into the stream for a long time. She hadn't expected to find him there—everyone for miles around knew he was busy rebuilding the family homestead—but she felt closer to him in that place of sunshine and sweet grass and whispering water. She remembered her quest for the magic frog, that long-ago day, that might well have ended both their lives, and found herself thinking of fair-haired princes mounted on pinto geldings.

She was at the mission school just outside of Jubilee when she first glimpsed the vast cloud of dust on the horizon, first felt the faint tremors in the ground. Raoul was back with his cattle, she needed no one to tell her that. The long trail drive that had been her reprieve was over.

Father Elias startled her by laying a hand upon her shoulder; she hadn't known he was beside her. "You'll want to go and greet him, I think," he said gently. "We will be all right here without you."

She had not confided her reluctance to marry to the priest, and she could not do so now. Her father knew, of course, and by association, Blaise probably did, too, but it wouldn't be fair or honorable to tell anyone else before she'd spoken directly to Raoul.

With a nod, she untied her apron, said brief good-byes to the children, and went to find Taffeta. The animal was grazing in the high grass behind the chapel, and Charity quickly slipped a bridle over the mare's head and mounted with as much grace as she could manage. She seldom bothered with a saddle, and that day was no exception.

She was in a state of agitation by the time she reached the ranch house and it was a relief to find that her father was not there. Blaise, who quite properly shared a large upstairs sitting room and bedchamber with her young son, was in the kitchen, helping Peony peel potatoes for supper.

"Look at you," said Peony, who had been her mother's childhood nurse, long ago, before Rianna married Jonah Barnham and came west. "All flushed and breathless, as if the hounds of hell were on your heels."

Blaise waved Peony into silence, collected Charity, and ushered her quickly into the cool privacy of Jonah's large study.

"What is it?" the older woman asked, her pretty face filled with concern.

Charity struggled to recover her composure. She was being silly. Difficult though the prospect was, she had to go to Raoul—who had been her friend since he'd come to live on the neighboring ranch years before, as a boy—and

47

explain that she could not marry him. He was intelligent, he was reasonable, he was good. He would see what a mistake it would be for them to wed.

She smoothed her hair lightly with both palms and drew a deep breath. "I'm perfectly all right," she said. "And I'm sorry if I alarmed you. It's just that—that Raoul is back."

Blaise's kind eyes clouded. "I see. What will you do, Charity?"

Charity bit her lower lip, struggling against tears of frustration and dread. She couldn't marry Raoul, it would be a crime to deceive him like that, and yet she knew he would be deeply hurt by her rejection. He had gone to such trouble to prove himself a good provider and suitable husband.

"I have to tell him the truth," she whispered.

Blaise embraced her. "Yes," she said. "Your father will not be pleased, but you *are* right. You mustn't go ahead with this marriage if it isn't what you want. You deserve every chance to be happy and so does that young man."

"Papa will be furious," Charity said anxiously.

Her future stepmother nodded. "He will indeed, but I'll do what I can to soothe him, and you must know he would not do you violence for the world. He is quite impossible, where this situation is concerned, but Jonah loves you with his whole heart, my dear."

"I know," Charity agreed. Her hands were interlocked with Blaise's, and both women squeezed simultaneously. "I'd better make myself presentable," she said, with sorrow. "Will

48

you send word to the barn that I'll need a horse and buggy within the hour?"

Blaise agreed, and hastened out of the room, intent on her mission. Charity knew the other woman would go to the barn herself if necessary, and she loved her for it.

Within forty-five minutes, the buggy was hitched and Charity had washed, brushed her hair and pinned it into a loose chignon, and donned a fresh dress of soft blue. When she arrived at the main house on the neighboring ranch, a distance of several miles, the place was in an uproar. There were cattle and cowboys everywhere, and the air roiled with dust.

Choking and coughing, Charity secured the buggy and then stood up in the box, scanning the chaos of men and beasts for Raoul.

He was not hard to find, mounted on his dusty black horse. He was broad-shouldered, and his dark hair brushed the collar of his shirt. He was riding through the confusion toward her, his white teeth revealed by his broad smile.

"Help me," Charity prayed, under her breath.

At last Raoul reached the buggy and, before she could say a word, he'd swept her out of the rig and into the saddle in front of him. A moment later, his mouth was sealed to hers, and a cheer rose from the trail-weary cowhands maneuvering the sizable herd onto the fenced pasture land that awaited them.

Charity was not unmoved by that kiss—

she was a woman and she wanted the fullness of a woman's life—but the passion and the honest affection it conveyed nearly broke her heart.

"Raoul—" she began, but then he kissed her again, and she fell silent. She couldn't tell him there, in front of the whole ranch, but when she suggested that they speak in private, he laughed and said he could not trust himself to be alone with her. He was in the mood to celebrate the end of the drive with the cowboys and they had all earned a wild night. In the end, Charity simply went home, promising herself that she would break off the engagement first thing the next morning.

3

*W*hen Charity came downstairs the following morning, after a virtually sleepless night, a message awaited her. Raoul had sent an apologetic note, scrawled in his strong, elegant script. He couldn't see her that day, he had written, for, to his shame, he had overindulged in alcohol the night before, and as a result he was no fit company for a lady. He begged her forgiveness and promised to visit that evening, when he expected to be presentable.

Charity crumpled the paper in one hand and tossed it into the dining room fireplace. The grate was cold, so she struck a match and watched the small flame consume it. She would have the buggy hitched up again and ride back over to Raoul's grandfather's ranch straightaway. He was going to hear what she had to say, whether he was hung over or not. She had agonized over the conversation for weeks as it was, and she could bear no more delay.

Jonah, who had risen from his chair when she entered the room, raised both eyebrows. "Is everything all right, my dear?" he asked.

"You know very well that it isn't," Charity answered, respectfully but with an edge to her voice. She took her place at the table, although she knew she would not be able to swallow a bite of food. "Raoul is back."

Her father heaved a martyrly sigh as he sank back into his own chair. Blaise, complaining of a headache, had not come down to join them, and Aaron had long since left to ride over to the neighboring ranch, follow the cowboys around and generally get underfoot. "Raoul and his men have traveled a thousand miles with those cattle," he said. "It's understandable that they might want to wash the dust from their throats with a little whiskey."

She straightened her spine and gave Jonah a pointed look.

He flushed and hastily cleared his throat. "I have not taken to reading your correspondence, if that's what you're thinking. I had a word with Ben this morning; he told me the boy was a little the worse for wear."

51

Charity didn't bother to explain her dilemma; she and her father had had that conversation too many times already, without ever reaching an accord. "Raoul is a grown man," she said quietly. "If he wants to drink himself into a state of misery, that's his affair and his alone."

He passed her a plate of biscuits and she knew by his wary expression that he wanted to lecture her but was restraining himself. "That is a very reasonable attitude, Charity," he said.

She looked with distaste at the fluffy, steaming biscuit on her plate and was saved from trying to eat when the front door slammed open in the distance and Aaron bolted into the room.

He was a wiry child, with red hair and two freckles for every angel in heaven, and his brown eyes were enormous as they sought and found Charity. "Father Elias needs you right now—there's measles at the mission school. He sent a peddler this way with the news. Can I go with you?"

Jonah was on his feet immediately, but Charity was quicker still.

"You may not," Charity told her future stepbrother firmly. "Run to the barn and fetch Taffeta for me, please, and don't bother to saddle her."

Aaron hesitated for a moment, as though he might argue, and then bounded outside again.

"Charity," Jonah said, taking a loose hold on her elbow, "listen to me. It isn't safe for you to go there."

"I've had measles, Papa," she answered,

already on her way toward the dining room doors. "I may not be back for several days," she turned to say briskly, as an afterthought. "Would you mind explaining to Raoul? He's planning to pay us a call tonight. Tell him he mustn't come to the school—he's liable to break out in spots if he does."

"Charity—"

She did not wait to hear what else her father had been going to say. Father Elias was a good man and a fine, patient teacher, but he was over seventy, and none too well himself. He could not be expected to deal with such an outbreak by himself, nor was it realistic to hope for help from the people of Jubilee. Although there were many who might have come to his aid otherwise, they would most likely be afraid of carrying the disease home to their own children.

Aaron returned quickly, riding Taffeta, and jumped down to surrender the reins to Charity. Despite her ruffled and voluminous skirts, she mounted easily, and paid no more mind than usual to the fact that her ankles and petticoats were showing.

"Stay here, Aaron," she warned, in case he was planning to follow on his own pony, Trooper. "If I catch you near that mission school, I'll tell your mother plenty that you don't want her to know."

He swallowed and nodded.

Charity raised her gaze to Jonah, who was standing on the porch, watching her, his face in shadow. "Send to White Horse Junction for the doctor, Papa. And we'll need as much quinine as you can round up. Leave it under that old birch tree at the mission gate."

Jonah nodded, and with that, Charity reined Taffeta around and set out for the mission at top speed. She took the shortcut across the Shardlow place out of long habit, and nearly ran Luke down when she sent the mare springing over a fallen log. She hadn't seen him there, bare-chested and sweating, his suspenders making loops at his hips, an ax in his hands.

He jumped out of the way with a shout of affronted surprise, and Charity brought Taffeta around in a half-circle.

"I'm sorry," she said breathlessly, afraid to tarry more than a few moments. "Are you all right?"

Luke looked grim. "I reckon I'll live," he said. "Where are you headed in such a hurry?"

Just on the other side of the Shardlow land was the mission's orchard and beyond that, the tiny compound with its chapel, dormitory and schoolhouse. She cast a longing, frantic glance in that direction. "I've got to go— some of the children are sick—"

"Go," Luke said. "And be careful."

She was heartened, somehow, by that brief encounter. He hadn't tried to stop her, as her father had, as Raoul surely would have done, had he been given the opportunity. No, Luke had understood her haste, with very little explanation, and even urged her on.

Before she had reached the edge of his

property, he was beside her, riding the pinto gelding without a saddle. He had donned a shirt, and he bent from the horse's back to unlatch the gate in the orchard fence, waiting chivalrously while she rode through ahead of him.

"You mustn't stay here," she said, slipping off Taffeta and hurrying toward the open doorway of the chapel, where Father Elias stood waiting, his white hair a rumpled aureole around his head, his kind face strained and pale. "There could be an epidemic brewing."

Luke, keeping pace with her as he buttoned his shirt, would not be put off. "I might be able to help," he reasoned.

She whirled on him, there in the sunny chapel yard. "I do not have time to argue with you, Mr. Shardlow," she snapped. "There are sick children here, and that means there will be a great deal of work to do. Frankly, neither Father Elias nor I need you getting in our way!"

"Come quickly," the priest interceded, beckoning to Charity. "There are six of them down, and the others are very frightened."

Charity followed Father Elias into the dormitory, and noticed as she did so how stooped he was, and how his step had slowed. She felt a pang—he had been her friend for as long as she could remember. When had he begun to fail this way?

Luke was right on her heels, but she had already given up the idea of persuading him to leave. It was clear that he wouldn't be persuaded, and she would waste no more time on the effort.

The children slept in cots in two good-sized rooms, one for the boys, one for the girls. The kitchen that served them all was attached.

"I'll get some cold water," Luke said, taking up a bucket and heading for the well in the courtyard, and the priest spoke softly to Charity.

"Who is that?"

"I think he's a frog disguised as a prince," she replied cryptically. "I tried to send him away, but he wouldn't go."

Oddly, the priest smiled at that. "Then we shall have to make good use of his stubbornness. I will look after the boys, Charity—you go to the girls."

She obeyed, and found that the situation was worse than she'd imagined. Four little girls lay abed, their skin hot and dry, their lips swollen. They were covered from head to foot with small red bumps and tossing with fever. The remaining children looked on with wide, worried eyes, afraid to come too close, but unwilling to abandon their friends.

Despair swelled in Charity's heart for a moment, but then she put her fears aside and set the girls who had not been stricken to tearing rags. When Luke brought in two buckets full of cold well water, she looked up at him gratefully.

He laid a hand on her shoulder. "Is there a doctor on the way?" he asked quietly.

Charity began bathing one of the sickest children with a cloth soaked in water. "Yes," she replied miserably, "but it might be days before he arrives. It's a long way to White Horse Junction, and we are not a priority here."

His jaw tightened. "I can probably convince him otherwise," he said.

Charity shook her head. "You can't leave now," she replied, touched by his fierce desire to help but angry, too. "You've been exposed, and that means you could spread the disease, even if you're immune yourself. That's why I told you to keep away."

"Then I guess I'd better make myself useful. What can I do?"

"Go and help Father Elias with the boys. He'll show you what needs to be done." She managed a smile. "And since you're in a persuasive mood, get Father to lie down and rest for a while. He's probably been on his feet half the night."

Luke tilted his head in assent and left the room.

After that, time passed so quickly that hours seemed like mere moments; Charity went from one child to another, trying in vain to soothe them and bring down their fevers. By sunset, two more girls had broken out in rashes, and Luke reported that several more boys had fallen ill as well.

Charity wept as she worked, and would never have known she was crying if Luke hadn't handed her the blue bandanna he pulled from his hip pocket.

"It's clean," he said, with a grin, when she hesitated. "Come on, Charity. Let's go outside and get a breath of fresh air." When she still didn't move, he drew her gently to her feet and led her through the doorway.

She was flabbergasted to find the day gone and stars scattered across a bruise-colored sky. Wiping her face with the bandanna, she sat down on the ancient wooden bench that stood against the chapel's outer wall. "You were a fool to come here," she said uncharitably.

He grinned, undaunted. "You're welcome," he said. "I was glad to help."

"Father Elias and I would have handled the situation just fine."

His eyes softened, and his gaze seemed for a moment to caress her. "Father Elias is on the verge of collapse, and you will be too if you keep insisting that you don't need anybody to help you."

"I don't need *you* to help me," Charity clarified, after blowing her nose.

"Well, you've got me, whether that suits you or not. According to the priest, it might be as long as two weeks before we can leave this place."

Charity looked at him in alarm. "Two weeks? What about your place? Do you have animals that need to be fed?"

Luke let the back of his head rest against the chapel wall, closed his eyes, and permitted himself a sigh. "Just the team I bought to pull my wagon. There's plenty of grass for them to eat, and they know their way down to the spring."

"You are remarkably calm about this, Mr. Shardlow."

"Luke," he corrected, without opening his

eyes. After a long time, he looked at her again. She felt something wrench inside her; a sweet, fierce kind of sensation, made of both pleasure and pain. "You don't seem too anxious to leave yourself," he observed. "Two weeks is a long time when a person is planning to be married in a month."

She narrowed her eyes. "Who told you that?"

"Your father. But I would have heard it around Jubilee anyway. It was the main topic of conversation at the saloon last night."

Charity winced, but it was a slight motion, and she hoped Luke hadn't seen it. "I understand there was quite a celebration."

Luke smiled, but there was a cautious, distant expression in his eyes now. "Ummm," he agreed. "It was that all right."

"You were there?"

He pondered his answer for a few moments, then nodded. "I was," he affirmed. "Your intended is a fine figure of a man, but he drank a few too many toasts to your beauty and virtue for his own good, I'm afraid. His friends had to carry him out."

Charity blushed and then pushed back tendrils of hair that had fallen around her face. "Raoul is not a drunkard," she said stiffly, "if that's what you're thinking."

He laughed. "I'm the son of Trigg Shardlow," he said. "I'm not likely to be casting stones. Not where drinking is concerned, anyhow."

She bit her lip. "I'm sorry if I seemed unkind. I just wanted you to understand that

59

Raoul is a good man." *A man who doesn't deserve to have his heart broken.*

"I could see that," Luke answered. "Do you love him?"

She didn't answer for a few moments. "Raoul and I were children together. I didn't have an older brother, and I wanted one in the worst way, so I tagged after him something awful. He never chased me away, though I must have driven him mad, sticking to his heels the way I did."

"That doesn't answer my question, but that's all right. It's none of my business any way you look at it, and I was out of line asking."

Charity shook her head. "No, Luke, you weren't. I need to tell *someone* how I feel. My father won't listen, and Father Elias is too burdened for such frivolous confidences. I can't marry Raoul. I simply can't do that to him—or to myself."

Luke's mouth tilted up slightly, just at one corner. "Would it be that bad, being married to you?"

He was teasing; she knew that by the light in his eyes, but she elbowed him in the ribs all the same. "For Raoul, yes. I don't love him the way a woman ought to love her husband."

"Then you oughtn't to marry him."

"I don't intend to. I was planning to tell him last night, but he wanted to go to the saloon with the others. I decided I would ride over this morning, but then I got word of what was happening here, and I couldn't take the time."

Tentatively, Luke took her hand in his and squeezed it. It was an encouraging gesture, but not an over-familiar one. "He's going to be a mighty unhappy man."

"Not as unhappy as he would be in a loveless marriage, year after year."

"There are men, Miss Barnham," Luke said gently, "who would count themselves lucky to have you for a wife, even if you just pretended to love them."

"But I couldn't pretend," Charity replied. "Don't you see? That's the problem."

"I don't know why I'm saying this—I ought to have my head examined for it. But it seems to me that you might grow to love a good man, if you gave the situation ample time. Raoul Montego has land and money, and he cares for you. I reckon most women would consider him to be handsome. He knows you, and you know him. Things like that matter a whole lot, Charity," he paused, pretending to be taken aback by her expression, which she knew was a stubborn one, "—whether that sets well with you or not."

"Suppose I *didn't* learn to love him? Suppose what Raoul feels for me isn't real at all, but just some romantic fancy that will die when the novelty wears off?"

He had released her hand, but his curved fingers brushed her beneath the chin, and she felt a jolt of something startling and elemental rush through her, like a hot wind. For a moment or so, she truly thought he would kiss her, and when he didn't, she was at once relieved and bitterly disappointed.

Before he could say anything, Father Elias

appeared, carrying a lantern. He looked as small and fragile as a bird in his familiar robes, and Charity was again struck by the fear that her dear friend was ill.

"You must lie down and rest, Charity," the priest said. "Perhaps the doctor will arrive tomorrow, and bring medicine."

Medicine. Charity remembered asking her father to get what quinine he could and place it by the birch tree at the mission's main gate. She bolted to her feet and, suddenly light-headed, swayed.

Rising, Luke steadied her by taking a firm hold on her arm.

"I'm not sick," she assured him quickly, but she was pleased and a little flattered by his concern. She was a strong woman and, as such, she was unused to being looked after. "I'm tired, that's all, and I got up too fast. I just wanted to go and see if my father's men brought the supplies I asked for. I said to leave them under the birch tree by the gate."

"I'll have a look," Luke said, after pressing her to sit down on the bench again. And he was away before she could make a protest.

Father Elias joined her, sighing as he did so. "I remember Luke's father," he said, gazing thoughtfully after Luke's retreating figure. "His mother, too. She was a good woman."

"I've been wondering why he came back to Jubilee," Charity admitted. "There's the land, of course, but I don't think that's it. He doesn't seem like the sort to settle down."

"Doesn't he?" Father Elias asked.

The question seemed odd, and Charity knew the priest didn't expect an answer, so she didn't attempt to come up with one.

Luke returned within a few moments, carrying a large wooden crate. "Where do you want this, Father?" he asked. "There are three more waiting out there."

Father Elias asked that the boxes be put in the kitchen, on one of the trestle tables, and Charity went back to her patients. Presently, when she had tucked those few children who had not broken out with measles into their beds and reassured them as best she could, Luke entered with a bottle of quinine and several of the small wooden spoons the mission students used to eat their porridges and stews.

Together they administered the medicine to each of the fevered children, and then Luke brought in a stack of blankets and made up an empty cot for Charity.

"You need something to eat," he said.

She shook her head. "I couldn't."

"I'll help you, then," he replied and, taking her hand, led her out of the room, with its dim, flickering kerosene lanterns, and across the courtyard to the small kitchen, where Father Elias was slicing bread. There was butter, too, and milk in crockery jars. An array of Peony's best preserves, a wheel of cheese, hard-boiled eggs and plenty of cold chicken and dried meat.

"Come the morning," Father Elias said, beaming, "the children will have a feast! God is good."

"God," Luke asked, "or Jonah Barnham?"

"Our heavenly Father works through all sorts of men to do His will," the priest insisted good-naturedly. He'd probably prayed for donations of food, as well as medicine, and here was his answer. "Women too, of course. He has an appreciation for irony, and often uses folks who've lost their way to guide the rest of us where He wants us to go."

Luke's jaw tightened, relaxed again. He put together a plate of food for Charity, pressed her into a chair, and set the meal in front of her. "Eat," he said, and sat crosswise on the bench beside her, apparently determined to watch every bite go into her mouth. Again, she felt that ache of tenderness in the most private regions of her heart.

"Let us thank the Lord," said the priest, and bowed his head.

The next morning, Charity was awakened by the sound of a male voice shouting her name. She hauled herself off the cot—she'd been up tending the children several times during the night—and staggered to the door of the girls' dormitory.

Raoul was at the gate, and he looked ready to get off his horse and break the thing down. Another few moments of that shouting and he'd awaken everybody at the mission.

"Stop it," Charity commanded. "There are children trying to sleep, and poor Father Elias is practically on his last legs."

Raoul's black eyes flashed with temper and

worry. He swung down from the saddle and started to open the gate.

"Don't," Charity said, and he froze. "There's sickness here. You mustn't let yourself be exposed."

Unlike Luke, Raoul heeded her warning. Though given to grand impulses and passionate declarations, he could be practical when it served him. He scowled, plainly pondering the possible consequences of stepping through that gate.

"What are you doing here?" he demanded, through his fine, perfect teeth.

"You know full well what I'm doing here," Charity replied quietly, folding her arms. She'd slept in her dress and her hair needed brushing, and she knew her appearance probably worried Raoul, but there wasn't much she could do about that. Oh, indeed, that was the least of her worries. "I've been helping Father Elias for five years. Now there's an outbreak of measles, and the children need me."

"I need you," Raoul said, thumping his chest. Just then, his gaze strayed past Charity's shoulder, and she knew without turning around that Luke was somewhere behind her. "Who's that?" he hissed.

Charity looked back then, like Lot's wife. Luke was standing in the doorway of the small dormitory building, arms folded, one shoulder braced against the jamb. "His name is—"

"I *know* who he is," Raoul growled.

"Then why the devil did you ask me?"

Charity snapped, out of patience. "He got stuck here by accident and, in case you're interested, he's been a great help." She glanced backwards again and saw Luke push himself away from the framework of the door and amble slowly toward them, looking unshaven and rumpled. His grin was either mischievous or insolent—or both.

"I'd shake your hand," he said to Raoul, stopping at Charity's side, "but I don't guess that would be a good idea. Unless you've already had the measles, of course."

Raoul retreated a step, frowning. He glared at Luke for a few moments, then shifted his gaze back to Charity's face. "What about our wedding?" he asked. "It's coming up soon—"

"I don't want to talk about that right now," Charity interrupted. She couldn't break their engagement in front of Luke or anyone else; Raoul's pride would be injured as it was. But she felt like a coward for letting the chance pass, even though she'd convinced herself her reasons for doing so were good ones.

"Well, I do," Raoul snapped. "I haven't seen you in three months. There are decisions to make, things we need to talk about."

"There surely are," Charity said, with a little sigh. She wished with all her heart for some way to keep from hurting her old friend, but no solutions presented themselves. "I'm sorry, Raoul, but I cannot—*will* not—abandon these children."

Raoul looked thunderous but then, like some majestic rooster settling his feathers, he began to collect himself. "You're going to have to give this up, once we're married," he said grudgingly. "We'll soon have babies of our own, you know."

Charity said nothing; she couldn't bear to speak. She wanted children more than anything else in life, but not by Raoul.

"If you want to help," Luke said, with a cordial bite to his words, "you might fetch some of Miss Barnham's things from the ranch. You know, dresses and brushes and books and the like."

"Give me a list," Raoul said, after an ominous, glowering silence. A few minutes later, he rode away, and Charity thought it was significant that he didn't look back even once.

For three days and nights, Charity, Luke and Father Elias labored, feeding the children, trying to bathe away their fevers, soothing them as best they could when they were at their most uncomfortable. In one instance, Luke held a little boy in his arms for the better part of eight hours, and when the child was fitful, he walked the floor with him.

On the morning of the fourth day, the doctor arrived and surprised them all.

She rode a brown mule, wore a cast-off coat that dragged on the ground when she walked, and called herself Dr. Molly. She was young, into the bargain, and had dark hair and great, serious violet eyes.

"You've done a good job here," she said, after she'd examined all the children thoroughly.

They sat at the long table in the kitchen, she and Charity drinking strong, sweet tea while Father Elias and Luke enjoyed coffee. "It looks like they'll all recover, but one or two of them might suffer hearing or vision problems afterwards. Measles is a serious disease as it is, but it's usually worse among Indians than among whites." She looked at Luke and Charity. "In a couple of days, it should be safe for the two of you to leave."

"I can't say I won't enjoy a little poker-playin' and some whiskey," Luke said.

Charity stared at him. He'd worked tirelessly throughout their ordeal and never said a word about missing those vices or any others. During the endless nights, they'd talked in quiet voices, exchanging confidences. She'd told him things she would never have told a stranger under any other circumstances, and he'd confided that his mother's elder sister, Rose, had been Trigg Shardlow's first wife, which meant, he supposed, that Vance was his cousin as well as his half-brother.

Now, suddenly, there was a distance yawning between them, and he was becoming a stranger again, drawing back inside himself.

The realization saddened her as few other things had done in her comfortable, privileged life. What had she expected? That he, a member of the notorious Shardlow family, would change because she wished it to be so?

She was twenty-three years old and it was time she stopped believing in fairy tales.

68

Dr. Molly stayed with them that night, and Charity got her first full eight hours sleep since she'd arrived at the mission almost a week before. In the morning, Luke left. He said good-bye to every one of the children and to Father Elias, but he seemed to have little to say to Charity, and she wondered if she'd done or said something to offend him.

The day after that, three women from the Holy Spirit Redemption and Glory Church in Jubilee arrived to help out, and Father Elias sent Charity home with strict orders not to come back too soon. Dr. Molly rode with her as far as the fork in the road that led through Jubilee to White Horse Junction in one direction, and onto the Double B in the other. Charity was in no particular hurry, and she had no cause to cut across the Shardlow place, so she steered clear of it.

She expected to be tired when she got home, but instead she was filled with a dangerous, vibrant sort of energy. She cajoled Peony into preparing an enormous breakfast, fit for a cowhand, then, in the privacy of her room, indulged in a long, hot bath. That done, she dressed carefully and sat at her dressing table, gazing blindly at her own reflection and practicing what she would say to Raoul when she called upon him later that day.

4

$\mathcal{B}$en Draper, Raoul's grandfather, came outside to greet Charity when she stopped the horse and buggy in front of their sprawling log home. Arthritic but full of energy nonetheless, Mr. Draper limped quickly down the front steps and extended a hand to help her out of the rig. His blue eyes twinkled with delight as he took in her tidy morning dress of light green cotton, and she realized with a pang that he too would be injured when she delivered her news. Perhaps they would no longer be friends...

"Ain't you a pretty sight," the old man crowed, staring down at her gloved hand for a moment and then pumping it vigorously. "I reckon you've come lookin' for Raoul, and it's my bad luck to be the one to disappoint you. He's gone over to White Horse Junction to sell off some of them cattle of his. I wouldn't be surprised if he came back home with a fancy weddin' ring in his pocket!" At this last, Mr. Draper winked.

Charity could have wept with frustration. It seemed that all of Creation was conspiring to keep her from having that crucial conversation with Raoul. "When will he be home?"

"Couple of days," Mr. Draper said. His kindly old face was wreathed with sympathy; he'd misread her consternation for the sorrow of a besotted bride-to-be who has been parted too long from her groom. "Why don't you come inside for a little while? I reckon I could rustle up some tea."

She was not in a sociable mood, but Mr. Draper had been a family friend for as long as she could remember and, like many widowers, he was starved for gentle company. She nodded, and took the arm he offered.

She had, of course, visited the house many times. It was a spacious place, with a certain rustic elegance, a fact that always seemed to take Charity by surprise. There had not been a woman residing under that roof for at least twenty years—an old wrangler and a Chinaman called Kwan did the cooking and cleaning between them, squabbling like a pair of spinster sisters all the while—and yet there were usually fresh flowers around. The curtains were of Irish lace, always pristine, despite the unremitting dust of summer, and there were brightly colored rugs scattered over the gleaming wooden floors.

After seeing Charity to the parlor, Mr. Draper took himself off in the direction of the kitchen, and returned presently to say that Kwan was brewing their tea.

They sat and chatted amicably, and then Kwan appeared with a tray, loaded with a plate of fussy little lemon cookies as well as a pot of steaming orange pekoe, delicate porcelain cups, fresh milk and lumps of sugar in a shining silver bowl.

Charity knew that Raoul was not the only member of that household who had been

71

looking forward to her coming to live on the ranch, and even though she enjoyed the visit, she felt weighed down by the sure and certain knowledge that there wasn't going to be a wedding. By that point she was so desperate to settle things with Raoul that she was ready to follow him to White Horse Junction.

Later, while she drove home from the Draper ranch, which would soon belong to Raoul, she imagined explaining the idea to her father. The prospect caused her to roll her eyes. No, she decided, she would stay home and bide her time until Raoul returned from selling his cattle. The winds of trouble were already blowing, and to whip them up further would be plain folly.

It was a time that demanded patience, the very trait that came least easily to Charity.

The following afternoon, she was in the small parlor, trying to keep her agitated mind on the straight and narrow path and playing a game of dominoes with Aaron, when the news came, brought by a cowboy dispatched from the Draper ranch.

Raoul had been set upon by bandits, behind a saloon in White Horse Junction, and during the fracas, he had been shot. His injuries were serious, but not fatal, and he would be brought home to his grandfather's ranch as soon as he was well enough to travel.

The message took the starch out of Charity's knees; she had risen from her chair, hearing the pounding hooves of the cowboy's horse, but when the announcement was made she sank down again.

"The boss said particular-like that you're not to go to him, ma'am," the cowboy told her solicitously, looking uncomfortable and out of place in a rich man's parlor. He cleared his throat and gulped. "Raoul says you should go right ahead with the wedding plans. He's got his heart set on bein' mainly recovered in time to stand up before the preacher."

Charity covered her face with both hands for a moment, then raised her head and straightened her shoulders. "You're certain that he's all right?"

"Well, ma'am, he's fine—for somebody who took a bullet in his thigh—" The man colored vividly as he realized that he'd mentioned a part of the human anatomy in the presence of a lady and looked as though he'd either swoon with mortification or whirl around and flee the room.

"Thank you," Charity said, eager to put the man out of his obvious misery. "How is Mr. Draper? This must have been a terrible shock to him."

"He's a tough old bird, Ben is. He turned a mite flimsy when I first told him, but then the Chinaman brought him a couple of shots of whiskey, and that fixed him up proper."

Charity had gotten to her feet, though she didn't remember doing so, and her hand rested on Aaron's thin, sharp little shoulder. "Has anyone told my father?" she asked. "He'll want to pay a call on Mr. Draper and ask if there's anything he can do."

The cowboy nodded. "My partner Jake

went lookin' for Mr. Barnham," he replied. "I reckon he knows what's happened by now."

Charity thanked the man and Blaise, who had come in from another room without calling attention to herself, saw him to the front door.

"What're you gonna do?" Aaron asked, gazing up at her with enormous eyes. Like practically everyone else in her life, he held Raoul in very high regard, and she couldn't help wondering if she was going to have a friend in the world once she'd called off the wedding.

"Wait," she answered. "There isn't much else I *can* do." She hated that, for she was not one to dillydally, once she'd made a decision. Not usually, anyway.

Blaise returned, looking pale. "Aaron," she said, "Peony needs some things from the garden. Go and help her, please."

The boy erupted from the room, and the two women were alone.

"You look absolutely desolate," Blaise said softly, taking Charity's upper arms in a gentle grasp, meant to brace her up, and brushing her cheek with a light kiss. "Don't worry so much, darling. The man said Raoul will be all right, and I'm sure he's right."

Charity felt tears spring to her eyes and blinked them back. "What am I to do now?" she whispered miserably. "I can't very well go to Raoul and tell him I don't love him—not under these circumstances—and yet with every day that passes, the lie gets bigger."

"Have you ever told Raoul that you loved him?"

Charity shook her head. He'd made his own declaration, Raoul had, and simply assumed that she felt the same way. The wedding had been his idea, too—he'd never formally proposed—and she had not spoken up because she'd thought it was just one of his spectacular whims. Then, a few months before, he'd arbitrarily set the date, without bothering to mention it to Charity. She had learned of her fate from her father, one night at supper.

She knew she should have gone straight to Raoul then, set matters right in no uncertain terms, but it was as if she'd been swept up in some sort of whirlwind. The moment never seemed quite right.

She sighed. Perhaps the marriage was fated after all.

Luke Shardlow's image came to mind, and she knew that wasn't the case. If she loved Raoul the way a wife should love a husband, Jonah's theories about arranged marriages to the contrary, surely she wouldn't think of Luke with such frequency, and such heat.

She went upstairs, changed into boots, a blouse and a riding skirt, and then proceeded to the barn, where she led Taffeta out of a stall and threw a bridle on over the mare's head. She knew that had it been her father who had been shot, or Luke, nothing could have kept her from going to them. The fact that she could so easily heed Raoul's decree that she stay at home was enough to put away any lingering doubts she might have had.

She planned to ride to the creek bank, always her favorite retreat, but somehow she ended up at Luke Shardlow's cabin instead. He was on the roof, shirtless and astraddle of the support beam, driving nails with hard, swift blows of a hammer.

He had noticed her right away, she knew that, but he took his time turning to acknowledge her. When he did, he swept off his sweat-soaked leather hat, then plunked it back onto his head again. That maddening grin of his, usually so frequent, was not in evidence. "Is something wrong?"

Everything is wrong, she thought. "Does something have to be the matter for a person to be neighborly?" she retorted, shading her eyes with one hand as she gazed up at him. If only Raoul made her feel the way this man did—exasperated, breathless, sweetly anxious—there wouldn't be a problem.

He swung one leg over the beam, stood, and made his way down the side of the roof with the deftness of a mountain-raised Indian descending a steep hill. Reaching the ladder that rested against the eave, he moved quickly to the ground. Pausing in front of a large barrel, he reached in with a dipper, drew out water, and splashed it over the back of his neck. He shook his head and made a sputtery sound of exultant shock, then came toward her, his flesh beaded with moisture.

Charity gaped at him—he was beautifully

76

made, like some living statue—and he had already snatched his shirt from a sawhorse and shrugged into it before she could make herself look away. Her own immodesty caused her to blush.

"I would invite you into my parlor," he said, with a teasing gesture toward the little house, "but I don't think that would be proper." He turned a small barrel onto one end and invited her to sit. "What are you doing here?" he asked then, his arms folded and his expression solemn.

"I don't have anyone else to talk to," Charity lamented. It was true, too—her best friend, Rose-Ellen Crawford, had married at the beginning of summer and moved to the next county. Her father wouldn't listen, Blaise was torn between sympathy for Charity's situation and loyalty to Jonah, the man she loved. Father Elias had enough on his mind, running the mission all by himself.

Luke rubbed the back of his neck with one hand. His hair was tied back with a strip of leather, though bits of it were coming loose here and there. "I imagine the topic hasn't changed since the last time we spoke," he said, pulling off his hat and swatting his thigh with it once. "This is about Montego, isn't it?"

Charity noticed that the ominous firearm was strapped onto his hip, as always. Even at the mission school, she'd never seen him without it. "Do you sleep wearing that thing?" she asked, pointing.

He chuckled. "No," he said. "But it's always within reach. And stop hedging."

"All right," she agreed grimly, "yes. It's about Raoul." She looked up at him and felt sudden tears stinging in her eyes. "He's been shot."

Luke crouched beside her, his brow furrowed. "I'm sorry," he said. "What happened?"

Something in his expression, in the way he took her hand and interlocked his fingers loosely with hers, made Charity's heart constrict. "There was a robbery, and he was shot. He–he's going to be all right—"

"Wait a minute," Luke interrupted. "Where did this robbery take place? And when?"

"Last night," Charity explained, a little taken aback by the intensity of his interest. "Over in White Horse Junction."

"Who did it? Did Montego get a look at them?" The questions were strangely urgent. His grasp on her hand had tightened.

She frowned. "I don't know if anyone was caught, or whether Raoul saw anything. He was shot, that's what's important."

"You're right," he agreed. He looked preoccupied and, releasing her hand, rose from his haunches. In the same distracted way that some men will fondle a watch fob or flip a coin end over end between two fingers, he drew the pistol, snapped open the cylinder, and spun it once with the pad of his thumb. "White Horse Junction," he muttered, shoving the .45 back into its battered holster. Then, as if he'd forgotten that Charity was even there, he whistled through his teeth for the horse and then fetched some personal gear and his tack from a little lean-to he'd built at one side of the cabin.

The gelding came at a trot, a fact which vaguely irritated Charity. If the moon had been out, she supposed that would have answered his summons too, trailing a sky full of stars.

"You're not just going to—to *leave*—?"

He kissed her forehead with such force that she rocked on her heels and felt even more annoyed than before. "That's exactly what I'm going to do," he said. "You wouldn't mind putting my tools away, would you? I'm in kind of a hurry."

"I think I have the right to ask where you're going."

He grinned. "Do you?" he countered. The bridle was already in place, and he was tugging at the saddle to make sure the cinch was tight enough to support his weight.

"Well, maybe I *don't* exactly have the right—" Charity hurried along beside his horse when he swung up into the saddle.

The pinto danced with impatience, wanting to be gone, and Luke seemed only slightly less eager. He tugged at his hat brim and smiled, but Charity knew by the look in his eyes that his mind was already far down the road.

She followed after him for a few steps, before her innate sense of dignity came to the fore, and she realized what she was doing and stood still. This, she reflected, was one of the many reasons why she shouldn't fall in love with Luke Shardlow. Because one day she would stand watching him ride away, there on his family homestead or somewhere else, and know that he was never coming back. She could survive that—she could survive anything, given the time—but the pain would be almost beyond enduring.

Stricken, as much by her insights into her own emotions as by his departure, she watched until he and the horse had vanished from sight before gathering up his tools—a hammer, an ax, a planing knife—and putting them inside the cabin.

She shouldn't have lingered there, should have had better things to do, but she stood in the shadowy quiet of the one-room structure, blinking a couple of times before her eyes adjusted to the dim light. There was no real furniture, just an old stove—surely the very one on which poor Marietta Shardlow had struck her head that long ago night—a large wooden crate with a candle in the center, obviously his table, and a smaller one that served as a chair. Several volumes with tattered covers were stacked on a shelf behind the stove, and Charity was inexorably drawn to them. She had never been able to resist looking at people's books when she visited their homes; in most cases, this habit told her more about their minds and spirits than a private diary could ever have done.

She smiled, running a fingertip over the worn spines. *Paradise Lost. A Rancher's Guide to Animal Husbandry. Theories of Advanced Mathematics.* Two novels by Sir Walter Scott, a Bible, and a small dictionary with a great many of the words circled in dark pencil.

Encouraged, though she could not have said why, Charity turned and left Luke's cabin, closing the door softly behind her.

He reached White Horse Junction at sunset, paid cash at the livery stable for a stall for the pinto and a place in the hayloft for himself, and headed toward the saloon. He could usually trust his instincts, which said that Vance was around somewhere, and that he'd had a part in the shooting the night before, but his nerves were oddly jangled and his inner balance was off. It might be nothing more than wishful thinking, his expecting to find his half-brother somewhere in or around that small town.

The saloon was quiet, a drunk brooding at a table, a couple of cowboys and peddlers at the bar. Everyone looked at him when he came through the door, and quickly looked away again. They'd read him accurately enough; the .45 told the whole story, except for the ending, which might or might not be happy.

He bought a single shot of whiskey and tossed it back.

"I heard there was a shooting around here last night," he said, when the barkeeper, probably more out of curiosity than friendliness, drew nigh and lingered, polishing a glass that would never be clean.

"Yeah," the barkeeper said. "So what?"

Luke took a five-dollar gold piece from a pocket of his vest and laid it on the bar with a minimum of fanfare.

"It was a rancher from over by Jubilee someplace. Some kinda Messican."

"Where is he now?"

The barkeeper pressed the tip of a fat finger to the coin and slid it over to the edge of the bar, enclosed it with his fist. His eyes were small and bright and somehow feral and Luke made a mental note not to turn his back on him. "Over at Miss Della's rooming house, I heard. He ain't in no fit shape to travel."

"Is there any kind of a law around here?" Luke inclined his head slightly, and the bartender refilled his glass. He was a bounty hunter, bent on drawing his outlaw half-brother out of whatever hole he might be hiding in, and as such, he had to keep his intentions to himself. Nor could he have folks around Jubilee talking about how much Luke Shardlow had changed from the old days, because that might get Vance to thinking too much.

"None to speak of. Marshal Dan Higgins rides over from Jubilee once a month, to make sure folks are behavin' themselves. Why? You wanted or something?"

Luke scanned the reflection in the murky mirror over the bar, glass raised to his lips, to make sure there wasn't any trouble taking shape behind him. "Depends," he said. "There was a dance-hall girl down in Laramie that seemed to want me pretty bad."

The bartender snickered. "Maybe so, but Miss Della is a good Christian woman, and she'd be plain scairt, findin' an armed man at her door. You want to speak with that Messican, you better wait till he's out and about, 'cause you ain't gonna get past Miss Della's front gate with that iron on your hip."

Luke tugged at his hat. "Thanks for the advice," he said. Then he took the whiskey bottle, corked it, and shoved it into the pocket of his coat. "I'm much obliged to you."

He paid a kid on the street a penny to show him where Miss Della's house was, and grinned when he saw that he'd been taken. There was a big sign on the front porch.

Covering his gunbelt with his coat, Luke mounted the front steps, tapped at the door, and removed his hat. A curtain moved in a nearby window, and a woman's face appeared, thoughtful and prim in the lamplight.

Luke straightened and summoned up his most boyish grin, calculated to say that yes, he was wild, but he might be set back onto the straight-and-narrow by kindness and the firm, guiding hand of a good woman.

The door opened a crack. "Yes?" Miss Della demanded.

"I'm sorry to trouble you, ma'am," he said, pressing his hat to his heart, "but I've been on the trail a long time, and I heard over at the general store—" he hoped there *was* a general store, he hadn't looked, "—that a man could buy a bath and a hot meal at your house. I don't mind confessin' that I've been missin' my ma's cookin' more than commonly of late."

The spinster's face was a study in caution, but she hadn't slammed the door. "I don't know—"

Luke was just drawing a breath to say he'd eat his supper on the back step if that would ease her mind, when a familiar figure appeared, and edged Miss Della aside.

Dr. Molly regarded him without a smile, but he knew she recognized him.

"Mr. Shardlow?" She opened the door, stepped out onto the porch. "Did I hear you say you'd been on the trail for a while?"

Hell, he thought, but his grin never faltered. The woman had seen him at the mission only a few days before; he could only hope she wouldn't flat-out call him a liar in front of the landlady. "Well, I did ride over here from Jubilee," he said winsomely. "I'm hungrier than a bear, and I do need a bath."

The young woman assessed him quickly, then turned to Miss Della, who fidgeted behind her, like a candle flame in a draft, squinting at Luke in the thin moonlight. "I've met this man," Dr. Molly said. She didn't actually vouch for him, but something in her tone gave the impression that she had. "He was of some help to Father Elias, at the mission."

Luke broadened his grin. "Thank you, Doc," he said, as the two women stepped back to let him in.

The place was clean and well-lit, and it smelled of fresh-baked bread, cleaning solvent, talcum powder and cold ashes. A sharp, singular loneliness, always a step or two behind Luke, caught up and walked abreast of him for a moment. He thought of Charity Barnham, of all people, then quickly put her out of his mind.

He took his time, consuming chicken and dumplings in the kitchen, complimenting Miss Della on the room she showed him, with its slanted ceiling and narrow brass bed. He paid his money, careful to keep his coat on, thus hiding the Colt, and asked Miss Della if there were any other guests in the house.

"Oh, my, yes," she replied, with a glance at one particular door down the corridor, where a bar of light glowed along the floor. Her voice dropped to a confidential whisper. "There's a young man here, recovering from a gunshot wound. Terrible thing. I've never forgiven Papa for bringing Mama and me to this wild place. It simply wasn't very thoughtful of him."

"No, indeed," Luke said sympathetically. From the looks of that house, he figured Papa had done all right by his family, but it wouldn't do to contradict a lady. Unless that lady was Charity Barnham, of course.

"I'll heat your bathwater," Miss Della said. "The tub's in a small room back of the kitchen. You get one towel, and the soap is home-made, so if you've got delicate skin, you'd better make do without it. Has lye. Water ought to be ready in half an hour."

He thanked her, and she left, intent upon her errand.

He waited for a few moments, then went to the door with the light under it and knocked softly. He heard the distinctive sound of a pistol being cocked on the other side, and decided he liked Raoul Montego. He pitied the poor bastard, too, for more than the bullet he'd taken; when he got back to Jubilee, and was fit for spurning, Miss Charity Barnham was going to show him the road.

Luke's spirits rose a little further. He opened the door and stepped inside, hands slightly raised, fingers spread. Montego, though reclining on a sickbed, was holding a big hog-leg on him, with the hammer drawn back.

"You," Montego said.

"I was counting on you to remember me," Luke said, and drew up a chair just as cordially as if he and Montego were old friends. Charity's fiancé rested with one leg sticking out from under the blankets, a thick bandage around his right thigh. He looked gaunt, and there were dark circles under his eyes, but there was a fire blazing inside him, all right. He'd probably be healed up proper, soon enough, though he'd be longer getting over Charity's news.

Luke turned the chair around and straddled it, resting his arms across the back. "Looks like you've had some bad luck."

"Bad luck?" Montego eased the hammer forward and set the pistol aside on the bedside table. He took a porcelain carafe into his hand—it looked silly there, speckled with little bees and flowers as it was—and poured water into an equally unlikely cup. He threw the stuff back as though it were whiskey. "Hell, that doesn't say half of it. I got myself shot and lost a good watch and ten dollars to boot."

"Did you see who jumped you?"

Montego frowned, obviously pondering the events of the night before. "There were four of them, I think, and they were wearing masks."

"Do you remember anything else?"

"What are you, some kind of lawman?"

"Something like that," Luke said easily, and waited. He could lie to most anybody without averting his gaze; it was a Shardlow trait. Anybody, that is, except Charity.

"One of them had yellow hair, like yours. That's all I saw. I was busy trying to stay alive."

Vance's name was pulsing in his mind like a heartbeat. Vance, with his golden hair. The fingers of Luke's left hand flexed unconsciously; he resisted an urge to rest his palm on the butt of his pistol.

"You didn't recognize any of them, or hear a name?"

Montego shook his head and sagged back onto the pillows. "It's my turn to ask questions, Shardlow. What's Charity to you? Why were you there at the mission, when all those kids were sick?"

Fair was fair. Montego had told him what he wanted to know, and he would return the favor. "I knew Charity when we were kids. And I was at the mission because she took a shortcut across my land and I followed her there, to find out what the all-fired hurry was. Turned out we didn't have the option of leaving again."

"You're aware," Montego said carefully, "that Charity and I are going to be married."

87

Luke made sure nothing showed in his face. No emotion, no opinion, no special knowledge. "So I've heard." He paused. "You're a brave man by anybody's reckoning."

Montego laughed, and that changed his whole countenance, if only for a moment. "I plan on going back to her as soon as I'm fit to ride."

"When will that be?" Luke stood, and put the chair back against the wall.

"Tomorrow or the next day, if I have my way. I can recover there just as well as here."

Luke's hand was on the doorknob. "I'll be headed that way myself, in a day or two, if you want company. Or have you got some of your men with you?"

Montego assessed him with solemn eyes. "My men have gone back to the ranch. Tell me, why did you come here? Did Charity send you to play nursemaid?"

He considered saying she had, and decided she would kill him if he did any such thing. "I've got business with one of the men who may have made off with your watch. Are you sure you don't want to hang around here for a while, let that pretty little lady doctor look after you?"

As if on cue, there was another tap at the door, and then Molly came in, carrying a medical bag. "So I was right," she said, gazing impassively at Luke. She'd been calm like that at the mission, too, even during the worst of it, and he wondered now, as then, whether anything ever brought up the fire in her. "You weren't just looking for a meal and a bath."

Luke smiled. "On the contrary, ma'am," he said, with a little bow, "those were the best dumplings I've ever had, and a bath and a good clean bed will be welcome luxuries. Much more to my liking than the hayloft at the livery stable, I'm sure."

Her mouth flicked briefly at one corner, but the large, luminous eyes remained serious.

"Good night, Mr. Shardlow," she said.

He opened the door, stepped out into the hallway. From downstairs, he could hear Miss Della singing "Shall We Gather at the River?" with stalwart Christian fervor. He waited until she'd rendered a few more rousing selections from the family hymnal, then descended the back steps.

The bath was steaming hot, and the soap strong enough to strip the prickly hairs off a boar's hide, but Luke gave himself a good scrubbing, put his clothes back on, and went upstairs to his room.

He slept only intermittently, the .45 on the floor beside his bed, within easy reach. A man never knew when he might get company.

5

Luke awakened before dawn the next morning, and when he descended to the kitchen, he found Montego already there, fully dressed, sipping coffee and looking as though he would fall off his chair. That the man could even hope to sit a horse without being tied to the saddle in his condition was beyond comprehension.

"Morning, Shardlow," Montego said.

Luke nodded and helped himself to a mug from the shelf and coffee from the stove. It was a stout brew, the way he made it when the cards had been running in his favor and he had plenty of change in his pockets. He joined Charity's fiancé at the table. "You look like hell," he said companionably. "And if we're going to hit the trail together, I guess you'd better call me Luke."

"My name is Raoul," the other man said. "And my appearance is not at issue here. I'm heading for home as soon as I've had some breakfast and settled up with Miss Della."

Luke reckoned it was a good sign that his traveling companion could even think about eating, but he still had his doubts. He hoped Vance would try to ambush him along the road, but Raoul's presence was bound to complicate matters. He couldn't reasonably expect to deal with his half-brother and protect Charity's beau at the same time. "Hadn't you better run that idea past the doctor?"

Raoul's smile had something of mischief in it, and something of fondness. Enlightened, Luke wondered if the man even knew that he had at least some tender feelings for Molly. "She'd keep me here for a month if I let her."

"Hmmm," Luke said, reflectively.

Montego's dark eyes flashed in a face pale as a winter moon. "Have a care what you say," he warned. "I only meant that Molly believes I need more time to recover before I make the trip back to Jubilee."

"No offense intended," Luke replied mildly. He baited the trap. "I've been thinking of settling down. You suppose the lady doctor would be interested in a man with a lively history behind him?"

Raoul took the whole hook. "The last thing she needs is a drifter," he said, glaring. "You leave her be and we'll get along just fine, you and I."

Before Luke could respond, Molly herself entered the kitchen, wearing a man's shirt, boots and a skirt fashioned of buckskin. She'd braided her dark hair into a single long plait. "If you two don't mind," she said dryly, shaking her head when both men moved to rise, "I'll choose my own suitors."

Luke hid a grin behind the rim of his coffee mug. Raoul was blushing like a spinster.

Molly didn't sit down, but consumed her coffee leaning against the cast-iron sink under the window. She was a beautiful woman, the kind Luke would normally have pursued, if he hadn't been so damn intrigued by Charity Barnham. His lack of interest worried him more than a little.

"Did you go to school back east?" he asked, in an attempt to diffuse the tension a little.

She lowered her eyes for a moment, plainly

reluctant to answer. "I grew up here in White Horse Junction," she said, when she was good and ready to speak. "My father was a surgeon in General Grant's army, before he came out west. I helped him as much as he'd let me, from the time I could see over the edge of a table without getting up on a chair. He taught me midwifery, how to treat common injuries and the like. Folks have been calling me "Doc" since Papa died, but I don't have a medical degree."

Miss Della interrupted the course of the conversation then by bustling in and rattling stove lids, kettles and pots. Plainly, breakfast was going to be a production.

Molly ate a light meal and left to make her rounds, Luke put away a plateful of bacon, eggs and fried potatoes, and Raoul pushed his food around on his plate with a slice of toasted bread.

Half an hour later, when Luke left Miss Della's rooming house, Raoul was hobbling along beside him.

Watching the other man mount his horse was a grim experience, but Montego wasn't about to accept help from anybody. He dragged himself into the saddle and took a death grip on the horn and pommel to keep from pitching headfirst onto the ground.

"Shit," Luke said, under his breath. If they met up with Vance and his gang on the road to Jubilee, they were screwed. Hell, Miss Della would be more help in a fight than this rock-jawed invalid.

Luke'd have his hands full, and Montego to

nursemaid into the bargain, and he had a whole passel of wanted posters, not to mention memories, to prove that Vance Shardlow was vicious as a sow bear with bad teeth. Two months before, in fact, Vance had killed a woman in southern Nevada, and that had made finding him Luke's personal business. It was plain bad luck that his half-brother's trail led back to Jubilee.

They rode out of town at a slow pace, and traveled some distance in silence. They'd been on the road maybe an hour when, in a sidelong glance, Luke saw Montego's eyes roll back in his head. He caught hold of Raoul's arm just when he would have taken a dive.

"Damn it," he spat, "we're going back. Right now."

Raoul coughed convulsively. "No," he managed to rasp, just when Luke thought he'd spit out a vital organ. "You do what you want, but I'm heading home."

"You love her that much?"

Montego met his gaze and plainly saw too much in Luke's face. "Yes."

"Doesn't it matter to you at all that Charity wouldn't want you to take a chance like this?"

Another spasm of coughing overtook Montego, and it was a while before he could speak. "How do you know what she wants?" he demanded, his eyes blazing.

Luke's sigh came all the way from his lower belly. "If you've got something to say," he snapped, "let's hear it."

"Charity belongs to me."

"She's a woman, not a horse," Luke heard himself say. "She belongs to herself." He paused, lifted his eyes to assess the darkening sky, and growled a curse. "I'll be damned if it isn't about to rain."

Raoul began to chortle, then to laugh. "Whether we go backwards or forwards," he said, over the rising wind, "we're sure to get wet. We might as well be going in the right direction." With that, leaning low over the saddle horn, he spurred his horse into motion and set off down the road at a dead run.

Left behind, Luke took the time to whip off his hat and slap his thigh with it a couple of times. Then he caught up with Montego.

The rain held off for another hour or so, but when it finally came, it was a deluge, and both men were instantly drenched to the skin. They sought refuge under a tree, willing to take their chances with lightning, and after a while the torrent slacked off to a drizzle, and they rode grimly on. Luke knew Montego was hurting, that, in fact, he was only partially conscious a good part of the time, but when they reached the homestead, Raoul insisted on pushing on toward his grandfather's ranch. That, of course, left Luke with no choice but to accompany him.

At the Draper place, Raoul immediately fell out of the saddle and was carried inside by several ranch hands. Luke accepted the old man's wary thanks for seeing Montego safely home, but politely refused to pass the night.

He felt a peculiar sense of agitation, a need to return to his own land, and take his rest beneath the roof he'd nailed into place himself.

He cut across Draper's pasture land and part of the Double B to the creek, now swollen with the warm, pounding rain. The pinto panicked a little on the steep bank, then plunged into the stream, the powerful muscles in his flanks and withers pulling against the flow. Luke felt his boots fill with icy water, then reached beneath his sodden coat to make sure the Colt was secure.

They scrambled up the opposite bank, horse and man, the gelding slipping, struggling for purchase, finally gaining solid ground. Though it was still fairly early, the light was almost gone, diffused in the gray weight of the sky. Luke assessed his position and realized he was near the place where he had first met Charity, some fifteen years before.

The thought had distracted him just long enough to give the riders a chance to surround him. They came out of the trees, guns drawn, rain running off the brims of their hats. Before Luke could reach the .45, the butt of a rifle struck him in the face and sent him sprawling backwards over the horse's rump. Half-blinded by a torrent of rainwater and blood, he rolled, and the Colt was in his hand when he came to his feet.

He fired, saw one of the riders slump over in the saddle, but it was already too late. Vance caught him in the side of the head with a well-aimed boot, and Luke's knees buckled beneath him as light exploded behind his eyes. For a heartbeat, he thought he'd been struck by lightning.

Things went straight downhill from there; he tried to get up, but Vance had already dismounted and was coming after him in earnest. For the second time, he kicked Luke, this time in the solar plexus.

Blood and bile surged up into the back of Luke's throat; he fell forward onto the wet grass, and struggled in vain to rise. Vance and his partners set about killing him then, and when he finally collapsed for the last time, it was as if the earth had become a great, frigid seething beast, yawning and then swallowing him whole.

Waking up came as a not-entirely-pleasant surprise; it was late, he was chilled, and the rain was still coming down. He listened, heard only the splattering chatter of the creek. He rolled onto his back and let the cool night shower rouse him. Pain surged into every nerve ending, thundered in every pulse. He sought the Colt with a groping motion of his hand and miraculously found it in his holster. Vance's idea of humor, no doubt. He thanked God that his brother's imagination was limited and, after several attempts, dragged himself to his knees.

They would be back, he knew, if only to make sure he was dead.

He started toward the oak, moving in something between a crouch and a crawl, stopping often to retch. He wasn't conscious of climbing through the branches to the place where he had so often hidden as a child, but his muscles, bruised though they were, must have remembered.

When Vance and his men returned, he heard their voices, angry and low. Heard the fitful jingle of the fittings on their horses' bridles. He lay holding his breath, holding his heartbeat, aware of the .45 clasped in his left hand.

He passed out, came to again, and knew that they were gone. "Shit," he murmured.

Charity saddled Taffeta and rode to the creek that rain-washed morning because she'd dreamed so vividly of the place the night before, because she'd awakened in the darkest folds of the night, gasping with terror, her whole body reverberating with the hard, painful beat of her heart.

The leaves of the oak dripped rainwater as she climbed; when she reached the tree house, she was at once vindicated and horrified. Luke lay before her, broken and still, his face so swollen that he looked like a grotesque parody of himself.

"What happened?" she cried, dropping to her knees beside him. He was sprawled on his back, with one knee drawn up. His arms fell wide of his body and in his left hand he clasped that ominous pistol of his. His hair and clothes were stained with blood.

Painfully, he laid an index finger to his

lips. "Keep your voice down," he whispered hoarsely. "They might—come back."

"Who?"

He laughed, and the sound was ludicrous, coming from that battered face. "The Ladies' Aid Society," he said. "Sweet God, Charity, I hurt everywhere."

"What can I do? Shall I go and get my father?" She didn't give him a chance to answer. "No, I'd better not leave you. Can you walk? Where is your horse?"

Luke put his arms around her, drew her down beside him. He was soaked through and through, but he was alive, and when she laid her hand on his chest she felt his heart beating steadily against her palm. The rhythm echoed through her like a promise shouted into a canyon; instinctively, she nestled close to him.

"We can't stay here," she said, after a long time.

"I know," he answered, with obvious effort. "The problem is, we can't leave, either. I'm all right, Charity, but I need some time to knit myself back together here."

She raised herself onto one elbow, brushed his discolored cheek with the slightest pass of her lips. "What happened, Luke?" she asked. "Tell me, please—if you don't, I'll go crazy."

"I wasn't paying attention—had my mind on other things. And I got the—some men jumped me."

"Who?"

"I don't know."

He was lying, she knew that immediately,

but she didn't pursue the subject. He was as stubborn as she was and besides, it didn't matter. Nothing mattered except that he was alive. "Is anything broken?" she asked.

He rolled, wincing, onto his side. "No," he said. Awkwardly, he pressed the heavy .45 into her hand. "Listen to me, Charity," he went on. "Take this and go back to the Double B. It's not safe out here."

She laid the pistol aside. "I'm not leaving until you can go with me," she told him.

He drifted off, although whether he was unconscious or merely asleep Charity did not know. She held him in a loose, gentle embrace, and the droplets from the leaves soaked her—secondhand rain, causing her riding skirt to cling to her legs and saturating her white blouse.

She was twenty-three, and despite Jonah's ceaseless efforts to shelter her, she had lived her life on a ranch. She understood the smoldering ache in the most secret parts of her body only too clearly, even though she had never felt anything like it before. Something was unfolding within her, an achy, heated sweetness that both puzzled and exhilarated her.

As emboldened as if she'd swallowed some gypsy love potion, she laid Luke's hand upon her breast, gloried in the sensation of his fingers closing gently around her. Fire raced through her system, like a thousand tiny flames following a network of fuses, spreading in seconds from her straining nipple to the core of her womb.

Luke moved to withdraw, but she covered his hand with her own, held it in place.

"Charity," he ground out, in miserable protest. "Stop it. You don't know what you're doing. Besides that—just in case you haven't noticed—I'm in no shape to deflower a maiden."

Her faced burned, and she laughed and cried, both at the same time. What a tangle this man had made of her emotions. Had he not been so beaten and battered, she might actually have seduced him, right there in the tree house, with the rain soaking them both. Was she losing her mind?

Luke groaned as she kissed his bruised face with no more pressure than the flick of a butterfly's wings, then snuggled close once more, wrapping her arms around him. The innocent ecstasy of that contact was dazzling, searing her from the inside, filling her heart to bursting. She felt as though she'd been struck to the ground by a vision, been blinded by it, like Paul on the road to Damascus.

She kissed the top of Luke's head, kissed his wet, bloodied hair.

"Go home," he murmured. "Now."

She held him tighter, though she was careful not to hurt him. "No," she said.

The nickering of a horse reminded Charity that she had left Taffeta untethered, but when she looked over the edge of the tree-house floor, she saw Luke's pinto below, reins dangling in the wet grass.

"Come on," Charity said, coming swiftly to

her senses. "You're going to die of pneumonia if we don't get you out of this weather."

He got up, with extraordinary effort, and followed Charity down out of the tree with deliberate, agonizing motions. Mounting the horse was another challenge but, with her help, he managed it. Grasping the saddle horn with one hand and placing her foot in the stirrup, Charity swung up behind him.

They rode slowly through another summer shower, headed toward Luke's cabin. Taffeta, who had been grazing in the meadow above the creek, trotted after them.

There was no bed, only a narrow pallet on the floor. Charity helped Luke out of his wet clothes, wrapped him in a musty blanket, and made him lie down while she built a fire in the stove. She fetched water from a rain barrel outside and put coffee on to brew before exchanging her wet outer garments for a blue chambray shirt, which she wore over her camisole and petticoats.

When the coffee was ready, she laced it with whiskey from a bottle she'd found among Luke's supplies and knelt beside him, holding the cup while he drank.

"Bar the door," he said, when he lay back, unable to hold his bruised eye open any longer. "Keep the pistol close at hand—"

She kissed his forehead. "Shhh. We'll be all right," she promised. But when he slept, she lowered the bar across the door and then sat studying the Colt until she was sure she knew how to fire it. Pretty sure, anyway.

Luke slept soundly until sunset, his breathing deep and even, his color improving with every passing hour. Although he was still brilliantly bruised, he got up from the pallet, moving with remarkable agility, and ate hungrily of the tinned meat and boiled turnips Charity had prepared for him. She sensed that his recovery stemmed as much from mental control as physical resilience, and she marveled. Such powers, she theorized privately, must exist in all human beings, but Luke had taken pains to develop them.

"Are you going to tell me what happened to you?" she asked. By then, she had had several cups of coffee, and generous portions of her own wretched food, and her resolve was at a high level.

He stood facing her, his abraded fingers curved beneath her chin, and she was glad that she'd put her semidry clothes back on while he was sleeping. "We have something more important to discuss right now," he said. "Or did I dream what happened in that tree house?"

Charity's cheeks burned; she tried to look away but he wouldn't allow it. "What is there to talk about?" she asked. Nothing had happened. Everything had happened. She was so confused, she didn't know what to do.

He raised one eyebrow. "Charity, something changed between us today. You know that as well as I do." He paused, drew a deep breath, and released it. "Now maybe that is of no great moment to you, but I have my reputation to think of." He grinned, but his eyes were somber. "You and I laid down together in that tree house, and there was some kind of spark and your father is going to have my hide for that. We might as well have—"

"Don't," she whispered, and pressed a finger lightly to his mouth. She doubted that even Luke could guess how tempted she'd been, and she needed time to sort through her own feelings about the matter. All she knew for certain was that she'd behaved in an inexcusably reckless and forward manner.

He simply kissed her fingertip and went right on. "And to put a fine finish to it all, here you are, alone with me, in my cabin, with the sun going down."

She blinked, lest tears come to her eyes. "We didn't do anything wrong," she protested, and sniffled.

"Charity, I'm a Shardlow, and Jubilee is a small town. And somehow, word always gets around." He kissed her forehead with such tenderness that she gave up her efforts not to cry. "For a start," he went on, "we've got to get you home before your father raises a posse. I'll ride with you—" he silenced her when she attempted to protest by kissing her lightly, briefly, on the mouth, "—and then we'll both take a step back, think things over for a couple of days."

Charity straightened her spine and swallowed a couple of times, until she could speak without her voice wobbling. "I can take myself home. I don't need any help from you. If there's been any harm to my reputation—

103

and I don't see how there could have been—
I'll take the consequences."

Luke's smile was no less engaging, no less
winsome, for being misshapen. He touched her
hair, his gaze holding hers fast, even though
she would have liked to look away. "I'm sure
you can. But what about me? How do I live
with the consequences, Charity? I know what
you felt—it went through you like lightning.
And I felt the same thing."

"My father doesn't need to know, if that's
what you're afraid of."

"I'm not afraid of your father," he said,
and she knew he was telling the truth. Which
wasn't to say it wouldn't have been wiser to
beware of Jonah's temper. When roused to right-
eous fury, he could be formidable. "This has
nothing to do with him and everything to do
with us. And what about Raoul? Unless you've
spoken to him, and I think that's very unlikely,
given the condition he was in when I left him
with his grandfather last night, you're still
betrothed. This is not a simple situation,
Charity."

Charity's mind was reeling; she was nearly
overwhelmed by an odd mixture of hope and
scandal. "We could get married," she said, and
could have bitten off her tongue and spat it out.

Luke looked pained. "Have you forgotten
who I am?" he asked gently. "How could you
wear my name and still hold your head up?"

She met his gaze. She could wear his name
for precisely that reason: because it was *his*
name, but she didn't say so. It wasn't the

proper time to talk; too much had happened, he was right about that, and they needed time to work things out in their own minds.

She groomed her hair as best she could, and smoothed her rumpled clothes, and then Luke, refusing to be turned from his purpose, mounted his horse and escorted her all the way to the door of the ranch house on the Double B.

Jonah was waiting on the threshold, his expression grim. When Luke stepped into the light from the entry hall, however, and Jonah saw the marks his visitor wore, his countenance changed.

He guided Charity past him, into the house, and stepped out onto the porch to speak with Luke. Charity followed, and even when Jonah gave her a withering look over one shoulder, she stood her ground.

He turned back to Luke, who waited with a sort of resigned patience.

"I ought to horsewhip you," Jonah told the other man, "but from the look of things, you've already been worked over pretty well. It's late. There's room for you in the bunkhouse—I hope you will pass the night there, as the roads are not safe. You and I will come to terms in the morning."

Charity had seen other men tremble before Jonah, but Luke stood firm and proud. "I'm obliged to you for the offer of a bed," he replied in even tones, "but if you want an explanation, you'll have to ask your daughter for it."

Out of the corner of her eye, Charity saw Jonah's jaw tighten. He turned to her, although his words were directed to Luke. "You may rest assured that Charity and I will have words," he said. "I will not have my daughter out roaming the countryside at all hours, in the company of a—"

"Of a Shardlow?" Luke asked softly, and the very air seemed to crackle around the three of them.

Jonah clamped his jaw down hard. His dark eyes flashed with barely contained fury, but he held his peace.

Charity was suddenly weary, through and through. "Good night," she said to Luke and then, after meeting Jonah's hard gaze straight on, she excused herself and went inside, up the stairs, and into her bedroom.

She expected to lie awake the whole night through, searching her heart, for she had fallen permanently and profoundly in love on that day of days, but instead she slept soundly, without dreaming. When she went downstairs the next morning, she found Blaise alone in the dining room, sipping tea and waiting.

"Your father and Mr. Shardlow are in the study," she said. "Poor Jonah, he looks terrible, and he confessed to me that he barely closed his eyes last night, but he would say little else."

Charity went to the sideboard, poured tea for herself, and joined her future stepmother at the table. She was furious with Jonah; the way he was behaving, anyone would have thought she was fourteen years old, instead of twenty-three. Whatever the constraints of society, and they were many, she was a woman, not an errant girl, and she would not explain her actions to anyone, including Jonah. Besides, all she'd done was lie on the tree-house floor, sheltering Luke in her arms. All she'd done was give away her heart forever and ever.

"Charity?" Blaise prompted.

Her cup rattled in its saucer as she set it down. "What?" she snapped.

"Why is Jonah so upset?"

Charity was not given an opportunity to reply, for at that instant shouts erupted behind the doors of the study, clashing like swords and clearly audible even from that considerable distance. Both women leaped to their feet and hurried out into the entryway, just in time to see Luke come out, his poor scraped and swollen face clenched in outrage. Without a word, without even a glance in Charity's direction, he stormed out into the bright, hot morning, slamming the front door hard behind him.

6

"What did you say to him?" Charity demanded, sweeping into her father's study without bothering to knock. There was little point in confronting Luke while he was in such an angry state; she would gain nothing by doing so.

The interview with Jonah, if the grim pallor of his face was any sign, promised to be only slightly more fruitful. He glared at her, but she stood her ground, arms folded, awaiting his answer.

"I forbid you to see that man again," Jonah said, through his teeth. "Ever."

She was possessed of a sudden and potentially fatal urge to laugh, which was strange given the fact that her head was light with anger and her stomach was churning. "Impossible," she said. She could not, *would not,* say that it was too late, that she had already fallen in love with Luke Shardlow, and thus changed the whole course of her life. His image was branded on her mind, and the sensations of his touch, his brief, tender kiss, impressed into every fiber and nerve, to be remembered, cherished and regretted for all time.

Jonah's jaw clamped down with such force that Charity saw the muscles bunch. "You are a headstrong woman," he said. "Perhaps I was wrong to let you grow up on the Double B, instead of sending you back east to school."

"There is no changing the past." She stated the obvious quietly, keeping her chin at an angle that was almost, but not quite, obstinate, and the words were directed as much to herself as to Jonah. "We have to go forward from here."

Jonah went to the window and stood gazing out for a long time, his back turned to her. When he faced her again, he seemed a little more composed than before, but his emotions were no less earnest. "You are betrothed to another man," he said, "and yet you come to this house with your clothes rumpled and your hair unpinned. What possessed you? You know how fast scandal spreads in a place like this, especially when the Shardlow name is involved."

He wasn't asking her to explain the events of the day, not really, but he clearly suspected that if she hadn't made love with Luke Shardlow, she'd come perilously close to doing so. It was a good thing he didn't know how right he was.

Jonah Barnham hadn't carved out a ranch and a life in that hard and inhospitable place by being stupid; what he really wanted from her now, Charity knew, was the assurance that her penchant for Luke was temporary, essentially meaningless, that she would follow his plan for her and go through with the long-anticipated marriage to Raoul—the very things she could never, ever give.

He knew her reply without her having to speak, had only to look upon her proud, desperate countenance to read her heart. In that moment a chasm opened between them that was a pledge of lasting sorrow.

"You know my terms, Charity," Jonah said evenly. "If you refuse to marry Raoul, you will have no part of this ranch."

Jonah was not a cruel man, nor was he unreasonable; he was doing what he believed to be right, and would not be turned aside from it. She had known that all along, of course, but even so, in the face of his decree, it was only the last tattered shreds of her pride that kept her from throwing herself upon his mercy, from wheedling and begging. Or, conversely, from throwing things and screaming in frustration and fury.

Except for children by the man she was destined to marry—Luke or a man she had not yet met—there was nothing in all the universe Charity wanted as much as she wanted that ranch. Had she been born male, it would have come to her by right of birth, whether she was suited to manage the place or not. Because she was female, she was considered too flighty and weak to take effective command.

"Then it would seem that there is no place for me here," she said, with wretched dignity. Where had that come from? In all the times she and Jonah had disagreed, and there had been many of those, given the fact that they were fundamentally alike, not once had she even considered leaving—the Double B was her home, the landscape of her very soul, made visible. Now, suddenly, it seemed she could not stay.

Jonah looked stunned, but he did not move from his place beside the window. Grief showed in every line of his imposing frame, as did the stubbornness that was to his nature as blue was to a summer sky. "Where would you go?" he asked, after a few moments of painful silence.

Her reply, like the announcement that she meant to leave the ranch, came from some mysterious place inside her that she had been aware of but never dared to explore, except on a very superficial level. "To the mission," she said. A vision filled her mind, seeped into her spirit; she saw herself as an old woman, still at the Indian school, stooped and gray and weathered, like Father Elias was now. It would be a useful life, and a satisfying one, teaching children, nursing them through the inevitable maladies of youth, but it wasn't the one she'd chosen for herself, and planned on. For however much she loved them, they weren't *her* children, and the future before her was one that should have belonged to someone else—by following this path, she would live out her days as a usurper, a thief, a person sorrowing behind a smile.

Jonah lowered his head, but his shoulders were straight and square. "You would truly do that?" he asked, after a short interval during which the gap between them widened again. His eyes searched hers, fierce and fiery and full of suffering.

"Yes," she replied.

"For Shardlow?"

"For myself. Luke has nothing to do with this."

He studied her for a long while, as though they were setting out on separate journeys, their destinations as far as east is from west, never to meet again. In a way, of course, that was exactly what they were doing. "I wish I believed that," he said, at great length.

There was no more to say after that—or at least, no more that either of them were willing to say—so Charity turned and left the room. Quietly she mounted the stairs, tears standing in her eyes, feeling as though she would splinter into thin, wafting billows of dust at any moment, and blow away in the slightest draft.

She fetched an old satchel from the shelf of her free-standing oak wardrobe, filled it with her three simplest, most serviceable dresses, two nightgowns, and assorted underthings. Her brushes and combs fit in, too, and the book of fairy tales that had seen her through an oft-times lonely childhood. The last item she packed was a small photographic likeness of her mother and father, made on their wedding day. After changing into a riding skirt, a blouse and boots, she went down the rear stairs and out through the back door.

Peony was working in the kitchen garden, an old-fashioned bonnet shading her face from the bright sunlight. Seeing Charity, and the bag, she started to speak, then thought better of the idea and remained silent.

Reaching the barn, Charity asked one of the

men to hitch up a horse and buggy for her, and managed to maintain her dignity when the ranch hand looked at her in curious concern. He too had taken note of the valise she carried, of course, but in the end, like Peony, he held his peace.

Since her mare was not trained to pull a rig, one of the animals from the stable was substituted, and Taffeta was tied behind. Charity tucked her bag under the seat, then climbed up to take the reins. Although all outward sign of tears had gone, she was weeping on the inside as she drove away from the only home she had ever known.

Before going to the mission, however, she meant to stop at the Draper ranch. She had put off speaking to Raoul long enough; for the sake of her own sanity, as well as for honor, she must tell him the truth.

Filled with resolve and sorrow, she made her way over the rutted, dusty roads that connected the two pieces of land like blood vessels. Friendship had flowed back and forth between the ranches for years; they were like separate parts of the same whole, sharing hay and grain in hard winters, joining forces to fight off rustlers and disease and, in the old days, marauding Indians. Both Jonah and Ben Draper had lost wives to the land; each had buried children there—Jonah, twin sons who died at eighteen months, Ben, two daughters struck down by smallpox, and each man, in those hard times, had found a measure of solace in the other's quiet understanding and stolid presence.

The bond linking the two families was a deep-rooted one, but what Charity was about to do might well sever it permanently, and it was like performing an amputation. Even if Ben and Jonah managed to weather the inevitable rift, and most likely they would, given time, she could not help considering what incalculable pain, what trouble it would have saved them all, if only she could make herself love Raoul as anything other than a brother. She had tried, but it was useless; her heart had simply refused to obey.

The exchange with Jonah Barnham had seared Luke's insides like a branding iron, and when he reached his own place, he was still simmering in a brew of temper and pride. Swinging down from the pinto's back, he removed the saddle with a series of wrenching motions and flung it aside. The bridle came next, and when he swatted the horse on one flank, it bolted for the sanctuary of pasture and springs.

Watching the animal trot away, Luke hurled his hat to the ground and shouted a curse to the hot August sky.

It helped a little, releasing a measure of his fury that way, but in his mind he still heard Jonah Barnham offering him money, an insulting amount in fact, to leave Jubilee and never come back.

Looking at the situation from a purely detached standpoint—if he could have done that, which he found he couldn't—the best course of action would surely have been to swallow his humiliation, accept the payoff and hit the road. The sum, added to what he had methodically tucked away in a big eastern bank, was enough to stock the ranch he'd dreamed of and worked for since he was fifteen. With Barnham's bank draft in his hip pocket, he could have put aside his carefully-made plans to bring Vance in, dead or alive, thereby collecting the bounty and settling another, older debt.

His jaw clenched at the thought, and he swore again. Even if his self-respect would have allowed him to be bought off, he had to get Vance. Their shared blood, rather than creating a tie between them, burned like kerosene in Luke's veins. The reward notwithstanding, and it was a sizable sum, payable in federal gold, no power in heaven or on earth could redeem him if he turned his back, walked away and left that mad dog to roam free. If he did that, then every robbery, every killing that followed would leave a stain on his own soul, as well as Vance's, and rightfully so. Oh, yes, Luke wanted even more than a prospering ranch, a loving wife, and a passel of kids. He wanted vindication for every cruelty his mother had ever suffered at the hands of the Shardlow men, for the young woman Vance had killed in a fit of drunken rage, and for who he was.

With an effort, he collected his wits, picked up his hat, stepped over the threshold of the cabin where he'd been born, bearing the mark of Cain from his first breath. The sweet and singular scent of Charity was there to greet him; he heard her laughter, saw her smile, felt the warm comfort of her body pressed to his, not only on the surface, in his flesh, but deep down, where no one else had ever touched him.

Desiring her was a distraction he didn't need, but for once his formidable will power would not serve him. She haunted him, with her luminous gray eyes and her lively mind, every bit as quick as his own. He ached to unpin those masses of light gold hair and bury his hands and face in them, to kiss her the way a woman like her should be kissed and, yes, to lay her down. Oh, God, to lay her down.

By sheer force, he turned his thoughts to his prey, to Vance.

He assessed his bruised face in the small shaving mirror he normally carried in his saddlebags, cataloged every cut and every cracked rib, every throbbing lump on his body. He might have wished for a different sort of opening gambit, it was true, but the important thing was that his efforts to smoke his half-brother out had produced the desired effect. Whatever his other problems, Luke was jubilant; the game was under way, and he meant to win it.

Vance was no genius, but he'd probably figured out by now that Luke wasn't dead. Nobody needed to know that every part of him hurt, inside and out. The next step, then, was to put on some kind of public show, make himself as conspicuous as possible. Vance might get careless then, come right out into the open.

Sweating with pain, full of anticipation at the challenges ahead, he dragged the copper tub around from the lean-to, lugged in bucketloads of water, heated them on that little piece-of-shit stove, and then poured a fifth of cheap whiskey into the mix. The rotgut would serve two purposes: it might have an antiseptic effect on the lacework of cuts and abrasions covering his body, and it would make him smell like a true Shardlow.

Dragging a crate up beside the tub, Luke laid the .45 upon it, within easy reach, then began stripping off his clothes.

Raoul was ensconced in a downstairs bedroom, propped on pillows, his hair rumpled and his face unshaven, languishing in cozy malaise. He was like an old maid, relishing a case of the vapors, and poor Kwan had obviously been on his feet since sunrise, fetching and carrying and commiserating.

Charity, admitted by a beaming Ben Draper, stood stiffly at the foot of the bed, waited in polite silence until she and Raoul were alone.

Raoul was cussed as a post on the best of days, and he could be downright overbearing, without even trying. All the same, he was smart and uncommonly perceptive—for a man—when he bothered to pay attention. He narrowed his eyes. "Why do I think you haven't come to stroke my fevered brow?"

She might have laughed, under other circumstances. As it was, her knees felt like last night's noodles and her head didn't seem to be anchored to her neck. She and Raoul had practically grown up together, and she dreaded the imminent loss of their old accord as much as she had ever dreaded anything.

"I can't marry you," she said. The words, though spoken softly, seemed to clatter off the walls, like stones flung in reckless fury.

For a moment, Raoul just stared at her, as though she were some mad stranger who had found her way in, raving and tearing her hair. Then he paled beneath his tan and his dark beard, and his near-black eyes reflected a bewilderment that wounded Charity to the quick. His voice was a rasp, like a handsaw tearing through hardwood. "What?"

She wet her lips and tried again. "You heard me, Raoul. I'm calling off the wedding. It would be a terrible mistake if we—"

He interrupted her with a bellow so sudden and so furious that it made her start, and set her heart to pounding. He wore a dressing gown of dark silk, and when he flung the sheet away and surged out of bed, she saw that his right thigh was heavily bandaged.

"No," he thundered, advancing on her. "I won't let you do this!"

Although Charity never for a moment thought he would do her any sort of physical harm, she retreated instinctively. "You don't have any say in the matter, I'm afraid," she said bravely, already retrenching. Her fists were clenched at her sides, she'd raised her chin, and she knew her eyes were blazing. She was grateful because, in a small way, he had made things easier for her; sad acquiescence would have been so much harder to deal with. "I care about you too much to marry you, Raoul. You would be miserably unhappy and so would I."

He was crestfallen, his former towering passion gone in the space of a moment. Facing her now, he brushed her cheek tentatively with the backs of his fingers, frowning as though he feared she might vanish at his touch, like a spirit. "But we agreed—"

She suppressed a sigh. "We did *not* agree," she pointed out gently. "*You* decided, and my father was so pleased, and before I knew what was happening, we were planning a wedding. I should have spoken up sooner, Raoul, I know that. And I'm so sorry."

Pain flashed in Raoul's brilliant eyes, followed quickly by anger. "This is nonsense," he boomed. "I won't have it!"

"You have no choice in the matter," Charity persisted, softening her voice in the hope that Raoul would follow suit. "There isn't going to be a wedding. And that's final."

He surprised her again by grasping her upper arms, wrenching her forward onto the balls of her feet, and planting a crushing kiss on her mouth. She stood rigidly until he released her, plainly both wounded and baffled by her lack of response. Although they had never been intimate, they had experimented with kissing over the long years of their acquaintance, and Charity had enjoyed those innocent encounters.

Now there was Luke.

"You actually think you mean this!" Raoul marveled.

She rolled her eyes and sighed, but said nothing.

The realization of what she might have to sacrifice for this decision dawned in Raoul's handsome, gaunt face. "The ranch—your father's will—"

She ached. "I can't go against my own best judgment, even if it means I have to lose the ranch. My father is very upset. I hope he'll come to see that I'm right, but if he doesn't, I'm prepared—"

"But you *aren't* right—"

"Raoul, please," she interrupted wearily. "I don't love you, not in the way I want to love my husband. That should be enough for you."

He cupped her face now, tenderly, and she dared to hope, for the first time, that their friendship might actually survive. "I can make you love me," he said, in the tone of one offering a solemn vow. "Give me a chance, Charity, and I'll prove that what I say is true."

Tears burned behind her eyes, but she would not release them. Not while Raoul or anyone else was looking on. She shook her head and stepped back and then back again, to a place where he could not reach her. After pulling off the modest ring he had given her before his journey to Texas to buy cattle and setting it on top of the bureau next to the door, she hurried out.

When she arrived at the mission school,

the voices of the children rode the heavy August air. Normally, Charity would have rejoiced—not so long ago, there had been tragedy in this place—but that day the sound was at such variance with her emotions that she could hardly bear it. She parked the buggy behind the chapel, hoping not to be noticed, secured the brake lever, and hurried into the orchard.

There, alone and utterly bereft, she wept.

Presently, a gentle hand touched her shoulder; she turned her head and saw Father Elias standing next to her. "What's happened, child?" he asked, his faded eyes bright with affection and concern.

Stumbling over the words, she explained that she had left her father's home, and her reason for doing so.

"Of course there is a place for you here," the priest said, when she had finished. He produced a clean handkerchief from a pocket in his plain brown robe and extended it.

She had thought she was through crying, that she had spent her supply of tears, but at Father Elias's statement and kindly gesture, she sobbed anew.

The priest took her hand, led her to a rough-hewn bench under an apple tree, and they sat down together. "Please do not despair so," he said quietly. "Things are never as bad as they first appear. You must give God a chance to work in the situation, my dear."

Charity loved her work at the mission, but she was neither Catholic nor especially religious; she had learned from Jonah to depend upon herself, solve her own problems, and not run wailing to the gates of heaven whenever some difficulty came her way. At the same time, however, she deeply respected Father Elias and others like him, sincere believers who found solace in their faith and actually practiced its tenets, so she did not give voice to her doubts.

Father Elias patted her hand. "Take the advice of an old man, my little friend; think of this experience as a gift, and be grateful for it. Such things often herald new beginnings and great growth." With that, he rose and moved slowly away, toward the small chapel yard, where the children were playing. Two of the older girls, both of whom usually worked in town as servants, were there to help.

Charity remained on the bench until she had composed herself, then she dried her face and returned to the buggy. She had asked the stable man who had hitched it up for her to come and fetch both rig and horse at the mission sometime that afternoon, so she did not remove the harness. She untied Taffeta and turned her loose to graze in the deep grass of the orchard, then went into the tiny dormitory to look in on those children who were still confined to bed with the last vestiges of measles.

Two of the boys were ill, though their impatience to join in the games outside indicated that they would soon recover. Only one of the girls was still sick, a three-year-old who sat list-lessly in Charity's lap while she told a lively story. The tale, much embellished, featured a princess who dropped her favorite play-thing, a golden ball, into a spring, and the frog who, for a price, retrieved it for her.

Susan listened with enormous brown eyes, winding one tiny finger in a tendril of hair that had escaped to bounce against Charity's cheek. It seemed foolish, that story, even as she told it—how could an orphaned child, sick and destined to be scorned by much of society, be expected to sympathize with a spoiled, greedy and dishonorable princess? Was she more like that story-princess than she would have liked to admit, the privileged daughter of a rich rancher, unfamiliar with hunger or prejudice, at least of the racial variety? Raoul was a fine and honorable man, a passionate man with property and good looks; surely many women would have been delighted to be his bride. Was her refusal to marry him really the right thing to do, or was it simply petulance and vanity?

She brushed the top of the child's silken black hair with her lips. If a flicker of love for Raoul existed somewhere inside her, waiting to be fanned to life, then why was she so com-pletely, so undeniably attracted to Luke Shardlow? She knew she was a moral person, usually sensible, and yet she felt herself tee-tering on the edge of becoming someone else entirely whenever she was around Luke, someone reckless and filled with wild, almost ungovernable passions. The most disturbing fact of all was the sure and certain knowledge that, given the opportunity, she might allow matters to advance considerably beyond skilled, tender kisses and caresses that set her flesh aflame.

Presently, the little girl slept, and Charity tucked her in and tiptoed out into the quiet afternoon. The children were back at their lessons again, sitting stoically while Father Elias explained the mysteries of numbers.

Two men came for the horse and buggy, and took it away, as Charity had asked. She tried not to think of the house on the Double B, of the beloved people who lived there, but it was impossible. She already missed her father and Blaise, Aaron and Peony, with an intensity that constricted her throat and made her stomach hurt, but for the time being, she must remain parted from them.

Still, when it was supper time, and she and Father Elias had fed the children from a great kettle of boiled pinto beans, Charity could not eat for thinking of the dining room at home. Peony would be laying the table about then, Blaise was surely playing the piano in the main parlor, same as every evening, believing as she did that music was an aid to good digestion. Aaron, always ravenous, was no doubt splashing his hands and face at the basin on the back porch and Jonah—well, Jonah would have finished the day's work by now, and retreated to his bedroom to wash and change into the garb of a gentleman. Although he worked as hard as any man on the ranch, he liked to enjoy his leisure time to the fullest, and dressing for the evening meal was a part of his ritual.

Was he thinking of her, Charity wondered, as she forced herself to eat, there at the trestle table in the mission kitchen. No doubt he regretted the impasse they had reached as much as she did, but he was willful and old-fashioned, with very rigid ideas of right and wrong. He was no more likely to give in than she was, and Charity could think of no way to mend the breach between them and still heed the dictates of her conscience.

She resigned herself to staying at the mission for the rest of her life, to growing old there, and watching helplessly when, on her father's hopefully distant death, the bankers and lawyers took over the Double B. City men, they would run the ranch at a distance, never feeling the heart-quickening love for the land that Charity did, never breathing the pure air or spreading their arms to embrace the wide sky. Without that love, without the fervor to fight the elements and the rustlers, the wild animals and the financial panics and the diseases that cattle and horses were prey to, the place as they knew it would not survive.

At sunset, reeking of whiskey, and artfully red-eyed, Luke rode into Jubilee and established a place for himself at the long bar in the saloon. There was a poker game going on at the back of the room, and several of the tables

125

were occupied by cowboys who looked as though they wouldn't be able to find their way back to the bunkhouse without the help of their horses. Luke smiled into his glass and set it down again without tasting the stuff inside.

He had been there an hour, carefully minding his own business and, at the same time, noticing everything that happened, when at last his patience was rewarded. A small, mean-eyed man came in, plainly looking for trouble. A filthy bandage showed beneath his shirt, and an equally unsanitary sling supported his left arm.

Luke didn't recognize him, and yet the pit of his belly quivered and the hairs on his nape stood straight out. His instincts, well-honed by years of practice, were demanding his attention.

The newcomer scanned the room, dismissing everyone—until his narrow gaze found Luke, standing at the end of the bar farthest from the swinging doors at the front of the saloon. If Luke had had any doubts before, the silent exchange that passed between him and the other man in that moment put an end to them all. This was one of Vance's business associates, and the damage to his arm had been done by Luke's own pistol the night before.

Apparently, Luke thought, with a bland expression meant to mask his interest, he wasn't the only one around who mended quickly. He turned back to his drink.

Sure enough, the outlaw came to stand right beside him. Luke waited for the message he was sure was forthcoming; Vance was no strategist, but he had sent this little sidewinder meandering into the busiest place in town for a reason. As a challenge, and a warning, to Luke. *Go away, Kid. You're in over your head here. Way over.*

"What're ya drinkin'?" the miscreant wanted to know. He tried to sound neighborly, Luke reflected, but his future, if indeed he had one, did not lie in the art of performance.

Luke gave him a bleary look that had taken a long time to cultivate. He was good at it, though; he'd had the best possible teachers, Trigg Shardlow and Vance. "Mare's milk," he said. The worm was expecting a smart-ass, and Luke wasn't going to do anything—yet—to throw him off balance. Let him think he was fooling God and all His angels, not to mention the populace of that saloon.

"You got a name?"

Luke bit back a grin. "Look, mister," he drawled, "I didn't come in here to make friends. I just want to have my drink and head home. That all right with you?" Out of the corner of his eye, he saw the other man blush. Socially delicate, evidently.

A brief silence ensued, during which, no doubt, the messenger considered the consequences of going back to the hideout, wherever it was, and telling Vance that he'd *tried* to carry out his orders, but it just hadn't worked out. After buying a bottle, he poured himself a drink, then shoved the jug toward Luke.

127

"You live around here?" he pressed, going red around the base of his jaw.

Luke turned and glared at his inquisitor. "Yes," he said acidly. "You slow or something, friend? I believe I told you I don't feel like chatting." He watched as the man ground his back teeth.

"Look," he growled, his beady pig-eyes hot. Plainly, the gentleman was affronted. "Far as I'm concerned, it's a pity you ain't layin' by a creek with a bullet in your head right now. I'm just talkin' to you because I was told to do it."

"You always do what you're told, little man?"

It was then, damn it all to hell, *then,* that someone came up from behind and tapped Luke on the shoulder. He cursed himself for becoming too absorbed in the game to keep track of what else was going on in that room, and turned to see Raoul Montego standing there, snorting like a bull.

"What the hell—?" Before the whole sentence was out of Luke's mouth, Montego's fist landed square in the middle of his face and, to his furious surprise, he went down like an anvil dropped from a hayloft.

He sat up, leaning back against the bar, dazed and feeling his jaw to see if it was broken. His face felt like somebody had taken a crowbar and pried it apart at the hinges; he spit some blood and part of a tooth into the filthy sawdust covering the floor and watched in helpless irritation as Vance's minion fled through the swinging doors.

Montego, still looming over him, reached down to offer a hand up and Luke, against his better judgment, accepted it, let the other man hoist him to his feet.

"I hope you have an explanation for that," he said.

Raoul looked like he was going to knock him down again. "Stay away from Charity," he said, and then he made the mistake of turning his back.

7

$\mathcal{I}$t was just plain, dumb luck that, somewhere between his horse and the wooden sidewalk out in front of the saloon, Vance's emissary managed to run afoul of the law. That, Luke had to confess, took no small degree of talent.

Luke secured his own place in the hoosegow by knocking Montego on his ass. Given that Raoul was only slightly more ambulatory than Luke himself, it was shamefully easy, and in no way a victory. The marshal, a tall, spare man called Dan Higgins, anything but garrulous and obviously not given to nonsense, arrested Luke and then personally escorted Raoul back to the Draper ranch.

Since there was only one cell in Jubilee's town jail, Luke found himself bunking in with Vance's man, who claimed his name was

Andrews. He admitted that after Luke had bounced him off the cell bars three or four times, but gently. After all, the poor little fellow was wounded. Mustn't handle him too roughly.

"Where is my brother?" was Luke's second question.

Andrews was definitely caught between a rock and a hard place; if he told, Vance would kill him, surely, soundly and slowly. If he didn't, Luke would. He came down on the side of expediency, which showed more good sense than Luke would have given him credit for.

"You shouldn't hold it against us, our workin' you over like we did, I mean. It was all Vance's idea."

"Thanks," Luke answered, "but that isn't what I asked you." Clasping Andrews's shirt front in both hands, he gave him another thump, to make sure he was paying attention. "Where—is—he?"

Hatred and fear gleamed in the man's eyes. His breath was foul and he'd probably been wearing the same clothes for months. "Won't do you no good, my tellin' you. We was holed up in an old miner's shack up in the hills, but Vance said we had to move on, stay ahead of you. I could take you right to the place, but you won't find nothin'." He chewed on that for a while. "Hell, I don't even know where to look for 'em myself. Nobody told me."

Luke let him go. "That's because Vance didn't expect you to come back."

Andrews looked perturbed. "That ain't true. Vance is a friend of mine."

130

"Vance," Luke responded, easing himself onto the edge of one of the two cots squeezed into the cell, "is nobody's friend but the devil's. By now he knows you've met up with Marshal Higgins, and he won't risk crossing your path again, in case you're followed. Unless, of course, he solves the whole problem by killing you." He stretched out, crossed his ankles and cupped his hands behind his head. The pull on his bruised ribs was enough to stop his breath, but he made sure it didn't show. "That would be like Vance. Killing you, I mean."

Andrews was sweating, and his eyes gleamed with the terror of a cornered animal. "Vance warned me about you. He said you could talk a fox right into a steel-jawed trap."

"Then what was the point of your coming into the saloon at all?"

Silence.

Luke heaved a long-suffering sigh and moved as if to hoist himself up off the cot, and Andrews looked like he might try to melt like candle wax and ooze between the floorboards.

"Vance thought you was dead the other night. He was real pissed off when we went back to the creek to make sure, and you was no place to be found. Where'd you get to, anyhow?" When Luke ignored the question, Andrews looked resentful, and scared shitless into the bargain, but he went right on running off at the mouth. "Vance said you'd follow me, when I left the saloon, and then he and Tom and Royce—well, they were going to jump you. Finish the job."

131

"Why go to all that trouble? He must have been watching me if he knew I was in the saloon tonight. Wouldn't it have been easier just to bushwhack me between here and the homestead?"

"He didn't want to tackle you on your own ground, I guess. Vance don't explain much of anything. He just gives orders. 'Sides, he's a little crazy—you ought to know that as well as anybody."

Luke pondered Andrews's words in silence for a time, but found no great revelation in them. He might have guessed most of it. Mostly, he'd just wanted to keep the little man talking, just in case something worthwhile spilled out by accident.

"How'd you contrive to get yourself arrested tonight?" he asked.

Andrews flushed with indignation. "I didn't even do nothin'. That marshal, he asked me where I got my horse—said the brand looked like somebody had been foolin' with it. I told him I bought it down in San Antone, and he said he hoped I wouldn't mind passin' the night as a guest of the town of Jubilee, so's he could send a few telegrams."

Luke yawned, still lying full-out on the cot; narrow and hard as it was, that sorry excuse for a bed was still better than the pallet he slept on at the cabin. Sighing, he watched the progress of a rat skittering along one of the low rafters. "Horse thievin' can get a man hanged," he observed calmly.

Andrews turned his back and said nothing,

but he made a forlorn figure, standing there staring out through the bars. He was probably looking for Vance to ride to the rescue, guns blazing. If so, he was even stupider than Luke had first reckoned.

Presently, the marshal came back from his stroll down to the telegraph office. Andrews was lying on his bunk by then, curled up on one side, facing the wall, and he didn't move when Higgins spoke to Luke.

"You in need of a doctor, friend?" he asked.

Luke was hurting, all right; he'd been worked over pretty thoroughly the day before, and Montego had gotten in a solid punch in the saloon that night, but he reckoned it wasn't worth dragging Molly all the way over there from White Horse Junction. "I'll be fine," he said.

The marshal remained, leaning against the wall opposite the bars and striking a match to a cheroot. A tall, thin man, balding, with a good-natured glint in his eyes, he might have been in a voluble mood, but it was more likely that he knew the family history and suspected Luke of being in cahoots with Vance.

Luke smiled at the irony. Because he had his own plans for Andrews, he didn't set the marshal straight. Vengeance belonged to him, for all the Lord's claims to the contrary, and so did the reward on his brother's head.

"I knew your daddy," Higgins said.

"I'll just bet you did," Luke agreed, though he knew the marshal hadn't been wearing a badge when Trigg was arrested. After all, he himself had been the one to bring the law down on the old man, and in those days, Asa McCallum had held down the job.

"Knew your brother, too."

"Half-brother," Luke clarified easily. "We had different mothers."

"But I reckon I remember your ma best of all," Higgins went on reflectively, as if Luke hadn't spoken.

That got Luke's attention; he drew himself up far enough to rest his shoulders against the wall. As far as he could recall, Marietta had never left the homestead; she hadn't gone to the general store, like other women did, or even to church. She certainly hadn't had any friends to speak of, though there were plenty of folks who pitied her. And that had made everything so much worse.

"How's that?" Luke asked. "My ma didn't socialize much as I recollect."

Higgins tossed an unlighted cheroot and a box of matches through the bars; they landed on Luke's chest. The marshal waited while his prisoner lit a smoke and drew on it.

"We came down here from Canada, my pa and me, about a year before you were born. Trigg was working for Jonah Barnham back then, swinging a pick in one of his mines. That was before the silver played out and Jonah turned his interests to cattle. Anyway, Pa took a job there, too, to earn some ready cash."

Luke felt an old, familiar hope swirl up from the pit of his belly, like a miniature tornado, but his manner was calm, like always.

He drew on the cheroot and expelled the smoke. "You must have been pretty young then."

"I was seven or eight," Higgins answered. "We staked a claim to some land over near where the mission is now, and we bought eggs and garden truck from your ma. She was gentle-voiced, I remember, and a mighty pretty woman, with that yeller hair of hers." He paused, measured Luke with a sweep of his eyes, and pushed away from the wall to stand straight. "My pa liked her, too."

For the first time, Luke was glad of the bars that stood between them. He waited, saying nothing. Trigg had accused his young wife of whoring as many times as there were stars in the sky, and Luke had never been able to do anything to shut the old man's mouth. Now, things had changed, and he wasn't about to listen to a word against Marietta.

"She was like an angel," Higgins recalled, in a wistful tone that didn't jibe with his lean, tough exterior. "I wanted her to be my ma. I used to pretend that she was."

Luke closed his eyes, remembering his own childhood, when he'd wished so fervently that Marietta would leave Trigg forever, taking him along with her, of course. He could well imagine how she'd have looked to a motherless boy, half-starved for some kind of tenderness.

Higgins sighed. "Something happened between her and my pa—I didn't know what it was until later. They were going to run off

135

together, him and her. The three of us would have started over someplace else. But there was an accident down in the mine one day; a crossbeam came down on Pa and broke his back. He died before they could get him aboveground."

"Jesus," Luke whispered, absorbing all the implications of what Higgins had told him. He shook his head. "Are you saying what I think you're saying?"

The marshal hesitated, and that in itself was an answer to Luke's question. "You anything like Trigg Shardlow?" he asked. "The color of your hair and your eyes, you got them from your ma."

Easy, he told himself. *Don't go jumping to any convenient conclusions.* "You said you knew Vance. He and I had different mothers, but he's fair-haired, like me. His eyes are light, too."

"The way I understood things, your ma and his were sisters. Couldn't that account for any resemblance between the two of you?"

Luke swung his legs over the side of the cot, stood up, and crossed the cell to stand facing Higgins through the bars. "What the hell are you trying to say?" As if he didn't know. As if he hadn't wished for just this sort of impossibly good news ever since he was a kid.

"Is this a family reunion?" he asked, with a note of false lightness in his voice. Higgins was implying that he and Luke were half-brothers, of course, that sweet, shy Marietta had turned to another man for solace. Few people would have blamed her, he supposed;

136

God knew, she'd never found the slightest tenderness with Trigg.

"Maybe," Higgins replied. "I guess we'll never know for sure."

"I don't suppose you feel obliged to let me out of here, on account of how we might have common blood, the two of us?"

The marshal chuckled. "You're staying right where you are, at least until daybreak. I can't take a chance on your going after Raoul Montego again." Having said that, Dan Higgins left him alone with his thoughts.

Luke had long since stubbed out the cheroot on the dirt floor. Now he lay down again, rested his hat over his eyes, and wondered.

The next morning, true to his promise, Higgins turned Luke loose, after returning his .45. But the erstwhile prisoner tarried, while Andrews snored in the cell.

"I've got some questions for you," Luke said.

Higgins spread his hands in a silent invitation.

"Where did you go after your pa was killed? If you'd lived in or around Jubilee, I'd remember you."

The lawman folded his arms. "I went back up to Canada to live with my grandparents after Pa died. Once I was grown up, I took to the wandering life. Spent some time in the cavalry, too. Then, a few years ago, I passed this way—I guess I wanted to see if things had changed any. This job happened to be open, so I took it and put down some roots."

Luke wanted to believe he was anybody's son but Trigg Shardlow's, wanted to believe that his mother had known at least a little joy, amidst all that misery. He remembered Trigg's constant accusations; even on the night of her death, the son-of-a-bitch had called Marietta a whore and shouted that Luke wasn't his. Still, it seemed too easy, Higgins's coming out of the woodwork the way he had, and spilling the whole story. It was pretty personal stuff, too, even if it had happened a long time ago. The kind of story it usually took some doing to tell.

Of course, Higgins couldn't have presented the theory much before then, given the fact that Luke hadn't been near Jubilee since the day Trigg was convicted of murder. He hadn't had the opportunity.

Luke put forward his second question. "Why would you want to tell me what you have, or anybody else for that matter? My knowing couldn't make much difference to you, one way or the other."

Higgins's gaze was direct, but that didn't convince Luke, either. The ability to look into a man's eyes and lie like a card sharp was one hallmark of a master. Luke had seen it before; hell, he'd done it himself, many a time. And he wasn't buying the marshal's claim, bad as he wanted to do exactly that.

The marshal moved the match stick he'd been chewing from one side of his mouth to the other. "The Shardlow name isn't exactly a matter of pride," he said plainly. "Besides, I thought you might like to know somebody loved her once, your ma. Treated her like a lady."

"I reckon Trigg would take issue with that last part," he replied. He put on his hat. "I'm obliged," he added, and then walked away.

Charity sat beneath one of the apple trees in the orchard, her skirts modestly arranged, the smaller children gathered around her in an irregular crescent while she read aloud from her book of fairy tales. She had chosen "Cinderella: Or the Little Glass Slipper," and was in the thick of the story, when a little boy named Hawk waved one hand wildly to interrupt.

"Yes?" Charity asked, with patience and genuine interest. She'd been living at the mission for a week by then and, although she still felt oddly hollow, an effigy of herself, made of dry and crumbling stuff, she no longer cried late at night after the lamps had been extinguished.

"Why would anybody wear glass shoes?" Hawk wanted to know.

Charity bit back a smile, and before she could reply, someone spoke from outside the circle.

"Why indeed?"

She looked up quickly and saw Luke standing there, hat in hand, grinning in that lopsided way of his. His appearance had improved greatly in the time since she had seen him; his bruises were fading, and the swelling that had distorted his face was almost gone, though he still had a fat lip. A swift and most unseemly heat surged through her and, to her chagrin, pulsed in her cheeks, surely visible.

"Cinderella," said one of the girls, with

authority, "wore glass slippers because she had dainty little feet and she wanted everybody to see them, see how pretty they were."

The boys hooted with disdain.

"They didn't show," asserted another female member of the audience. "Her long skirts covered them up."

Luke gave a philosophical smile and sat on his haunches to listen.

Charity made her stoic way through what remained of the story and then, to her relief, Father Elias summoned the students inside for catechism. Luke watched them file past, but remained where he was, and with the children gone, that seemed ever so much closer than before.

"You appear to be mending nicely," she remarked, and then felt foolish.

The grin flashed, then subsided into a sort of mischievous sobriety. "Thank you," he said. "I hear you've left the Double B."

She was taken unawares by the statement, which seemed odd, since she'd had two recurrent thoughts for much of the past week—how much she missed her family and the ranch, and how wonderful it would have been to go ahead and make love with Luke Shardlow, up there in the tree house above the whispering creek. She looked down at the book in her hands, and thought of the innocent dreams she'd cherished for so much of her life. And suddenly she was so choked up that she couldn't utter a word.

"Charity," Luke persisted, in a gruff yet gentle

voice. "Why are you here? The Double B is your home."

She shook her head, and dabbed furtively at the outside corners of her eyes with the back of one hand. "Not anymore," she replied, and sniffled. "Papa is furious because I refuse to marry Raoul. The situation became unbearable, and I—I had to leave."

Luke considered her words thoughtfully before answering. "You don't look very happy," he observed, after a few moments had passed. "Charity, you're wonderful with these kids, anybody could see that, but this life doesn't suit you. Why don't you go back home and talk things through with Jonah?"

"It isn't that easy," she said, with a sniffle. Her right index finger still marked the page of the story she had just read to the children—the ending, in which Cinderella had married her prince, and was destined to live happily ever after. "I've never lived anywhere but on that ranch. I never wanted to be anywhere else, not really. I grew up thinking I would marry one day, that my husband and I would run the Double B when Papa was no longer able. Now it isn't my home anymore, and I couldn't bear staying there, knowing that."

Luke came to sit beside her, one knee drawn up, his hat resting on the grass beside him. "Jonah and I have our differences," he said, "but he's a good man, Charity. He loves you. Go home and talk with him. Talk until he listens."

She began plucking blades of grass, tossing them aside. "If Papa wanted me to come back, he'd have come for me by now."

"He's stiff-necked. So are you. Somebody has to give in, take the first step."

Charity drew a deep breath, and let it out shakily. "You know what I think?" she countered. "I think Papa never wanted a daughter at all. All these years, he's just pretended to love me, and secretly wished I'd been a boy."

"Now you're being just plain silly," Luke said, studying her solemnly. "Jonah's your father, and maybe he's feeling his age a little these days. He wants to know you'll be loved and looked after when he's gone."

Charity looked away, looked back, her cheeks flaring with conviction. "If he'd give me the chance," she ranted, "I could learn to run the Double B. I could be a real help to him, now and in the future. I'm very good with numbers; I could do the books and manage investments. But he won't let me try because I'm a woman!" With considerable effort, she caught hold of her runaway tongue and spent several moments struggling for composure. "I'm twenty-three years old, Luke. If I'd been a man, and refused to marry someone he had chosen for me, Papa would *never* have taken away my birthright."

He was quiet for a time, and when he spoke, his voice was gentle. "That's probably so," he allowed, "and it's not right or fair. Lot of things want changing in this world. I've got no doubts at all that you're as smart or smarter than most of the men around here—you can probably ride, shoot and think as well as a lot of them. But you're still vulnerable, Charity; it's a question of physical strength. So even though I don't agree with Jonah's approach, I can understand his thinking."

"It's old-fashioned."

Luke nodded. "Intellectually, I agree with you. But emotionally, well, that's another matter. In Jonah's place, I might do the same thing. I'd want to know that my daughter, if I had one, was protected. And I'd lots rather have her mad at me than leave her at the mercy of some of the people out there." He made a small gesture that was nonetheless calculated to take in the whole world. "Maybe you don't want to hear this, Charity, but you've been sheltered. You couldn't possibly know what life can be like—" Seeing a protest brewing in her eyes, he lifted a hand, palm out, but she wouldn't be stopped.

"So you think I should marry Raoul?" she burst out. "Be a good girl and do what my father says?"

Luke remained calm, which only fueled Charity's need to throttle him. "The last thing I want," he said quietly, reaching for his hat and rising to his feet, "is to see you become another man's wife. If I had anything to offer besides a run-down homestead and a bad reputation, I'd speak for you myself. The point is, somebody suitable will come along in time. You'll get what you want, and so will Jonah." He glanced down at the book in her lap. "Bide your time, Cinderella. The prince will show up one of these days, and the slipper will fit your foot."

With that, he turned and walked away, leaving Charity to stare after him, open-mouthed. She wasn't thinking about any storybook prince, though—her mind was stuck on something else Luke had said. *If I had anything to offer besides a run-down homestead and a bad reputation, I'd speak for you myself.*

Did that mean he cared for her? She considered the question throughout the busy afternoon, the quiet evening, and in her dreams that night.

Blaise arrived first thing the following morning, driving a buggy at breakneck speed, while Father Elias and Charity were overseeing breakfast in the mission kitchen. Peony was perched beside Blaise, white in the face and gripping the edges of the buggy seat with both hands, Blaise being a wild driver with a tendency to round curves on one wheel.

Having seen their approach through a window, Charity hurried out to meet the visitors, now coming to a lurching stop in front of the chapel.

"You must come home immediately," Blaise announced, without preamble. "Your father is very ill. I've brought Peony to take care of your work here."

Charity felt as if every drop of blood in her body had suddenly drained into the ground through the soles of her feet. She swayed, and Father Elias steadied her with a surprisingly strong grasp.

"Go to Jonah," he said, with gentle urgency. "I will pray."

Charity nodded and climbed up into the buggy, edging Blaise over to take the reins herself. Peony stood on the grass, satchel in hand, watching, unmoving and bewildered, as they made a wide turn and sped away.

During their hurried trip back to the ranch house, Blaise explained, with unconscious tears shimmering on her cheeks, that when Jonah had not come out of his room that morning, she had gone in to check on him. He had been awake, staring up at her with frantic eyes, but he seemed unable to move at all, let alone rise from the bed. His face had been distorted, as though crumbling in on itself.

She had immediately sent a ranch hand over to White Horse Junction, to fetch the doctor. She'd come for Charity herself, because she'd sensed that was what Jonah wanted her to do, but she'd stationed Aaron at his bedside before going, and left him with only the greatest reluctance.

Charity asked no questions; the answers she wanted could only come by seeing Jonah and assessing his condition with her own eyes.

When they reached the ranch house, Ben Draper's horse was out front, as was Raoul's. Charity left the rig to a waiting stable hand and raced inside and up the stairs to Jonah's room.

The door stood open, and both Ben and Raoul were there, standing at the foot of the

145

huge mahogany bed, hats in hand. They stepped aside at Charity's entrance, and she swept between them to her father's bedside.

Jonah's face looked as though it had fallen into parts, like the scattered pieces of a puzzle that would not go together again. He seemed shrunken, his hair was in disarray, his eyes frenzied. He was helpless, trapped in a body that had served him well all his life; helplessness was a completely foreign circumstance for him, a torture, and his flesh was an alarming shade of gray.

Charity dropped to her knees beside the bed, grasping one of his hands in both her own, raising it to her lips for the brush of a kiss. She was full of tears, but she would not let them fall, not in Jonah's presence at least, for that would only increase his agitation. This was a time to project strength, even if she didn't feel it.

"Papa," she said gently, when she could trust her voice. "You mustn't worry, do you hear me? Everything is going to be all right. Everything."

His gaze found Raoul, with a visible struggle, and then groped back to Charity's face. The meaning of that look was as clear as if Jonah had spoken out loud. *Marry him. Marry Raoul, so I can die knowing you're safe.*

She straightened her spine. "Trust me," she whispered, half pleading, half insisting. "Believe in me. I'm *enough*, Papa—strong enough, smart enough, brave enough. I'll prove that to you. But you must give me a chance."

Jonah might have nodded slightly, Charity couldn't be certain. He closed his eyes then, and slept, and she did not move, but remained there, praying without words. Presently, she felt two strong hands take hold of her shoulders as Raoul lifted her to her feet and turned her into his embrace. She did not resist him; he was her oldest friend, and she needed the brotherly solace he offered.

"Tell me what I can do to help," he said.

Charity buried her face in Raoul's shoulder and clung to him for a long moment. Then, somewhat restored, she stepped back. "Find the foreman," she answered. "Tell him I want to see him right away."

Raoul looked stunned. "What?"

Ben, silent since Charity had entered the room, brought a chair close to the bed, and she sank into it with a nod of gratitude. She noticed Blaise then, standing on the other side of the room, staring at Jonah as though to will her own life-force into him. If Charity had ever had any doubts about the strength of this woman's love for her father, they were gone in that brief flicker of time.

Raoul crouched beside Charity's chair. "Sweetheart, listen to me. I'll take care of the ranch; that's what Jonah would want right now. You've got enough to worry about without your father's business affairs."

He meant well, Charity knew that, and she wasn't about to deplete her personal resources by arguing, for she had none to spare. "Fetch the foreman," she said quietly, evenly. "Please."

Raoul emitted a great sigh, but at a gesture from his grandfather, he stood, bent to kiss Charity's forehead lightly, and then left the room to do her bidding. Ben followed, after a nod to each of the women.

Alone with Jonah, Charity and Blaise kept their vigil in silence for a long time. Blaise's fingers were so tightly interlocked that the knuckles showed white, and her eyes did not stray from Jonah's face even when she began to speak.

"He's the finest man I've ever known," she said. "So stubborn, but so strong. So kind. Why, he treats Aaron like he was his own flesh and blood. It's a privilege to be loved by Jonah Barnham."

"Did he show any signs of being ill before this?" Charity asked, very softly. She couldn't help wondering if she'd been the cause of this tragedy, refusing to marry Raoul, severing her ties with him and with the ranch.

Blaise rounded the end of the bed and came to stand beside Charity's chair, one hand resting on her shoulder. Though she could be flighty, Blaise was a perceptive woman, and plainly knew what thoughts were going through Charity's mind. "He's been working too hard, but he's always done that. You mustn't blame yourself."

Charity sniffled, battled hard against a fresh onslaught of tears, and prevailed. "I was so blind. I should have guessed that there was a reason why Papa was so fiercely determined to see me married. He felt this coming, didn't he?"

Blaise retreated to the opposite side of the bed, sat down on the mattress, and reached across to stroke Jonah's hair with the tenderest possible pass of her fingers. "If he did, he didn't let on to me. But it's true that there are problems."

A great hand seemed to reach into Charity's chest and squeeze her heart to near bursting. How she'd yammered and howled and fussed, fearing that the ranch would be lost to her, handed over to lawyers and bankers. Yet never once had she considered that the place might be threatened in other, less obvious ways.

She closed her eyes briefly, in order to hold on to her composure, and then opened them again. "What sort of problems?"

"Jonah won't thank me for telling you," Blaise said, and a soft, fond smile touched her mouth. "He thought he could manage." She paused, looking across the expanse of the bed to meet Charity's questioning gaze straight on. "There's been some rustling, and he's made some investments that went bad." A short, painful silence fell. "He hasn't admitted as much, but I think someone might be black-mailing him, too."

"Why?" Charity whispered.

Blaise shrugged. All during their conversation, she had kept her gaze fixed on Jonah. "I don't know," she answered. "It's just a feeling, really."

"There must be more," Charity said.

A sigh. "He's been turning a blind eye to

things," Blaise responded. "That isn't like him."

Charity closed her eyes for a moment. *What's happened, Papa?* She asked silently. *Did it drive you to this, whatever it was?*

8

$\mathcal{W}$ith every passing hour spent at Jonah's bedside, his chances of recovery seemed to shrink. By force of will, Charity continued to believe he would pull through, and Blaise was no less devoted, no less determined. Charity, for her part, put every other worry aside.

At first, neither woman dared to sleep, but as time plodded mercilessly on, and Jonah sank deeper into himself, it became clear that this approach was not merely impractical, but impossible. They agreed to divide the vigil into four hour shifts, and Blaise insisted on taking the first. When Charity returned, rumpled and unrested, to take her turn, she found her father's intended wife lying beside him on the bed, head upon his shoulder, one arm flung protectively across his chest.

Jonah, for his part, was wide awake, and his somber eyes, turned upon Charity, were beseeching. She could have pretended not to notice, not to know what he was trying to communicate to her, but she would have despised herself for it.

She raised the window to the fresh summer morning then, letting Blaise slumber on, snoring prettily. She pulled a chair up close on her father's side and sat down. His gaze seemed to burn straight through flesh and bone to touch her very soul.

"I said I would take care of everything," she reminded him quietly, "and I will. You've got to trust me, just as I have always trusted you."

Nothing short of her parading Raoul into that room in his wedding clothes would satisfy her father, she knew that, and she had formulated a plan during the long watch, but she could not be certain it would work until she had read through Jonah's will and examined the books of account. She hadn't reconciled herself to doing those things just yet, though she did not dare procrastinate for long, so they were at an impasse.

She leaned forward in her chair. "I will do whatever I must to hold on to this ranch. I promise you that. Close your eyes for a moment if you understand."

Jonah blinked, and Charity was jubilant at this small accomplishment, this voluntary response. It was a beginning, and a reason to go on hoping, but the expression in those beleaguered eyes had not changed. Jonah wanted reassurance, and he wanted it desperately. He wanted her to marry Raoul and put the reins of the Double B in her husband's hands.

Charity had not overlooked the possibility

that her father's recovery might hinge on the actions she took in the next few days and weeks. She leaned forward and kissed his forehead. "Try to rest, Papa. You'll soon be up and around again, running everything. In the meantime, you can depend on me."

It was then that Blaise stirred and awakened, her wealth of lovely auburn hair charmingly disheveled. She sat up, yawning a little, and blushed when she realized she had been lying on Jonah's bed. Despite the inevitable rumors, Charity was positive the relationship was a virtuous one.

Charity flushed with chagrin. She hadn't made love with Luke Shardlow, but she'd wanted to, lying with him in the tree house the way she had, holding him in her arms and guiding his hand to her breast. The worst thing was, she would have done it again, given the opportunity. Done much more, in fact.

"Has the doctor come yet?" Blaise asked, rising gracefully from the bed. The tenderness in the look she gave Jonah tugged at Charity's heart.

She shook her head. Jonah, heaven be thanked, had drifted off to sleep again.

Blaise stood at the foot of the bed. "He'll refuse to marry me now," she said, as much to herself as anyone else. Her tone and countenance were so thoroughly bleak that Charity had to look away for a moment, lest her own resolve to be strong should be shaken. Nor did she try to counter Blaise's statement, because she knew it was true. Jonah, proud to a fault, would no longer regard himself as a suitable husband and protector; he was almost sure to send Blaise and Aaron away.

They would not go empty-handed, the mere prospect was antithetical to Jonah's every principle, but go they would, to Seattle or San Francisco, Denver or Boston, never to return.

Pig-headed fool, Charity thought, with fathomless love and a despair almost as deep. *Sweet, dear, pig-headed fool.* She bent to kiss his forehead then, smiling through tears, and found no particular comfort in the knowledge that she herself was at least as stubborn as her father.

Blaise straightened her shoulders and stood tall. Looking at Charity she said, with a sort of fretful resolution, "I will make some breakfast and bring it to you."

"I don't want to eat," Charity protested. Her stomach seemed to be gone, vanished, as if it had shrunk to nothing.

"I don't care," Blaise retorted. "Your father needs you. And you need food."

Charity deferred with an inclination of her head, knowing this was one battle she wouldn't win. Blaise was right, of course; a body required sufficient nourishment to meet the demands of the day. And Charity was set on doing that.

The instant the door closed behind Blaise, Jonah opened his eyes, the devious old devil, and glared at her so intensely that she could actually feel the weight of his will. Was he trying

153

to force her to the altar, even now, flat on his back and unable to speak or move? Despite her worry over him, it was galling to think he considered her so helpless that she could not even survive, let alone prosper, without a husband. From the time she was ten years old, Charity had gone on trail drives, helped with branding and de-horning, stayed up nights birthing calves and foals, ridden through near blizzards at Jonah's side, looking for strays. Of an evening, she had pored over the books, bank accounts and investments, asking questions until things made sense. Then, inexplicably, somewhere around her eighteenth birthday, everything changed. She became a mere hostess; clothes and charm and the running of a household were to be her only concerns. If Jonah could have kept her from riding and driving the buggy, he would have done it.

What did I do wrong? she thought, as they stared at each other, father and daughter. But she knew the answer: she had grown up, become a woman. Jonah had expected her to simply shed her wild, rambunctious nature, like a snake's skin, thus transforming herself into a fluttering female, concerned only with ruffles and ribbons and dance cards.

Once the joy of Jonah's life, she had not been able to please him since that confusing time. The awareness, she realized now, had broken her heart, and her sense of betrayal went bone-deep.

Blaise returned in half an hour, bearing a

tray. Jonah had either gone to sleep or chosen to pretend again, and the two women spoke in hushed tones, sitting at the small, round table over by the window, sharing toasted bread and coffee, fried eggs and bacon.

Just as they were finishing, Molly arrived, small in her odd, ill-fitting clothes, a battered medical bag in one hand. Raoul, apparently keeping a vigil of his own downstairs, had shown her to Jonah's room. Charity had not known, until then, that her childhood friend, her fiancé, was still in the house.

She was at once touched by the realization and frustrated that she should have to deal with Raoul now, of all times, when her personal resources were at such a low ebb. She needed every ounce of her strength for the challenges ahead, and she meant to conserve it.

The look she gave Raoul, as she stepped out into the hallway with Blaise, so that Molly could examine Jonah, was one of mild irritation.

Typically, Raoul ignored her expression. "How is he?"

"There's no change," Charity responded.

Blaise, no doubt hearing Aaron down in the kitchen, as Charity did, excused herself and left the two of them standing there in the corridor.

"Charity," Raoul began, "the ranch—"

"Don't," she interrupted, raising one hand, palm out, to stem the flow of his words. "I appreciate your concern, Raoul, but you have your own place to look after."

He was silent for a few moments, his right

155

temple throbbing visibly as he made an effort, a noble one for Raoul, to speak calmly. No doubt it was his genuine concern for Jonah's well-being that inspired this singular restraint.

"Look, I promised Jonah a long time ago that if he ever—"

Charity could not hold her peace as far as the end of that sentence. "Wait," she insisted. "What, exactly, did you promise Jonah? And when?"

A muscle bunched in Raoul's jaw, then relaxed again. "I said I'd marry you, right away, if anything ever happened to him. And now, Charity, whether any of us care for it or not, something *has* happened. Let me send to town for the preacher. We'll say the words, and then we won't have two ranches to worry about—just one big one."

Although it went against everything Charity felt, wanted and believed in, she was still sorely tempted to give in. It would surely make Jonah happy, perhaps even restore him to health, and Raoul was not a bad man. He was handsome, he was intelligent, he was devoted. He would make a fine husband and an exemplary father.

Maybe it shouldn't matter so much, that she didn't love him. Thousands, no millions, of women had entered into such unions throughout history, and made a success of them. Her own mother, for one.

And yet there was that other aspect of marriage, the intimacy of sharing a bed, of becoming, as the Bible said, "one flesh." Now that she'd found

Luke again, she was giving that more thought than was strictly proper—a lot more. She knew full well what that meant, and could imagine how wonderful it might be, with the man she loved. To her mind, lying with the wrong man, whether he was her husband or not, would be akin to harlotry. Society might approve of the arrangement, but paradox though it was, Charity knew she would never be able to square such a thing with her principles.

She leaned back against the hallway wall and squeezed her eyes shut in an effort to restore some order to her emotions.

Raoul cupped his hands around her head, ever so gently, and raised her face so that she had to look at him. The pads of his thumbs traced her cheekbones. "Am I so terrible?" he asked, and there was something broken in his voice.

"No," Charity said quickly. Desperately. "It's just that—" She swallowed hard and took the plunge. "I'm—I want someone else."

Raoul knew what she meant, that was plain, for he looked as though she had run him through with a pitchfork. "*What*?" he rasped, as all the color drained from his face.

"Don't ask me to explain," Charity pleaded, but her chin was high.

"Who?" Raoul demanded, as though she hadn't spoken. Then she saw a horrible realization dawn in his face. "Luke Shardlow. I'll be god-dammed—I'll kill that son-of-a-bitch!"

It was all she could do not to raise her hand

to him. Jonah was lying in the next room, critically ill, perhaps even dying, and besides, Raoul had no claim on her, whatever devious and high-handed agreements he might have made with her father.

"I'm not going to discuss this with you, Raoul. Not now, and not ever, because it's none of your business!"

Worse than his fury was the look of stricken injury that followed on its heels. For an awful moment, she thought he might break down and weep. "How—how could you do this?" he asked, in a hoarse whisper. "How, Charity? We made plans—"

She blinked rapidly and swallowed again, lest she be swamped by tears of desolation, of confusion, of longing. "I love him," she said simply.

Raoul grew still—she had heard of men doing murder in just his circumstances—but when she gazed up into his dark eyes, she saw a fierce tenderness there. "Are you going to marry him? Does he want you the way—the way you want him? If he takes advantage, if he hurts you, I swear by every star in the heavens, I'll cut out his liver!" He paused, gave a raw, rueful chuckle that was hard for Charity to bear, resembling a sob the way it did. "Don't be surprised if he shows up at the wedding, be it his or mine, with a fat lip and a few new bruises."

"Raoul," she said gently. "I need a friend right now. And you were always that."

He nodded, then put his arms around her,

pulled her close, placed a light kiss on the bridge of her nose. She clung to him, and that's how they were standing when Molly came out of the sickroom.

Something flickered in the lady doctor's violet eyes; temper, maybe, or sorrow, even jealousy, perhaps. But it was quickly gone.

"How is he?" Raoul and Charity asked in perfect unison.

Molly's smile was sad. "Could we discuss this downstairs—in the kitchen, say? I've got a powerful need for a cup of coffee, and the answer isn't all that simple."

Blaise was waiting for them when they descended the rear stairway; she had already put coffee on to brew. Charity knew without asking that she had overheard the conversation, and she touched the other woman's shoulder lightly, offering what comfort she could.

"Is Jonah going to die?" Blaise wanted to know, the moment all four of them were seated around the kitchen table, like gamblers with no game to play.

Charity's heartbeat quickened painfully as she leaned forward, waiting for Molly to speak.

"Probably not," the doctor said, but the look in her eyes was not one to inspire celebration, or even relief. Blaise, Charity and Raoul all held their breaths, and their tongues, waiting for her to go on. "As you've probably guessed, Mr. Barnham has suffered an apoplexy. He could recover to a very great extent, or he could

159

deteriorate, and remain an invalid until the end of his days." She stopped, fixed a level look on Blaise, then Charity. "I don't want to hold out false hope. Mr. Barnham's symptoms are severe, and he will most likely never be quite the same man you knew before this happened. I'm sorry."

"Tell us what we can expect," Blaise said, with brave impatience, filling each of their cups from the pot of coffee she had brought to the table. "Please."

Molly sighed, cupped her hands around the mug as if for warmth. "There has been some disfigurement, and that probably won't change. He may speak with a slur, if he can speak at all—it will require a great deal of patience and determination on his part, and on yours, for that to happen. He could walk—that too will be a fight—or he might be confined to an invalid's chair. If he's been active for most of his life, as I assume he has, Mr. Barnham will no doubt chafe at the restrictions his illness places upon him. His state of mind will be the most important factor in all of this."

Charity sagged back in her chair, absorbing what she had heard. Raoul and Blaise, too, were silent. Perhaps too stunned to say anything.

The little group sat, sipping their coffee and thinking private thoughts, for a long while. Then Blaise, apparently forgetting it wasn't her turn to sit with Jonah, excused herself and went upstairs.

Charity, realizing that Molly had probably traveled a great distance, went about preparing

160

a meal for her. Raoul, noticeably restless, scraped back his chair and left the house. When he was coming to terms with something, Charity knew, Raoul liked to be around horses, so he was most likely headed for the corral. He would ride, no doubt, until both he and his mount were exhausted; Raoul solved his problems by hurling himself at them, bombarding them.

It wasn't until later that day that Charity could make herself enter Jonah's study, unlock his desk drawer, and go through his private papers.

She found the will easily enough; he had wanted it to come easily to hand, in case of disaster. Sitting in her father's big leather chair, beside the cold and empty fireplace, Charity unfolded the thick document and began to read.

The last will and testament of Jonah Barnham was fairly complicated; there were bequests to various individuals, such as the foreman, Alec Hager, who had worked on the Double B for two strenuous decades, before his rheumatism forced him to retire three years before. There was a respectable sum set aside for Father Elias and the mission school and, as Charity had expected, Blaise and Aaron were both well provided for, too.

At last, virtually holding her breath, Charity reached the main body of the will, which concerned her inheritance. Jonah had left her everything—the land, the mines and timber, the cattle and horses, and the bulk of his money. These were, as she had known, to pass to her control not only in the event of his death, but upon his incapacitation by illness or injury. The terms he'd set did not surprise her, either. She had to be married, or control of the property would pass to the board of directors of a bank in San Francisco and the firm of lawyers he had retained in case his stipulations were not met.

Charity bit her lower lip. It went without saying that she would rather have her father, sound and well, than all the ranches west of the Mississippi, but the foremost reality of all their lives, hers and Blaise's and Aaron's, was not an encouraging one: Jonah was in no fit condition to look after his own affairs. She must marry, if she wished to hold on to the ranch.

She read the pertinent line again, and the paragraphs that followed, her heart pulsing thickly in her throat. It was a shock to realize that Jonah had neglected one small detail: he had failed to specify *who* she should take for a husband. Raoul's name, amazing as it seemed, was nowhere in the document— probably he had assumed, as everyone had, that the match was inevitable. After all, she and Raoul had been practically inseparable all the time they were growing up.

Carefully, Charity folded the will, put it back into its place, and locked the drawer. Her mind was racing like the creek when the snows melted, moving swiftly over many possibilities, wearing them smooth like stones, and returning over and over again to the same one.

While she read the ledgers covering the last several years, she continued to worry that single idea, somewhere in the back of her mind, like a cat with a ball of yarn.

The Double B was profitable, despite the usual problems and struggles, and Jonah not only had money in banks in Boston, San Francisco and Denver, he had purchased a small hotel in Seattle and was half-owner of a wheat farm near Spokane into the bargain. These investments seemed sound, but the ranch itself was plainly struggling. It was, in fact, the least profitable of all his holdings. But why?

Charity was still pondering that question an hour later, when she sent Aaron out in search of the current foreman, an ex-soldier, tough and seasoned by years of work on the range. His name was Hector Tillmont and he was short and very muscular, with bad teeth, leathery skin, and long, mouse-colored hair that could have done with a washing. When he entered the study, only about twenty minutes after the summons was sent out, the smell of whiskey came with him. He carried his hat in one hand and stood just inside the double doors.

"Ma'am," he said, as a greeting, his voice deep and somber. "Me and the boys were real sorry to hear that Mr. Barnham's took sick."

"Thank you," Charity answered primly. She remained in her seat behind Jonah's massive, highly-polished desk, quietly assessing the man before her. She had paid little attention to him, in the three years since he had replaced Mr. Hager, but now she found her-

163

self wondering what special skills he possessed that had inspired Jonah to keep him on.
Her father, though not exactly a member of
the Temperance movement, did not countenance hard drinking among his men. Even at
the end of a trail drive, they were expected to
mind their manners, and Jonah had shown many
a cowpoke the road after bailing him out of the
Jubilee town jail.

Tillmont hovered in the doorway, uncertain
what was expected of him.

"Please," Charity said, indicating a chair.
"Sit down."

After looking behind him, as if seeking
someone who would clear up some perplexing
mystery, he accepted the offer. Charity found
the man too comfortable, and mildly smug,
and she decided she disliked him.

"Yes, ma'am? What might I do for you?"

"I want a report on the current state of the
ranch. A head count of the cattle and horses,
of course. And send some men out to ride the
fence lines. See that they're repaired and let
me know where the work was done." She
would have overseen the tasks personally, if
she'd felt free to leave the house for more
than a few hours at a time.

Tillmont gaped at her as if she'd told him
to climb up on the church steeple and drop his
clothes one garment at a time. "I beg your
pardon, ma'am, but—well—I work for Jonah
Barnham. And that's who I take my orders from,
and nobody else."

Charity let out a long breath. "It really

would be better to do as I tell you," she said. "My father is certainly your employer, but he is ill and I intend to make sure the ranch is here for him when he recovers. If that means firing you and hiring a new foreman, Mr. Tillmont, I will do precisely that."

The man peered at her through narrowed eyes. "I thought Montego would be runnin' the show," he persisted evenly. "In the event that anything like this ever happened, I mean."

She rubbed her eyes with one hand. "You were misinformed," she replied flatly, as the full extent of her problem began to come clear. Every accomplishment would come after a fight, she could see that. "Please do as I tell you. I know my father will appreciate that. I'll be giving him reports right along, naturally, and we all hope that he'll be back in charge very soon."

The foreman glanced behind him again, found no help there, and stood. "I'll see about those fence lines in the morning," he grumbled. Then, after excusing himself, he left.

Charity's head throbbed. She went back upstairs, intending to look in on Jonah, and found Aaron in the hallway, pale behind his freckles and pacing. When he looked up at her, she saw that his green eyes were enormous with fear and suspiciously red-rimmed.

She ruffled his carrot-colored hair and, in the same gesture, pulled him close in a brief embrace. He tolerated that, and sniffled once, exuberantly.

"I don't even remember my real pa," he confided, in a soft voice. "Try though I might, I can't recollect a thing about him."

Charity smiled, though tears stung smartly behind her eyes. "That's all right. You've still got Jonah."

"Ma says he'll send us away, once he's better. I don't want to go nowheres."

She forced herself to hold the child's gaze, though she wanted, powerfully, to look aside. "Anywhere," she corrected softly. "And I wouldn't borrow trouble if I were you. Jonah is a strong man, Aaron, and I know he'll do his best to get well."

"Can I see him? Please?"

Charity hesitated; the stroke had ravaged Jonah, and he looked more like a corpse than a living, breathing man. Even to Charity, his appearance was downright unsettling—how would it affect Aaron? Then she had second thoughts, though, and put an arm around the boy's thin shoulder, reaching for the knob with her other hand. Wondering would be far worse for Aaron than seeing the man he loved as a father with his own eyes. He needed to know the truth, difficult as it was.

"Come with me," she whispered.

Molly was attending Jonah, listening to his heart through a stethoscope, while Blaise stood at the window, staring out over the landscape. Charity could well imagine the other woman's thoughts, and her heart went out to her. Jonah himself appeared to be sleeping, but when Aaron crept up to the foot of the bed to peer at him hopefully, the patient opened his eyes.

It would not be strictly true, Charity later reflected, to claim that Jonah had actually smiled. Still, something in his distorted face seemed to reassure the child, and Aaron crept closer. Molly made way for him, exchanging a look with Charity before dropping the stethoscope into that ancient bag of hers.

Charity had spent several days in Molly's company, during the outbreak of measles at the mission school, but for all that she was no closer to knowing this quiet, strangely-dressed lady doctor. Molly kept to herself, even when she was in the company of several other people, and though there was nothing furtive about her, she gave the impression of a deer poised to go springing away into the forest at the slightest provocation.

Molly cast one glance at Blaise, who still had not turned around, and indicated with a nod that she wanted to speak with Charity privately. Before they slipped out into the corridor, Charity saw that Aaron was sitting on Jonah's bed, earnestly explaining that he was old enough to be a ranch hand and do his share of the work.

Charity sympathized, but she didn't think his chances of winning Jonah over to his way of thinking were any better than her own. They would have to use subterfuge if they wanted to help, she and Aaron both.

"There isn't much I can do for your father," Molly admitted, when they were alone in the hallway, with the bedroom door closed. "And I have so many other patients—"

167

Charity glanced at the arched window above the main staircase. Somehow, the day had slipped away, and although there was still plenty of light, a lavender dusk was beginning to seep in, strewing shadows in its path. "We would be glad to put you up tonight, and between Blaise and me, we should be able to come up with a passable supper. Won't you please stay?"

Molly gave one of her fleeting, ghost-smiles, and Charity thought she saw a flicker of longing in those wary eyes. "I couldn't. I've got two women over in White Horse Junction who are having trouble holding onto their babies, and there's a man who sliced his foot open, chopping wood. I'm worried about septicemia—" Her voice fell away, and she looked down at her dusty boots, for all the world like a shy spinster at a barn dance. "I'm sorry it took me so long to get here," she rushed on, after a moment or so, "but I can barely keep up with my rounds, what with so many folks falling sick and hurting themselves."

"I understand," Charity said. She felt sorry for Molly, obviously overworked and harried, but in another way, she was keenly envious. Whatever this young woman's difficulties, and they appeared to be considerable, she had valid, responsible, *necessary* work to do. People trusted her, depended on her, watched the road for any sign of her.

They descended the stairs together, and Charity paid the doctor's modest fee in cash, then walked with her onto the porch. There

168

were many things she wanted to ask Molly, but she didn't feel she knew her well enough, and didn't wish to pry.

The first stars were just beginning to show through the clouds of roiling August dust stirred by cattle and horses and men. In the corral, Charity saw Raoul, mounted on a roan stallion the hands had been trying, without success, to break to ride. It was strictly an accident that Charity looked away first and caught Molly staring in the same direction—watching Raoul with an expression of quiet hunger.

"I'll stop by again in a week or ten days," the lady doctor said, her cheeks tinged with pink as she realized that Charity had been watching her, had noticed her undisguised absorption in Raoul. "Unless I can get back here sooner, that is." Molly looked doubtful. "In the meantime, don't fuss over your father too much. He needs care, that's true, but you've got to find just the right balance. You don't want him thinking he doesn't have to try anymore. Or worse still, that it's no use if he *does* try."

Molly's mule was brought around then, freshly fed, groomed and watered, and a ranch hand helped her up into the saddle, though that was mere courtesy. The doctor was, of necessity, an experienced rider.

Charity watched as Raoul, having subdued the recalcitrant stallion, dismounted and came toward Molly in long strides. He took the mule's halter in one hand and spoke to the

169

pretty physician, his handsome face upturned and awash in the changing gold and crimson light of sunset. Molly listened intently, nodded once, and then rode away.

Raoul saw Charity on the porch and walked over to stand in the yard, gazing up at her. "You look all done in," he said. "Get some rest tonight, Charity. You'll be no good to Jonah or anyone else if you collapse."

"I will," she promised. For the second time in a few minutes she felt a pang of emotion; first she had coveted Molly her independence, however hard it was, and now there was the almost certain loss of the long friendship she and this man had shared. Even if Raoul forgave her for spurning his suit and loving someone else, things would never be quite the same between them.

After one long, searching look at her, Raoul turned and went back to the corral.

Charity lingered for a few moments, wishing on stars, then turned and headed into the house. In the kitchen, she and Aaron busied themselves making a simple supper of sliced cheese, buttered bread, canned crabapples in tangy sauce, and late string beans purloined from the garden.

Blaise joined them, but she was preoccupied, and there were dark circles under her eyes. She ate without speaking, and then sent Aaron to the spring house for milk. When he returned, she emptied the crockery jug into a pan and set it on to heat.

The kitchen was broiling hot, and Aaron soon

fled to tag after ranch hands in the thickening twilight, but Charity remained, watching in silence as Blaise added cinnamon and a dash of sugar to the foamy milk. When its warmth suited her, she poured it into a bowl, got a small spoon from a drawer, and started up the rear stairs.

Jonah had eaten very little in the week since he had taken ill, only broth and water and weak tea, and Charity had her doubts that he would accept this offering, but she was devoutly grateful to Blaise for the attempt. She hadn't even thought of it.

Charity discovered, when she went to spell Blaise, that she had indeed managed to get a little of the heated milk into Jonah, and now he was sleeping. The woman he had planned to make his wife sat on the edge of the mattress, gazing down at him.

"I can't leave him," Blaise murmured, and though she spoke softly, Charity had no doubt that she meant what she'd said. "I won't." She sighed, came back to herself. "You might as well go to bed, dear. Tomorrow is bound to be hard."

Charity hesitated only briefly, then went wearily to her own room, stripped off her clothes, washed, and tumbled into bed. Blaise's words, she thought, as she teetered on the verge of sleep, were probably prophetic ones. Tomorrow, and all the days after it, promised to be very difficult indeed.

9

$\mathcal{L}$uke waited a full week after his release from the Jubilee town jail, mostly to give the fact of his arrest time to settle in folks' minds, then rode up to the abandoned mine Andrews had mentioned while they were confined together. He'd been certain Vance would leave some sign there, if only to taunt him, and his conviction proved justified.

A lone, scrubby oak stood sentinel near the opening of the boarded-over shaft, and from its sturdiest branch hung the body of a small man. Andrews had been dead several days, and he was in no condition to entertain company.

Cursing, Luke cut down the body and laid it out at the foot of the tree. His eyes watered from the stink, and the pinto made it plain that he was not amenable to the idea of carrying a corpse for any significant distance, but Luke never questioned that the horse would come to see matters his way. Unpleasant though it was, you didn't leave a man's mortal remains out for the buzzards, no matter how he'd lived his life.

So, after a thorough and fruitless look around—he was pretty certain he'd already found all Vance had intended to reveal— Luke settled the debate with the gelding, tied Andrews on behind his saddle, using the noose for binding, and started for town at a cautious pace. To say they attracted attention when Jubilee took note of them, he and the dead man and the reluctant horse, would be to seriously understate the situation.

Dan Higgins was outside waiting when Luke reached his office, and the barber, the closest thing to a doctor or a coroner the town could boast, was with him.

"Damnation," the barber said, in retching disgust, when the miasma of death rolled over him like a dust storm in the desert. It was only a little stronger, Luke reflected, than the odors of rotgut whiskey, sweat and decaying teeth that emanated from the complaint department.

Higgins strolled over, jerked Andrews's head up by the hair to get a look at his swollen, purple face, and spat. "You do this, Shardlow?"

Luke had anticipated the question, but that didn't mean it set well with him. "No," he said. "Somebody strung him up. If I wanted to kill a man, I'd just shoot his ass and be done with it."

The marshal spoke to the barber, whose name turned out to be Clive. "Get a wheelbarrow or something and haul this poor bastard over to the cemetery. Some of those fellas biding their time in the saloon might want to take on the job of buryin' him. The town'll pay two bits apiece, and I'm gonna check to make sure that hole is six feet deep, so if anybody's lookin' for easy money, they'd best look someplace else."

Clive, pressing a wadded bandanna to his face, nodded and fled. Within a few minutes,

173

Andrews was gone, hauled away ignobly in the suggested wheelbarrow, which had been borrowed from the livery stable and was generally employed, from the looks of it, for transporting stall muck. The stench clung, however, and the whole experience left Luke's horse downright testy.

Inside the marshal's office, where wanted posters fluttered on one wall like feathers on some large, rectangular bird, Higgins brought a bottle out of a drawer and set it in the center of his cluttered desk.

Luke straddled the only extra chair in the room, a high-backed one with a hard seat. Higgins, too, sat down. His sigh was heavy and, in the clear light of day, the lines in his face looked more deeply etched than before. Not for the first time, Luke pondered the possibility that this man was his half-brother but, as was usual for him, he kept his own counsel.

Higgins offered him the bottle first, and Luke did not falter, but took it, tilted it back, drank deeply. His stomach roiled, but he knew he appeared to enjoy the wretched stuff. He handed the whiskey back to the marshal, watched as he took a gulp.

"You hear about old Jonah Barnham?" Higgins asked, after clearing his throat and wiping his mouth with the back of one hand.

Luke's manner was easy, his speech slow, but mentally he was leaning forward, listening hard. "What about him?" he inquired, with little apparent interest, and took another

174

deep draught from the bottle, for good measure. He wondered if the other man was just shooting the breeze, or if he had some purpose in telling Luke about Barnham's bad luck.

"Took sick a while back," Higgins answered. "The way I heard it, he can't move or talk. He's just lyin' there, in his bed, Jonah is, waitin' to die."

Luke felt a rush of sympathy for Charity that might have swept him off balance, if he hadn't schooled himself so well, for so long, to reveal nothing of what he was thinking or feeling. "You know him?" Luke asked, plucking a cheroot from his shirt pocket, while the marshal, after ferreting out a bag and papers from the litter on his desk, squeaked back in his chair to roll his own.

"A man can't live or work in these parts for long without gettin' acquainted with Barnham. I reckon that daughter of his will stop diggin' in her heels now and marry Montego. It will take a man to run that place."

"Strange nobody's spoken for her before now," Luke said, squinting in the smoke that curled past his eyes. He was going to give up the smoking habit one day soon; a thing like that couldn't be good for a man's health. "She's a fine looking woman."

Higgins smiled at that observation. "Plenty of men have gone a-courtin' on the Double B, but old Barnham, he cut Montego out of the herd a long time back. Wants her to marry him so they can join the Double B with the Draper

175

place. Miss Charity's mighty sweet to look at, but I hear tell she's strong-minded. I can't abide a woman like that."

Luke suppressed a smile. "That so?" he asked idly. "I like a lady to have some spirit, myself. Brains, too."

The marshal laughed. "You're a fool, then. Smart females are nothin' but trouble. No time at all, they're tellin' you how to run things."

"You sound like a man with experience."

"I've thought about settlin' down a few times, but I always came to my senses in time. What about you, Shardlow? You ever tied the knot?"

Luke indulged in a long pause before answering. "No," he said finally. "Never really stayed in one place long enough."

Higgins nodded thoughtfully. "Well, maybe you'll meet somebody right here in Jubilee. There's a dance Saturday night, east of town, out at the old Meddly place. They just raised a new barn, and this is their way of showin' it off. Folks will come from all over for a gatherin' like that."

Luke wondered if Higgins fancied himself a subtle man, conveying the message the way he had. While the lawman rolled another smoke, Luke stretched in a leisurely way, then rose and swung the chair against the wall, where he'd found it. He took care to do most everything slowly; people tended to spook at sudden moves when a man was armed. "I might be there. Thing is, though, I've kind of taken a shine to Charity Barnham."

The marshal gave another low guffaw and sat back in his chair, arms folded. "Good luck with that," he said, "but I don't think you've got the kinda pedigree old Jonah is looking for. Montego may be a bastard, but his mother's people can trace their blood-lines back a thousand years."

Luke ignored that, sniffed at his shirt sleeve, and grimaced. He was going to have to strip down, scrub off, and boil his clothes to get rid of the stink of Vance's dramatic announcement. "Guess I'll go home," he said. "Thanks for the whiskey."

"You gonna be at that dance?"

Pitiful, Luke thought. Just plain pitiful. He shrugged. "That depends."

"On what?"

Luke grinned. "On whether or not Miss Charity Barnham plans to attend."

Higgins was still chewing on that when Luke turned around and ambled out. Conversely, his mind was racing, sorting, drawing conclusions.

Shit, Vance, he thought, swinging up into the saddle and wheeling the fitful gelding toward home, *you don't have to beat me over the head. I'm paying attention.*

When Charity arrived at the Shardlow place, mounted on Taffeta and full of high resolve, her eyes widened at the sight that awaited her. It wasn't so much the large cauldron of hot water steaming over a slow fire that came as a surprise—people did laundry and made soap that way all the time—but the fact that Luke was sitting in it, like a cartoon missionary in a cannibal camp, wearing his hat and nothing else.

He smiled through the rising vapor, but she saw the knowledge of Jonah's illness in his eyes, and it touched her in a way words of sympathy could never have done. "You'll pardon me," he said, tipping his limp hat, "if I don't stand."

In spite of all the sorrow and distress of past days, Charity laughed. "I won't ask why you're taking a bath in the dooryard in the bright light of day," she said, dismounting but keeping a cautious distance, "but I will surely perish of curiosity if you don't explain the hat."

The grin widened. "Habit," he said. "Pure habit. Guess I've been a bachelor too long—getting set in my ways. Would you mind adding a few chunks of wood to the fire? I don't want the water to get cold."

Charity complied, though her nerves were rattled and her heart was thumping away in the pit of her stomach. "Mind you don't stay in there too long," she fussed. "You might just boil right down to the bone, like a stewed chicken. Doesn't the bottom burn your—feet?"

The brim of the disreputable hat moved upward as Luke raised his eyebrows. "You could always join me in here and find out for yourself," he suggested.

"Don't be lewd," Charity scolded. She felt color pounding in her cheeks, and wouldn't meet his eyes for a few moments. When she had a better grip on her composure, she placed her hands on her hips and fixed him with a level gaze.

"I have serious business with you, Mr. Shardlow," she went on. "Frankly, I would have preferred to find you fully clothed and in a slightly more circumspect state of mind."

He produced a bar of yellow soap from somewhere and began to lather himself about the chest and underarms, and Charity squirmed imperceptibly as a flock of unseemly sensations beat their wings inside her, then took flight. "I'm sorry to disappoint you," he said. "Fact is, I'm feeling pretty cheerful."

Charity recalled the state of her father's health and the old heaviness of spirit overtook her. Her shoulders, held rigid beneath her burdens for days, ached with the strain. "You may have heard that we are experiencing difficult times on the Double B," she said.

Luke's gaze conveyed an understanding so gentle that, once again, she came perilously close to weeping. "I've heard," he affirmed. "And I'm sorry, Charity. How is Jonah?"

She sighed. It was a question she'd been asking herself, at all hours of the day and night. He was like a husk, her father, and yet a fire of determination burned within him, flickered behind his expressive eyes. "He is very ill," she said, because that was the fundamental truth. "He cannot run the ranch, of course, and yet the terms of his will—"

"His will?" Luke interrupted. "What's that

got to do with anything, given that he's not dead?"

"Papa's papers take all possible circumstances into consideration," Charity answered, wondering how on earth she was going to make herself say what she had to say, ask what she had to ask. "He's made sure of that."

Luke sank into the water, up to his stubbled chin, and reflected at length. "And now you've got to marry Raoul Montego or give the place up to a pack of greenhorns in some city," he said, eventually.

Charity fairly trembled, trying to contain her anxiety. "Well, I've got to marry, that's true. But there is no stipulation in the papers as to who my husband should be." She thought she saw him stiffen, hoped she had imagined it. Lest she lose her courage, she dove into the subject headfirst. "That's what I've come to talk to you about. I'm willing to pay you ten thousand dollars to marry me, Mr. Shardlow. It's just for a year—long enough for me to prove to Papa that I am perfectly capable of taking over the management of the Double B. We won't sleep together, of course, and—"

"Wait a second," Luke broke in. "Why don't you offer this deal to Raoul?"

Charity's face grew hotter; she attributed it to the heat of the fire and the steam from the kettle in which Luke Shardlow was slowly parboiling. "Because I'd never get rid of him, for one thing. And for another, he would expect me to—well—"

"He would expect you to share his bed," Luke said, in a voice that revealed nothing of what he was thinking. He might have been insulted, he might have been considering her offer. His next words cleared the matter up. "So would I," he told her plainly. "Furthermore, I am not flattered to be chosen as your throw-away husband."

Charity wished she could dissolve and blow away in the breeze, like the delicate white down of a dandelion going to seed. "I simply thought—"

His face was hard. "You simply thought," he outlined bitterly, "that I'd go away like a kicked dog when you figured I'd served my purpose. Hand me that towel over there on the woodpile."

"Get it yourself," Charity snapped, and then hurriedly turned her back, knowing he was just audacious enough to rise right out of that big kettle and fetch the towel. Behind her, she heard considerable splashing, followed by a muffled curse. Just when she'd broken her paralysis, and started toward the mare, waiting with its reins dangling, he caught hold of her arm and spun her around to face him.

Her heart fairly stopped at the sight of him, beaded with moisture, a scanty cloth around his middle, and that hat resting insolently on the back of his head. "Just hold on a minute here," he snapped. "*Damn* it, you're not going to hit me with a suggestion like that and then ride out like it never happened!"

Charity trembled with the effort to maintain her dignity, but maintain it she did. Her throat was constricted to the point of pain, though, and her stomach felt as if it had been shot from a catapult. "I didn't mean to insult you," she said, with effort.

"Well," said Luke, easing up a little, "you did, all the same." Furrows took shape in his forehead. "What makes you think Jonah wouldn't blow another blood vessel if we actually went through with this—this scheme of yours?"

Was he considering the proposition? Charity was jubilant, almost dizzy with relief, but there was bitterness, too. How she wished things could have been different between her and Luke, but there was no sense in dwelling on that. "I don't think Jonah would care if I dragged a saddle bum in off the trail, as long as I had a husband."

Luke rolled his eyes. "If that doesn't beat all," he said, with a note of quiet fury. "Now I'm a saddle bum. Well, I have *some* pride, you know." It seemed an ironic statement, given the fact that he was standing there before her in a towel and a hat and an attitude, and absolutely nothing else. "Maybe the Shardlow name isn't one you'd want to shout from the rooftops, darlin', but it's mine and I'll expect my wife to use it." He paused, doing battle with some private demon. "As for the ten thousand dollars, Miss Barnham, you can just take that and—"

She could bear no more; she'd already made enough of a fool of herself, and if she

182

remained, she would surely break down and sob. Maybe even beg. So she whirled again and started for the horse, planning to ride away without looking back.

Once more, however, he stopped her. "Let me finish," he said, holding her arm with one hand and the towel with the other. "You can put the money in trust someplace. We'll decide what happens to it on our first anniversary."

Her mouth fell open; for a moment her amazement was such that she could not speak. "Are you saying that you'll do it?" she cried, once the verbal stranglehold was broken. "You'll marry me?"

"Yes," he said. "But I've got some terms of my own, and I won't give ground, so don't plague me about it. I'll tell Jonah myself that I mean to take you for a wife and if that doesn't kill him, we'll go ahead with the ceremony." His aquamarine eyes snapped with barely-controlled irritation, and he cocked one thumb toward the cabin looming behind him. "But we'll live right here in this house, and you'll wear the clothes I buy for you and eat the food I provide."

Charity had not envisioned the plan unfolding in quite that way, but she supposed they might work out a reasonable compromise. "The whole point of our getting married at all," she said, mildly exasperated, and a little thrilled as well, "is so that I can run the Double B instead of seeing it turned over to strangers. I don't see how I can do that, if I don't live there."

183

"That's my offer," Luke said. "Take it or leave it."

"Well, I'll leave it, then," Charity bluffed. She could—conceivably—return to this cabin each day, when the work was done, and they both knew it. The whole idea was impractical, that's all.

"Fine," he replied, and turned his back on her. He picked his barefoot way through the deep grass toward the cabin door, stooping at the threshold to pick up his boots. He paused and looked back at her over one naked shoulder.

She spread her hands wide. "This is ridiculous." She followed that up with a wild gesture, in the direction of the Double B. "There's that huge house over there, with every comfort, and you want to live *here*?"

"That's right," Luke said. Then, unbelievably, he went inside the cabin and shut the door, leaving Charity with an untenable choice. She could knock, like some beggar, and agree to his demands, she could marry Raoul, who would settle for nothing less than the rest of her life, or she could lose the ranch.

"Damnation," she sputtered and, hoisting her skirts, swept grandly up to the door and pounded on it.

Luke's voice was chime-like. "Who's there?"

Charity stormed into the cabin, realized what she might find, and covered her eyes. "If this is any indication of how you intend to behave when we are married," she said, "I can't imagine how we shall keep from killing each other!"

184

"I'll be happy to demonstrate how I intend to behave when we're married," he retorted. "Uncover your eyes, Charity. I've got pants on."

She peered through latticed fingers, not entirely ready to trust him. Sure enough, he was wearing trousers, and he'd pulled on his boots at some point, too. Between his spectacularly bare chest, however, and what he'd just said, he might as well have been stark naked.

"I'm ready to agree to your terms," she said primly, "although I don't mind telling you that I consider them quite extreme."

His stare was pointed, and he said nothing at all.

"The next year is going to be very difficult," she persisted.

Luke shrugged into a clean shirt, plucked from a peg on the wall. "You have no idea how difficult," he said. The statement sounded ominous, and Charity didn't pursue it.

"I can't possibly be ready for a wedding before next week," she said, pulling the door open to leave. "Good-bye, Mr. Shardlow." She stepped outside, then paused and turned. "Oh, and one last thing. If you ever lay a hand on me in anger, or take your pleasure with another woman, I shall shoot you without so much as faltering."

He chuckled. "Fair enough," he said.

When she was gone, Luke stood there in the center of his cabin, half-dressed and wondering what in the hell had made him agree to marry Charity Barnham or any other woman. He didn't mind the idea of bedding her—in fact, he was hard, well in advance of the event—but a year of his life was a year of his life, and he had plenty of problems without taking a bride. Call him old-fashioned, but he'd planned to marry just once, and he didn't relish the prospect of explaining to some unknown woman, a ways down the line, that he'd traded vows with somebody else just because she offered him ten thousand dollars. And he was pretty sure what *his* opinion of such an arrangement would be, if the situation were reversed.

Outside again, Luke gathered up the clothes he'd worn earlier, started to throw them into the still-steaming cauldron, then changed his mind and kicked them into the embers instead. They smoldered for a while, then took fire and burned.

Satisfied that they had been consumed, and the smell of death with them, he returned to the cabin, strapped on his gunbelt, drew the .45 and gave the cylinder a spin to make sure it was loaded. Then he went back out again, and whistled for the pinto.

The gelding played deaf, though he could see the animal clearly, grazing down by the spring, ears raised and twitching. Old Shiloh was taking no chances on being made to haul another dead man, and when Luke whistled again, piercingly, the s.o.b. ignored that, too. "Dogmeat," Luke muttered, and started striding through the grass toward the horse.

186

The pinto eluded him for a few more minutes, then relented and came trotting over, nickering. Luke changed his mind about shooting him and eventually they reached a shaky accord where a saddle and bridle were concerned. By the time twilight crawled over the hills and spilled into the low country, Luke was mounted and he and the horse were both headed in the same direction.

Reaching the cemetery, he saw that the drunks Higgins had sent the barber to recruit were still digging, sending plumes of dirt into the air from the bottom of Andrews's grave. It was clear from their nervous talk and their hurry that they didn't care to stay in that place after sundown, and Luke smiled at that. The dead gave no cause for fear, but the living, now, that was another matter entirely.

He dismounted by the rear fence, vaulted over it, and made his way to his mother's grave. The roses Charity had laid beneath the marker that first day after his return had faded and died, leaving spindly skeletons behind. He leaned down to toss them aside.

The wooden cross was weather-beaten and a little askew. Luke straightened it gently, and waited. Over on the other side of the graveyard, the diggers argued as they scrambled up out of the ground. The cheap pine box beside the hole must have been heavy; the two men huffed and cursed in the attempt to lift it, then gave up and shoved it in.

Luke looked up at the stars, remembering the day they'd laid his mother to rest in this spot. Remembered Trigg standing just about where he was standing now, handcuffed and sobbing. He could still feel the rain, cold and heavy, wetting his clothes clean through to the skin, and, with it, the sorrow that went so much deeper.

It was the prickling sensation at the back of his neck that brought Luke out of his reverie; he eased the .45 from its holster but did not turn around.

"Drop it," Vance said.

Luke sighed. After all his planning, was it going to end like this? "Don't be stupid," he answered. "You're not fast enough to take me."

Vance laughed. By the sound, he was no more than six feet away, and Luke reflected with chagrin that he deserved shooting, letting himself be sneaked up on that way. He'd been woolgathering ever since Charity's visit to the homestead, and now he might have to pay the price.

"That's confidence," Vance said.

Still holding the .45, Luke turned. His half-brother stood among shafts of shadow, his features hidden by the brim of his hat. Instead of a pistol, Vance held his weapon of choice, a Bowie knife that glinted even in the fading light. The blade, Luke knew, was razor sharp, and as much a part of the other man's anatomy as the Colt was of his.

"What do you want?" he asked.

Vance's white teeth gleamed, wolflike, in the thickening gloom. "Peculiar," he countered. "I came here to put the same question to you, little brother."

188

"All right," Luke said, "I'll play the game. I want the bounty on your head, *big* brother, and I mean to collect it."

"Here I am," Vance said, spreading his hands, the blade protruding like a sixth finger. "Take me in."

"So your friend Higgins can turn you loose again? That would be impractical."

Vance laughed again. There seemed to be no end to his good cheer. "I should have known you wouldn't swallow that story about his father and your pretty little mama. Genius that you are, you've probably figured out that my men are watching right now, and you're covered from about six directions?"

"I'm disappointed in myself," Luke lamented, and he was. "I should have expected something like this."

"Believe it or not," Vance said, "I don't want to have to kill you. I'm asking you to get on your horse and ride out of here. The solution is that simple."

Luke ran his tongue along the inside of his lower lip. "Your brotherly sentiments surprise me, given the fact that you and those jackasses you ride with tried to stomp me into the ground by the creek that night. What are you doing in Jubilee, Vance?"

"I'm just passing through," the other man replied, sounding aggrieved.

"Seems like you're taking your sweet time doing it," Luke observed. "I'm not about to back down and you must know that. So why are we really having this conversation? Just for old times' sake?" He paused to draw and expel a long breath. "How does Higgins figure into this?"

"Questions, questions. You have always asked too many questions, little brother. I've tried to deal with you gently—your sweet mother was kind to me, treated me like her own, and I owe her a debt for that—but I'm losing patience with you. Just move on. That's all I'm asking you to do. Move on." Vance sheathed the knife, brought out a smoke, and struck a match off the nearest grave marker. The tip of the cheroot glowed crimson as he drew on it, the smell curled around Luke's head like fingers reaching out of hell.

"Pure poetry," Luke mocked, spreading his free hand, fingers splayed, over his heart. "If I didn't know you were an asshole, Vance, I'd probably break right down and cry."

"I could kill you, here and now. You know that, of course." Vance's voice had hardened, and the ease with which he'd stood up to that moment gave way to a certain wary stiffness of countenance. "All I've got to do is give the signal, and you're a dead man."

"That's probably true," Luke agreed affably. "But there's an obvious hitch in your plan. Before my knees bend, before my heart stops beating, I'll have put a bullet through your forehead. It's just too tragic to think about."

"Luke," Vance said. "I know about the woman. I don't want to hurt her, but I will, if you don't do as I tell you."

A chill twined itself through Luke's insides like a silvery snake, but he didn't allow himself so much as the flicker of an eyelash or the twitch of a muscle. "A word of advice, Vance," he said moderately. "Kill me first. That way, what I do to you won't win me a place in hell, at the devil's right hand."

Vance chuckled, but the sound was raspy, and completely devoid of humor. "You are trying my patience," he said.

On the other side of the cemetery, the grave diggers finished their task, paying no apparent mind to the confrontation between Luke and Vance. Andrews was tucked safely away in the ground, put there by a man he was gullible enough to trust.

Luke, for all his admitted faults, was no fool. Vance was roughly as predictable as a rattler prodded with a sharp stick; he would strike if the odds seemed favorable to him.

The whole of Luke's consciousness was focused on the .45, still held loosely in his left hand. It seemed that his blood vessels ran right through his fingers into the cold steel of that gun, that his pulse beat in the trigger. He would not have to move to fire, only to let a mental picture take shape in his mind.

Sweat itched between his shoulder blades as Vance turned his back and walked away, certain that Luke wouldn't shoot him unless he could look into his eyes. He was right, as it happened, but until the moment had passed, Luke himself hadn't been quite so sure.

10

Charity stood at the foot of Jonah's bed, the morning after her proposal to Luke Shardlow, twisting her mother's pearl ring round and round upon her finger while her thoughts raced. Jonah sat almost upright, with pillows fluffed behind him, and though he still could neither speak nor walk, his dark eyes were ablaze with conviction. Whatever his outer limitations, inwardly he seemed to grow more robust with every passing moment, and to Charity he seemed anything but helpless.

Aaron had brought him a small slate and a stick of chalk, and although the process was painfully slow, Jonah was able to manage a rudimentary sort of communication. He and the boy had worked out a system—an X for no, a check mark for yes; they were in the process of creating a language all their own.

Now, seeing Jonah's fingers curled awkwardly around the stub of chalk, Charity braced herself for an argument that promised to be no less arduous for the fact that one side of it would be nonverbal.

"I'm going to be married," Charity announced bluntly, with the same grim look she might have employed in pulling off an old bandage or removing a splinter from a grizzly's paw.

Jonah's eyes glittered. He made a check mark on the slate.

Charity swallowed and held up one hand,

palm out. "Listen to me, Papa," she said respectfully. "I've complied with your wishes, unreasonable though they are, but it's only fair to tell you that I have chosen someone other than Raoul."

Jonah's gaze narrowed; he did not need to speak, for she felt his question like the impact of a stiff and sudden wind. *Who?*

She wet her lips and her anxiety heightened so that she grew dizzy with the altitude. "I've asked Luke Shardlow to marry me," she blurted out. "He has accepted." *However ungraciously,* she thought.

Jonah's reaction was far worse than she had expected: color surged into his neck, pulsing crimson and then purple. His strong jaw grew rigid, his eyes flashed, and Charity watched in horror and chagrin as the slate board slipped to the floor. Fearing that he would suffer another spell of apoplexy, she rushed to his side and grasped both his hands in hers. Tears slipped down her cheeks.

"Don't do this to me, you old tyrant," she pleaded, furious and desperately afraid. "I love you so much, and I'm doing the best I can to please you—"

His grip surprised and reassured her, for it was vital, powerful. He made a garbled, murmuring sound in his throat, and when Charity let her head fall to his shoulder, sobbing softly, his right hand found its way to her shoulder and rested gently there.

She collected herself, sniffling, and looked deep into his eyes.

He raised one brow and, as before, his question was clear.

She considered. "Yes," she confessed, in a wet whisper. "Yes, I love him."

It seemed to Charity that Jonah smiled, though of course his mouth didn't move. He made a slight movement with the chalk, and she hastened to retrieve the fallen slate. With heartrending determination, Jonah contrived to reply to her admission, and his answer was another shaky check mark.

He had given his blessing.

Laughing and crying, both at once, she kissed her father's forehead. "Thank you," she whispered. "Thank you."

The exchange had clearly exhausted Jonah; he sank back upon his pillows, pale and somewhat tremulous.

"That was a terrible risk," Blaise said coolly, from the doorway.

Charity stood, adjusted Jonah's covers in an effort to make him more comfortable, and turned to face the woman she hoped would become her stepmother. Taking Blaise's arm, she ushered her gently into the corridor and closed the door before speaking.

Color flared in Blaise's high cheekbones. "What were you thinking of, opposing him that way?" she demanded, in an outraged whisper.

Charity was stung by the rebuke, partly because she knew it was not entirely unfounded, and partly because she and Blaise had always been allies, with never a harsh word passing between them. "What would you have had me

194

do?" she asked, in a low voice. "Simply sweep in one day, with Luke on my arm, and announce that I've taken him as a husband?"

Blaise sighed. "He looked—"

Charity took her friend's arm in a light, supportive grasp. "I know," she agreed contritely. "Papa looked dreadful when I broke the news, didn't he? But can you imagine how he would have reacted to the *fait accompli?*"

Tugging a lace-edged handkerchief from the bodice of her dress, Blaise dabbed delicately at both eyes, then her nose. "I should not have spoken so sharply," she said, in tremulous tones. "It frightened me so, that's all. I cannot spare that man, Charity. I simply cannot."

Charity embraced the other woman, found her small and fragile and sweetly scented, like the first spring lilacs. "Hush," she said. "We're not going to lose Papa. Before we know it, he'll be out of that bed, striding about and bossing all of us around again."

Blaise's eyes were enormous and shimmering with tears as she looked up into Charity's face. "I pray God you are right," she said softly. Then, drawing a deep breath, she squared her shoulders and stood a bit taller. "He wants me to leave, you know. To take Aaron and go."

Charity knew her hard-headed father, knew that what Blaise said was probably true, but she could not bring herself to say as much. "My dear papa has gotten his way too often, for far too long," she said. "You aren't actually planning to go, surely?"

For all her small stature, Blaise looked fierce. "If Jonah Barnham wants me out of this house, he'd better get himself well enough to remove me personally. Until that day, I shall remain, whether he likes it or not." With that announcement, Blaise opened the door to Jonah's room and disappeared inside.

Half an hour later, Charity was seated on the screened sun porch, on the quiet side of the house, where the garden bloomed, reading one of her father's ledgers, when a team and wagon clattered to a stop beyond the picket fence out front. Everything within her quickened when she saw Luke wrap the reins around the brake lever and spring down from the box.

Seeing Charity open the porch door and start down the steps, he tossed her a grin and tugged at the brim of his hat.

"Afternoon," he said, going around to the back of the rig and opening the tailgate. Then he dragged an object wrapped in a blanket—a large contraption of some sort—out of the rig and set it on the ground.

Charity approached, puzzled, but when he removed the blanket, she saw that it was a battered invalid's chair, with great wire-spoked wheels, a high wicker back, and a worn leather seat. She stared at it in amazement, touched it with a tentative hand. Jonah would despise the thing, but it might well be his salvation.

"Where on earth—?"

Luke took a few moments to admire the apparatus. "I put it together myself from a few pieces

196

of junk old Pete had stuck away in the back of the livery stable. The wheels are from some kid's pony cart, and the chair used to be a rocker. What do you think?"

Charity was hard put not to commence weeping again. "I think he'll hate it," she said. Then, impulsively, she threw both arms around his neck and planted a smacking kiss on his cheek. "Oh, Luke, it's wonderful!"

He laughed and held her away from him, but his hands rested firm and possessive on her waist, and she felt a great burst of heat roll over her, like a fireball from some unseen explosion, scorching her senses and nearly taking her breath away. She could not help imagining what it would be like to be Luke's wife, and explore, with impunity, the strange fiery country of their intimacy. "You told him, didn't you?" he asked.

She sighed. "Yes."

"And?"

"And, for a few moments, I thought he was going to have another stroke. Then I told him that—well, anyway, he relented. I think he's actually pleased."

Luke looked skeptical, but he hoisted the invalid's chair up into his arms for transport into the house and replied, "Well, this ought to piss him off."

They entered the house by way of the cool, shadowy sun porch, and being alone in that confined and quiet place with Luke, if only long enough to pass through, awakened new yearnings in Charity, and stirred a powerful, com-

197

bustible ache in the heart of her womb. She pictured a child there, tightly curled, and the image shook her so profoundly that she stretched out one arm, just briefly, to steady herself against the framework of the kitchen door.

Luke, being behind her, almost certainly saw the gesture; though he offered no comment, she could feel his gaze burning into her, laying silent claim not only to her body, but to the plains and peaks and valleys of her spirit.

They passed through the dining room and into the entry hall, where they encountered Blaise, descending the stairs. She smiled charmingly at Luke, and responded with lady-like pleasure to Charity's introduction.

"Where did you find that marvelous chair, Mr. Shardlow?" she asked. "I declare, it's just what Jonah requires. He won't care for the thing a bit, mind you, but I'm sure he'd go mad if he had to spend another whole day and night in that bed of his."

"I'd like you to call me Luke, if you would, ma'am," Luke responded. "It's nothing much, this chair, though it might serve a purpose. Is Mr. Barnham awake?"

Blaise nodded. "He was staring up at the ceiling when I left him, like to set the place on fire." Her gaze slipped to Charity, then went back to Luke. "I think you should see him on your own, this first time. Without Charity or me there to look on while he makes peace with the idea of needing that chair."

Luke glanced questioningly at Charity,

beside him on the stairs, and she sighed. "Blaise is right." She paused, gazed earnestly into Luke's eyes. "Don't let him buffalo you, Luke. Papa's a stubborn old devil and he won't make things easy for you."

He chuckled. "I don't trust easy things anyway," he said. He'd taken his hat off outside, and tossed it up onto the wagon seat, and his sun-streaked hair was in charming disarray. His blue-green eyes danced with mischief as he indicated the pistol on his hip with a tilt of his chin. "You'd better take this hog-leg, Charity." Simple courtesy required that he disarm himself, they both knew that, but Luke grinned and confided, "Jonah might get hold of it and make me dance."

Charity had been around guns all her life, could shoot as well as many of the men on the Double B, but there was something dizzyingly intimate about the act of removing Luke's pistol from its holster, and she did so gingerly, holding the handle between two fingers. Then, automatically, she flipped open the chamber, shook the shells into her palm and dropped them into her apron pocket.

Blaise looked at the pistol with round-eyed distaste. "Do put that dreadful thing away, Charity, before Aaron sees it."

Charity nodded, but her words were addressed to Luke. "I'll lock this up in my bureau drawer," she said. Then she blushed hotly, foolishly, not so much because it was taboo to speak of the place where she kept her most intimate articles of clothing, which it was,

199

but because the images of linen and lace roused the very feelings of unseemly longing she had been trying to quell since Luke's arrival.

He read her expression accurately, if the grin that curved his mouth was any indication, then proceeded up the stairs, with Blaise swishing along ahead, showing him the way.

Charity hurried into her bedroom, locked the .45 safely away, and then went over to her washstand, poured tepid water from the pitcher into the basin, and splashed her face repeatedly.

Jonah glared at Luke all the while he was wrestling the invalid's chair over the threshold and set it down with a thump beside the bed.

"I guess you know by now that Charity and I plan to be married," he announced.

Jonah scowled, and one of his hands curled into a fist.

"The way I figure things," Luke went cheerfully on, "if you don't want to turn into one big bedsore, you'd better roll out of the hay and get some fresh air." He nodded toward the terrace, visible through the double doors on the other side of the room. "I reckon you can see what's going on down at the corral from over there. Make sure things are to your liking."

Jonah looked grim at that, and the message was clear enough. Nothing was to Jonah's liking at the moment, not his physical condition, not his future son-in-law.

Luke chuckled. "Well, Jonah, I guess if you feel that way about it, you'd better get well, hadn't you?" He approached the bed and, with a philosophical sigh, flung back the thin covers, revealing the rancher's striped nightshirt and hairy legs. With as little fuss as possible, he hoisted the other man off the mattress and into the chair.

Jonah sat stiff as a tamarack tree, and Luke felt a pang of pity, though he would have died before letting it be seen. He found a lap robe and put it over Jonah's knees, then wheeled him out onto the balcony.

There, while Jonah drank in the sight of the land, the horizon and the sky, plainly as thirsty for it as a sojourner in the desert would be for water, Luke leaned against the heavy wooden railing and folded his arms.

"I'll be good to her," he said.

Jonah didn't look at him, maybe he couldn't have turned his head even if he'd chosen to do so, but there was no doubting that he heard. The angle of his chin told Luke that, and the set of those bearlike shoulders.

"The thing is, Jonah," Luke went on, "if Charity's going to be my wife, and it appears she is, she'll have to live under my roof."

At that, Jonah turned his head, pierced Luke with an arrow-sharp gaze.

"Oh, you don't need to worry," Luke answered, as if the other man had spoken aloud. "She's set on looking after this ranch, and I imagine she can do a proper job of it, too, being every bit as cussed as you are. But this is her place, not mine, and I won't live here like some pet rabbit. Besides, I've got one or two of my own objectives and, believe it or not, they've got nothing to do with you or your daughter."

Jonah groped for the wheels of his chair as he listened, found them, made an awkward effort at moving himself. He managed a couple of inches forward, then a couple of inches back, and the look of triumph in his eyes brushed a tender place inside Luke, a patch of soul that had not been touched since well before his mother's death.

Luke expelled a sigh. "I wasn't meant to be a preacher," he said, "but I'm going to try to set you straight anyhow. You have a fine place here, Jonah. You've got a woman who loves you, and a boy who wants to grow up to be just like you, which is about the best compliment a kid can pay, and then there's Charity. If you won't get better for yourself, then do it for your daughter. She loves this ranch, old man, but she loves you more. That's why she's fighting for her birthright, why she's ready to take on a task a lot of good men would shrink from. And it's why she's willing to marry me, too. She isn't looking to take over. She wants to preserve this place for you. She figures if she can hold the light high, you'll follow it back out of that place you're hiding in right now and join the rest of us in the real world."

Jonah reddened along the lower part of his jaw, which looked rock-solid to Luke, even if it was a little out of kilter.

Luke watched in silence for a while as Jonah continued his subtle attempts to maneuver the chair. Then he laid one hand to the other man's shoulder.

"I'm sorry about what happened to you, Jonah," he said quietly. "You didn't deserve it. And that's the last of my sympathy, so make the most of it. From now on, I plan to ride you like the last horse out of hell. You'll either get better out of sheer spite, or die of vexation, but your days of languishing in peace and pity are over."

With that, Luke left the other man to the healing powers of the land and the sky and his own fury, grinning to himself as he turned his thoughts to Charity, tucking his .45 away among the bits of dainty frippery in her bureau drawer.

She was waiting downstairs, on the screened porch, and he found her unerringly, as if led by some sixth sense that would concern itself with nothing else but this woman and her whereabouts.

"How was he?" she asked, in a voice that made Luke want to comfort her.

He joined her on the porch swing. "Right about now, he's probably mad as a rooster dunked headfirst in cornmeal mush," he said. "I did my best to be diplomatic, but it still isn't easy for a man like Jonah, needing so much help with ordinary things."

Her chin had been wobbling a little, but at Luke's words, she worked up a watery smile that was gone again as quickly as it appeared.

"Blaise and I will turn the small parlor into a bedroom and move Papa downstairs. That way he won't be so cut off from things."

"He's going to be fine," Luke said and, on an impulse, he leaned forward slightly and brushed her mouth with his. A jolt of pure, unrefined need went through him, and he shifted uncomfortably, trying to accommodate the undignified change she'd worked in his anatomy. Lordy, but he'd have taken her right there, if she'd been his wife, just set her on his lap, opened his trousers, and eased her right down onto him. He'd massage her plump breasts while she rocked slowly on him, and crooned...

"Luke?"

He stifled a groan and made to stand, so he could turn his back and thus hide the proof that his thoughts had gone astray from the conversation.

She stopped him cold just by laying a hand on his arm. "Are you all right?" she asked, with a concern so genuine that he was further unnerved.

"I'm fine," he said hoarsely. A swim in the creek would make truth of the lie, as soon as he could get away. He got up, and that process, simple as it was, caused him no little pain.

Charity stood too, her eyes wide and somehow troubled. "You'll want your pistol," she reminded him.

He would have forgotten it if it hadn't been for her speaking up. Hell, if he didn't stop letting her distract him the way she did, he'd end up dead one of these days. "Oh," he said stupidly. "Yes."

A brief smile flitted across her mouth, and then flew away. "I'll fetch it for you," she said, and was gone.

Luke shoved a hand through his hair and muttered a curse. Any other time, with any other woman on his mind but Charity, he would have ridden into town and bought himself a session with one of the girls who plied their trade above the saloon. What would have been a mere expediency before his return to Jubilee had taken on the singular shape and substance of betrayal.

"Shit," he murmured.

Charity returned, handed him the .45, and he shoved it thoughtlessly into his holster. His collar cinched up like a noose, and he tugged at it with one finger.

"When did you plan on holding this wedding?" he asked.

She looked up at him through her lashes, and that slight tilt at the corners of her mouth was back, telling him plainly that she knew how she moved him, and that she loved it.

"I think that should be a mutual decision, don't you?"

Some passing demon must have taken him over then; he took her face in his hands, tilted her head back, and kissed her, softly at first and then, when she opened for him, with a promise of all that he was holding in restraint.

She swayed when it was over, and looked up at him with enormous, dazed eyes. "Would tonight be too soon?" she asked.

He laughed. "I believe so, yes," he said. "We'd better start by courting a little, I suppose. Be seen together now and again. Like at the dance over at the Meddly place, on Saturday night. Will you go with me, Charity?"

She blinked, as though surprised by the request, and just when he was beginning to despair, a beaming smile transformed her face into something too glorious for any mere mortal to look upon and live. "Yes," she said, in a breathless rush, sending that one word tumbling over itself, end over end.

He traced the outline of her jaw with the tip of one finger. "Good day, then," he said gruffly, and turned to go.

She caught hold of his sleeve. "Do you think we should practice?"

Luke swallowed. "Practice?" he echoed.

She rose on tiptoe and spoke close by his ear, her breath a sweet, ruffling softness that made a hard tightening inside him, as well as out. "Dancing," she whispered.

"Dancing," he repeated, bewildered.

She took one of his hands in her own, and laid the other lightly upon his shoulder, and began to move within his embrace. "You know. Like this. To music."

"Oh, God," he said, because he couldn't help himself.

She began to hum, pulling him into a pattern of small steps, as graceful, as spectacularly beautiful, as the flight of a bird rising against a blazing sunset.

"Do you remember," he managed to ask, after

a long interval of exquisite torture, "when I pulled you out of the creek and you promised me a wish?"

Her gray eyes sparkled with magic and mischief, and the dance went on, a thing of eternity. "I remember. I offered you a kiss first, as a reward, and you turned up your nose."

"I was eleven, for God's sake," he said, a little desperately.

Charity's smile widened, revealing her small, strong, perfect teeth. "It's true that I promised you a wish. Are you ready to make one?"

Blood rushed up his neck into his face and he felt like a bumbling adolescent. "Oh, I've got one, all right, but I don't think this is the place to grant it."

Her laugh was like music. "You ought to save that wish," she said. "It might be a very handy thing to have in reserve."

He took her by the hips, pulled her gently but firmly against him, held her there until he saw a pink flush rise in her cheeks. "You're right, Miss Charity," he said. "I believe I'll save that wish after all."

She did not pull away from him, although her color heightened and a sleepy languor seeped into her eyes. Silently, she dared him to go further and it was all he could do to resist the challenge. And so they stood, their bodies pressed together in a tender impasse, neither one willing to break the spell and step back.

They might have stayed like that until Luke died of needing her, if they hadn't heard the distinct sound of someone approaching. A mere moment after they drew apart, the boy appeared, his freckles standing out so vividly that they seemed to get there before he did.

"Mr. Shardlow?" he asked, breathless.

Luke smiled down at him. "Luke," he corrected. "You must be Aaron."

Aaron came cautiously toward them. "It was you that made that invalid's chair for my pa—" he glanced uneasily at Charity, "—for Mr. Barnham, I mean?"

Charity's arm slipped through Luke's, but she spoke to the boy. "He's your pa, too," she said gently. "What would he think, if he heard you call him 'Mr. Barnham'?"

Aaron colored brightly, behind that field of freckles, and swallowed. He stared straight up into Luke's face. "I want to thank you for what you did. And to tell you that you mustn't pay too much mind when he's contrary, because he doesn't mean nothin' by it. It's just the way he is."

Luke was touched. "Thanks," he said. "You ever have time for fishing?"

A light went on in the boy's troubled eyes, and he was quick to nod. "I'm pretty good at it, too. There's a real good hole in Jubilee Creek, just around that bend where the willow trees grow."

"So there is," Luke agreed. And he put out his hand to shake. "Maybe you can give me a few pointers one of these fine days."

"You going to live here?" Aaron blurted eagerly. "In our house, I mean?"

Luke was sorry to disappoint him. "No," he said. "I've got a place over on the other side of the creek. You're welcome to pay me a visit any time you feel the inclination, though."

Aaron worked that through, then smiled. "I'll bring my fishin' pole," he said. His mother called to him, from somewhere inside the cool, spacious house, and he turned reluctantly to answer the summons, leaving Luke and Charity alone again.

Seeing a book on the floor of the porch, Luke leaned down to retrieve it, wanting to delay his departure a little while longer. Charity's presence was a balm to all his sore spots; he thrived on the sight of her, the scent of her, the feel of her smooth skin under his hands. Best not pursue that last thought any further, he reflected.

The volume opened in his hand and, seeing columns of tidy figures, he couldn't help scanning them. Mathematics was a game to him, and a peculiar solace, and the numbers automatically sorted themselves in his mind.

"Somebody's been stealing you blind," he said, with a frown.

Charity looked at him, then at the account book. "What?"

He ran a finger down one column, then another, just to make sure. "Yes," he reiterated thoughtfully. He consulted the notes at the front of the book—it was a record of the spring roundup and subsequent sales of beef to the army, the railroad, and several packing companies—then flipped back to the numbers, which were crying foul just as clearly as if they'd had voices. "There are some major discrepancies here. They're carefully disguised, but I still can't believe Jonah didn't see them."

"Why, that's impossible," Charity said, white-faced. "My father kept those records himself."

Luke sat down on the porch swing and Charity joined him immediately. He showed her where the numbers didn't tally the way they should have done, and she examined them closely for herself.

"It doesn't make sense that Jonah would juggle his own funds like this. Either he knew what was happening and looked the other way, or he was mighty distracted by something else."

Charity took the ledger into her hands and studied it, brow furrowed, lower lip caught between her teeth. "Why didn't I see it?"

It hurt him to hear the quiet, self-directed fury in her voice. He wanted to defend her, even from herself. "Sometimes an outsider has a better perspective on things like this," he said. He gave a gusty sigh. "We'd better look over the other records right now."

Charity nodded, and thoughts of leaving were put aside as Luke rose and followed her into the house. Soon, they were in Jonah's study, seated on the same side of the massive wooden desk, with papers and ledgers spread out everywhere. The situation was unquestionably serious, and yet Luke felt, for the first time, as though he might have a place in the scheme of things after all.

11

*C*harity sat at her father's desk, the open ledgers spread before her, long after Luke had planted a light kiss upon her forehead and taken his leave for the evening. To his credit, he had not given her advice before going; he had simply shown her the pattern in the numbers and left her to decipher them for herself. He clearly believed she was capable of doing just that, and she would have loved him for that alone, if there hadn't been a thousand other reasons.

Jonah, regrettably, would be less certain of her abilities, and because she needed to work things through on her own, prove that she could make a success of running the Double B. Her father had enough on his mind, between his own illness and her refusal to marry the man he had chosen for her; he must pour his energy and, if need be, his fury, into the struggle for recovery.

Full night had fallen when she finally closed the account books, locked them away in a drawer, and, carrying a small lamp in one hand, made her way slowly up the stairs. A soft, flickering light showed beneath her father's door, but she merely paused in the corridor outside his room, trying to will some of her own strength into him.

In the morning, she and Blaise would prepare the small parlor downstairs for Jonah's occupation. The wheeled chair Luke had improvised was sure to restore some of his lost mobility and thus raise his spirits, but it would not be an easy task. Jonah's immense pride, at once an attribute and a distinct liability, fierce enough to sustain him through so many other trials throughout his life, now lay in ruins.

Filled with sorrow and, in paradoxically equal measure, determination, Charity proceeded to her room. She had exchanged her clothing for a nightdress and wrapper, and was seated at her vanity, brushing her hair, when a rap sounded at the door.

She turned on the bench and called out a soft, "Come in."

It was no surprise that her visitor was Blaise, but the other woman's tear-swollen eyes and wobbling chin certainly alarmed her. At first, Charity thought Jonah had passed away, so great and so plain was Blaise's misery, and it seemed that her own heart stopped for a moment, bracing itself for an onslaught of grief.

"What is it?" she whispered, when she was able to speak. Only then did she notice that Blaise was clutching Jonah's slate against her chest.

Blaise took a moment to compose herself, and the effort was painful to see. She crossed the room, without a word, and held out the slate. Upon it, in wavering and awkward letters, Jonah had written a single word, *Go*.

Charity stood and briefly embraced her friend. "You predicted this," she reminded

212

Blaise gently. "Remember? And you said nothing would make you leave him. That he would have to remove you from this house himself if he wanted you to leave."

Blaise nodded, sniffling, and accepted the fresh linen handkerchief Charity rummaged for with gratitude. "I know," she admitted. "But I had not taken the force of his will into account. He turns his head away when I speak to him, or closes his eyes or—and this is the most terrible thing of all—he just looks through me as though I weren't even there. Why won't he let me into his suffering, so I can share the burden?"

"You know the answer to that," Charity responded sadly. "He's ashamed of his weakness."

Blaise dabbed at her puffy face with the wadded handkerchief. "Blast," she said furiously. It was a rash term, for her. "I can be just as stubborn as he is. More so!"

Charity smiled. "That's the spirit. Now, try to get some rest. I'll look in on Papa once or twice during the night. Tomorrow, we'll see about hiring someone to help with his care—that might restore some of his dignity and smooth his feathers down a little."

Blaise sniffled again, her red-rimmed eyes large and hopeful. "Who, Charity? Jonah will not tolerate any of those town women—why, he'd die of mortification if they saw him this way. Besides, they'd snoop and carry tales."

"Father Elias will know of someone," Charity said, with a certainty that was at least part bravado. "I'll ride over to the mission and speak to him in the morning."

"You have a great deal planned for tomorrow," Blaise observed, but she was smiling slightly now, encouraged, Charity hoped.

"All our days will be long ones from now on," she confirmed, with an inward sigh, thinking of the disparities in the ledgers and of Raoul's inevitable anger when he learned of her impending marriage to Luke. There were sure to be other difficulties, too, but she could think of no alternative but to go forward boldly, pretending to whatever graces and confidences she lacked if she could not find them within herself. "Sleep, Blaise. Rest in your own bed, and take your time over breakfast in the morning. It would do Jonah no harm to wonder, at least for a little while, if you haven't honored his demand and left him, after all."

Blaise kissed Charity's cheek. "I could not love you more, or be more grateful for you, if you were my own daughter," she said. Then, turning away, she left the room.

The night passed with fitful haste, full of tangled dreams and sudden wakening. Twice, Charity visited Jonah's room and, twice, she found him staring blankly up at the lacy web of shadows on his ceiling. She gave him water on both occasions, and sat for a time at his bedside, speaking softly, telling stories they both knew, tales of Charity's childhood, when he had taught her to ride, taught her to shoot and to recognize trees and birds and animals and call them by their right names. She talked about Christmases and birthdays, and recounted, for the first time, how Luke Shardlow had pulled her out of the creek that day, when she was just eight years old, and almost certainly saved her life.

Jonah listened solemnly, his gaze fixed upon her face, but his despair was palpable, almost an entity in its own right. Not for the first time, Charity considered the possibility that her father might give up the fight, might actually choose to die. He certainly wouldn't be the first to do so in the face of such odds.

When morning came, she did not feel rested, but quietly frenzied instead. There was a great deal to do, and only a few hours to do it in.

Father Elias saved her one task, however, by arriving only minutes before she would have gone to find him at the mission. He had heard of Jonah's misfortune, of course, but because of his responsibilities he had not been able to pay a call until now. His own health, Charity knew, was precarious, and he had to conserve his personal stamina carefully in order to cope with the many and varied demands of his vocation.

His call upon Jonah was private and short, and when the old priest descended the stairs again, Aaron led him to the small parlor, where Charity and Blaise were supervising the removal of chairs, tables and settees to make room for a bed. Two ranch hands were busily carrying out the unnecessary furniture and taking the heavy pieces up to the attic, via the rear stairs.

Both women gave up the project when the priest appeared; Charity hurried off to brew fresh tea, and Blaise saw Father Elias settled in one of the few remaining chairs.

By the time Charity returned with refreshments, the tea and some sweet biscuits Blaise had baked earlier, as much to keep herself busy as to fill the culinary gaps left by Peony's departure for the mission school as anything else, the two were deep in conversation.

It was agreed that Peony, though able to cook for the children and look after them to some extent, would not make a suitable nurse for Jonah. She was as bristly and opinionated as he was, and there was little to be gained by pitting the two of them against each other. Father Elias had someone else in mind, he said, and he would bring her to the Double B himself, as soon as possible. When pressed for further information, he would give none and, though curious and not a little exasperated, Charity had too much on her mind to wrangle with him.

She escorted him down the front walk to the gate, but her thoughts were disorderly, like a team of ill-trained horses, straining to escape the harness.

"What of your situation, child?" he asked, pausing beside his patient old mule, Solomon, reins in hand.

"I have decided to marry," she replied.

Father Elias smiled. "Raoul must be very pleased."

Charity bit her lower lip before answering.

"Actually, I don't think he'll be happy at all. Not at first, at least. You see, it's Luke I've chosen for a husband."

If the priest was surprised by this announcement, he gave no sign of it. Charity had, after all, explained at least part of her dilemma to him days before, when she'd taken refuge at the mission. "I see. And when is the ceremony to take place?"

Charity sighed. All her life, she'd dreamed of a big, romantic wedding, something right out of one of the fairy tales she'd loved so much as a child, but such a celebration would hardly be appropriate under the circumstances. Jonah was too ill, her engagement to Raoul too recently dissolved and, worst of all, the marriage was a sham, from Luke's viewpoint anyway. Just remembering his initial reaction to the idea brought a quick, fierce sting of humiliation.

"Soon, I suppose," she said. "You will perform the services, won't you?"

Father Elias responded with a searching look. "That depends," he answered, at length. "Do you love Mr. Shardlow?"

Charity felt hot tears behind her eyes. "Yes," she said, nearly choking on her accursed Barnham pride. "But I am not sure the sentiment is mutual." She could not make herself admit to Father Elias that she didn't expect the alliance to last; the knowledge shamed her too greatly, pained her too deeply.

The priest's gaze was soft and, at the same time, piercing. "Marriage is a holy sacrament, Charity. The vows, once taken, bind not merely the body and mind, but the spirit as well. To enter into such a union for the wrong reasons is not only dangerous, not only foolhardy, but wicked."

She felt heat flare under the flesh of her face, and it was all she could do not to avert her eyes. "Will you marry us, Father? Or must we go before the circuit judge next time he passes through Jubilee?"

Father Elias sighed again. There was such weariness in the sound that Charity was distracted from her own cares, however briefly, and could not help laying a hand upon his arm in concern.

"Bring your young man to the mission," he said. "I will marry the two of you in the chapel."

"Are you all right?" Charity asked, barely taking note of the promise she had wanted so badly only moments before.

Another smile. "I am an old man," he said. "I am weary. I have had word from my bishop in San Francisco that a younger priest will arrive soon, to assist me in my work. Two women, spinster sisters I am told, will accompany him."

Charity felt relief for her friend's sake—the church had taken its precious time sending someone to help carry Father Elias's burdens—but she was concerned, even frightened, by his readiness to surrender his place in temporal matters. He seemed as fragile and ethereal as a wisp of smoke, the fading reflection of his own substance as a man. "The

218

children love you so much," she said helplessly. *And so do I.*

It was clear by the compassionate look he gave her that Father Elias knew her thoughts. In his years of selfless ministry to others, he had no doubt learned many such skills. "No one," he said, "is indispensable. I shall be glad of company, and content with humble tasks. Now, I must get back to the mission, for poor Peony is neither able nor inclined to manage the place by herself." He mounted the mule with a difficulty Charity had not noticed before. "Ask your young man to pay me a visit," he said in parting. "I would like a word with him."

Charity nodded, and stood at the gate watching Father Elias until he and the mule had melded into a single figure, disappearing into the distance.

Then she went back inside the house. Within the hour, a bed had been erected facing the windows of the small parlor, and the two ranch hands had carried a stone-faced, glaring Jonah down the stairs.

He continued to treat Blaise as though she were invisible, and the looks he gave Charity were alternately furious and bleak. By noon, when she had spoon-fed him a bowl of chicken broth—he would not even take food from Blaise—Charity's nerves seemed to be standing out from her skin like hairs bristling on a hog.

"You are behaving like a beast!" she accused, when Blaise finally fled the room in tears.

Jonah merely glowered at his daughter.

219

Chalk in hand, he slashed an X onto the slate board, then another over it, and another over that. Then, with a strength Charity had not known he possessed, he flung both board and chalk away, so that they clattered across the bare wood floor. The rugs had been removed earlier, to facilitate use of the wheeled chair.

Charity bent down, hands braced on the armrests of that very chair, her nose within an inch of Jonah's. "So you're angry!" she shouted. "Good! That is a vast improvement over self-pity!"

It was plain from his sudden pallor and the set of his jaw that he was stunned by her response to his outburst—though surely no more so than Charity herself—and his eyes blazed with dark fire. In any other set of circumstances, she would not have had the courage, much less the cause, to speak to Jonah Barnham in such a way, but she understood now that he was drowning, that tenderness was a weighted cable that would drag him under.

For all of that, Charity might have apologized, had it not been for quiet applause coming from the direction of the arched entry. Both father and daughter turned at the sound, and Charity knew a sense of sweet alarm when she saw Luke there, one shoulder braced indolently against the door frame.

"That's telling him," Luke said, shoving away from the jamb and walking toward them at an easy, unhurried pace. "Anybody ever dare to point out to you, Mr. Barnham, that you've got the disposition of a jackass with one tooth and a muzzleful of rock candy?"

Charity straightened, smoothed her skirts and hair, and briefly hated herself for revealing what she had in those small, innocent motions. In a vain attempt to undo the damage, she stiffened. "This argument is between my father and me," she said.

"Is it?" Luke countered. The .45, which Charity hated, was prominent on his hip, and looked as though it would spring into his hand of its own volition if he merely spread his fingers above the handle. "If I'm going to marry into this family, I mean to be a part of it. Jonah, somebody is robbing you blind, and they've been at it for at least five years. I'd like to know why you haven't done anything about it."

Charity was flabbergasted by Luke's audacity; she had made it clear to him that the discovery they'd made in the account books was not to be mentioned in front of Jonah. Indeed, she was so angry that, for those few moments at least, she could not speak.

Luke took advantage of the interval to bend down and gather up the slate and chalk, then press them both into Jonah's hands. The chalk snapped into two pieces between the latter's powerful fingers.

"It was Tillmont, wasn't it?" Luke went on. "The foreman."

Jonah sat rigid in his chair, looking through Luke the way he had looked through Blaise. Luke, however, was undaunted.

"What does he know, Jonah? What did he threaten you with?"

The muscles in Jonah's neck corded with such violence that Charity was afraid for him. She started to step between the two men, one standing, one in a wheeled chair, but Luke put out an arm, without so much as a glance in her direction, barring the way.

"Tillmont," Luke persisted quietly.

Jonah sat trembling for a moment, not with fear, Charity was absolutely sure of that, but helpless fury. The chalk squealed against the slate as he made a check mark.

"That means 'yes,' " Charity murmured.

"I know," Luke replied mildly. He was still gazing at Jonah.

"I'm going to fire him. Right now." Charity would have left the room, intent on her mission to send the foreman packing, but incredibly Jonah wheeled his chair into her path, effectively stopping her. His hand shaking violently, he made an X on the slate, and the expression in his eyes was one of desperation.

Luke crouched beside Jonah's chair, and in that moment Charity felt a sharp deepening of the love she had for him. He was on his haunches, she knew, so that a proud man would not be forced to look up.

"I don't know if you can talk, Jonah. I imagine you've tried, once or twice, when you were by yourself. If you can get the words out, or scribble them on that little chalkboard, tell me how to help you."

222

Jonah tried to speak, and the effort was so painful to see that Charity longed to turn away, though she did not. Nothing came from her father's mouth but garbled, meaningless sounds. He made another X on the slate and was, by the time he'd finished even that small task, so enervated that the color had drained from his skin, leaving a pasty gray pallor in its wake.

"All right," Luke said, rising and laying a hand on Jonah's unsteady shoulder. "All right. We'll deal with the situation some other way."

A tear spilled over and trickled down Jonah's left cheek. Jonah, who had never wept in Charity's presence, not even on the day of her mother's funeral. Using all that remained of his strength, he wheeled himself away and sat slumped in his chair, before the open windows at the foot of his bed.

Charity took Luke's arm and half-dragged him out of the room. In the corridor outside the kitchen, she suppressed the urge to punch him in the chest only by dint of enormous willpower. "Why did you do that? You knew I didn't want him to know we discovered the trouble in the books!"

Luke folded his arms and regarded her calmly. "That wouldn't be honest," he said. "I would hate to think I'd agreed to take a deceitful woman to wife. I hope you're not one of those people who think that not saying something that ought to be said isn't the same as lying. It is."

Charity rolled her eyes. "The point is, you've upset my father!"

"He was 'upset' when I got here," Luke retorted, leaning in close. "Or hadn't you noticed?"

She set her hands on her hips. "I will not have you interfering—"

"Oh, lady," Luke interrupted, without backing off so much as a fraction of an inch, "you can *count* on my interfering. A lot. If you want a husband you can boss around, marry one of the ranch hands."

"Maybe I will!"

"Go ahead."

Charity expelled an irritated sigh. "I believe you must have misunderstood our bargain," she said, with overstated patience. "I do not need a husband to take over my responsibilities, which include this ranch and my father's well-being. Nor do I require a protector."

"What exactly *do* you need from me? Besides my name on a marriage license?"

She ran her teeth over her lower lip. "Nothing," she answered warily, and at some length. They both knew it wasn't true. "Our agreement—"

"Our agreement," Luke amended, "was that I would be your husband and you would be my wife. It seems likely that we don't agree on the exact definitions of those words, so I'll just state my side of things, for the sake of clarity." He laid his index finger to his own chest. "I'll be the husband, which means it's my job to look out for you and for anybody and anything you happen to love." That same finger came to rest lightly, tantalizingly, on Charity's lower lip. "You, lovely lady, will be the wife." A quicksilver grin flashed across his mouth, full of mischief and lethal charm. "I suspect you understand your duties fairly well."

Charity flushed. "If you expect to dominate me—"

"I only plan on doing that in one place. Our bed. But don't worry—we can take turns."

Lightning streaked through Charity's veins, glanced off the insides of her pelvic bones, and took fire in her womb. "You are deliberately confusing the issue."

He laughed and he was so close that she could feel the heat and the hard substance of him in every muscle and tissue. "You're as stubborn as your father," he drawled, his blue-green eyes twinkling. "About that wish I've got coming. Suppose I wanted to kiss you, right here and now?"

"Is that what you want?"

He had pinned her against the wall by then, but the sensation was dizzyingly pleasant. His mouth was almost touching hers. Almost, but not quite. "Umm-hmm," he said. "But I confess I'd sure like to save that wish for another time, though."

"Sounds like you want to have your cake and eat it, too," Charity breathed, only a little miffed. God help her, she wanted him to kiss her.

He tasted her mouth, sent more lightning

shooting through her. "That," he said, "would require a lot more privacy than we've got here."

Charity was both embarrassed and excited by that remark, though she wasn't sure precisely what he was talking about. "If you think you can bamboozle me with a few kisses, you are perfectly—perfectly—wrong."

He chuckled, and then he took her mouth, and she couldn't imagine being in any other place, with any other man, doing any other thing. She raised herself onto her tiptoes, and put her very soul into the kiss. When it ended, it seemed to Charity that the earth's poles must surely have exchanged places in one swift flip of the axis, and she was certain that her knees would have buckled if Luke hadn't held her upright. His hands were grasping her hips, tilting them at an angle that made perspiration spring out between her breasts, on her upper lip, and her belly and the small of her back.

She made a soft, fitful sound, then slipped her arms around his neck. "Kiss me again," she said.

"Will that count as my wish?" he teased, raising one eyebrow.

She laughed. "No," she answered, with a little twist of her hips. "It will count as mine."

He kissed her again, more thoroughly that time, and her senses were spinning when he raised his head. God only knew what would have happened after that, she thought later, if a great clamor hadn't been raised at the front of the house.

Luke stood with his arms out straight and his palms pressed to the wall, and Charity ducked out of his embrace and hurried down the corridor. After a few moments, he followed.

Father Elias was standing in the entryway, and beside him stood a buxom woman wedged into a cast-off calico dress, almost certainly plucked from the poor box at the mission. Her hair was a bright and unlikely shade of yellow, and the remains of old rouge, kohl and paint glowed from deep beneath the surface of her soap-chafed skin, as though tattooed there.

"This," Father Elias said, rather grandly, "is Genesis Wickam. She is here to look after Mr. Barnham."

"I've had experience lookin' after men," Genesis put in eagerly. Charity's heart, still pounding from the episode with Luke in the rear hallway, went out to her, welcoming.

"I'll just bet you have," replied Blaise, who stood with her arms folded and her chin several notches above its normal setting.

Charity watched the new arrival in fascination, conscious of Luke standing just behind her and at a slight angle. By what magic, she wondered, could she feel his size and shape as surely as if he'd been touching her, skin to skin?

"My father is not an easy man to deal with," she said, and had to pause once in the middle of the sentence to clear her throat.

Genesis was gazing warily at Blaise, plainly seeing a potential enemy there and, just as plainly, hoping against hope that she would not be turned away.

"Mrs. Wickam is a widow," Father Elias interjected kindly, pushing the front door closed between his charge and a cruel and unfeeling world. "She's got a young son, back in Kansas, boarding with her sister."

Blaise, herself the mother of a son, showed signs of relenting. "How have you been earning your living of late, Mrs. Wickam?" she asked, nonetheless. Her voice was gentle, and her gaze sympathetic, but she would have her answer, that was plain.

Tears welled in Genesis's large and slightly myopic blue eyes. She turned and would have fled, abashed, except that the priest prevented her going by some subtle and indiscernible means.

"We was travelin' west, me and my Frank, some years back. He was goin' to work in the big timber, north of Seattle, and start puttin' money by so we could have our own fishin' boat." Her eyes glowed in the reflected glory of that lost dream. "We had to leave our boy, little Frank, with my sister—we could hardly feed ourselves, and we knew he'd be safe with Minerva. Her Walter has a good farm there, and a few cattle." She paused and sniffled. "We were going to send for Frankie when we got settled, but Frank took sick just outside of White Horse Junction and we didn't get no further. He died and I—well—I took the only work I could find."

A throbbing silence descended, and all eyes turned to Blaise. Although Charity regarded herself as mistress of the house, and would not under any circumstances allow poor Genesis to be sent back to the infamous rooms above some saloon, the nature of Blaise's relationship with her father demanded that she defer to her in this case.

Blaise, a perceptive woman, was plainly imagining herself in Genesis Wickam's place. "Come along, then," she said, with bright resolve. "I'll show you to your room, and then introduce you to the patient. You will find my Jonah only slightly less difficult than a bull backed up to a hot branding iron, I'm afraid, but you look strong enough to manage a good day's work. How old is your son?"

Genesis's face was alight as she scrambled to follow Blaise up the main staircase, her one battered satchel hastily gathered from the floor. "He's going on ten, my Frankie," she answered eagerly. "I haven't seen him in five years, but he writes me often. Knows his letters and numbers real good, and he's a hard worker, too. No doubt there's things he could do right here on this ranch."

Blaise's voice trailed back down the stairs like music, although she herself was already out of sight. "My Aaron is ten, too," she said companionably. "I cannot imagine what I would do, if I were parted from him—"

Charity crossed the entryway to take both Father Elias's old, gnarled hands into her own and kiss his papery cheek. "You," she said, "are quite the miracle-worker."

The priest smiled, but set aside her praise. "Genesis appeared at the mission last week with

229

her satchel and a black eye," he explained. "She could have stayed on with us, of course, but when you mentioned needing help with Jonah, I knew she would be perfect."

Luke's gaze was fond as he stood next to the door. "Thanks, Father," he said. "For every-thing."

The old man beamed. "I'm told you and Charity mean to be married."

"That's right," Luke confirmed wryly. "And the sooner, the better."

12

Father Elias's mule had been tethered to the front fence, busily nibbling at the lilac bushes, and when Luke returned from seeing that the older man was mounted and on his way, he found Charity waiting in the entryway, arms folded.

"I suppose I shouldn't have said what I did," he grinned. "How the sooner we get mar-ried, the better it will be, I mean. I only meant—"

Charity's nerve endings were still thrumming from those kisses stolen in the corridor off the kitchen, and her cheeks felt hot. "I know pre-cisely what you meant," she interrupted, in a hissy whisper. "Unfortunately, so did Father Elias!"

He cupped a hand under her chin, raised her

face, and looked deep into her eyes. "Would you like to revoke our agreement?" he asked quietly.

She shook her head, and he ran the pad of his thumb across her lower lip.

"Good," he said, and placed a light kiss on her mouth. He stepped back and assessed her riding skirt, cotton shirtwaist, and boots. "Planning to ride the range?" he asked, with a low, teasing lilt in his voice.

Charity braced herself for another quarrel. "I've been expecting Mr. Tillmont with a report on the fence lines. He's had more than enough time to make an appearance, so I've decided to go out and find him."

Luke leaned slightly forward, his nose almost touching hers. "You saw how Jonah reacted, when Tillmont's name came up. Do you figure on ignoring that?"

She sighed. "Yes," she said, after a moment spent considering the alternative which, though appealing, would be flagrant cowardice. If she was going to take over the running of the Double B, she could not afford to shrink from unpleasant duties. "Don't you see, Luke? I *have* to ignore it. There is a great deal at stake."

"I think Jonah sees things the same way, but from another angle. Let me handle Tillmont." Luke's tone did not leave much room for negotiation, and his eyes, bright with humor and mischief only moments before, were suddenly as cold as the steel barrel of that dreadful pistol he carried.

"That's my responsibility."

The muscles at the joint of his jaw bunched, as though he'd bitten down hard on a walnut or an apricot pit, and relaxed only with a visible effort. "Be that as it may, I'm sure you can understand why I'm not about to let you do that alone. I owe Jonah an old debt, and this is as good a time to settle up as any."

She was briefly taken aback, and she knew her eyes were wide as she looked up at him. "What sort of debt?"

Luke expelled a sigh. "He saw that we shared in the meat, whenever a hog or a steer was butchered on the Double B. My pa didn't need food, he lived on whiskey and meanness. Vance was gone most of the time, and I could have done with trout and dandelion greens and the occasional stolen egg. But Ma was gently raised, and setting a decent table meant a lot to her. She would have gone hungry if it hadn't been for Jonah."

Tentatively, Charity touched Luke's face. It didn't occur to her to pity him, but she was moved by the kindly picture he painted of her father. For a few precious seconds, that image brought Jonah back from the remote place where his illness had taken him, and she was grateful. "If you wish," she conceded, "you may go with me to find Mr. Tillmont. But I'll do the talking, Luke."

The grin was back, fleeting and sweet. "Fair enough," he said. "Just be advised that if Tillmont doesn't answer back politely, I'll have a thing or two to add to the conversation."

Blaise descended the stairway then, trailed by a gawking Genesis.

"We've gotten Genesis settled in the room across from Aaron's," Blaise said. She looked as though she'd never entertained the slightest reservation about letting the other woman move in and help with Jonah's care. "Now it's time to introduce that old devil to his nurse."

"Best of luck," Luke said, with a smile.

Charity rubbed her temples with the fingers of both hands. "I hope he won't be rude," she murmured.

Luke chuckled. "After what Genesis has been through," he answered softly, watching the women disappear into Jonah's downstairs bedchamber, "your old daddy won't so much as ruffle her feathers." He touched a kiss to her forehead. "Come on, sweetheart. Let's track down Mr. Tillmont."

They found the foreman an hour later, at some distance from the ranch house, overseeing the branding of several stray calves. Although he flicked a glance at Luke, Charity might have been a horsefly, for all the attention he paid to her.

She dismounted and strode over to him, and although she did not look back, she was fully aware of Luke, still mounted on his gelding, just behind her.

Tillmont was forced to acknowledge her, and tugged at the brim of his filthy hat as he favored her with a seamy smile. "Ma'am," he said, acting surprised.

"I believe I asked for a report on the fence

lines," she said. "Perhaps you've forgotten?"

The foreman's attitude was condescending, though he was plainly keeping one eye on Luke. "It's a big ranch, ma'am. There's a lot to do, especially now that Mr. Barnham's confined to his bed."

"He's getting better every day," Charity said, with a confidence that was almost wholly false. What hold did this man have over her father, she wondered, that would cause Jonah to overlook stealing? "In the meantime, Mr. Tillmont, I'm looking after the ranch. And when I give an order, I expect it to be obeyed."

Tillmont squinted against the August sun as he glanced up at Luke again, then spat tobacco juice into the dirt. "You're the boss's daughter, ma'am," he said, "and that's reason enough to respect your wishes. But I been ridin' for the Double B brand for a long time, and I believe I know a thing or two about the way the place works. Fact is, I take direction from Jonah Barnham and nobody else."

Two of the cowboys wandered over from the branding fire, sweating and dirty. Charity could not tell whether they were friends or foes but, with Luke at her back, she didn't much care, one way or the other.

"You and I need to speak in private, Mr. Tillmont," she said, as if he had not uttered a word. When she leveled her gaze at the cowboys, they turned on their heels and went back to work. "There are some discrepancies in the books, you see."

"I don't keep the books, ma'am," Tillmont

answered, in that same blithe and patronizing tone. He was already turning away, dismissing her, dismissing her authority.

She'd be damned if she'd allow it. "Come and collect your pay," she said clearly, halting the big man in his boot prints. "We won't be needing your services any longer."

Tillmont spun on her, one index finger raised to waggle in her face, but the distinctive metallic click of a gun being cocked made him stand as still as a buck deer scenting the wind. His gaze ricocheted off Charity to collide with Luke's.

"You don't want to pull that trigger, boy," he said.

"That's what you think," Luke replied. Charity glanced back then, and saw him leaning indolently on the pommel of his saddle, the .45 pointed directly at Tillmont's chest. "As it happens, I can only think of a few things I want more."

"Just take it easy," Tillmont said, in a wheedling tone. The cowboys had left off their hot, dirty work, and were looking on with wary interest, though none, Charity noticed right away, seemed inclined to come to their foreman's aid. "Take it easy. I don't want no trouble."

"Then I'd recommend," Luke answered, "that you don't make any."

"What have you got to do with this, Shardlow?" Tillmont demanded, but he'd retreated a few steps, and he was holding both hands away from his body, to show that he didn't mean to draw.

"You know old Jonah wouldn't have the likes of you on the place for five minutes if he was well enough to throw you off." He paused and glared at Charity. "You ought to be home getting ready to marry Montego, 'stead of runnin' around the countryside with a no-good gunslinger like Shardlow."

Charity saw no earthly reason to explain her plans to this man or to make excuses for Luke's presence. She ignored Tillmont's remarks and moved past him to address the half-dozen men around the fire. The irons were heating in the embers, and several calves awaited attention, while others, hides smoking, bawled in complaint.

The smell of singed fur and flesh turned her stomach, even though she knew the animals had thick hides, and that livestock had to be branded. Cattle were the life's blood of a ranch like the Double B, and lately it had been hemorrhaging not only beef, but money. She met each of the cowboys' gazes once, and squarely, before speaking.

"If any of you feel sympathetic to Mr. Tillmont here, you can get your gear and your pay and ride out."

Nobody spoke.

Charity waited, then turned and walked away, grasping Taffeta by the dangling reins, swinging deftly up into the saddle. Tillmont, erstwhile foreman, was already riding toward the ranch house. He'd want to collect his belongings before coming in to get his wages, so there was no great need to hurry.

Luke had long since holstered his pistol, and as she turned the mare toward home, he watched her with a half-grin from under the brim of his hat. "Feeling pretty cocky, aren't you?" he teased.

"Shouldn't I?" She nudged Taffeta into a trot, and Luke rode up beside her.

"I guess that depends," he answered.

The horses picked up speed, moving into an easy lope. "On what?" Charity asked.

"On whether or not you noticed the brand on those calves."

The truth was, she hadn't looked, and she didn't like admitting it. So she didn't say anything at all.

"Whatever irons those boys were using, they didn't come from the Double B," he said. Charity would have wheeled Taffeta around and turned back, but Luke reached out and caught hold of the mare's bridle before she could execute the move. "No point in your confronting them now, boss lady. They think they were caught red-handed, those cowboys, and if you look over your shoulder, you'll likely see them headed for the proverbial hills."

Charity glanced back and, sure enough, the men had abandoned both calves and fire to mount up and flee in a torrent of dust. Apparently, they weren't planning to pick up either their possessions or their money.

"Why didn't you say something?" she demanded.

Luke laughed and resettled his hat. He

looked at home on that horse, and since he didn't slow, Charity had to work at keeping up. "I believe you told me not to interfere in ranch business," he observed. "I wouldn't want to undermine your authority or anything like that."

"You didn't hesitate to draw that pistol," Charity pointed out, with a little sniff.

"I never have," Luke agreed easily.

A chill took Charity and, thinking a cloud must have blocked the sun, she looked up. The sky was clear. "What about those calves? We can't just leave them out here."

Luke didn't look at her. His quicksilver mind, it seemed, had already moved on to some other matter.

Luke stood by in Jonah's study while Charity tallied up Tillmont's wages, got the money from the safe, and counted it out. The foreman himself was grudgingly silent, snatching his salary from Charity's hand before she could offer it and stuffing the bills into an inside pocket of his vest.

It was only when Luke stepped aside to let the other man leave the room that Tillmont spoke. "I want to see Mr. Barnham."

"I'm afraid that won't be possible," Charity said. "As you know, my father isn't well."

"Just head out, friend," Luke advised Tillmont calmly. "Jonah won't be kindly disposed toward you once he hears about those branding irons you were using, anyway."

"I can explain that."

238

Luke's smile was slow and wholly unfriendly. "I'll mention to Dan Higgins that you want to unburden your soul. I'm sure he'll be eager to listen."

Tillmont colored dangerously and, forgetting himself, poked at Luke's chest with one index finger. "Now you listen here, you damned saddle bum—"

Luke caught Tillmont's wrist in a hard grasp. "No," he said. "*You* listen. I can have this .45 out of the holster and half an inch up your left nostril before you take another breath. I won't shoot you here—that would make a mess and upset the lady—but believe me, where I lead, you'll follow. Whatever your game is, you'd be smart to content yourself with what you've already stolen, fold your cards and take to the trail." He waited a beat, and then spoke very softly. "Are you, Tillmont? Smart, I mean?"

Charity swallowed hard, waiting for the answer.

The ex-foreman wrenched free of Luke's hold. "I'll go, all right. But you and I, Shardlow, we'll meet down the road a ways, and we'll settle our business then." He glanced back at Charity. "As for you, little lady, well, you might just want to ask your daddy why he hasn't gone ahead and married that pretty woman of his, after all this time. Ask him for the truth about your sweet mama."

"Get out," Luke breathed, and flung Tillmont over the threshold into the hallway.

Charity stood stricken in front of her father's

desk, while Tillmont's words quivered in her breast like the point of a poison arrow. She doubted she had moved when Luke returned, took her upper arms in his hands. The other man's cruel tone echoed in her mind. *Ask him for the truth about your sweet mama.*

"My mother is dead," she said woodenly. "She was killed in a fall from a horse. I remember the funeral."

Luke eased her into one of the leather upholstered chairs facing Jonah's desk. "It's not important, sweetheart," he said gently. "All of that happened a long time ago."

"But it was important to Jonah, wasn't it?" Her voice was small, childlike. She sat very straight, and drew a deep breath. "Luke, you remember it, don't you? When Mama died?"

He looked grim as he dragged another chair over and sat down facing her. He was holding both her hands in his. "I remember."

"You saw her, then." For some reason, the idea made her feel hopeful.

But Luke shook his head. "I didn't go to the services, Charity. They were private, if I recall correctly. Father Elias was around back then, wasn't he? Maybe he could tell you more."

"I was so small. I can see the coffin in my mind, but I think it was closed."

"Tillmont was just trying to make trouble, sweetheart. Let it go."

Charity made to rise, then sat down again, when Luke didn't release her hands. "No," she said. "There's more to it, you know that.

You saw how Papa was when I said I was going to fire that dreadful man. He was fierce, Luke. He was—he was *afraid*."

Luke's thumbs made easy, comforting circles on her palms, the insides of her wrists. She wondered outlandishly, insensibly, if he might be persuaded to rub her feet, once they were married. She thought she'd swoon with pleasure if he ever did that.

"When Jonah's himself again," he said, "the two of you can talk things over. In the meantime, there's no sense in chewing on it. Whatever the truth turns out to be, it can't make much difference now, when so many years have gone by."

Charity knew it *would* make a difference. Old secrets didn't just die, they fomented, sprouted tentacles that reached into every part of a person's life. This one, if Jonah's terror of it was anything to judge by, might put the lie to everything Charity believed herself to be.

"Marry me," Luke said. "Tonight. At the chapel, at sundown."

She blinked. "Tonight?"

He smiled, but there was none of the usual mischief in the curve of his mouth or the light in his eyes. "You having second thoughts?" he teased.

"No." She shook her head quickly. Anxiously. "We'd need flowers, and cake, and I don't have a ring to put on your finger—"

Luke kissed the tip of her nose and somehow that simple, silly gesture was more reassuring than anything else he could have done. "No,

241

darlin'," he said. "We need ourselves and Father Elias. That's all."

Of course he wouldn't want any of the trimmings usual to a wedding, Charity thought, deflated. She'd forgotten—again—that this particular marriage was a business arrangement. "You're right," she said sorrowfully.

He lifted her hands, kissed one palm and then the other. "I've got things to do," he told her, rising from his chair. Her eyes followed him, seemingly of their own accord. "I'll come for you in my wagon, Charity, at twilight. Wait for me here. And if you go out again today for any reason, be careful. All right?"

She swallowed. "All right." Her head was spinning with questions she could not put to Jonah, questions only he could really answer. If Father Elias knew anything—and he might, for her mother had been Catholic, and he had been her priest, her confessor—he would never tell.

After planting a kiss on the top of her head, Luke left, and Charity sat still for a long time, wondering until she was dizzy with it.

Much later, she went to Jonah's new room, knowing he could not explain, might not be willing to do so even if the stroke hadn't rendered him mute. He was sleeping, in any case, sprawled on his back. Genesis sat contentedly in a chair nearby, darning a stocking.

Jonah kept journals and various personal papers in the safe in his study, Charity had seen them there many times, but she would not read them. To do so would be an unconscionable violation of his privacy.

"Have you seen Blaise?" she asked softly.

Genesis's smile was blissful. Life had handed her one hardship after another, but now she had every hope of peace and plenty, and soon she could send for her son. "She's resting," she replied. "I don't think she's had much sleep lately."

Charity nodded, approached the bed to look fondly down at her father for a few moments, then slipped out of the room.

Upstairs, she packed underthings, a nightgown, soap and perfume in a small carrying case. Then, after much consideration, she chose a pale peach-colored dress from her wardrobe, and petticoats, and laid them all out on the bed for inspection.

One year when the cattle prices were especially good, Jonah had had a modern bathing chamber installed at the opposite end of the hall, and it was still the envy of most of Jubilee. Rainwater, collected in a special drum hidden away among the peaks and valleys of the ranch house roof, came in through copper pipes at the turn of a spigot, and Charity filled the tub in something of a stupor.

Memories came back to her as she stripped off her clothes and stepped into a tepid bath—in winter the water would be heated by means of a special burner under the interior tank—but they were not recollections of her mother's death. Instead, she recalled when Marietta

Shardlow had died, a few years later, and Jonah had come home from the funeral looking dismal.

The next day, the marshal—his name, Charity recalled, had been Asa McCallum—had come to the ranch. Charity, listening at the closed doors of the study, had heard him telling her father how he'd found Luke stretched out on the ground beside Mrs. Shardlow's grave, clothes wet through, burning with fever and trembling with chills. He and the missus were going to take the boy in and look after him, Asa had said. He was almost grown, of course, but they'd always wanted a son of their own, and they reckoned young Luke would do just fine.

Jonah must have given McCallum money— Charity clearly remembered hearing the safe open and close—but that in itself was nothing out of the ordinary. Her father had always been generous, and not just with the Shardlows. When anybody around Jubilee fell on hard times, he'd invariably helped out in whatever way he could. So had Ben Draper.

Charity sat up a little straighter in the tub. Ben Draper—of course. He had been Jonah's closest friend for years. He would know what Tillmont had been talking about if anyone did. The trouble was, she was hardly in a position to question him, given the fact that she'd spurned his grandson and would be married to another man before the evening was over.

Her hair piled on top of her head, Charity sank to her chin in the water and sighed.

244

Maybe Luke had been right, she reflected. Maybe her father's secret, whatever it was, simply didn't matter anymore. But if that was true, why had he protected Tillmont for so many years? It was utterly unlike Jonah to look the other way while one of his men stole from him, to submit to blackmail in any form, for that matter. But he had done both those things, obviously, and he would have gone right on guarding the mystery to the end of his days, given his druthers. His behavior that day was proof enough of that.

Charity took up a washcloth and a bar of lavender scented soap and began to scrub, but her mind kept working all the while. In all these years, she had rarely, if ever, thought of Mrs. Shardlow and the marshal's visit to the ranch the day after her burial, much less entertained the image of Luke sprawled beside her grave, drenched with rain and too grief-stricken to care. The McCallums had left town soon after, and never returned.

Her bath finished, Charity rose out of the tub, pulled the plug that would allow the water to drain out of the house through another system of pipes, and began to dry herself. When that was done, she applied talcum powder all over, and generously, and her thoughts turned then to the grown-up Luke who would be her husband. That night, that very night, she would lie with him in his bed, as his lawful wife.

She smiled a little, remembering that he had no bed. On her one visit to his cabin, she'd seen that he slept on a pallet on the floor. Since he'd made it clear from the first that he wouldn't share her room at the ranch, she wasn't quite sure what to expect. Maybe they would pass their wedding night in the tree house that had been a refuge to them both, at various times in their lives, or in the sweet, soft grass beside the creek.

Charity didn't care where it happened, so long as it did. What mattered was that she would finally, finally feel the glorious, soaring emotions Luke had promised her, with his eyes, with his kisses, with the touch of his hand. The desires he aroused in her were profound ones and for her, a marriage of their two bodies would also be a marriage of their souls.

When she had donned drawers and a camisole, Charity put on a wrapper and stepped out into the hall. Pausing outside Blaise's door, she heard the woman humming softly within, and knocked.

At Blaise's cheerful invitation, she went in.

"I'm going to be married tonight," she said, standing just over the threshold and feeling ridiculously shy. "At the mission chapel."

Blaise, also wearing a wrapper, crossed the room to kiss Charity lightly on both cheeks. "Are you sure this is what you want, darling? Luke is a very attractive man, but we don't really know very much about him, do we?"

"I know all I need to," Charity replied. And it was true. Her intuition, always a formidable force, had tested Luke, long since, and found him sound in every way that counted. The years ahead would surely bring a great many surprises, good and bad, but Luke was Luke; she knew his best qualities, and honored them, knew his faults, and accepted them. Most of all, she loved him with her whole heart.

"Blaise, I have no right to ask you this, I'm not even sure you have the answer, but I must put the question anyway. You and Papa have been deeply in love for what—five years? You've lived in this house—chastely, I know—for two. Why haven't you married?"

Blaise's large, luminous eyes contained no secrecy, but puzzlement instead, and a certain sadness. "I—I've always thought your father had— well—reservations."

"He hasn't explained?"

Tiny lines appeared in the space above Blaise's perfect nose. "I haven't pressed him, darling. I've been content with our life as it is." Color flared along her fine, high cheekbones. "Well, mostly content. It *is* unconventional, my living under Jonah's roof this way, without benefit of clergy, but we've avoided scandal because you've been here with us."

Charity felt a dull weight rise into her throat and settle there, and when she responded, it was with difficulty. "Luke insists that I live with him, on the homestead," she said.

"Oh, dear," Blaise breathed. Then her face brightened again. "But I am forgetting Genesis. She'll serve as a chaperone, I'm sure."

"Blaise," Charity reminded the other woman

247

reluctantly, "Genesis, however fine a person she may be, is a former prostitute. Her presence here will create talk, not prevent it."

Blaise spread one hand over her heart, made her way to her vanity table, and sat down, looking pale. "What am I going to do?"

"I've said too much," Charity lamented, backing toward the door. "I'm sorry, Blaise. I didn't mean to upset you."

"I know that," Blaise replied, rallying visibly. Lifting her chin, squaring her shoulders. She was probably the most resilient woman Charity knew. "You are simply direct, like your father. And what you've said is quite true. I must think, come up with a course of action."

"Maybe I can persuade Luke to stay here, after all—just until Papa is better." But even as she spoke Charity knew the idea was hopeless. Luke was proud, as proud as Jonah in his own way, and he would never live in another man's house.

Blaise shook her head. "You needn't try to solve my problems," she said gently. "That's for me to do. Will you tell your father—about the wedding, I mean?"

"Tomorrow," Charity made the decision as she spoke. "It won't come as any surprise to him, I'm sure. I've told him that I meant to marry Luke."

"Shall I come with you? To be a witness or anything?"

"Stay with Papa," Charity answered, in a soft

voice. "Perhaps we'll have a celebration of some sort, in a few months, when Papa is feeling better."

Blaise pondered that, then nodded and smiled. "Be happy, darling. You deserve the very best of everything."

Charity blew her friend a kiss and then turned and walked out, afraid of dissolving into a puddle of silly, sentimental tears if she remained.

When Luke returned to the ranch house to fetch her, several hours later, she was wearing the peach silk dress she had selected earlier, and her hair was wound into a single thick plait, braided through with tiny white rosebuds taken from the garden. At the sight of her, Luke took a quick step backwards, as though he'd been struck by something. He recovered in a few moments, though, and his lopsided grin was only a little unsteady.

"You do look beautiful," he said, on a long breath. His movements were unusually awkward as he helped her up onto the wagon seat, then came around to the other side, passing in front of the horses, to climb up and take the reins.

She did not thank him, for that same strange shyness that had afflicted her earlier, during her conversation with Blaise, was upon her again. She simply sat there beside him, holding her wedding bouquet of dark red roses in her lap, her heart dancing ahead of the wagon like a merry wraith.

13

They traveled over a road awash in the glow of a broad harvest moon, though the sun was not entirely gone, and Charity, stricken by the sight in a way she could not define, searched within herself for her voice, usually so ready, for boldness or at least bravado. She found only the wild, sweet reticence of a bride.

Long before they reached the mission gate, Charity heard the voices of laughing children, then glimpsed them running and playing in the tall, lush grass, chasing the last elusive minutes of daylight with the sort of frenzied joy that belongs only to the very young. She smiled, and followed the sound from moment to moment, like a golden rope that could guide her through the inevitable doubts.

One of the smaller boys ran to unlatch the gate, riding gleefully on the lower rail as it swung open in a slow, creaking arch. The others soon surrounded them, frolicking around the wagon like curious wolf cubs, crowing their exuberant greetings to Charity and to Luke. Trying to buy time, precious time, before being sent off to their prayers and their beds.

Charity laughed at their antics, laughed again when Peony came out into the large yard, fluttering her apron at the children as though they were a flock of noisy birds to be shooed back to their proper perches. They paid no mind to the elderly cook; only Father

Elias's appearance and smiling commands dispersed them, sent them toward their dormitories, heads bent, feet shuffling, voices low and petulant.

They begrudged every moment, Charity knew, and would not have given so much as a heartbeat up to sleep if they had had an alternative. Even when they had gone inside, and lighted their lamps, heads showed at both windows and in the doorway.

In a sidelong glance at Luke, Charity saw that he was grinning. "I remember how it was," he said quietly. There was nothing of sadness in him, only a certain nostalgia. Plainly, for all the trouble in the Shardlow household, Luke had known at least some happiness as a child. She had not suspected that before.

"They would make lively wedding guests," Charity mused, with a smile of her own.

"Indeed they would," Luke agreed, securing the brake lever and then jumping down to greet Father Elias, who labored slowly toward them. Overhead, the first stars shimmered in a soft twilight sky.

The priest had known, of course, that Luke and Charity planned to be wed. It was certainly nothing unusual—many men and women came to be married in his chapel, in all seasons and at all different hours of the day and night.

Beaming, the old man pumped Luke's hand. Charity would normally have jumped down from the wagon and hurried over to offer a greeting of her own, but the skirts of her appointed wedding dress were voluminous, and she did not want to tear or soil them.

After a few words with Father Elias, Luke came back, raised his hands to encompass her waist, and lifted her easily to the ground. She flushed, because he was standing so close, and because she thought, for a moment, that he would kiss her, right there in the mission yard, with the priest and Peony, a gaggle of children and the moon and stars looking on.

He must have read her mind, for he chuckled, took her chin between his thumb and curved fingers, and smiled down into her eyes. "Later," he promised, so that only she heard.

Peony, looking less gleeful than Father Elias, nonetheless drew nigh, and walked with Charity into the chapel. A communal shout of exultation from the children signaled that either Luke or the priest had invited them to witness the wedding, and they stampeded in, to take their places in the pews.

Father Elias lighted the candles on the altar, and then arranged the bride and groom before him, careful and earnest in this work. The children fidgeted until Peony shushed them with a fierce gust of air, and then she and one of the older girls took their places at the front of the chapel, as witnesses.

The ceremony was almost intolerably beautiful, from Charity's dazed perspective anyway, with the dancing candlelight and the gentle exhortations of the priest, and she never missed the embellishments she would have had if they had exchanged vows at the ranch. She did, for all her happiness, sorely miss Jonah and Blaise and Aaron; they should have been present for the occasion, there was no denying that.

In good time, the holy words were said, the tender pledges made. When the priest asked if there were rings, Charity shook her head, but Luke produced a golden band from the pocket of his frock coat and slipped it easily onto her finger. She looked down at the ring, then upwards, quickly, into his eyes.

He smiled at her surprise, and turned his attention back to the priest. The children, lining the rough-hewn pews, must have been spellbound, for they were utterly silent.

Father Elias pronounced them man and wife, and enjoined Luke to kiss his bride. He did so, and though he was outwardly circumspect, an inaudible growl reverberated against Charity's mouth when their lips touched.

The children cheered raucously, while Peony wailed with romantic sentiment.

Luke paid the priest with a gold coin, and the old man held it in his palm for a long moment, squinting in amazement. Then papers were signed, and the world was a blur around them, it seemed to Charity—she kissed Peony's wet cheek, and then Father Elias's dry, crinkled one, and the children nearly toppled her with their ebullient congratulations.

Finally, Luke took her by the arm, and guided her back to the wagon—it seemed to her later that her feet never touched the grass, that instead of walking she had floated over the ground, like some stray angel flying low—and helped her into the seat.

More words passed between Luke and Father Elias, quick and fervent ones, and then Luke was beside her, taking up the reins, bringing the rig around in a wide turn. The heavens poured silvery brilliance before them, to light their way, and the night sang a summer chorus.

The very spirit of the earth seemed to rise up and embrace them both in those precious moments; Charity felt its great, thunderous pulse enfold her. She had not thought it possible to know such joy, even though she must have read a thousand fairy tales in her life, and made up a thousand more all her own. But sitting there beside Luke, in that battered old wagon, wearing one of last year's party dresses for a wedding gown, she knew a bliss so complete that it seemed downright greedy to expect anything more.

She and Luke did not speak during that interval; Charity was too moved, too fearful of breaking the spell, and Luke was whistling softly through his teeth, keeping the team to a steady, unhurried pace. She knew he was wearing his gunbelt, that indeed he had worn it even during the marriage ceremony, but for once that didn't trouble her. For good or ill, he would not have been Luke without it.

Presently, the team and wagon rattled into the dooryard of Luke's cabin, and a shiver of reckless anticipation spiraled down Charity's spine and burst in a place deep and private, like a fire-flower unfurling against an Independence Day sky.

Luke got down first, of course, and this time when he took Charity into his arms, he didn't set her down, but carried her through the waving grass to the door. After pushing that open with one foot, he brought her over the threshold, into the intimate darkness of that tiny house.

It was a crude place, but it might have been a castle, for all Charity knew. She heard music in the silence, felt warmth and welcome in the darkness.

Still holding Charity, Luke bent his head to hers, and the kiss they exchanged was tender, and lasted a long time. Charity was unsteady when at last Luke set her on her feet; she might actually have fallen if he hadn't steadied her.

His hair glistened like gold in the gloom, and his laugh was as private, as personal, as a caress. "Stand right there, and don't move," he said. "I'll light a lamp."

She did not want him to leave her, even long enough to strike a match and hold it to a wick, but she made no protest when he stepped away, and merely blinked when light flared, flickered and then took hold. The smoky scent of kerosene rose from the plain lantern sitting in the middle of the improvised table.

"I've got to put away the team," Luke said, a little gruffly, keeping his distance. He looked like an archangel in the light of that single lamp, impossibly handsome, too perfect to be mortal. His eyes were serious as he gazed at her, and she saw his throat move with a swallow. "I'll bring in your satchel and give you some time to—well, some time."

Charity might have laughed, if her heart hadn't been pounding fit to suck up every drop of blood in her body. She was so frightened, so uncertain, so utterly glad to be who she was, and where she was. She nodded her assent, momentarily unable to speak, and Luke rushed out of the cabin as though demons were chasing him, overturning one of the apple-crate chairs in the process.

There was a fire laid on the hearth, and Charity took a match from the box on the mantel and crouched down, her silk skirts pooling around her, to start the blaze. The pungent scent of burning applewood filled the air, and a sound behind her indicated that Luke was back with her traveling case. She didn't turn to look at him because something else had taken her attention.

A bed stood against the far wall. A real and very regal bed, with a carved mahogany headboard and creamy linen sheets, fat pillows and a clean, brightly colored blanket.

She rose slowly to her feet, staring in wonder. Where could he have gotten so fine a piece of furniture, on such short notice? She turned to ask, but he was gone again, leaving the door ajar to the consensus of crickets and the nickering of the horses.

Biting her lip, Charity opened the valise, took out her nightgown, and removed her dress and petticoats as quickly as she could. She had just taken her hair down when Luke returned, his gaze at once reverent and hungry as he looked upon her, and he latched the door without a moment's distraction.

"You look—sort of bulky," he observed, sounding hoarse again.

Charity, primed for a compliment, was more than a little stung. Then she realized that she'd forgotten to take off her camisole and drawers, and she didn't expect an opportunity to remove them gracefully, either. Judging by the expression on Luke's face, he wasn't ever going to look away from her again, let alone turn his back like a gentleman.

"Where did you get the bed?" she blurted, because she couldn't bring herself to respond to his earlier remark directly.

He chuckled, and the sound broke some of the tension that sizzled between them, though it still felt as though all the thunder and lightning in the world had found its way into that little cabin, and gotten trapped there. "I bought it from the storekeeper in town," he said. "He's probably talking pretty fast, right about now, trying to explain an empty boudoir to the missus."

"You mean Mr. Witchell sold you his *own* bed?"

He shrugged, but the set of his chin and the look in his eyes made for a cocky countenance. "I am a persuasive man," he said.

Charity had recovered some of her normal sass. "You are an arrogant one, too," she said, "though I must confess I'm grateful not to have to sleep on a straw pallet."

Luke bent over the lamp, his hair gilded by its glow, and extinguished it. Except for the dim light of the fire, the cabin was dark again. "You were planning on sleeping?" he asked, with a smile in his voice.

Charity glanced nervously toward the bed. What was she supposed to do? Climb onto the mattress and lie there like an Apache's captive staked out on an ant hill? Wait for Luke to guide her? She was, for all the furious passion that had been raging in her fertile imagination of late, woefully innocent. Fairy tales always stopped short of the bridal chamber, after all, and she had no idea how to proceed.

Luke gave a low, throaty laugh. "So that's it," he said. "You're still wearing your drawers."

She was startled by the observation, having been lost in thoughts of romantic protocol and sheer, delicious terror, and so gasped softly and crossed her arms over her breasts. "How—?"

"You're standing in front of the fire, Charity," he told her. "I can see through your nightgown."

Grateful for the lack of light, since her face was pounding with renewed heat, she moved to turn away, and somehow divest herself of the camisole and pantaloons, but Luke spoke again, and stopped her.

"Don't," he said. "I want to undress you."

A great tremor went through Charity, but

it was made of eagerness as much as trepidation. She froze, with her back to Luke, not daring to get into bed, unwilling to flee into the starry night beyond those thick cabin walls.

He came to her, laid gentle hands on her shoulders, and turned her around to face him. "Let me," he said, and bunched the fabric of her nightdress in loose fists. He waited then, his gaze locked with hers, until she nodded her permission.

Slowly, with the care of a shaman performing a holy ritual, he raised the gown up and up, past her knees, her thighs, her hips. Over her head, and away.

She bowed her head, shy of his inspection; he curved a finger under her chin and raised her face, held her captive with only his eyes.

"You are so beautiful," he murmured, tossing the gown aside. It curled around one of the great posts at the foot of the bed, like a pale ghost collapsed in exhaustion.

"So are you," Charity answered, in all sincerity, and he laughed, and drew her close by cupping his hands lightly beneath her jaw. His kiss was deep and soft, possessive and yet cautious, as though she were some wild and splendid creature, wont to take wing and fly away.

She was trembling when he drew back, and she whispered her confession. "I—don't know what to do. You see, I've never—"

He smiled, his eyes shining. "I know, and I'm glad." He wound a finger in a loose tendril of her hair. "Don't worry, Charity," he said.

"I'll teach you everything you need to know."
His voice had turned solemn when he went on.
"I want to look at you. It's about all I've been
thinking of since I came back to Jubilee." He
paused. "Is it all right?"

She nodded, and he untied the laces that held
her camisole closed, and spread the cloth,
baring her bosom. Her nipples tightened
under his gaze, and Charity shivered as Luke
cupped one breast in a callused hand, stroked
her with his thumb.

"Cold?" he whispered, with genuine concern.

She shook her head, and with his free hand
he caught hold of her plaited hair, and unwound
it, combing it through with his fingers. When
it fell loose down her back, he smoothed away
the open camisole, letting it spill onto the
wooden floor, and held both her breasts like
ripe fruits. He frowned, as if choosing between
them, and then ducked his head and took a
nipple full into his mouth.

Charity cried out in surprise and in pleasure,
and plunged her fingers into his hair, straw spun
into gold it was, and held him to her, lest he
stop. Dear heaven, but this was so much
better than anything she'd ever imagined,
and she'd imagined plenty.

He continued to enjoy her, divesting her of
the drawers while he suckled, attending to the
second breast only when he had taken his fill
of the first. Charity, her head flung back in surrender, whimpered and writhed, able to stand
only because Luke had taken a firm hold on
both her hips.

She was making a soft sound, half sob, half plea, when he lifted her into his arms again, and carried her to the bed. The sheets were smooth with scented powder against the flesh of her back and her thighs, and her heels were already scrabbling for purchase.

Luke stretched out beside Charity, and she wanted him inside her, but she soon learned that his preparations for her conquering had only begun. He kissed her repeatedly, deeply and slowly, stroked and explored her with his hands until she thought she would go mad with the delay. She pleaded, arching her back in the firelight, and it was then that he eased her legs apart, and knelt between her thighs.

She was exultant, thinking he would have her at last, and quench the sweet fire that was already consuming her from the inside. Instead, he bowed down over her, and kissed her belly, and teased her navel with the tip of his tongue.

She sobbed aloud, and dragged at him, her hands frantic in his hair, wanting him on top of her, needing him there. Instead, he trailed his lips down farther, over the secret silk, and set her ablaze with his breath. Then, with a quick, nuzzling motion, he breached the veil of curls and took her boldly, greedily, into his mouth.

She screamed, like a jungle creature with its mate, and thrust her hips upward, seeking. He held her buttocks in his hands and raised her high, like a chalice, so high that her feet no longer touched the bed.

The pleasure grew more and more intense, and every time it seemed that the universe would fold in upon itself, stars and moons and other worlds tumbling into its dark center, Luke paused, kissing her belly and the insides of her thighs. Letting her dangle there, between heaven and earth, utterly vulnerable to him and wanting nothing else but to give herself up to him completely.

She was wet with perspiration when he finally parted her, laved her with his tongue, and then suckled hard while she pitched beneath him, and splintered into a million pieces, each one trailing fire.

Tenderly, he lowered her onto the feather-filled mattress, and gathered her into his arms, soothing her with tender, senseless words and light caresses until her quivering had ceased, until she lay warm and pliant and bedazzled beside him.

With slow motions of his hands, with lingering kisses, he took her back to the edge of the sky, and when he mounted her, and filled her with himself, she barely noticed the breaching pain, brief and sharp as it was. At the first long stroke of his hips, she shattered like a clay pot dipped in ice water and then thrust into a kiln, and had to be led back to herself, one step at a time, when it was over.

True to his word, Luke did not allow her to sleep, but roused her, again and again, and took her soaring against the night sky. Only when the dawn poured pink-gold light through the windows did he relent, and they both rested, fitted one against the other, like the interlocking parts of something once broken, but now restored.

The sun was up when he awakened her, and moved over her, and guided her once more through the intricate dance their bodies had learned so well in the night. She called his name when her release came, and he plunged into her hard after that, and she stroked his back and whispered, urging him onward, into the very heart of the fire.

With a low groan, his gaze holding hers even as he flexed upon her, Luke spilled his warmth into her very depths.

Let there be a child, she prayed silently, as she received him. *Let there be a child and I will never ask You for anything else.*

Sometime later, Luke climbed out of bed and dragged on plain trousers and a cotton shirt. His wedding clothes, like Charity's, were scattered from one end of the cabin to the other.

"I'm going out to check on the horses," he said. He was sitting on the edge of the mattress as he spoke, pulling on his boots.

"I want to sleep." She stretched and then turned onto her side.

Luke swatted her smartly on the bottom. "Too bad," he said. "You've got a ranch to run, boss lady. Or had you forgotten?"

Charity groaned and tried to pull the sheets up over her head, but Luke dragged them down, until she was lying naked in the bright spill of sunshine flowing in through the window.

"I hardly think the Double B will go under if I take one day for a honeymoon."

Luke was already halfway to the door. He threw her camisole and drawers to her from there. "Well, then, you'd better think again," he counseled cheerfully, picking up their scattered garments and laying them carelessly across the foot of the bed. "Soon as word gets around that you've gotten yourself hitched to the likes of me, every snake-oil salesman in the territory will be headed straight for your daddy's front door, full of sympathy and solutions. And that's only the subtle ones."

Resigned, and not a little hungry, Charity squirmed into her underthings, then her petticoats. She had packed a blue morning gown in her valise the day before, at the Double B, and she was wearing that when Luke returned from outside, carrying a bucket of spring water. She scrambled some eggs, and now that he was back with the pail, she made coffee, too.

"You can cook?" he marveled. His eyes were twinkling; that was all that saved him from retaliatory action.

She was indignant, if inclined to be merciful. "Do I seem helpless to you?"

He crossed the cabin floor and stood beside her, inspecting the contents of the skillet. "Oh, no, boss lady. Never that. I just figured you were used to the high life."

"It's true that Peony made most of our meals," Charity admitted, slapping his hand when he reached for a piece of scrambled egg, "but Papa insisted that I learn to run a proper household." She felt a touch of sadness at the memory of that decree, and it must have shown on her face, for Luke pushed the skillet to the back of the stove and turned her around to meet his gaze.

"And therein," he said gently, "hangs a tale?"

She sighed. "I didn't mind learning to cook and sew and clean. Truly, I didn't. It's just that Papa expected me to give up riding astride, and shooting, and all the other things that were perfectly all right before."

"Before?" he prompted.

"Before I turned eighteen. Everything changed on that day. I was supposed to ride sidesaddle, if I rode at all. I wasn't allowed to help round up strays anymore, or go along on cattle drives. In the fall, when Papa and the men went hunting for deer and bear in the mountains, I had to stay home. And I was absolutely forbidden to get into any more horse races."

Luke's expression was one of tender amusement. The coffee started to boil over, so he picked up a ragged pot holder and pulled the pot off the heat. "Sit down, Mrs. Shardlow," he said. "The eggs are getting cold."

Charity went to the large cable spool, which she had set with chipped metal dishes and cups and mismatched cutlery. "I suppose you think he was right," she speculated, stung by the mere possibility. "Women ought to know their proper places, and never take a risk. Is that your opinion?"

He shook his head, pouring their coffee, setting the skillet in the middle of their makeshift table. "The way I see it, folks should be able to follow their inclinations, insofar as nobody else gets hurt. For what it's worth, I'm pretty sure Jonah was just trying to protect you." They might have been sitting down at a grand banquet table, the way he waited for her to be seated before dropping onto his own upturned crate. "Did you win any of those horse races?"

"Yes," she said, scooping eggs onto her plate. "I've won plenty." She paused. "If Jonah wanted to keep me safe, why did he teach me to ride and shoot in the first place?"

Luke smiled at whatever images happened to be passing through his mind just then. "He was always around to look after you when you were younger. But when a girl turns into a young woman, there are obvious complications."

"Such as?"

He let his gaze linger on her full breasts for a moment, breasts he had thoroughly enjoyed during the night. "I don't think you really need me to answer that question," he said simply, chewing. "These eggs are good."

Charity was flustered, partly because it seemed as though he could see through her bodice, when he looked at her that way, and partly because he was right. She knew well enough what the "complications" were that had changed her life so drastically, but the feelings of abandonment and betrayal were with her still.

"I didn't do anything wrong," she protested.

Luke laid down his fork and fixed his full attention on her. It was a thing she loved about him, that way he had of really seeing her, really hearing what she said. "No, darlin'," he said. "All you did was grow up, that's all. Jonah loves you, and he did what he thought was right. You can't ask more than that of anybody."

"I guess not," she allowed.

After that, they talked about inconsequential things. Luke went outside and hitched up the wagon when they'd finished eating, while Charity cleaned up, made the bed, and relished a second cup of coffee.

Stepping out into the bright morning sunshine, Charity felt like spreading her arms and whirling for joy, just as she had often done as a child. The sight of Luke saddling his gelding, Shiloh, distracted her.

"I'll ride over with you," he said, in reply to her unasked question. "I want to look in on old Jonah. See if he's still as ornery as he was yesterday."

Charity was at once pleased and concerned. She certainly welcomed Luke's company, but she was afraid he intended to follow her all over the ranch, playing nursemaid. "I can do this," she said firmly. "I might make a few mistakes, but I can run the Double B as well as any man could."

He handed her up into the wagon with the elegance of a liveried footman settling milady into her carriage. "Like I said," he replied, "I want to pay Jonah a call. And if you're going to manage the Double B, you'd better arm yourself, because there are apt to be plenty of people inclined to take your authority lightly."

She took up the reins and released the wagon's long brake lever, glancing pointedly at the pistol riding low on her husband's hip. "I intend to use reason to get my way, not bullets," she said, in a tone that sounded insufferably prim, even to her.

Luke mounted his horse, leaned down to pat its muscular neck with affection, though he was looking at Charity when he spoke. "You're a fool, then," he said, cheerfully. "Maybe Jonah had cause to think you couldn't take care of yourself. There are a good many trolls and monsters and evil sorcerers in the real world, Charity, and they're not always so easy to recognize as the ones in those fairy tales of yours."

The jibe irritated her thoroughly, and she did not reply, but simply brought down the reins and called crisply to the team, which stumbled into noisy motion at her bidding.

Luke rode quietly beside her, all the way to the ranch, thinking his own thoughts and apparently seeing no reason to share them. In the night, even at breakfast, they had been as intimate as two human beings could be, though in different ways, of course.

Now, as Charity drew the wagon to a stop in front of her father's house, she felt the complicated variances between herself and Luke very poignantly indeed. It was more than their backgrounds: he wore that .45 as easily as a shirt or a comfortable pair of boots, and he seemed to have few qualms about using it. Although Charity loved to shoot, and was at home with firearms, she did not see gunplay as the solution to any kind of problem.

There were other things, too. She was not the sort of woman Luke would have chosen, if left to his own devices. It was obvious, from his skill at lovemaking, that he had been tutored in places no true lady would ever have frequented.

He stood by while she climbed down from the wagon, using the spokes of the wheels like the rungs of a ladder. Before either of them could speak, however, they became aware of a rider, approaching fast.

Raoul, Charity saw, with a sinking heart.

She waited, with Luke beside her, one hand shading her eyes from the bright sun, and soon Raoul was there, dismounting in a single furious motion, flinging his horses's reins in the general direction of the ranch hand who had come to take care of Charity's wagon.

"Is it true?" Raoul demanded, seething. His dark eyes blazed as he glared at Charity.

"Yes," she answered, knowing full well what he meant. Word traveled fast around Jubilee, and he had learned of her marriage.

Luke took a step closer to Charity, and the atmosphere between the two men was tumultuous, like thunder trapped inside a metal barrel. "You have something to say, Montego?" he asked calmly.

Raoul let his gaze fall to the .45 in Luke's holster before rising back to his face again. "Yes," he replied. "I'm going to kill you."

14

I'm going to kill you.

Raoul's dark eyes were narrowed to slits, his nostrils flared. He wore a shoulder holster, with a .38 caliber pistol inside, and to Charity he looked as though he meant exactly what he'd said. She was livid, and made a move toward him, but Luke immediately put one arm out and stopped her.

"This is between Montego and me," he said, without so much as glancing her way. "Go inside, Charity."

"I'm not going anywhere," she replied, almost as furious with Luke as she was with Raoul. "If you two think you're going to stand here and shoot at each other, you are sadly mistaken!"

Luke chuckled at that, but Raoul was literally seething. "Do you know what this man is?" he demanded, advancing on Charity and stabbing an index finger in Luke's direction. "He's a common outlaw, a gunslinger!"

"He's my husband," Charity said quietly. "And I love him." She had not meant to make that last declaration, and having said it she did not dare to look at Luke.

Raoul looked stricken. "You don't mean that," he rasped, and shoved one hand through his glossy black hair. His clothes looked uncharacteristically disheveled; he was gaunt from the wound he'd suffered in the robbery, too, though he seemed as agile as ever.

"I do mean it," she insisted, in a very soft voice. He had been a loyal friend for a long time; she did not want to be harsh with him. "Now get on your horse, Raoul, and ride out of here. Don't come back unless you're prepared to apologize."

He reminded Charity, in those moments, of a majestic mountain, shuddering and rumbling, ready to spew molten lava in every direction. *"Never,"* he hissed. He paused, closed his eyes, drew in a deep breath and released it. He looked only slightly less volcanic, after this noble effort. "I will forgive you, in time, and I am still willing to marry you. You will see reason once this road agent is gone, and we will be wed." While Charity was still reeling from that pronouncement, Raoul turned again to Luke. "There is a knoll a mile east of my grandfather's home," he said coldly, and cocked a gloved thumb toward the sun. "I'll expect you at noon."

"I'll be there," Luke said grimly.

A gunfight. Panic swept through Charity; she, who had never fainted in her life, felt as though she would swoon. And that outraged her.

"If you go along with this idiocy," she said to Luke, in furious desperation, "don't bother to come back."

271

"Don't worry," Raoul interceded. "He won't be back."

"Why wait until noon?" Luke asked. "Come to that, why even bother to ride all the way over there at all? I'll just kick your ass right here."

Raoul pitched forward then, breathing fire, and promptly caught the knuckles of Luke's left hand square on the chin. He crashed backwards into the picket fence, which teetered back and forth under his weight, but held. Blood poured from a gash in his lip, and he wiped it with the back of one hand before flinging himself forward again into the teeth of the buzz saw.

Luke had a distinct advantage, though not in size, nor in strength; in these areas, both men were fairly well matched. No, it was his calm, deliberate manner, as opposed to Raoul's unbridled fury, that gave him the edge. Luke landed a punch in the other man's midsection that made Charity wince, and most of the power in that blow came from Raoul's own momentum.

"Stop this!" she cried, and when neither man paid her any heed, she went back to the wagon, climbed up into the box, and dredged a long forgotten driving whip out from under the seat. She jumped down again, drew back her arm, and gave Luke a good whack across the shoulders. He was still yowling when she struck the small of Raoul's back with a wicked snap.

Both men stared at her, angry and amazed, Raoul bleeding from his nose and a cut in his lip and breathing hard, Luke glowering like a bull about to lower his horns and charge. A soundless drone arose, like invisible bees swarming in a hive.

Charity stood up very straight and squared her shoulders. "I warned you to stop," she said priggishly. A tense moment passed while the two men simply stood there in ominous silence, but she held her ground.

Then, suddenly, Luke began to laugh. He picked up his hat, which had fallen into the dirt in the midst of the scuffle, and slapped his thigh with it. "I will be damned," he reveled, "if I haven't married myself a wildcat."

"I'll whack you again," Charity said, giddy with bravado and waving the whip at Luke and then Raoul, "if you don't give up this nonsense and—and shake hands!"

"Shake hands?" Raoul echoed. He was grim, and uncommonly pale.

"Not if you whipped the hide right off me," Luke added.

Charity raised the lash, though she really hoped they wouldn't force the issue. The horrid echo of that long strip of braided leather striking flesh and bone still resonated in her inner ear. "All right, then," she suggested, "just promise not to gun each other down."

"I wasn't going to shoot him," Luke said reasonably, spreading his hands wide in exclamation. "I just meant to beat hell out of the damn fool."

Raoul opened his mouth to argue, but before he got a word out, the loud metallic rasp of a rifle being cocked put a sudden end to the discussion.

Charity sought the source with her eyes, found it on the front porch, where Jonah stood, leaning against one of the pillars supporting the slanted roof, a double-barrel shotgun in his hands.

"Enough," he said clearly, and the look on his ashen, distorted face was a ferocious one.

Luke and Raoul seemed stunned, but Charity gave a cry of joy, dropped the whip, and ran toward her father. Having spent the strength he'd somehow summoned to intercede, Jonah now looked as though he would collapse. The shotgun clattered to the porch floor and discharged, splintering the umbrella urn full of flowers and pocking the wall behind it.

Just as Charity reached the top step, Genesis dashed out of the front door, closely followed by Blaise, and between them the three women struggled to hold Jonah upright. Luke vaulted over the picket fence and up the steps, bracing his father-in-law, draping one of Jonah's arms over his own shoulder.

"Enough," Jonah repeated. The word was garbled, and hollow with exhaustion.

"Are you satisfied now?" Charity snapped, meeting Luke's gaze briefly before he turned and hauled a stumbling Jonah back into the house.

"Don't start in on me," Luke warned. "Last time I looked, I was still wearing the pants in this family."

Out of the corner of her eye, Charity saw

274

Blaise and Genesis exchange an amused look, and she wanted to throttle them, one in each hand. Might have tried, too, but for the overriding and miraculous fact that her father had not only transported himself from inside the house, under his own power, but brought his favorite shotgun along with him.

The wheeled chair was in the middle of the entryway, lying on its side. Genesis hastily righted it, and Luke eased Jonah, now only half-conscious, onto the seat.

Raoul came in behind them, carrying the gun Jonah had dropped on the porch. He took the weapon into the study without a word, and Charity didn't have to look to know he'd returned it to the gun rack over the fireplace. He'd spent almost as much time on the Double B as on his grandfather's ranch, and he knew his way around the house.

Overwrought, Charity blinked back sudden, burning tears.

Luke wheeled Jonah back to his bedroom, while Blaise and Genesis hurried ahead, like two billowing winds driven along ahead of a rising storm. Charity, seeing that Jonah was being looked after, went slowly back to the doorway of the study.

Raoul stood before the empty fireplace, his back to the room, both hands braced against the heavy wooden mantel piece. His head was down.

"I'm sorry," Charity said.

He did not turn to face her, or raise his head. "So am I," he replied gruffly. "How is Jonah?"

"I'm not sure," Charity answered, with a sniffle. "I couldn't get close enough to him to find out."

At last, Raoul pushed away from the mantel and faced her. His stance was one she recognized; proud, arrogant. Even aristocratic. He was a grayish-white under the natural bronze tone of his skin, and his eyes were bleak. "Did you mean what you said, *Conchita?* Do you love him—that drifter, with a murderer's blood flowing in his veins?"

Charity simply nodded. It would do no good to defend Luke to Raoul.

"He will destroy you."

"I am not so easily destroyed," she answered quietly. "And if I do wind up with a broken heart, I won't be the first woman it's happened to, will I?"

"Come to me," Raoul whispered. "When he rides away, come to me."

She pretended not to know what he meant— come to the heart of my life, come to the marriage bed, come to a future spent together. "You'll still be my friend, then?"

"You will need a husband when that day comes, not a friend."

"Don't wait for me, Raoul," she said, in a small voice. Then she turned and walked away, toward the room where Jonah lay, recovering from his rescue effort on the front porch. Her head lowered, she collided with Luke's chest in the corridor.

He steadied her by gripping her shoulders. "He's all right, Charity," he said, with a tenderness that made a lump swell in her throat. "Just a little tired, that's all."

"I want to see him."

"He's resting," Luke said. The words, though gently spoken, filled Charity with foreboding.

"But he walked—he spoke—"

Luke cupped her face in his hands, brushed aside tears she had not been aware of shedding with the sides of his thumbs. "He did," he agreed. "But the effort set him back a little, Charity." He paused. "I blame myself for that. He must have thought you were in danger."

She moved around him and he didn't try to stop her. Didn't speak.

Genesis and Blaise had undressed Jonah, and even managed to put him into a nightshirt. He lay propped on pillows, his eyes closed, his face slack. His flesh was waxen, and Charity's heart, so hopeful before that moment, folded in upon itself.

The two women made way for her, and she sat on the side of Jonah's bed, and took his motionless hands into her own. She kissed the bony, work-roughened knuckles, and his eyes rolled open.

"For-give me," he murmured painfully.

She shook her head. Surely it was a good sign that he was talking, when he had been silent for so many days. "There is no need, Papa. Nothing to forgive."

"Your...mother," he said.

Instantly, Charity was brittle with dread; dizzy

with it. She had put the secret out of her mind, but now the fear of it filled her like a second soul. "No," she said, and started to stand up, to step away, but he held onto her hands with something like the old strength.

"I lied," he said, very slowly, and the words made an awful, scraping sound in his throat. "Lied—"

Charity could not protect herself from the revelation to come, she knew. Could not retreat from it. And yet she did not feel ready to hear what her father had to tell her. Genesis had left the room, but Blaise remained, gripping the footboard of the bed, her eyes wide and worried.

Jonah's effort to speak was excruciating. "Letters...my bureau—"

Eyes brimming, Charity nodded. "I'll get them, Papa. I promise. You rest now. You just rest, and everything will be all right."

He managed a semblance of a nod, and slept.

"Where is Luke?" she asked, finding Genesis outside her father's room, patiently waiting to be needed.

"He and that other fella lit out for somewheres. Said they had things to see to, and you weren't to worry."

Not worry? Charity sagged against the wall for a moment and rubbed both temples with her fingertips. A quarter of an hour before, Luke and Raoul had been indulging in fisticuffs. Had they gone to the appointed knoll on the Draper ranch, to settle their differences with guns?

If so, Charity reasoned, straightening her spine, there wasn't much she could do about it now. In fact, she decided, if they were stupid enough to do such a thing, they deserved whatever happened.

She put the whole matter forcibly out of her mind and headed for the stairs, bent on finding the letters Jonah had told her about. If she didn't read them right away, she might lose her courage.

They were in an old cigar box, under a stack of pressed handkerchiefs, three thin letters, crumbling with age. Charity carried them, box and all, to a chair near the windows, and sat down. Her heart raced painfully—poor heart, she had asked so much of it in recent days and nights—and she spread her right hand upon her chest, trying to confer peace upon herself.

The envelopes were addressed to Rianna Barnham, in care of the Double B, in a strong, unfamiliar and distinctly masculine hand. From the first line she knew they were love letters, and that they had not been written by her father.

Come back to me...I have never stopped loving you...Bring your little girl and come home to me, darling Rianna. We will make a family...Leave Jonah these letters, not to cause him pain, but so that he will know I truly love you, that you were mine first...mine always...mine forever.

Charity read every word of all three letters, then read them again.

When she had finished, she folded them

slowly, tucked them back into their envelopes and their cigar box, and put them back under the handkerchiefs in her father's bureau drawer.

She descended the rear stairway, walked through the empty kitchen, over the back porch, through the tall grass to the barn. There, motioning away several ranch hands who offered to help, she saddled Taffeta herself, and mounted.

She took the short way to the mission, passing through Luke's land.

Father Elias must have seen her from a distance, for he was waiting at the main gate when she arrived.

"I've seen the letters," she said.

The priest had grown smaller, and wearier, it seemed to Charity, just since the night before, when he had joined her to Luke by the sacrament of marriage. He fumbled with the latch on the gate, and opened it just far enough for Charity to ride through.

The yard was quiet, which indicated that the children were inside, at their lessons. She wondered briefly if Peony was with them.

Father Elias waited while Charity dismounted and tethered Taffeta loosely to a low tree branch, then led the way into the quiet, shadowy chapel. The smells of candle wax and incense were familiar and therefore comforting.

"Sit down, child," the priest said, taking a seat on the front pew and patting the place next to him.

Charity sat, battling a storm of emotions—anger, hurt, confusion and a dozen others without names. She did not meet his gaze. "My mother didn't die. She left. She left Papa and me."

"Yes," Father Elias said gently. He had known it all along, of course. Had probably arranged the false funeral, overseen the burial of an empty box, marked all these years by a monument bearing a live woman's name.

"Why?" she whispered.

He laid a frail hand on her shoulder. "She was engaged to another man, before she met your father. They quarreled, and Rianna married Jonah and came west with him. Gave birth to you. Jonah loved her deeply, even desperately, but she—well, she'd left her heart behind, in the east, in the keeping of her first love. When she received the initial letter, she came to me, she wept and begged me for absolution. For release from her marriage vows. Of course, I could not give this last."

"He asked her to bring me back with her." She couldn't make herself say the other man's name, even then, with all those years in between now and the day of her mother's betrayal.

"Jonah wouldn't allow it," the priest explained heavily. "He could not bear to lose both of you."

"His pride."

"No, child. His love. He had no pride left when she went away. He was a broken man; he wept in this chapel many, many times."

The image filled Charity's mind; pushed hard

281

from behind her forehead, pounded under her temples. She thought of Blaise, patiently waiting for a wedding band. For respectability. "They are still married, my father and mother."

Father Elias sighed. "In Jonah's heart, perhaps," he said. "They were never divorced—such things are difficult. But Rianna died three years ago."

Charity clasped the edges of the pew with both hands; suddenly, the familiar smells were not holy, but cloying. "Papa knew."

Father Elias nodded. "Rianna's lover wrote to him. It was a very kind letter, considering all that had gone before."

She was silent for a long time, absorbing, realigning everything she had thought of as truth. She did not grieve for Rianna Barnham; she had done that long ago, and for her the woman Father Elias described, the woman who had lived an unknown life and finally died three years before, seemed unreal. She was like a tragic heroine in one of Charity's stories.

"That sham of a funeral. That grave—" Her voice fell away. That grave she had visited so many times, prayed over and wept over and confided in.

"For Jonah, she truly was dead. He had to act it all out, I think, in order to square everything in his mind. Too, he didn't want you to know, ever, that she had left you."

"Even though he forbid her to take me with her."

"Yes," the priest said sadly. "How she cried, that rainy night, when Hector Tillmont took her to Spokane to board the train. Jonah put it about that Rianna had not come back from her afternoon ride, told everybody he'd found her lying in a ravine, that she'd fallen and broken her neck. He and Hector and I were the only ones who knew the truth. He built the coffin with his own hands, Jonah did, in the barn at the Double B—had it done before dawn. He put two sacks full of grain inside, to give it weight, and the next day we held a funeral."

"I guess I understand what moved Papa to do such a thing, misguided as it was," Charity reflected, though she felt hollowed-out by the knowledge, stricken to the heart. "Tillmont was probably well paid, and I'm sure he's been blackmailing my father ever since, in one way or another. But why did *you* go along with the deception, Father?"

The priest took a few moments to ponder the question. "I have never seen a man suffer as much pain as Jonah Barnham did, losing that woman. It was wrong, what I did, and God will have His accounting for it when I leave this earth, but it was the only mercy I could offer just then." He looked pensively at the simple crucifix suspended above the altar. "I've implored Jonah, many times since, to put the matter right, to tell you what really happened, but he could not bring himself to do it. I know he feared that you would despise him, and that was a prospect he could never abide."

Charity dried her cheeks with the back of one hand. "He's paid the greatest price of all,

Papa has. And the money Tillmont extorted from him was the least of it."

Father Elias patted her shoulder again and got to his feet. "I will leave you to your thoughts, and to your God," he said. "Do not judge Jonah too harshly, Charity. He loves you, has always loved you. Nor should you blame your mother. We can never really know the forces that drive others to do what they do."

She gave no answer, for none was necessary. She knew what the priest had said was true, but she also needed time to sort out her feelings. For most of her life, the hours, days, weeks and years had seemed to creep by, uneventful, requiring little or nothing of her, but since Luke's return to Jubilee, things had happened with a vengeance—Jonah's stroke. Her marriage. And now this discovery, this shattering discovery.

So much.

She rose from the pew presently, and went out to mount Taffeta. Father Elias was nowhere in sight, and inside the mission school, the children were singing a song she did not recognize, in a language she could not speak.

She was not angry with Jonah, but she wasn't ready to face him, either. Nor could she go to the empty grave in the churchyard, where she had poured out her soul, again and again, ever since she was old enough to make her way there alone. Oddly, she had never noticed that her father did not visit the place himself, though in retrospect the fact seemed starkly obvious.

She wanted to return to the homestead. When Luke got back from wherever he had gone with Raoul, she would tell him what she had learned, and having related the tale, begin to heal. She rode there in a daze, surfacing from her thoughts only to guide the horse.

The men came, mounted, from the thick copse of trees to one side of the cabin, and surrounded her, without haste, before she could escape.

There were six of them, but their spokesman was a blond man, handsome in a hard-edged sort of way, and so like Luke that Charity's stomach did a sickening flip.

"Name's Vance Shardlow," he said, touching the brim of his hat. "I believe we're family now, you and me."

Charity did not waste time on courtesy. She knew these men were outlaws; Vance's name was as well-known in those parts as that of Jessie James or Butch Cassidy. He was wanted for a dozen robberies, and almost that many assaults and murders. "What do you want?" she demanded.

"Just paying a neighborly visit," Vance said. His eyes were blue-green, like Luke's, but cold as creek water running beneath winter ice. She shivered. "Luke around?" he asked.

"I imagine you've already surmised that he isn't," Charity said. She was more annoyed than frightened at that point. She had enough on her mind as it was, blast it, without a surprise visit from a pack of bandits.

A smile spread across Vance's mouth, but his eyes didn't change. They were remote. Empty. "That's a real pity." He looked back at the five men ranged behind him, their faces shadowed by the brims of their hats. "Isn't it, boys?" No one so much as flicked an eyelash, as far as Charity could tell, but Vance seemed to take their silence for hearty affirmation. "We wanted to congratulate him. He's a lucky man."

"Lucky to be alive, after the beating you gave him," Charity said. Luke still carried a number of bruises and scrapes from the night he'd been ambushed. *Please God,* she prayed silently, *don't let Luke come home now. They'll kill him for sure.*

Vance's frigid grin neither faded nor faltered. He made her think of a leering skull, mounted on a body of flesh and blood. "We'll leave a message for my little brother, if you don't mind," he said. He was beside her in an instant, and a knife gleamed in his right hand. Grasping Taffeta's bridle in one hand, he sliced the bodice of Charity's dress from her neck to her waist, the point of the blade skimming along her skin. Leaving a mark, without drawing blood. He laughed when she clutched at the severed fabric with both hands. "Yes, sir, he's a lucky man. One hell of a lot luckier than he deserves to be, after what he did to my daddy."

Precarious as her situation was, it was all Charity could do to keep herself from spitting straight into Vance Shardlow's face. He'd wanted to scare her, and he had succeeded at that, but she wouldn't let him have Luke. Not if she had to creep into hell, steal from the devil, and walk back over hot coals.

"He tell you what happened to old Trigg Shardlow?" Vance leaned in close to ask the question, and he smelled of whiskey, sweat, tobacco and evil.

She raised her chin a notch. "He was hanged, at the territorial prison," she said clearly. "For murdering his wife."

Vance gave a bitter, humorless laugh. "That what Luke told you? That Trigg killed that pretty little thing? It isn't true, you know. She jumped out of the hayloft window, Marietta did. Broke her lovely neck." He made a sharp snapping sound with two fingers, causing Charity to start. "Just like that."

"He threw her down, in a drunken rage," Charity countered. "She struck her head on the edge of the stove."

Vance shook his head, his face a parody of sorrow. "Why that little brother of mine would rather climb a tall tree and lie than stand flat-footed on the ground and tell the truth." He swept the "boys" up in another look before turning back to her. "Don't think I'm done with you yet, either. What happened today, that's just a warning. Next time I congratulate you, Mrs. Shardlow, things might get a bit rough."

That did it; she spat in his face, and she didn't regret it, even when he raised his hand and slapped her so hard that she lost her balance and struck the ground hard. Taffeta nickered and danced, and nearly stepped on her before she gained her feet and calmed the animal by murmuring and stroking its long neck.

Vance looked down at her, laughed again, and then wheeled his horse around and spurred it away, toward the trees. The silent marauders followed, and their backward glances made Charity's skin crawl.

Knees wobbling, back stubbornly straight, she took off Taffeta's saddle and bridle before shooing the mare away, toward the deep grass and the bubbling spring. Only then did Charity go inside the house, close the door, and throw the bar across it.

The cabin had been a happy place to her, because of the joy she and Luke had shared there, but now, fresh from an encounter with Vance, she saw in her mind's eye the murder of Marietta Shardlow. She felt the child Luke's grief, his helpless rage, his hatred, and it became her own as well. She took a rifle down from a rack on the wall, loaded the chamber, and propped it against the face of the fireplace, within easy reach.

Her dress was ruined, and so was the camisole beneath. She took them both off and put on the only other gown she had on hand, the one she had worn to be married. She yearned to take a long, hot bath, to scrub away the look in Vance's eyes, the filthy trail of his touch, but that wasn't practical.

To keep herself occupied, she made biscuits, never straying too far from the rifle, and sliced salt pork taken from a chipped crockery jar. It seemed that a very long time had passed before she heard an approaching rider and knew that Luke had returned.

She rushed to wrench open the door, flung herself into his surprised embrace before he'd gotten halfway across the yard.

"Am I to conclude that I'm forgiven?" he asked.

Charity clung to him. Began to sob. "He was here."

Luke stiffened, held her away to look into her face. There wasn't a trace of a smile anywhere in him by then. "Who, Charity? Who was here?"

He knew before she answered, she could see that. She guessed he'd needed to hear it anyway. "Vance," she said.

Luke went white, and the aquamarine in his eyes sharpened to a color that could cut through bone. "What happened? Are you hurt?"

She shook her head. Then, grasping his hand, she pulled him into the cabin, into the negligible shelter of four walls and a roof, and showed him the dress and camisole, before stuffing them into the cookstove to burn. Showed him the red scratch the point of Vance's knife had made.

He traced its path from the hollow of her throat to the middle of her belly with the tip of one finger. Then, without saying another word, he checked the pistol on his hip, to make sure it was loaded, and stormed out of the cabin, slamming the door shut behind him.

15

Charity caught up to Luke in the dooryard of the cabin, grasped at his arm, was shaken off in a single, furious motion. He whistled through his teeth for the pinto, already far away, and the beast raised its head from the sweet grass, pricked its ears at the sound. Perhaps sensing its master's fury, the horse hesitated.

"Luke." Charity took his arm again, and held on with all the determination Jonah had passed down to her, but this time she was standing so close that he could not throw her off without hurting her. She felt his muscles go rigid beneath her palms and fingers. "Listen to me. There were five men with Vance—you can't go after him alone. That's just what he wants you to do, isn't it? Luke, have you forgotten—these are the same people who nearly beat you to death. They thought they'd killed you, and now they want to finish the job."

His face was stiff, hard, the face of a stranger, not the man who had held her so tenderly in the night. "I'm not afraid of Vance."

She spoke softly. Swiftly. "Then you're a fool. He's a killer, Luke. He's set a trap for you, and he's trying to use me as the bait. Maybe you're willing to let that happen, but I'm not."

A muscle in his cheek knotted as he ground his back teeth. His gaze, every bit as cold as Vance's had been, was fixed on the tree line, as though he could see the shades of his half-brother and the others, mounted on their ill-kept horses, vanishing into the woods. A sheen glittered in his eyes, was blinked away.

"You're right," he said, but each word seemed torn from him, like a strip of hide. Then, in a raw whisper, "You're right."

She moved in front of him, slipped her arms around his waist. Only when he relaxed in her embrace a little did she put the question that was uppermost in her mind. "Why did Vance come here, Luke?"

He met her eyes, but his expression was hardly less forbidding than before. "He and I have something to settle. That's all you need to know right now."

"It isn't," Charity replied, but she had no intention of pursuing an argument just then. Luke was still with her and for the moment that was victory enough. Gently, carefully, one arm loosely around his waist, she steered him back toward the cabin. It was cool and quiet inside, a tiny fortress, a refuge that was theirs alone.

"Give me the gunbelt," she said, holding out one hand. She felt his heat and his weight, standing there facing him, even though they weren't touching. The sensation rushed through her, a burning ache, and she stiffened her knees to steady herself.

Luke regarded her for a long, pensive moment, then sighed, unbuckled the belt, and handed it over, .45 and all. It was unbelievably heavy, that weapon, but he clearly didn't feel as though he'd been relieved of a burden.

"Now," she said, when he didn't speak. "Sit down."

He dragged one of the upended crates back from the spool-table and sat. His eyes still snapped with fury and as he gazed at Charity, he seemed to be daring her to suggest something better to do than go out and kill his half-brother.

She stood behind him, laid her hands to the place where his neck and shoulders met, and began to knead the ungiving muscles with strong, persistent fingers. Slowly, grudgingly, he began to relax under her attentions, in spite of himself.

She bent once, and kissed the top of his golden head. "I suppose I can assume," she ventured, when some considerable time had passed, "that you and Raoul managed to settle your differences in a sensible fashion?"

Luke rolled his head and made a low, lusty sound of enjoyment somewhere in the depths of his throat. "Montego is alive and well," he said. "Well, all right, alive."

"I hope you didn't hurt him."

"How do you know he didn't hurt me?" There was a teasing note in his voice, though she sensed that he still hadn't come all the way back from that inner place where his rage had taken him earlier.

She leaned down again, and kissed the side of his neck. "Did he?" she countered lightly. The muscles in his shoulders were more pliant now, and he allowed his spine to curve a little. Then, in one easy, unexpected motion, he pulled her down onto his lap. "If I said yes," he drawled, raising both eyebrows, "would you feel called upon to soothe me?"

With as little effort as that, he'd aroused her. The need of him pulsed everywhere inside her, and his own desire rose hard and high against her hip. "Maybe," she replied. "Of course, it's still light outside and everything."

He chuckled. Using one hand, he began opening the buttons at the front of her dress; her wedding gown. His voice was low, sleepy and slow. "What does that have to do with anything?"

"Well, I just thought...maybe we should wait until it got dark—" Why, she wondered, even as the words came out of her mouth, was she saying that? If she had to wait, she would die. She would flare up and burn, like a single broom straw held to the flame of a candle.

Luke uncovered one of her breasts, caressed its peak with the hardened pad of his thumb, smiled at its instant obedience. "We're going to start now," he said, almost as an afterthought, just before he ducked his head and took the nipple into his mouth.

Charity cried out in delighted alarm and rose a little way off his lap; he pressed her down again, with a motion of one hand, and continued to suckle. She plunged all ten fingers into his hair, held him so tightly to her that she could feel the contours of his skull. "The window...is uncovered—" she gasped.

Luke released her nipple, only to lash it mischievously with the tip of his tongue.

Then, with a philosophical sigh, he rose from the apple crate, bringing her with him, carrying her to the bed.

He laid her there, then went to the cabin's only window, and covered it with an empty burlap sack. He kicked off his boots and shed his clothes as he crossed to her, leaving a trail of garments behind. Reaching the bed-side again, he removed her shoes, unrolled her stockings, pulled down her drawers and tossed them away. She trembled as he paused to stroke the insides of her thighs, made no sound of protest when he slipped the dress off over her head. She was naked then, for she had not put on another camisole after shedding the one Vance had torn.

Kneeling astride her, Luke leaned down and laid his lips lightly to that place just beneath her throat, where the line Vance had carved into her flesh began. With just the tip of his tongue, and in no discernible hurry, he traced the passage of the mark down between her breasts and over her belly, healing it with his notice and his breath.

Charity moaned and arched her back, a pagan priestess offering herself in sacrifice, and he slipped one hand under her buttocks as he kissed the hollows of her hipbones. Then he raised her up, nuzzled his way in, and feasted. There was nothing tentative, nothing gentle about the exchange; he wanted to consume her and she, alternately sobbing and gasping, wanted to be consumed.

He brought her to the brink of sweet cataclysm, then kissed his way back up the length of her body to her mouth. Feverish, she tasted herself on his mouth as he kissed her.

"I need to be inside you," he whispered. He lay between her legs; she felt him seeking the place of entrance, finding it, hesitating at the threshold.

She nodded, and he accepted the invitation with a single, powerful thrust of his hips. They moved together, as one, their pace increasing each time they met in the most intimate place, the furthest reaches of Charity's straining body. Their satisfaction was simultaneous, a fiery collision, full of sound and fury.

When it was over at last, when they had both slid, clutching, slippery-fleshed and breathless, from the heights, to lie curled together in the crater they'd made in the feather mattress, Charity was encompassed by a state of blissful exhaustion.

Luke held her tenderly, as though she were some fragile thing, fallen broken-winged from a dark and raging sky. He murmured words that made no sense, and she was comforted, even in the violence of her joy.

She could barely keep her eyes open— dreams pulled at her from below, dragging her down and down, toward the blessed solace of sleep—but after a little while she began to tell him what she had learned that day about Jonah, about her mother.

He listened and, more importantly, he heard. He kissed her eyelids closed, and told her that everything would be all right. He bade her rest and she gave herself up to sweet oblivion, lying safe and spent in his arms.

She was aware first of the stillness of gathering night, when she began to rise out of that deep slumber, and before she opened her eyes, Charity knew that she'd been had, in both senses of the term. Luke had gone, leaving the loaded shotgun beside her, in his place, and she felt his absence like a blow.

Shifting onto her back, tangled in strands of her own waist-length hair, like a fish caught in a net, she bit down hard on her lower lip to keep from crying. She had been changed, transported, mended by their lovemaking, but the experience had probably been nothing more to Luke than a calculated seduction. He'd known, damn him, that he could melt her, with his hands, his lips, his promises, that he could render her boneless, blind her with sleep—and then go merrily about his deadly business, without interference.

Sniffling, Charity wriggled out of bed and put on her discarded wedding dress. By now, Luke was God-knew-where, chasing a band of outlaws by himself, too proud and stupid to ask for help in town, or at the Double B. Searching for him would be an exercise in futility; she knew by the quality of the emptiness in that cabin that he'd been gone a long while. He was probably miles away.

Wrapped in her wedding gown, now beginning to look a bit bedraggled, Charity found her way to the table, struck a match, and lit a kerosene lantern. The shadows receded a little, but the gloom was dense, and her senses, having been sent spinning earlier, were still out of kilter.

When her eyes had adjusted, she saw the note propped on the fireplace mantel, and snatched it down.

Sorry, Luke had written. *Bolt the door.* That was all; no salutation, no explanation and certainly no "love, Luke." The word "sorry," written in his bold, strong letters, contained nothing of contrition.

She crumpled the paper and tossed it onto the cold grate, then shuffled over to the door and pulled the latch bar into place. Some husband, some protector Luke Shardlow made, riding off and leaving her to defend herself. Her utter conviction that she could do just that did nothing to calm her rising temper; she'd been tricked, made to willingly—*eagerly*—participate in her own deception, and the realization stung like a slap.

"Fool," she chided herself. She put on the dress, then found her hairbrush and began to subdue her wild mane with long and angry strokes. When the snarls were gone—the brisk exercise of the task calmed her somewhat—she made a single thick braid and secured the plait with a small ribbon. She promised herself that when Luke came home—she was afraid to consider the possibility, even for a moment, that he might never return—she would give him a piece of her mind.

The prospect of vindication offered small comfort, as the evening wore on and there was no sign of Luke. Charity made a scant meal of tinned meat and coffee, then paced back and forth in front of the hearth, filled with that ancient and singular agitation of a woman waiting for a man who should have reappeared hours before.

The lamp was burning low when she heard the sound of an approaching horse and rushed toward the door. She had her hand on the latch, ready to raise it, when it came to her that the rider might not be Luke. Returning to the bed, she took up the shotgun, then went to the window and pushed the burlap curtain aside.

At first she did not recognize the lone rider just swinging down from the saddle, for it was late and the moon, swathed in clouds, gave thin light. All she knew was that it wasn't Luke, and her disappointment was profound, and prickled behind her eyes and at the back of her throat like nettles. When the visitor drew nearer, and she could see his face, she nearly cried out in despair.

Marshal Higgins approached the door. At that hour, he surely bore bad tidings.

Charity set the shotgun aside with haste, and had the door open before the lawman had contrived to knock. "What is it?" she said. "Luke—my father?"

He looked at her in silence for a long time, and her heartbeat got faster and louder with every passing second until her own pulse seemed to pound at her from outside her skin.

"Tell me!" she finally demanded, unable to bear the waiting any longer.

Higgins eased her back over the threshold, guided her to a seat. "I'm afraid it's Luke," he said quietly. "He's been hurt pretty bad, and he's calling for you."

She sprang off the apple crate, fluttered from one place to another, frenzied, accomplishing nothing. "Where is he? What's happened? Take me to him, right now!"

The marshal finally stopped her, taking her upper arms into his hands. It was too intimate, too familiar, a gesture she would not have permitted under other circumstances. She saw his throat move as he swallowed. "He was shot."

The words seemed to tear through her flesh, to splinter inside her, sundering, severing, burning, like the bullets that had felled Luke. "Take me to him," she reiterated, and he nodded.

Later, she would have no memory of finding and saddling Taffeta—Higgins had probably done that—or of the headlong ride into the heavy summer darkness. The marshal led the way, and she followed in heedless, unquestioning fright.

She had lived in those parts all her life, and she knew them well, from the days when she had worked with Jonah and rambled near and far with Raoul, and yet she might have been in another country that night, or even another world. Her thoughts had gone ahead, seeking Luke, and she paid little attention to landmarks, could not have retraced her path. Only when she saw the tent up ahead, glowing golden, with moving shadows inside, did she begin to suspect that she would not find Luke in this place.

She reined in and turned to the marshal in outraged amazement when a familiar figure came out of the tent. *Vance.* Marshal Higgins, a man she had every reason to trust, had led her to Vance. There was a moment of fierce relief—Luke was surely unharmed—amidst a maelstrom of less pleasant emotions.

"Why?" she whispered.

"Don't bother your head about it," the lawman answered, reaching over and taking hold of Taffeta's bridle an instant before Charity would have spun the horse around and fled. "Once we've got him, we'll let you go."

Charity clung to her saddle horn, her palms sweating, as Vance ambled toward them. She knew the marshal's promise for a lie, of course; she was a mere drawing card, a pawn, and once she'd served the obvious purpose, she would be raped and killed. That didn't bother her nearly as much as the sure and certain knowledge that Luke would come for her, and get himself shot—for real—in the process.

Vance reached up and offered his hand, for all the world like a country gentleman welcoming a neighbor on the lawn of a mansion. Charity slipped her foot out of the stirrup and planted it squarely in the hollow of his throat, heel first, and he stumbled backwards from the force of the impact, spitting swear words and, she hoped, blood.

"Damn idiot woman," the marshal fretted. Vance had recovered himself by then, and was advancing again. Higgins stepped between them, the reins of Charity's horse wrapped securely around the fingers of one hand. "Take it easy, Vance," he cajoled. "She'll be no use to us if you take her apart now."

Vance rolled to a stop. "Get her down," he said reluctantly.

Charity clung to the saddle horn, trying to kick again, but it was no use. Higgins still had the reins, and he was much stronger. He curved an arm around her waist, swearing, and hauled her down off the horse, holding her backwards against his chest.

"Did you show my brother the message I left for him?" Vance asked, in a lascivious drawl. He sounded gruff, and Charity hoped she'd get another chance to cave in his voice box.

A tremor went through her, of fear, of anger. She spat in his face.

Before the marshal could intercede again, Vance had backhanded her so hard that Higgins, still holding her, nearly lost his footing. Taffeta whinnied and pranced behind them, ready to bolt.

The pain of the slap was brief but searing; it brought blood rushing to her head, though, and cleared her mind. She sagged against the marshal, letting Vance think he'd knocked her unconscious, and when he moved in to grab her and wrench her out of Higgins's grasp, she brought her knee up between his legs with all the force she could summon.

Vance screamed and doubled over, and his cry brought the others running from in and around the tent.

"Damn it all to hell," complained the marshal. "You got more guts than sense, lady."

After a few moments of retching and groaning, Vance straightened his spine, and his eyes glittered in the darkness as he unsheathed his knife. "I'm gonna kill her," he vowed. "Right here, right now."

"No, Vance." It was one of the other men, drawn close, features hidden in shadow. Nonetheless, Charity recognized the man as Hector Tillmont, the recently dismissed foreman of the Double B. His presence answered a lot of questions. "We need her. Until we've got Luke, until we *know* he's dead, we can't touch her."

"I don't like this," another outlaw contributed. "He's one crazy son-of-a-bitch, Luke Shardlow is. I heard he skinned a man once, down in Nogales, just for beating up a whore out back of a saloon one night."

Vance made a pitiful attempt at laughter and spat. "Luke? He hasn't got the stomach for killin'."

"I didn't say he kilt the feller," the other man insisted. "I said he skinned him. There's a difference."

Charity felt her stomach roll, but now that her head was cooler, she'd stopped struggling. If there was any hope of escaping, of intercepting Luke, it lay in her ability to stay calm and think straight. She'd wasted a lot of energy, striking out at Vance, but she wouldn't make that mistake again.

Vance traced her jawline with the side of his knife. "Take her into the shed and tie her up," he said. "We know she enjoys keeping company with rats." He cast a look around him. "And keep your hands to yourselves. One of you touches her improper-like, I'll cut your fingers off."

Suddenly, she was lightheaded again. They'd brought her to a tumbledown shack at the base of a hill, just outside one of the mines her father had closed down years before—she was at home, on the Double B. The irony of that brought bile surging into the back of her throat. Luke, she knew, had found the body of the man called Andrews here, hanging from a tree branch, and he was certain to guess where she was being held. *Stay away,* she pleaded silently, but the certainty that he would come was a solid weight within her.

Higgins stayed behind to argue with Vance while two of the outlaws took her by the arms and thrust her toward the shack. The others returned to the tent. It would be darker than dark inside that cabin, Charity reflected miserably, as she stumbled along. She resisted a frantic urge to dig her heels in and fight against being imprisoned in such a place, against what might happen to her there, and walked with her eyes closed, counting her heartbeats, finding courage in the spaces between.

A chill rushed out of the windowless box to

greet her, enfold her, pull her forward, like some mythic beast with tentacles and claws. She raised her chin and contained her rising fear within a thin-walled silence.

"That weren't no yarn about Shardlow peelin' that poor bastard alive, down there at Nogales," one of her escorts muttered. "It happened, Wylie."

"I know it," the other answered bleakly.

"He'll probably do the same thing to you," Charity put in, her tone deliberately light and cheerful. She didn't believe the skinning story for a moment; in fact, she was pretty sure Luke himself had been the one to put it around, but it might serve a purpose. "Let me go and I'll take your part when the time comes. You might have a chance then. Otherwise, there'll be worse stories to tell, and they'll all be about you—each one bloodier than the last."

One of the outlaws shuddered, but the other one, Wylie, flung Charity over the threshold with a murmured curse. "There's only one man meaner than Luke Shardlow," he said. "And that's his big brother, Vance. You forget that, Ernie, and you'll suffer for it. We all will."

"Luke will kill Vance for sure," Charity said. Unlike the gruesome Nogales myth, she thought grimly, that statement was undoubtedly true. "Then you'll be easy pickings."

"Shut up," barked Wylie. He wrenched Charity's hands behind her back and bound them with a strand of rawhide, pulled painfully tight. "Damnation, but you yammer more than any ten women I ever knowed. Get out the way, Ernie. How you expect me to get past, when you're standin' there like a barn door?"

"I'm ridin' out of here afore daybreak," said Ernie, but he stepped aside.

"You ain't neither," Wylie replied, unruffled. "Get me a lantern from the tent. I don't want to fall through the floorboards and break my neck."

Charity held her tongue while Ernie went to fetch a light. Obviously, Wylie wasn't as easily swayed as his friend. All too soon, Ernie returned, and the glow of the lantern offered no solace at all. The place was filthy, and there was a rat-chewed mattress ticking in the middle of the floor. Vance, Charity knew, had specific—and very ugly—plans for her, though he meant to kill Luke first.

Wylie flung her onto the mattress, her hands still bound. Her head struck the floor with bruising force, and she bit her tongue in the fall.

"You just lie there, little lady, and think about entertainin' visitors."

Charity wanted to vomit, but she controlled herself. She had to stay calm, think clearly. Be ready for a chance to escape and warn Luke.

Fear bit into the very marrow of her bones, and she was almost as afraid of being left alone in the dark, with the rodents and spiders, as she was of Vance and his men. She could barely breathe, and the sensation was like being buried alive.

"We'll be back," Wylie said, holding the inadequate lantern high, casting looming shadows all around. Charity heard rustling and saw the gleam of little eyes in the gloom, feral and patient. "You can be sure o' that."

"We can leave her the lamp, though, can't we?" Ernie asked. He was looking around nervously, as though he expected a demon or a mama bear to come howling out of a murky corner.

Wylie punched him hard in the arm. "This ain't no fancy ranch house."

Charity had to use all the fortitude she possessed to keep from begging them not to leave her there, in the dark, not to hurt Luke, not to hurt *her*. She bit down on her lip and tasted blood.

Wylie set the lantern carefully on the floor, evidently not trusting Ernie with it, and, pulling another strip of leather from the pocket of his shirt, hunkered down to pull off Charity's shoes and bind her ankles together. "You be real good," he crooned, patting her thigh, "and we'll come back for you."

"You *touched* her," Ernie accused, pointing. "You heard what Vance said about that."

"You ain't gonna tell," said Wylie, with a knowing grin, standing upright again. He leaned down and reclaimed the lamp.

"She's got a shiner comin' on, where Vance hit her," Ernie remarked. "Shardlow will be pissed when he sees that. Real pissed."

"Come on," Wylie said. "He'll be dead before he sees much of anything." Holding the

306

lantern aloft, he led the way out, and Ernie hurried after him, stopping in the glare of the doorway and casting one worried glance over his shoulder before he closed Charity in.

Once again, Charity struggled with rising panic. The darkness was so utterly complete that it made no difference at all whether her eyes were open or closed. She thought of Luke dying, and terror welled up within her. She passed the next five minutes or so battling back an urge to scream her throat raw.

She had barely mastered that ordeal when something skittered nearby, and fresh hysteria washed through her. She flailed wildly, in an effort to break free, but the bonds on her hands and ankles only tightened, and chewed more deeply, more cruelly, into her flesh. Common sense, eventually prevailed, and she persuaded herself to lie still, to breathe deeply, despite the moldering stink of the place, to think.

Luke left the pinto far back in the woods, reins dangling, and picked his way back to the edge of the clearing. There was a light burning inside the tent, and he could see the shadows of three men inside, playing cards. Two more stood guard outside the shack, arguing between themselves, and there was another with Vance, near the cook fire.

He pondered that. Apparently, Vance had already recruited a replacement for the dead Andrews. He thought he knew who it was, but at the moment he didn't care. They had

Charity, he had no doubt of that, and it was no great mental leap to figure out that she was inside the cabin. He also knew that she was relatively safe, for the moment at least. As long as he stayed alive, she would too. If, on the other hand, he was killed, as Vance surely intended, Charity was doomed.

He closed his eyes briefly. He'd dealt with other situations like this one many times, but there had never been quite so much at stake before.

Somewhere in the distance, a wolf howled. Vance raised his head at the sound, and a spark spiraled into the fire as he tossed down a cheroot. Luke sighed to himself; his half-brother feared wolves, feared so many things.

He moved back into the shelter of the trees. The horses were in a ramuda well back of the tent; he would start with a small stampede, he decided, and proceed from there.

The horses were easy to spook; he found a piece of dried wood on the ground, plunged it into a spill of pitch oozing out of a big pine, and struck a match to it. He flung the flaming brand into the middle of the impro-vised corral, Indian-style, and widespread consternation ensued. The animals tore down the ropes and scattered in every direction, ter-rified, but unhurt.

Vance broke into a run, though he moved with a peculiar limping hop, and the card players in the tent scrambled for the flap, but they were too slow, too frantic. Several of the escaping horses passed too close, and brought the canvas roof down onto the men's heads. While they flailed and bellowed curses, prayers and imprecations, the lantern must have tipped over, spilling kerosene and flame, because the tent went up with a memorable *whoosh*. After that, the boys inside grew more enterprising, and erupted through the burning sides, howling and rolling in the dirt to extinguish the scattered tongues of fire on their clothing.

Vance and Higgins were busy trying to catch the horses, and the other two had abandoned their lantern on an outcropping of rock next to the cabin to bolt into the heart of chaos. Luke made for the door of the shack, the .45 as at home in his left hand as any of his fingers.

He waited in the shadows, his back pressed against the wall of the shed.

"God damn it, you idiots," Vance roared, "he's here—he's here someplace, lookin' for the woman!"

Luke smiled grimly, cocked the .45. *Your move, brother,* he thought.

"Find him, damn it!" shouted Vance, running in six directions at once. "He'll head for the cabin!"

Nobody seemed to be paying much mind to their leader's commands; bullets flew in all directions, and Luke wasn't particularly worried about out-thinking this tribe of idiots. Hell, left to themselves, they'd kill each other.

No, it was the steep slope looming above the shack that troubled him; stones, dislodged by all the shooting, were already tumbling down like hail, pounding at the flimsy roof. Sweat broke out on Luke's upper lip as he made his way quickly along the cabin wall toward the door.

Hold on, Charity, he thought. *Hold on.*

16

Charity didn't waste a moment wondering about the thunderous downpour battering the roof over her head; she'd grown up around mines and mining, and she knew all too well what was happening. All that gunplay out there had loosened stones and dirt already undermined by years of digging and blasting. She was about to be buried alive, and with her hands and feet bound, she was helpless to escape.

All the same, she had to try. She rolled off the stinking mattress onto the splintery, debris-strewn floor, sat up, and tried to inch her way in the direction of the door. The problem was, she didn't know exactly where the door *was,* since the cabin was dark as the inside of a cow's belly.

Luke was out there somewhere; she knew that much, and he was most likely alone. Vance and the others could easily kill him; they'd lured him there for exactly that purpose. Hope and dismay did battle in her mind, equally weighted.

It was happening just as Vance had planned. Luke, the predator until now, had deliberately made himself the prey. For her. She bent double on that filth-strewn floor, eyes squeezed shut. The pain spawned by the mere prospect of Luke's capture or death was a thousand times what she felt in her wrists and ankles, where the rawhide strips were digging in deeper with every passing moment.

Stones continued to hammer at the roof, and several fell through, clattering on the wooden floor. Charity screamed, and in the same moment, the door sprang open, spilling thin light and a stumbling Luke over the threshold.

Without a word, he leaned down, closed his right arm around her waist, and hauled her to her feet. When she tripped, he realized her ankles were bound, as well as her wrists, and hoisted her against his side like an armload of books.

Under any other circumstances, Charity would have protested volubly, for the position was most uncomfortable, and it didn't help that Luke's .45 was in his free hand, mere inches from her head. It spat bullets even as the hillside rolled down behind them with a deafening roar. The air was so full of dust and dirt that she choked on every breath.

Some twenty feet from the shack—she didn't need to look back to know the place was crushed to splinters by then—Luke dumped her onto the ground, hunkered down to cut the ties from her hands and feet with a pocket knife. Then, taking her elbow, he flung her to her feet again and yelled, "Run!"

311

She stared at him stupidly for a few moments, amazed to find herself in such a ludicrous situation.

"I said *run!*" Luke bellowed.

She ran, heedless of the bands of pain left on her flesh by the rawhide ties. "The others—"

"Damn the others," Luke retorted. "Keep running."

Thunder rolled beneath the land, as if pursuing them, raising a fog of dirt all around, and they kept going, long past the point of collapse. Through the noise, she could hear, just faintly, the confused cries of the men they'd left behind.

Charity felt as though her heart would burst from the exertion when Luke finally lunged to the ground, taking her with him, covering her with his body.

The worst of it came then, the terrible tremors beneath the grass and topsoil, beneath the layers of rock and clay, seemed to crack the surface like an eggshell. Charity lay there beneath Luke, certain that they were about to die after all.

Maybe it was a minute later, maybe it was an hour, but the blessed silence came at last. Luke rolled over onto his back and stared up at the star-strewn sky, Charity alternately choked and sobbed.

"You could have been killed!" she cried.

He sat up, drew her into his arms, kissed the top of her head. "But I wasn't, and neither were you. Come on." He got to his feet and pulled Charity after him. "We'd better find the

312

horses and get you out of here before Vance figures out that we aren't under that pile of dirt. I'll come back and deal with him once I know you're safe on the Double B."

"How did you know?" Charity coughed, as Luke gave a low whistle through his teeth. "That I was in trouble, I mean?"

"When I got back, and you were gone, I looked for tracks and followed them here. It didn't exactly take a scholar to figure it out."

The spotted horse came out of the brush just then, reins dangling, saddle slightly askew. Luke grinned and patted the animal affectionately on its lathered neck.

"I thought you were off—"

"Off doing what?" Luke asked, securing the saddle and then helping Charity up into it before swinging on behind her. His arms were strong around her as he gripped the reins.

"Killing Raoul," she answered, only half in jest.

Luke's chuckle sounded hoarse. "Don't worry. Your friend is fine." He spurred the pinto into a lope, and his embrace tightened a little.

She turned to look up into his dusty face. "I was scared," she confessed, in a small voice.

He grinned and kissed the tip of her nose. "Just goes to show that you're a right smart female," he replied.

Hector Tillmont's betrayal hadn't really surprised Charity, for she'd never liked him, but Mr. Higgins's perfidy was quite another matter. The marshal was well-liked in Jubilee,

313

duly sworn and appointed to uphold the law; she knew her father trusted him, as did Ben Draper and a number of other astute men. The discovery that they'd all been wrong was disillusioning.

"Do you think Vance is dead?" she ventured.

"I couldn't be that lucky," he answered dryly. Then he leaned a little and kissed her left ear. "Let's discuss this some other time," he said. "Right now, I've got to get you home."

"My horse," Charity lamented, "is probably halfway to Canada by now."

Luke chuckled. "I don't mind sharing," he said magnanimously.

She rested the back of her head against his shoulder then, too worn out to talk or even think beyond the simplest things, like keeping her seat on the horse.

Luke too was silent but, presently, she began to sense a wild, restrained energy in him, and she knew his mind, engaged in some complicated plan, had long since left her behind.

It took more time than usual to reach the ranch house at the Double B, since they stayed off the main roads, and by the time Luke lifted Charity down from the saddle, she could hardly keep her eyes open. "Why are we here?"

He raised her into his arms with a groan that was uncalled-for, and she remembered fuzzily that she'd long since lost her shoes. "Try to keep up, darlin'," he teased, carrying her through the gate and up the shadowy walk toward the porch. "We're here because if we go back to the cabin, by now, Vance will have guessed that we're alive, and he'll be madder than a grizzly with a hornet up its—-" He paused, cleared his throat, and actually blushed a little. "My brother will be out for blood after this. And I don't want it to be yours."

She blinked. She was dirty and bruised, and her wrists and ankles burned painfully, but she was alive, and Luke was alive, and she was anything but defeated. "You don't expect me to hide?"

He maneuvered to reach for the door knob, then gave the door a vicarious nudge with Charity's left hip. It swung open with a slow squeal. The entryway was as dark as the inside of the shack that had so nearly become her coffin.

"Stop right there," said a female voice. The command was punctuated by the sharp, distinctive sound of a rifle being cocked. Apparently, Charity thought, Genesis could shoot, in addition to her other talents.

Luke gave a long-suffering sigh. "Tell her," he said, giving Charity a little jiggle, as if to jar her into cooperating.

"It's me, Genesis," she said wearily. "Charity. Luke—my husband—is with me."

They were still while Jonah's nurse found a lamp and struck a match to light it. The shotgun dangled from one large hand as she assessed them, frowning. "Lordy," she finally huffed, "what *happened* to you folks? A body could hardly recognize the pair of you, you look such a sight."

"We were set upon by road agents," Luke said, with comical formality.

Charity laughed, even though there wasn't one thing funny about the situation. She knew well enough that Luke planned to deposit her there, in the perceived safety of her father's house, and go after Vance in earnest. He might have been putting on a jovial front, but inside, Luke was coldly furious, and that frightened Charity more than anything that had happened that night.

"What did they do?" Genesis asked, keeping pace as Luke carried Charity up the stairs. "Drag you through a mud-hole?"

"They tried to drop a mountain on us," Luke replied. "Where's your room, Charity?"

"Put me down," Charity retorted. "I'm not an invalid, you know."

"I like the way you feel in my arms," he said, and kept walking. Genesis might not have been there at all. "You're pretty solid. About like a yearling calf."

"I'm too tired to hit you for that," Charity replied, "but you may be sure I won't forget that you said it. I don't want to go into my bedroom, covered with grime, and you're not going to, either. We've got to have baths."

Luke made a growling sound, low in his throat, and chuckled when she elbowed him in retribution. "'Baths'?" he mocked. "Sounds extravagant. We'll share."

"We will not."

"Want to make a bet?"

"Yesterday you wouldn't sleep in this house.

Now you're willing to—" She lowered her voice, remembering Genesis's dogged presence, "bathe here? With—with me?"

"We're married, aren't we?"

"Yes, but you said—"

"I said I wouldn't sleep here. I didn't say I wouldn't avail myself of a fine tub and hot water."

"Then you're leaving?" Charity didn't know why she'd asked the question at all, since she already knew the answer. She fought down a desperate urge to cling to Luke's neck and beg him to stay with her, at least until the sun was up and the world was recognizable again.

Genesis led the way into the bathroom, set the lamp down, and busied herself making a fire in the small burner under the inside water tank. Luke set Charity on the lid of the commode and squatted to examine her injured wrists and ankles, a task made difficult by the multiple layers of dirt that covered her skin.

"He wants to kill you!"

He sighed. "I think that's obvious," he said. Then he rose, found a washcloth, and soaked it under the single spigot in the basin. Lowering himself gracefully to one knee, he began to clean her wounds. Even in that poor light, she saw him turn pale when he got a close look at what the rawhide bands had done, saw his jaw tighten with resolve and knew that his eyes burned with banked fury. Maybe that awful story about him skinning a man in Nogales was true after all.

Charity had been in a daze those past few

minutes; she'd forgotten Jonah, forgotten his illness, forgotten the discovery she'd made, only that day, that he had lied to her, let her think she was motherless all those years. It would probably take a long while to work through that; she'd begin in the morning, when she hoped she'd be able to think clearly again. She gave a soft cry.

"Take it easy, sweetheart," Luke said. "You don't want to wake your father."

"Gabriel's trumpet wouldn't wake that man," Genesis said cheerfully. She had the fire going and was turning the valve that would send more water pouring into the tank from its larger counterpart on the roof. "He's tuckered plum out. All that walking around and shooting and everything."

Charity flinched and bit her lip as Luke continued to clean her cuts. They burned like thin strands of fire, wrapped around and pulled tight.

"You folks need anything to eat?" Genesis asked. "I could go downstairs and rustle up some leftovers from supper."

Luke looked at Charity, his eyes dancing in his dirt-masked face. "You hungry, Mrs. Shardlow?" he asked. When she shook her head, he addressed his words to Genesis. "No, thanks, ma'am. But we could use something to paint on these cuts and a few strips of cloth for bandages."

"Don't be silly," Charity said. "I'm perfectly fine."

"Whiskey will do," Luke went on, as if she

318

hadn't spoken, "if you haven't got anything else."

Genesis bustled out, apparently untroubled by the fact that it was the middle of the night. She had the air of a person who would be returning soon, bringing medicines that were guaranteed to sting like the very blazes of hell.

Luke stood up, assessed the water tank next to the tub, and shook his head in good-natured amazement. "What a contraption. Makes a man wonder what they'll invent next, doesn't it?"

"I wouldn't know," Charity answered, exasperated and bone weary. "I'm not a man."

He laughed. "No, indeed, Mrs. Shardlow, you are pure woman and that is a fact." He perched on the edge of the tub. "Now, tell me, if you will, what possessed you to go rushing off with Dan Higgins at a time when all God-fearing people are sound asleep?"

"You weren't sound asleep," she interjected, peevish because she sensed a lecture coming on and she wasn't up to fighting back.

"Never mind what I was doing."

She sighed. "Higgins said you'd been shot." Her eyes filled with tears at the memory. "Naturally, I believed him—anyone would have."

Luke leaned forward, and their gritty foreheads touched. "It was a trick," he whispered, as if imparting a great secret.

Charity might have shoved him backwards into the empty tub if she hadn't been so glad he was still breathing. "How was I supposed to know that? He's the marshal, for pity's sake. And if there was ever a man hell-bent on getting himself shot, you're him."

He kissed her, very lightly, very briefly. "I guess I might have made the same mistake," he admitted. "But from now on, we're not taking any chances. You're to stay right here, Charity, and lay low, no matter what you hear, until I've got Vance and Higgins and all the rest of them."

"I could get old and gray-headed waiting for that to happen."

He laughed again. "Thanks for your vote of confidence," he said. He touched her nose with the tip of one finger. "You're going to be a really mean old lady. But you *will* be an old lady—I intend to see to that. Now, stop talking, stop worrying, and let me take care of you."

Genesis returned with a shredded dish towel and a pint of rye whiskey. "Good night," she said brightly, and went her way.

Luke set the medical supplies aside, presumably for after the bath, and assessed the attending apparatus with a pensive frown. "How do you work this thing?"

Charity showed him, and soon the water was steaming hot and the tub was full and they were both lowering themselves in. They let the tank fill again and kept the burner going, knowing it would take more than one scrubbing to get down to bare skin.

They washed each other, Charity employing great industry, Luke working gently, with

320

the tenderest care. They drained the huge tub, rinsed it clean, and started all over again, repeating the whole process. After drying off with a similar ritual, Luke seated Charity on the commode seat once more and doused the lacerations with whiskey. She cried, because she'd had an incredibly long and difficult day, because she was tired and it hurt. Because she knew Luke would leave her alone soon, and that this time he might not come back.

"Stay with me," she said, with quavering dignity. "Just this one night."

Luke wrapped a towel around his middle, loincloth fashion, and pondered his ruined clothes. "I don't think I could bring myself to put these things back on even if it meant losing Vance's trail for good," he said thoughtfully. He was pretending he hadn't heard her injunction, and she didn't intend to let him get away with it.

"Luke," she insisted. "It makes no sense to go out again. What can you accomplish in the dark?"

"I did plenty of damage tonight," he said lightly.

"Are you going to make me beg?"

He laughed and cupped a hand under her chin. "I love it when you beg," he said. "But not in this context. I'll stay, sweetheart, just until daylight. Do you think any of Jonah's gear would fit me?"

Charity was so relieved that, for a few moments, she couldn't answer him. "He's—he's a little heavier than you are," she replied at last. "Maybe he's kept some things from a few years back. I'll check the cedar chest in his room." Since Jonah was now sleeping downstairs, they could enter the master bedroom without disturbing anyone.

After putting on a wrapper she'd left on a hook behind the bathroom door, Charity led the way down the corridor, carrying the lantern Genesis had used to light their way up the stairs earlier that night. Luke, of course, was still wearing the towel.

In the small dressing room off Jonah's bedchamber stood several sturdy chests. Blaise kept her things in her own room, at the opposite end of the hall, and yet the air smelled faintly of perfume and powder. The scent brought Rianna, her mother, back from the far reaches of her mind with a cruel clarity.

"He's never really let go of her," Charity reflected, and did not realize she'd spoken aloud until Luke replied.

"That's not surprising, considering the lengths he went to, trying to keep her here," he said. His voice was quiet, unhurried. Would Luke ever think of her, Charity, when the agreed-upon year was up and he finally went away? Would he remember her scent, the color of her eyes, the sound of her laugh? He was a drifter, maybe even an outlaw, she reminded herself. He probably wouldn't even look back, let alone linger over her memory.

She opened one of the trunks, rummaged for a while, and finally brought out trousers, a shirt, suspenders, and a pair of much-darned stockings. In a corner, they found an array of boots, lined up like old soldiers, past their prime. "These look as though they'll fit," she said sadly. "You ought to try everything on, of course."

"Thanks," Luke replied, draping the garments over one arm. "Let's go to bed, darlin'. It's been a long, hard day."

Charity nodded, appropriated one pair of the boots, and set out for her bedroom. It was odd, bringing Luke into that fussy, feminine place—he seemed too big for it, as though he might bump his elbows against the walls if he moved his arms. The bed looked small, for a presence such as his, and she fully expected his feet to stick out past the end of the mattress.

He set the clothes across a chair, took the boots and put them on the floor. She was still holding the lamp, and he took that, too. Then he drew the covers back, courteously waiting for her to precede him. The lamp, burning low on the bedside table, cast a warm glow over the sheets and glinted in the soft hair on his chest.

Charity shed the wrapper, knowing he had no intention of making love to her under Jonah's roof, and slipped naked into bed. He had not bandaged the cuts on her wrists and ankles, but he clearly hadn't forgotten her injuries, because he treated her as though she were made of dried butterfly wings. After extinguishing the lamp, he joined her under the covers.

"What will you do when you capture Vance

and the others?" She didn't mention the other possibility—that he would be killed instead—because she couldn't bear to think about it anymore.

He was silent for a long time, and although he had put his arm around her, and drawn her close against his side, she had never felt less secure. When he spoke at last, she wished she hadn't prodded him for an answer. "Good night, Charity," he said gravely. It was what he left *unsaid* that hurt so much.

He did not kiss her, and when she awakened in the morning to find the sun well up in the sky, he was gone. Had been, probably, for hours.

She did not weep, fearing that if she started, she would never stop, but instead rose and dressed herself in a sensible cambric dress of dark blue. Her wedding gown was ruined, and she made up her mind to burn it in the kitchen stove, first thing after breakfast. It would be a gesture for her inner knowledge, symbolic of letting go, and moving on.

When Charity descended the stairs, she found her father in the dining room, seated in his wheeled chair, occupying his normal place at the head of the table. He wore Sunday garments, and his hair was carefully brushed.

Charity leaned down to kiss his cheek. "Good morning, Papa."

He might have been surprised to see her there, but if he was, his eyes revealed none of it. She had not seen him since the morning before, when he had sent her to find the letters another man had written to her mother, and he was watching her with an expression of wary hopelessness.

She took the chair to his right, which would normally have been Blaise's, and enfolded one of his hands in both of hers. "You should have told me about Mama," she said. "I had a right to know she was alive. You were wrong, Papa, about so many things. But I love you, and much as I missed having a mother, I'm glad I didn't have to leave the Double B. I forgive you—or at least I think I can, in time—but you mustn't ever deceive me like that again. I won't tolerate it."

Jonah closed his eyes, visibly relieved, and gave her a semblance of the old smile. "Luke?" he strained to say.

Charity didn't know exactly what to make of the inquiry. Jonah hadn't approved of her choice in husbands, though he had given her his blessing, however reluctantly, when she confided that she loved Luke. Now he seemed almost fond of him. "He's gone off chasing outlaws," she said, trying not to sound petulant. She wasn't about to explain what had happened at the mine shack, not yet, anyway; Jonah wasn't ready to hear that story.

Her father's heavy brows knitted together in a frown.

Charity poured coffee for herself and warmed up Jonah's half-finished cup. "When are you going to marry Blaise?" she asked bluntly.

Jonah's frown deepened. His throat moved, and so did his mouth, but no sound came out.

"Yes," put in a feminine voice, from the doorway. "When?"

Jonah blushed furiously as Blaise entered the room, looking elegant in a crisp brown sateen dress. On anyone else, the gown might have seemed dowdy, even grim; on Blaise, it was the perfect accent for her translucent complexion and bright hair.

"Never," he said clearly.

17

The borrowed boots pinched something fierce; for a big man, Luke reflected, Jonah had dainty feet. Every stitch he had on at the moment, in point of fact, had belonged to Jonah first, but the trousers and shirt were from years back, and thus fit fairly well.

He lay belly down on the ridge behind the defunct copper mine, the sun rising behind him, and watched as Vance's camp began to stir. The shack where Charity had been held captive was buried under a hundred tons of rock, and there was nothing left of the tent but a pile of charred rags and ashes. The men slept in twisted bundles of blanket, wherever there was a patch of bare ground. Two bodies lay covered in the back of a wagon—Hector Tillmont and another no-good thief he remembered from the night he'd been bushwhacked and beaten half to death next to the creek. It seemed to Luke that if you were going to shoot a man to death, deserving of the favor though he might be, you ought to at least know his name.

Luke waited idly, sighting the .45 in on his half-brother's ass, just for practice. Vance and the marshal, stretched out on either side of the dead fire, showed signs of life, but they were the last to rise.

Luke shook his head in mock censure; Vance just wasn't cut out for leadership. Evidently, he'd been so certain his prey hadn't escaped that he hadn't even troubled himself to post a lookout. Luke allowed himself a grin, though he knew he was tempting fate. The Good Book said it, and so had old Asa McCallum, to whom he owed his life—*pride goeth before a fall.*

He wondered if the nickel-plated star Higgins usually wore was the same one Asa had carried, way back when. That would indeed be a travesty, since Asa had been one of the finest men ever to pin on a badge.

Vance got up, finally, looking peaked and cradling his crotch in one hand. Luke smiled again; Charity had told him, while they were sharing Jonah's fancy bathtub, how she'd used her knee to defend herself. God in heaven, he was going to miss her when he went away—he'd never met another woman like her, and he didn't expect that he ever would.

The thought of leaving sobered him. He had to move on when the job was done, he'd known that all along; he couldn't build a life and a ranch and rear his children in a place where the Shardlow name meant drunkenness and thievery and murder, like it did in Jubilee. He was equally certain that Charity would not consent to go with him; her roots went down deep into the soil of the Double B, and she loved her father. Yet if he stayed—well, even being born a Barnham wouldn't save her from the scorn and scandal of a marriage to him.

He dried his forehead on his sleeve. True enough, most everybody for miles around knew he and Charity were married, small communities being what they were, but once he was gone, she could quietly divorce him, and tie the knot with Montego in a year or so. Between them, the bride and groom would have enough land, money and good breeding to overcome most any kind of disgrace, and in time the talk would die down.

He and Montego had planned the whole thing the day before, when the two of them were supposed to be on a knoll on the Draper ranch, killing each other in a shoot-out. By means of a lot of discussion and some yelling, they'd agreed that Raoul would wait a few months after Luke left, then start courting Charity again, just like nothing had happened. The very fact that the other man loved her enough to do that more than qualified him for the privilege, as far as Luke was concerned.

Not that it didn't make him half sick to think of her lying down with Raoul, or anybody else, every night for the rest of her life. He wanted her for himself, there was no denying that, wanted her in all the stages she would pass through in future years—swollen with pregnancy, nursing a baby at her breast, a young matron, a middle-aged woman tending to plumpness, a wise and wiry old lady. He'd pictured Charity as every one of those selves, and loved them all.

Oh, yes, he thought, watching Vance's gang go about the business of breaking up their camp. He loved her, though he hadn't confessed as much to her, even in the scalding heights of their lovemaking. To tell her the truth about what he felt would only make everything harder. Better to pretend he didn't care at all.

Down in camp, Vance and his band of geniuses were saddling up. He and the marshal appeared to be arguing about something, and for a little while it looked as though they might draw on each other. Luke knew that was too much to hope for, however, and waited patiently.

To his mild surprise, the five remaining men rode out, singly and in pairs, headed in a variety of directions. Although there was no love lost between the members of the gang, it didn't figure that they were splitting up now. There had to be a big job ahead; that would explain, at least in part, what had prompted Higgins to turn his back on the law. People usually altered their courses like that for one of a few elementary reasons—money and revenge were the most popular choices. Since Higgins had never had the wild-eyed look of a man with a grudge, Luke concluded that they were planning a robbery. No great surprise there.

There was a bank in Jubilee, but even Vance was likely to know there wasn't much money there. Men like Jonah and Ben Draper kept their funds in more secure places, like San Francisco and Seattle. So, for that matter, did Luke himself. The nearest railroad terminal was seventy-five miles away, and the tracks gave Jubilee a wide berth, so a train robbery was out of the question.

He was still pondering the enigma when he heard a twig snap behind him. Rolling onto his back in the space of an instant, he aimed the .45 dead in the center of the visitor's chest, drew back the hammer, and damn near shot Raoul Montego.

"Shit!" he hissed. "Get down before they see you."

Montego looked intensely Latin for a few moments, but then he overcame his aristocratic pride and dropped to the ground beside Luke, peering through the deep Johnson grass at the scene below. "If you think I'm going to lie here and let you shoot the marshal of Jubilee, Shardlow," he said, in an undertone, "you're crazier than I ever imagined."

"Have you noticed anything about that little gathering down there, Montego?" Luke snapped. "That's my half-brother Vance he's riding with. They've been there all night, chummed up like a couple of hounds on a cold night. Now even *you* ought to be able to work out that something is wrong with that situation!"

Montego squinted. "I hate to admit it, but you're right. They're at each other's throats, but they're up to something."

Luke explained the events of the night before, quickly and in abbreviated form, and finished with, "The other five rode out about a quarter of an hour ago. Separately but together, if you follow me."

"I follow," Raoul answered thoughtfully, watching as Vance and the marshal finally left off bickering and started toward town. "The bank in Jubilee is empty as a parson's cupboard," he went on. He ruminated on that for a spell, then spat a curse. "Son-of-a-bitch. They must be after the gold shipment."

"*What* gold shipment?" If Luke hadn't been counting on Raoul to marry Charity, look after her, and keep her happy, he'd have throttled the answer out of him right then and there.

Vance and Higgins were out of sight now, so Raoul rolled over and sat up, just as if he had all the time in the world. Luke did the same.

"My grandfather and Jonah were planning to buy a piece of land, bordering the northern ends of both the Double B and our ranch. Before you came waltzing in and stole Charity, I mean. The owner is a crafty old codger, and he knows what his place is worth to the penny. There's copper and maybe silver on it, and he knows that, too. He wanted hard cash for the deed, and plenty of it, so Jonah sent to Seattle for gold."

"You might have mentioned that," Luke snapped.

"It was a secret," Raoul shot back. "Even Charity doesn't know."

The transaction didn't show in Jonah's books, either, unless he had another set tucked away somewhere. "How do you figure they found out?" Luke asked, with a toss of his head toward the empty camp.

"Higgins knew all along. He's the marshal."

"Shit," said Luke.

"Your vocabulary leaves something to be desired," Raoul replied.

Luke got to his feet. "Shut up," he said, and strode into the copse of trees where he'd left his horse. "How the hell did you stumble across me, anyway? I took care not to be seen."

Montego smiled, smug as a barn cat dipped in fresh cream. "You're lucky I'm not one of them," he answered, cocking a thumb. "You'd have a hole in the back of your head by now." He paused to relish Luke's discomfiture for a beat or two, then explained. "I was on my way to the Double B to look in on Jonah, and I saw you light out, so I trailed you."

It irritated Luke in no small measure that he'd never so much as guessed anyone was behind him. Hell, the moment he'd spotted Charity hiding in that tree house by the creek, he'd turned fool. He couldn't string two sensible thoughts together and, much as it pained him to acknowledge it, Montego was right. He was lucky he wasn't dead.

He thrust himself to his feet and slapped the

dust off the legs of his pants with a little more fervor than necessary. "What the hell were you doing, paying a call on a sick man before the sun was even up?"

Montego had no shame. "They get up pretty early, around that place, and if Charity's cooking breakfast, it's worth the trip."

It didn't seem right to get defensive about a woman's cooking, especially when he'd all but handed his wife over to this man already, but Luke got irritated just thinking about somebody else drinking coffee she'd brewed. And that was only the beginning of the list. "Well, why don't you just ride on back there, then?" he barked, begrudging every word, striding toward the pinto. "I've got work to do, and I can't be stumbling over you every time I turn around."

"I'll just ride along, if you don't mind," Raoul said. He summoned his own horse, a fine gelding, with a low whistle, and swung up into the saddle. "You could use somebody to cover your ass."

"We're not going to be friends, Montego."

Raoul's grin flashed, and he shrugged.

Luke simmered in silence for a few minutes. "And Vance is mine," he added, at length. "You can have any of the others, but you leave him to me."

Montego didn't say anything, he just saluted.

Jonah's *never* resounded in the dining room, bouncing off the walls like the clapper in some gigantic bell. Charity sprang out of her chair, ready to flee, but her father caught her forearm in one amazingly strong hand and made her sit down again.

"You, Jonah Barnham," Blaise thundered, sweeping across the carpet with all the dignity of a Viking queen, "are too cussed to live. If you weren't an invalid, I swear I'd take a horsewhip to you myself!"

Charity winced at the word 'invalid,' well aware of the effect it would have on Jonah. Blaise might as well have tossed a lighted stick of dynamite into the room. Out of the corner of her eye, she saw her father's face flood with crimson.

He raised himself to his feet, hands planted flat on the tabletop, and glared at Blaise with enough fury to set anybody else back on their heels.

Blaise was undaunted. She stepped in close and shook her finger under Jonah's nose. "You're not going to run me off," she warned. "I *know* you love me, because when you were still sane and rational, you told me so. I've lived under this roof and compromised my reputation just to be near you and *by God* you will marry me, and to hell with your blasted pride!"

Jonah blinked; probably, he had never heard the elegant, ladylike Blaise swear, and Charity couldn't think of another woman, besides herself, who would have dared stand up to him that way. He was an imposing man, strong as a bull ox and dead sure of every opinion he held, and his personality was a power in its own right.

"Sit down," Blaise commanded and, just like

that, she laid her small hands on Jonah's broad shoulders and pressed him into his chair. "You'll have another fit if you don't learn to conquer that temper of yours, and I swear by all that's holy, if you do that to yourself, I'll stay right here in this house and spoon-feed you until the day you die."

Charity swallowed a smile and looked down at her lap, waiting for the roof to fall in.

Jonah tried to speak, found it impossible, more because of his emotions than his medical condition, Charity guessed, and slammed one fist down onto the table with such force that all the crockery rattled. Then, overcome, he lowered his head and wept, his great, broad shoulders trembling with sorrow.

Charity was dumbstruck; she had never seen her father break down before. She pushed back her chair and rose, not knowing whether to leave or stay, while Blaise knelt beside Jonah's wheeled chair, took his knotted fist into her hand and, with infinite tenderness, unfurled the fingers one by one. Then she bent her head and softly kissed Jonah's palm.

"I won't *ever* leave you," she whispered, looking up into his face. Her heart was shining in her eyes like a star drawn too close to earth. "I love you, Jonah Barnham."

Charity turned, her vision blurred by tears of her own, and hurried out, closing the dining room doors softly behind her.

She and Luke had agreed, during the night, that she should stay close to the house for a few days, taking care not to be seen, but she knew it was going to be difficult. There was no foreman on the Double B, since Tillmont was gone, and although most of the hands working the ranch were good men, it bothered her to leave them to their own devices. Jonah had always taken an active role, and she wanted to do the same. Besides, she'd go mad if she didn't stay busy.

The garden was fairly private, so she cut an armload of lush red, yellow and white roses for the house, and the scent of them soothed her a little. She was in the kitchen, standing at the table and arranging the blossoms in a variety of vases, when Blaise came in, her eyes red and swollen.

"Is everything all right?" Charity asked, pausing in her work.

Blaise crossed to the stove and tapped a finger against the coffeepot to see if it was still hot, then got a mug and poured herself a dose. She sighed. "No," she answered. "No, I don't think *anything* is all right. I do believe Jonah would rather be dead than stuck in that chair the way he is. He's sitting in front of the windows in his room right now, staring out at the land as if he could somehow draw it all inside himself, just by looking." She sat at the table, picked up a white rose, and drew in its scent. "But it's not just the illness that's troubling Jonah. It's the guilt."

Here was ground Charity dared not tread upon. If Blaise didn't know about the false funeral and Rianna's flight back to her eastern lover, she wasn't going to be the one to tell her.

"Guilt?" she asked, in what she hoped was an even tone of voice.

Blaise traced the velvety petals of the rose with the tip of one finger. "You needn't pretend," she said gently. "Jonah showed me your mother's letters. I guessed the rest."

"She's dead, you know," Charity said. The statement sounded abrupt, though she hadn't meant it that way.

"Yes," Blaise reflected. "There was a letter from the man she—the man she loved. It was very sad."

Charity had not seen that final epistle, but it didn't matter. Father Elias had told her enough. She thought for a long time before speaking. "I was furious with Papa when I learned what he'd done, and with Mama for choosing that other man over her husband and child. Maybe I will always be a little angry. But I love Luke very much, and what I feel for him makes it easier to understand both Mama's actions and Papa's. He needs you, Blaise, and I hope you meant what you said about never leaving him."

Blaise took a sip of her coffee, and Charity noticed that she held the cup with both hands. "Jonah will recover," she said, her eyes bright. "I'm sure of that now. I mean to stay, but I confess I am afraid he means what he says, that he will never marry me."

"He loves you."

"He loved Rianna. When she left, he buried a big part of himself in her grave, Charity. He was so badly wounded that he's afraid to care deeply for another woman. That's why he's kept me at arm's length all this time. Now he's determined to send me away."

Charity sat down in the chair beside Blaise's, took her hand and squeezed it. "Wait for him, Blaise. He *does* love you, and he's coming to terms with that right now. He probably thinks he isn't a fit husband for you, that he ought to let you go so you can find someone stronger—someone better."

Blaise's eyes filled. "There is no one better!" she cried.

"Then wait," Charity persisted.

For a time, the two women just sat there in companionable silence, each reassuring the other merely by her presence and her sympathy. Then Blaise sniffled, straightened her shoulders and peered into Charity's eyes.

"What about you, darling? You fairly glow, and yet I see a certain sadness in you, too. Is that because of your father, or is there something more?"

Charity bit her lower lip. "Luke is going to leave me," she said. She had never made a more difficult admission.

"What?" Blaise looked genuinely startled. "Has he said that?"

She nodded. "He mentioned it only last night. Our marriage was—well, it was sort of a business arrangement." She blushed, realizing that, in her own way, she'd been as dishonest as Jonah. "Things haven't changed for Luke."

"But they have for you?"

"Yes," she said miserably. "Oh, yes."

"You married him to keep from having to marry Raoul."

"Yes," Charity repeated. "That was my reason, at first. I wanted my birthright, I wanted to help look after the Double B, but Papa wouldn't hear of it. I had to have a husband. He *decreed* that, like some feudal king. I knew Luke was just passing through, and I thought I wouldn't care when he left. I believed I could prove myself before then." She gave a small, bitter laugh. "What a fool I've been. I know nothing about running a ranch like this, and I've given myself, heart and soul, to a man who won't even remember my name six months from now."

"I don't believe that," Blaise insisted. "I've seen the way Luke looks at you."

Charity felt heat surge into her face. "He wants me," she said. "But no more than he'd want any other woman. When he rides out, he won't even look back."

Blaise looked as wretched as Charity felt. She laid one hand to her bosom, fingers splayed, and drew a deep and unsteady breath. "This is dreadful. Suppose—suppose there's a child?"

"I pray there is," Charity answered honestly, busying herself with the flowers again. "Under the circumstances, a baby is the most I can hope for, for I surely will not have a husband for much longer."

In a sidelong glance at Blaise, Charity saw that there were tears slipping down the other woman's cheeks. "And if no baby comes?" she asked, very softly.

"Then I shall be the loneliest woman on the face of the earth," Charity replied. Having finished filling the vases, she chose one for Jonah's room and took herself off in that direction.

Her father was on his terrace, looking just as Blaise had described him earlier—as if he wanted to take the land and the blue skies inside himself somehow, and hold them there forever.

She put the roses on a table near the bed and joined him, leaning back against the rough-hewn rail and folding her arms.

"Somebody tried to kill Luke and me," she announced. She had not intended to tell him so soon, but it was obvious that he needed a little shaking up.

He looked up sharply.

"Luke's half-brother, Vance. He sent Marshal Higgins to fetch me at the cabin—yes, that's right, Marshal Higgins. He told me Luke had been shot, and I believed him. It was a trick, of course—they took me up to the old copper mine, tied my hands and feet, and shut me up in a shack." She showed him one of her wrists as proof, and the look on his face was one of immediate and terrible fury. "They were after Luke, and he came for me, just as they hoped he would. It was Luke's doing, mostly, that they didn't succeed."

Jonah's eyes widened, then narrowed. His coloring was livid one moment, and pale the next. "I—will—kill—them—all," he said. The words were garbled, barely recognizable, but his tone would have made the meaning abundantly clear in any case.

She bent and kissed the top of his head. "Perhaps," she replied. If anybody killed Shardlow, it would be her husband, not her father. Vance's hatred was straightforward enough; he blamed Luke for their father's conviction and subsequent hanging in the territorial prison. Luke was harder to understand; he pursued Vance with a persistence that reminded Charity of a stalking wolf, but if he felt anything for his half-brother, it was cold indifference. "He saved my life, Luke did. At the mine, I mean."

Jonah found her hand, held it. Bent to examine the laceration encircling her wrist like a bracelet. "Be—careful—"

She looked at him. He'd spoken very clearly that time; Blaise was right. He was recovering.

"—of Luke—" he labored to add. He was visibly exhausted by the effort and closed his eyes, his head tilted back.

"Be careful of Luke?" Charity was puzzled.

Jonah looked at her again, his gaze reaching deep. He knew it all, she could see that— how much she loved Luke, how irrevocably she'd given herself to him, mind, body and spirit. His throat worked spasmodically and the cost of speaking was plain agony, etched into the lines his face. "Bounty—hunter—" he said.

341

Charity turned her back in a useless effort to hide her emotions. Luke, a *bounty hunter?* Such men were hardly better than the outlaws they pursued; many were gunslingers, bushwhackers and thieves. They lived by blood and by violence, and they took money for their dirty work.

"No," she whispered. It wasn't the Luke she knew, the slow, patient lover, the mischievous man-boy, the strategist and thinker. But at the same time she accepted the truth of it, admitted to herself that there was another Luke Shardlow who was virtually a stranger to her. A man marked by the brutal circumstances of his childhood and perhaps even given to some of those brutalities himself.

"Let—him—go," Jonah pleaded, in tones made of gravel and grief.

She turned back, her cheeks streaked with tears. "I thought I knew what you went through when Mama left us," she said. "God, how arrogant and presumptuous I was! However did you bear it, feeling like this days and nights and years on end?"

Jonah was a long time recovering from his own private storm of emotion, but finally he wheeled himself up beside her and clasped her hand. The sorrow she saw in his face reflected her own, and she was, in that situation, every bit as helpless as he was. "I—threw away—my life."

Charity knelt beside the chair. "But you have time left," she insisted. "You have Blaise."

"Too late," Jonah said, with a shake of his head.

"We are a miserable pair of proud and stupid fools," Charity lamented, sniffling. She sought a smile inside herself, but could find none. "Blaise loves you, Raoul loves me. Why can't we love them back?" She paused, studying her father's stricken face. "But you do love Blaise, don't you? You adore her. And you're just bullheaded enough to believe you aren't good enough for her."

"I—am—a *cripple!*"

"It's your heart that's crippled, Papa. The state of your health doesn't make any difference to Blaise, at least not in the way you think. Please—let Mama rest in peace, let her be dead. It's time and past that you were healed, on the inside, where it truly matters."

Jonah raised his hands, tremulously and with strenuous effort, and cupped Charity's face in them. "You never—understood." he said.

She was baffled. "What?"

"I would not trade you—for a dozen—sons."

It was the blessing, the birthright, she had yearned for all her life. With a great, choking sob of joy and sorrow, she leaned forward, and let her forehead rest against her father's once-strong shoulder. And as she cried, he stroked her hair.

Presently, when she had recovered herself a little, Charity realized how weary her father was. Although the day wasn't half over, he'd crossed a lot of bridges, and his strength was depleted. She dried her eyes, got to her feet, and wheeled him back inside. Genesis appeared immediately, as if summoned by some form of telepathy, and began the task of helping Jonah into bed.

Charity went back to the terrace and looked out over the land she loved. She'd won a great battle that day, and yet the victory was not entirely a triumph. She was still going to lose Luke and, while it was probably for the best that he would leave soon, knowing who and what he was wouldn't make the parting any easier to bear.

18

$\mathcal{L}$uke supposed he wouldn't have gotten the driver and guards to cooperate if Montego hadn't been with him, but he'd rather have worked alone all the same. As it was, the pair of them had been on the road for three solid days when they finally met up with the gold shipment some sixty miles outside of Jubilee, and they looked and smelled accordingly. The freight men were worse.

It took some doing, even with Montego there to vouch for him, to convince the driver to surrender his place in the wagon box to Luke. Once they'd explained that Vance Shardlow and his gang were lying in wait somewhere along the line, and how there was bound to be shooting even if everything went without a hitch, a prompt agreement was reached.

While traveling in the hope of meeting up with Jonah's gold, Luke had studied the countryside, memorizing every rock pile, hill and bend in the road. He had a good idea where Vance would strike—a place not too far from Jubilee, where the trail wound between two big boulders, left behind like sentries by some ancient glacier—but there were several other possibilities and he gave them equal weight. He couldn't afford to be wrong this time; Vance would kill him for sure if he got the chance. Worse still, Montego might take a bullet, and leave Charity alone in a world that could be a much worse place than she'd ever imagined.

He set his jaw, which bristled and itched with a new beard, and squinted into the blazing crimson and gold sunset. He was getting too old for this kind of life, he reasoned, and if he wasn't damn careful, he wouldn't get any older.

"When do you think they'll show up?" Montego asked.

"It could be at any time," he answered. He could hardly keep his mind on the task at hand, even now. When had it become so bitterly poignant, this yearning to buy land and build a house, stock the place with cattle and good horseflesh, make babies with a warm and willing woman? He sighed. He'd cherished that dream ever since he could remember, in one guise or another, but Charity Barnham hadn't figured into it anywhere, except maybe as a character in a yarn he'd tell when he was an old coot, wanting to make himself out as a hero. He'd once saved a pretty girl from drowning in a fast creek, he might have said. By then, storytelling being what it was, the stream would surely have transformed itself into a torrential river, and he'd have had one broken arm. Maybe a leg, too.

He looked into Montego's grim, sunburned face. "When they hit us," he said, "don't try anything fancy. Just lay low until it's over. Charity's going to need you."

They were standing alone, a dozen yards or so from the wagon, and the other men were making camp and the first watch of the night. "Is she?" Raoul asked. The expression in his eyes was bleak.

"Yes," Luke answered, shifting his gaze back to the horizon. He knew that Montego was in a certain amount of pain himself, and since it wasn't decent to pry or go blundering into private territory, he pretended not to notice. "I'm not going back after I'm through here," he said. "There's a wagon and team and some gear at the homestead. I'd appreciate it if you'd give those things to Father Elias, for the mission. The land is mine, since I paid the back taxes, and I've already signed that over to you and Charity for a wedding gift."

Montego stared at him. "If that doesn't beat hell," he marveled. "We've been riding together for three days, and in all that time you never mentioned any of this. It isn't right, your leaving without even saying good-bye to Charity. She deserves better."

"That's exactly it. She deserves better. My name is Shardlow. I'm a bounty hunter, and my old man was a murdering drunk. The only thing I can give Charity is a fresh chance now, and the best way to do that is to take to the road."

"Where will you go?"

"Does that matter? The point is, I won't be coming back."

"You know," Montego drawled, "I'd like to draw back my fist and knock you into the middle of next week. You married Charity, you bastard. You *slept* with her, and God knows

347

I ought to kill you just for that. But you're not going to leave her wondering what happened to you, I can promise you that. Not if I have to hog-tie you myself and take you back to face her!"

Luke was developing a headache. He rubbed the back of his neck and issued another sigh. "Because you've been halfway decent to me up until now," he said evenly, "I'm going to overlook the implication that you can hog-tie me and take me anyplace. What purpose would it serve, for me to see Charity again? It would only make everything more difficult for her."

"Would it?" Raoul challenged, jabbing at Luke's chest with a forefinger. "It seems to me you're more worried about making things easy for yourself!"

Luke held his temper; he didn't want to mark up Charity's next husband. "Do you think this is easy?" he rasped. "I *love* that woman. I'm never going to draw another breath without feeling the loss of her!"

"Then stay."

"I can't. We've been over that. Now, if you're through giving advice to the lovelorn, Montego, maybe we could get on with our business." With that, he walked around the other man and headed for the campfire, where there was coffee brewing.

Three long days had passed since Luke went away, and Charity had managed to fill them, going over the books with her father and laying plans for the running of the ranch. It was a painstaking process, since Jonah found it so difficult to communicate, and some of their sessions left him sweating and pale, but eventually they worked out a strategy that was acceptable to them both.

The nights were different, slow-moving and dismal. Charity tried to sleep, knowing she would need all her strength for the challenges ahead, but she was wakeful, haunted by the specters of children who would never be born, and dreams that would never come true. She did not weep, for her grief was an arid country, beyond the reach of tears.

On the morning of the fourth day, Father Elias came to call, in the company of a grave young priest he introduced as Father Michael. With them was Peony, who had heard about Genesis and wanted to take back her kitchen, by force if necessary. Father Michael, as the elder priest had predicted, had brought two female missionaries with him, sisters named Colleen and Susan O'Neal.

"Prissy spinsters, that's what they are," Peony scoffed, when she and Charity were in the kitchen, making coffee and assembling plates full of Genesis's cookies to serve to the priests. "Not even nuns."

Peony herself had never married, but Charity saw no virtue in pointing that out. "I'm sure they will be a great help. I'll go over and pay them a call, in a few days." Her voice sounded too cheerful in her own ears, too brittle and earnest. Where was Luke? Was he dead, or had he simply finished the tasks he had set for himself and ridden on to some new place? When he made love to another woman for the first time since they'd parted, would she, Charity, feel the betrayal like an arrow through her heart?

"Humph," scoffed Peony, who never looked beyond people's surfaces, and therefore did not see that Charity had been wounded, perhaps mortally. "Busybodies, those women. Snooty easterners. Like as not, you'll find no welcome with them."

"Nonsense," Charity said. "They've dedicated their lives to the service of others. How can they be anything but fine people?"

"Humph," Peony repeated and Charity gave up.

"You do not look well, child," Father Elias observed, an hour later, when Father Michael was occupied with introducing himself to Jonah. Charity and her friend were in the garden, where there was some shelter from the heat, and the air smelled of roses instead of dust and cow dung. "Perhaps you have overextended yourself, looking after your father with such diligence. Do not forget that there are others here to help."

Charity found a smile, though it took some effort. "It isn't that," she said. "I'm just missing my husband."

Father Elias raised his bushy white eyebrows. "Missing him? But where has he gone?" He looked around, as if Luke might simply have been mislaid somewhere, like a pair of garden shears or a favorite book.

350

"Away," Charity said, in a small voice, averting her gaze. "I don't think he ever meant to stay."

"But my dear, he married you—"

"That was my idea," Charity confessed. She plucked a leaf from the lilac bush, which had long since lost its fragrant purple blossoms, and split it with her thumbnail. "I needed a husband to claim the Double B."

"And what were his reasons for accepting such a bargain? Luke's, I mean?"

"I'm not sure," Charity said. "I thought it was money—I offered him a significant sum for a year of his time—but he's gone away and I really don't expect him to come back."

Father Elias sank onto the stone bench, looking winded. "This is dreadful," he said. "Marriage is a holy sacrament, blessed by God Himself. I cannot believe that either of you would enter into it for such frivolous and unsavory reasons."

Charity sat down beside him. "I love Luke, Father. I think I always have. And the truth is, I don't regret anything except losing him." She paused, drew a breath, and let it out slowly. "I'm never going to see him again. How will I bear that?"

The priest took her hand, patted it in a way that was comforting, if innocuous. "Surely you are overwrought, and your imagination has run away with you—"

"No, Father," she interrupted softly. "I'm tired, yes—we all are. Papa's illness has been grueling for him, and very difficult for the rest

351

of us. But I was a lonely child, and I've lived much of my life in my imagination; I know the terrain. This is something else—intuition, maybe. I knew he planned to leave, he told me so. But until about an hour after he left the house, I believed there was still time to change his mind. Now I know differently."

The priest's reply surprised her. "Perhaps you're right then. Luke has been plagued by various demons for most of his life; I'm sure he's confided in you. It's possible that he needs time away, on his own, to think things through."

Luke had told Charity very little about his past, and she'd had the strong impression that he wasn't one to dwell on matters that couldn't be changed. Now, though, she remembered how Luke had sat up late with Father Elias, every night during the measles epidemic at the mission. Their conversations had been earnest ones, and Charity had been either too tired or too busy to join in.

After a few minutes of reflection, she shook her head. "Luke knows his own mind. He accepts whatever comes to him and handles it in the best way he can, without flinching. No, Father, what Luke thinks of me today is what he will think of me ten, twenty or even fifty years from now."

"Wouldn't he want to say good-bye?" The question was put gently, and Father Elias was still holding her hand. She was grateful for that, because she felt as though she might dissolve.

She bit her lower lip. "I hope so," she answered forlornly. Hopelessly.

She kept watch at her window for most of that night, and there was no sign of Luke.

Vance made his presence known with a flair Luke had to admire; that Bowie knife of his came spiraling out of the sky and stuck with a resounding *thwack* in the seat of the freight wagon, no more than six inches from Luke's right thigh. In the next few seconds, gunfire erupted all around, peppering the ground surrounding the rig and raising puffs of dirt.

There was no place in the wagon bed to take cover; it was full, between Jonah's gold and various stock for the dry-goods store. Having no other choice, Luke dove straight down between the two rear horses and the wagon, catching hold of the under part of the harness and hanging on with both hands. The team was understandably panicked, and he was dragged a hundred yards or so before he managed to slow them down. All the while, he was thinking that he'd been wrong about Vance's choice of ambush sites. They'd been passing a farm, and the shots, like the knife, had come from high up in the branches of the peach trees growing on either side of the road.

When he crawled out from under the wagon, the .45 in one hand, the bullets were still flying, and Vance and his merry men were dropping out of the trees like bird shit. Montego was nowhere in sight, but the two freight guards were on the ground, bleeding and most likely dead.

Luke ran straight toward the center of the

fray, firing as he advanced. He had his eye on Vance, but he shot one of the outlaws in the shoulder and one in the thigh all the same.

Vance turned to face him and suddenly all the guns were still. There was no sound but for the squawking of the farmer's chickens and a few moans from the wounded.

"It *is* you," Vance said. He was holding a .38, with the hammer drawn back, and when he pulled the trigger, the bullet would strike roughly in the center of Luke's liver. "I must say, little brother, I truly hoped you were dead. I guess I'll just have to rectify that disappointment right now."

"Don't try it, Vance," Luke replied. "You aren't fast enough. You know that. Drop the pistol and step away from it."

Vance sighed. "You can't dodge this shot, Luke."

"Neither can you," Luke said. They were facing each other now, with no more than ten feet between them. "There's been a lot of gunplay here, Vance. You sure you've still got bullets in that cylinder?" He knew he had a single shot left in the .45; he always kept count.

The flicker of an eyelash revealed Vance's doubt, but he grinned and raised the pistol, extending his arm and taking careful aim at Luke's head. He looked more like Trigg in that moment than Luke would have thought possible.

"Say you're sorry," Vance said. "For what you did to our pa."

Luke didn't move. "Go to hell," he answered. "There's only one thing I'd do different if I could go back to that day, and that's kill the bastard myself."

"She was only a woman, not worth that much fuss. None of them are, when you get right down to cases."

Luke ground his jaw down, made himself relax a little. "Put the gun down," he said, though he wanted nothing so much as to shoot Vance where he stood. But Vance wasn't Trigg; he had to remember that. "I want to take you in alive if I can. The bounty's the same either way."

"You're not going to take me anywhere, little brother. You're gonna die, right here, just like me. It'll all be over then."

Luke's eyes burned with dust and sweat, and his back was bruised and scraped beneath his shredded shirt. He didn't get a chance to answer, because he could see that there was no more time. The .45 went off, and yet, somehow, he heard the simultaneous click of his half-brother's empty pistol.

A crimson blossom spread across the front of Vance's shirt, and he fell, slowly, gracefully, like a dancer with mush for knees. Luke raised his eyes, saw that two of the freight men, one wounded in the shoulder, the other in the side, were checking the outlaws and their fallen comrades for pulses. Montego came out of Luke's peripheral vision, unharmed.

"It's over, Luke," he said. "Take it easy. It's over."

Luke let out his breath, lowered the .45 to his side, dragged his free arm across his eyes. He felt the sticky moisture then, and knew he had a red streak across his face, like war paint. "How many men did we lose?"

"Just one," Montego answered. "The others will be all right. But you're hurt, Luke. Let's have a look at that arm."

Luke ignored the request and took a stumbling step toward Vance's body. "He knew he was out of ammunition," he said woodenly. "He knew it."

"You had to do what you did. He didn't give you a choice."

Luke knelt beside the man, the brother he'd shot to death, and rolled him onto his back. In death, Vance didn't look like the killer and thief he had been in life. His features had softened strangely; he might have been ten years younger than he was, an innocent ranch hand or a farmer, with a wife and kids waiting for him somewhere. He didn't see Trigg in Vance anymore, he saw himself. He saw the fair and fragile girl who had been Marietta's elder sister, Vance's mother, Luke's own aunt. Alice, her name had been. Marietta had treasured her photograph, kept the likeness hidden from her husband.

His stomach pitched upward into his throat. He turned his head and spat bile into the dirt.

"Luke," Montego insisted, crouching beside him now. "You're bleeding. Come over here and lie down in the grass, and let me fix you up."

Montego's voice seemed to echo inside

Luke's head, and the daylight dissipated into a thick, pounding gloom. The last thing he remembered was falling forward.

It was the pain that awakened him. He realized he was lying on something hard, the floor of that farmhouse, maybe. An old woman smiled down at him, missing a few teeth, and he heard Montego's voice close by, an even droning sound.

"You were hit in the shoulder," the woman said. "You ought to be all right, if you don't get up too soon."

"Raoul." He put enough force behind the name to shout it, but it came out as a raspy whisper.

Montego loomed over him, needing a shave and a bath as badly as before. "Shardlow," he said, with a grin, "You are one ugly-looking son-of-a-bitch."

"There's one missing," Luke said.

"One what?"

Luke closed his eyes for a moment. His mouth felt dry as drought dirt, and it hurt to talk. "Higgins. He wasn't with them."

"I noticed," Montego answered. "My guess is, he's probably dead. He and Vance didn't get on too well, remember? They most likely got into it somewhere along the way."

Luke accepted that, though he would have liked to see Higgins's body for himself. "What the hell am I lying on? A marble slab?"

Montego laughed. "A door, balanced between two chairs. I wouldn't toss around a lot if I were you."

"When was I hit?"

"Somewhere between the wagon seat and the ground, I suppose. I was pretty busy at the time myself. You were already bleeding like a pig when you drew on Vance."

"What about you? Are you all right?"

Montego nodded. "There's nothing wrong with me that a pint of whiskey wouldn't cure. I caught your horse about five miles from here, still running. He has more sense than you do, that gelding. He was headed straight for the Double B."

"Go to hell," Luke said. The anguish he felt, picturing Charity waiting for him, giving up and finally hating him, was worse than the gunshot wound that had torn open his flesh. He took refuge in sleep, the only place of escape.

At dawn, he was on his feet. He was weak as hell, and in more pain than he would have believed he could endure, but it would be infinitely worse to lie there, idle, going over and over the same mental ground.

With help from Montego, who bitched like a fishwife the whole while, he tied Vance's body to the back of a horse, saddled the pinto, and mounted.

"You idiot," Montego complained, looking up at him, "you'll never make it."

Luke touched the brim of his hat. "I guess that isn't your problem, is it? When you and Charity have been married a year or two, make my apologies. I've shown a real lack of manners, I know, but what can you expect? I'm Trigg Shardlow's baby boy."

"That's a bullshit excuse," Montego growled. "And if you have a message for Charity, you'd better deliver it yourself."

"Do you want her or not?"

"You're damn right I want her. You're the fool here, not me."

Luke clamped his back teeth together for a moment. "Take care of her. That's all."

Montego's face contorted with anger, frustration, sorrow. "Get out of here," he said. "You're a coward and I can't abide the sight of you."

Touching his hat brim again, Luke smiled wanly, reined the pinto around and rode out, leading Vance's burdened horse behind him.

Raoul came riding up to the house on a Tuesday morning, a full week after Luke had vanished, and Charity knew without being told that they'd been together. She ran out to the gate, her heart in her throat.

"Where is he?"

Raoul dismounted and tethered his horse to the hitching rail, then came over to her. His eyes were sunken and shadowed, and he'd lost a good deal of weight. He opened the gate and stepped through before answering. "He's gone, Charity."

"Not—not dead?"

He took a gentle hold on her shoulders. "No," he said gruffly. "Luke's alive. He got Vance and the last time I saw him, he was on the way to Seattle to collect the bounty."

Charity had known this was coming, and yet

the reality struck her like a battering ram. She let Raoul hold her up, clasped his leather vest in both hands and hung on. "No," she whispered. "It can't be. We were so happy—"

Raoul kissed her forehead. "I know," he said.

Tears stung her eyes. "Why? Why is he doing this?"

"He's stupid, that's why. And he's stubborn." He paused, then his next words tumbled out. "I want to help you forget him, if you'll let me." He pressed a finger to her mouth when she started to protest. "I know you're not ready, and I'll wait as long as I have to. Now, let me take you inside. You need to sit down."

A small, hysterical bubble of laughter welled up from her throat. She was breaking apart into pieces; how could sitting down help? She was lightheaded, blinded by grief, and she let Raoul lead her into the house because she couldn't have made it on her own.

"Did you hear about Marshal Higgins?" she asked, in a ragged, distracted tone, as Raoul set her in a chair in the main parlor. "They found his body behind the jailhouse— he'd been stabbed to death."

"Vance," Raoul said. When Genesis hovered in the doorway, looking fretful, he spoke to her firmly. "Would you bring some hot tea, please? Miss Barnham isn't feeling very well."

"Mrs. Shardlow," Charity corrected. "My name is Mrs. Luke Shardlow."

Raoul heaved a heavy sigh, but he was patient. He probably *would* wait for her, probably didn't even realize that it wasn't her he loved at all, but Molly, the lady doctor from White Horse Junction. It would be just like Raoul to throw away his chance at real happiness out of some misguided code of honor.

"I love Luke," she said, hoping to spare him. "That will never, ever change."

"Maybe not," Raoul agreed grimly. "We'll see. Tell me, how is Jonah?"

She sniffled. "Better. He's making Blaise's life a living hell, but he can talk if he takes his time, and he's getting less dependent on his wheeled chair, too." Fresh sorrow stabbed through her, sharp as an icicle. Luke glowed golden in her memory, grinning that singular grin as he carried the invalid's chair into the house, his gift to Jonah. "Tell me what happened," she said, with quiet desperation, her eyes following Raoul as he paced along the edge of the hearth. "Tell me everything, and I promise I'll never plague you about it again."

Raoul started to refuse, but then he thrust one hand through his hair and muttered some imprecation under his breath. "All right," he agreed. "It might as well be now as later." With that, he began the tale, starting with the morning Luke left and he, Raoul, had followed him to the outlaws' camp at the mine site. The story was long and involved, but he left nothing out, not even the showdown between Luke and Vance, and the fact that Luke had been shot in the ambush without realizing he was hit. "He got up before sunrise the next morning," he finished. "He was damn near too weak to stand, let alone ride, but he strapped Vance's body onto a horse all the same, and saddled his own. He and I had a few words, and then he left."

Charity nodded and swallowed hard. She was close to tears again. "I thought he loved me," she confessed.

"He does," Raoul replied, and then looked surprised by what he'd said. "But sometimes that doesn't matter, Charity. Luke's bent on getting over what he feels for you, and he's just fool enough to believe he can do that."

After that, they lapsed into an awkward silence. Raoul refused to leave, and presently Genesis served the tea he'd asked her to bring. Charity would have found it comical, his trying to sip from a translucent china cup, if her heart hadn't been broken.

In the weeks and months ahead, Charity would look back on that interview as the one that set the keynote for Raoul's courtship. He didn't seem to care that she was married, or that she loved another man. He came to see her every day, sometimes bringing a gift, sometimes dragging her out to ride with him, or simply to walk in the garden. He told her wild, improbable stories, in an effort to make her laugh. They were seen together at a dozen parties and dances, at his insistence, and Raoul was undaunted by even the most furious refusals. He threatened to carry her out of the house bodily if she didn't keep him company, and she knew he would do it, so she usually capitulated.

In November, Washington Territory became Washington State, and there were many celebrations. The place took on a more distinct identity, now that its borders were clearly defined, and back east new maps rolled off the presses day and night.

At Christmas, when the Double B lay beneath a blanket of pristine snow, a letter arrived from Luke, and Charity's hopes rose when she saw that envelope, with his handwriting on the outside. She let herself dream, just for a few moments, that he was coming back, that he loved her, that he knew somehow that he'd left a part of himself behind. The postmark was smudged, and she couldn't make out from that where he was.

He said he hoped she was well, and that Jonah was recovering. There had been a sizable price on Vance's head, and he'd collected that; a bank draft was enclosed, in case there was anything she needed. He was ready to give up the bounty hunter's life—her breath caught on that line—and he planned to settle down.

Probably in Montana.

Charity had been standing until that moment, but disappointment took the starch out of her knees, and she sat down hard in the nearest chair. She'd slipped into the main parlor when the new foreman brought the mail out from town, to be alone while she read.

She wasn't to worry, he finished, because he'd passed through Mexico in his travels, and secured a divorce; he'd enclosed the decree. He recommended that she marry Raoul, and get on with her life, and he gave no return address.

19

September 1890

It seemed the whole town of Jubilee was decked out for the wedding. There was snow-white bunting on the saloon's second floor balcony, across the facade of the jailhouse, somewhere on every building in between. Bright paper streamers of yellow and green fluttered in the mild afternoon breeze, pinned as they were to lampposts and even hitching rails. The pinto was bothered by the color and motion and started nickering and side-stepping, but a low word reassured him.

There was nobody in sight; even the whores, who usually lined the balcony rail over the saloon when anybody new rode in, were keeping to themselves. The dry-goods store and the livery stable were clearly closed, and the shade was pulled in the glass door panel of the telegraph office. If it hadn't been for the festive decorations, he would have thought there was a funeral planned for that day, rather than a wedding.

He took his watch from an inside pocket and snapped it open, fearing that he'd gotten the time wrong, but it was just 1:00 o'clock. According to the brief notice he'd seen, quite by accident, in a week-old newspaper over in Seattle, the ceremony was scheduled for 2:00 P.M. sharp, in the yard of the Protestant church.

It surprised him a little that she'd be married there, even though she wasn't Catholic, instead of having Father Elias officiate at the mission. The priest was an old man, of course; he might have retired or even passed on.

The sounds of lively music, talk and laughter reached his ears long before he came near the church. He made his way around the outermost edges of the celebration, and drew little notice from the townspeople, ranchers and farmers gathered to witness a marriage. There were relatively few joyous occasions in the lives of country folk, and when one came along, they tended to throw themselves into the merrymaking. Today, they could expect cake and champagne aplenty, and from the tireless exuberance of the fiddlers, a fair bit of dancing, too.

He smiled and took the long way around to the back of the cemetery, leaving the horse at the fence and vaulting over to stride through the tall grass.

There was a pink marble headstone where the wooden cross had been, and the area surrounding the grave was neatly tended. At the base of the marker lay the last roses of summer; yellow ones.

He took off his hat. He'd arranged for the stone himself, after leaving Jubilee, but the flowers might have gotten there on their own, for all he'd known of them. Still, it was no mystery who'd left them. He remembered standing with her here, at the very beginning; she'd brought yellow roses that time, too.

He sighed. If he had any sense, he told himself, he'd just get back on the pinto and ride. Keep on going until he'd outrun the memories, and the feelings, and the dreams. Trouble was, he'd already tried that, and it hadn't worked.

Still, he had no right to be there now, of all times, when he'd been gone for so long. No right at all.

He reflected for a while, there in that peaceful place, then turned and went back to his horse. He'd been half-crazy for thirteen months, and when he'd seen that newspaper piece, he'd covered the breach in the space of a few heartbeats. He'd given up on the idea of ranching and marriage by the time he'd reached Seattle, and planned on heading north, to try his luck in the gold fields. If he hadn't picked up that periodical in a restaurant one morning, while waiting for his bacon and eggs, he'd surely be freezing his ass off in some mining camp by now.

He got as close to the church as he could, without drawing too much notice, and scanned the crowd. He found her unerringly.

She was wearing pale ivory, and there were small flowers wound into her hair. To him, she looked like the queen of some ancient and mystical kingdom, mistress of magic, keeper of secrets. He watched her until she seemed to sense his regard, then turned his attention to Jonah.

He looked hale and hearty, did Jonah. There was no sign of his invalid's chair, and he was shaking hands and talking volubly with everybody who came past. Blaise, standing beside him, beamed with joy, and he reckoned Barnham had finally broken down and married her. It was past time for that.

He looked for Montego, but there was no sign of him anywhere. He checked the pocket watch again, and when he raised his eyes, she was staring at him. He couldn't make out her expression, but from the way she was standing, with her spine straight as a rifle barrel and her chin up high, it was clear enough that she hadn't expected him.

Of course, she wouldn't have.

She took a step toward him and in that instant he lost his head completely. He spurred the pinto forward into a lope, then a gallop. It cleared the picket fence surrounding the churchyard and landed a few feet from a little group of startled guests, who scattered and flapped like chickens with fancy feathers.

The next thing he knew, he was beside her. He leaned down, put his arm around her waist, and pulled her up onto the horse, in front of him. No doubt he would have headed for the hills with her if she hadn't smiled at him.

The sight brought him back to sanity; he felt like an idiot, sitting there in the middle of a wedding party, on the back of a horse that was only slightly dustier and more travel-worn than he was. He needed a shave, his hair was too long, his boots were scuffed, and his black canvas coat had seen uncommon wear. He probably looked like an outlaw.

She stared at him, and he saw a hundred emotions race through her eyes—fury, resistance, love.

"Luke," she whispered. That was all. Just his name. Her eyes were awash, but she was smiling a little.

She was about to send him away, he figured, and he couldn't deny that he deserved just that.

"I love you," he said. And he meant it. God in heaven, he'd never meant anything the way he meant that, and devil take the fact that it was her wedding day. Whether she was glad or sorry to see him, and he still didn't know which, he'd had to tell her. "I've loved you ever since that day you tried to drown the both of us in the creek."

She smiled, touched his lapel with tentative fingers, as though she couldn't quite believe he was there. Her lips moved, but no sound came out.

Luke was in agony, had been for months, but he made himself grin. If she'd fallen in love with Montego, he wasn't going to stand in her way. Nonetheless, he couldn't help putting a question. "What the devil do you mean by getting yourself married to somebody else?"

She laughed. This was going to be worse than he'd ever dreamed.

"Married?" she echoed, as though they were there alone, without the whole town and half the countryside looking on.

"The paper said the Barnham wedding was scheduled for today," he said. "This looks like a wedding, and you look like a bride."

"I'm the bride," a voice announced, from somewhere in the pounding blur that seemed to surround them, man, woman and horse.

Luke turned his head and looked down into Blaise's upturned and glowing face. He felt color surge up his neck, but he figured the grime and beard would hide most of it. He'd arrived too late for a bath and barbering, even though he'd gotten there as fast as he could.

Jonah stepped up beside her, slipped an arm around her waist. Up close, he looked even more spry than he had from a distance, but his smile wasn't all that friendly. He was showing a few too many teeth.

"If this wasn't the happiest day of my life," he said, "I'd take a bullwhip to you."

Blaise elbowed him. "That's enough, Jonah. He's back, that's the important thing."

They faded back into the haze, then, both of them, because Charity had laid her hand to the side of his face. "You are staying, aren't you?"

His throat was tight and dry; he swallowed hard. "If you'll have me."

The glimmer in her eyes was downright saucy. "Oh, I'll have you all right," she said. "But there's a problem. We're not married, remember? You divorced me."

A few loud organ chords sounded within the church. "I thought it was the best thing to do," he said.

"You were wrong," she replied, and placed a light, brief kiss on his mouth. "We'll settle

369

all that later. Right now, there's going to be a wedding, and I'm supposed to stand up for Blaise. I can't do that from the back of a horse."

He let her down, reluctantly, and then dismounted. The boy, Aaron, approached with big-eyed caution and led the pinto away, and the guests came into uncomfortably clear focus, pointing and whispering.

Luke ignored them. Charity wasn't being married that day, and she hadn't sent him packing. It was more than he had a right to expect, and if his ears and the back of his neck were burning a little, he reckoned he deserved it.

Charity left his side, because the ceremony was about to begin, and took her place next to Blaise. A tall man with a cap of freckles on his bald head brought out a Bible and positioned himself under an arbor of late-blooming flowers, the bride and groom before him.

"Dearly beloved," the preacher began, and at those words Jonah turned his head just long enough to glower at Luke, "we are gathered here—"

Luke's collar felt tight, and he tugged at it with one finger.

Aaron had posted himself at Luke's left elbow, and he must have grown a foot in the past year. "My pa says you're a no good polecat," the boy confided, in a cheerful stage whisper.

"He's right," Luke answered, more quietly.

The ceremony continued, came to a close. There were shouts and tears all around as Jonah and Blaise turned to face their family and friends as man and wife. Charity embraced them both, and earnest words were exchanged, then she turned and hurried toward Luke.

She seemed to be walking a few inches off the ground, and her face was as bright as Blaise's. He marveled that he'd lived a day after leaving her, let alone thirteen miserable months. She was as vital as his breath, his heartbeat.

"Come with me," she said and, linking her fingers with his, pulled him toward the shade of a maple tree. The leaves were just beginning to turn, and they made a crisp rustling sound in the breeze.

He squinted, peering into the shadows, and saw Genesis sitting quietly on a wooden bench, talking to a boy about Aaron's age. Beside her was a wheeled apparatus, made of wicker, with a handle at one end and a hood at the other.

He stopped. "My God," he said.

Charity brought him forward with a wrench on his arm. Genesis smiled, collected the boy, and made for the party.

A golden-haired, blue-eyed baby girl lay in the carriage, waving plump hands and feet and laughing up at her stunned father. He reached one faltering hand toward her, remembered that he was dirty, and drew back.

"You didn't tell me," he said to Charity, unable to look away from the wondrous child.

Had there ever been such a baby born, in all of time?

"I didn't know until you'd been gone two or three months," she answered. She'd linked her arm through his, Charity had, not seeming to care about the dried mud and the trail dust. "And maybe I wouldn't have told you even if I had known. A baby is not a fair way to hold a man."

"She's perfect." His eyes were stinging, and he blinked to clear them, but it didn't help much.

"Her name is Marietta. Do you want to hold her?"

"Do I want to hold her?" He wanted to shout, he wanted to ring bells and fire cannons. "Hell, yes, I want to hold her. But look at me."

"I don't think a little dirt will hurt her, Luke." Charity lifted the baby from the carriage and handed her to him, just like that. He had no choice but to accept the squirming, gurgling little form. "See? She already loves you."

Luke didn't trust himself to speak for a few moments, and when he finally tried, he had to clear his throat a couple of times first. "How—how old is she?"

"Nearly five months. She was born in the middle of May."

Luke let his forehead touch the baby's. "No wonder Jonah wants to kill me," he said. "Charity, I didn't know—I didn't even imagine—"

She stopped him. "It's all right," she said.

Very carefully, Luke laid his daughter back in her carriage and tucked the lightweight blanket in around her. She immediately kicked it away, and drew a smile from him.

He turned to face Charity. "Will you marry me?" he asked. "Now? Today?"

"Tonight," she agreed, "at the ranch house. After we've talked and—" she assessed him thoughtfully, "—you've had a hot bath and a shave. We'll send for Father Elias; he's living in your cabin now. And we'll have the whole ranch house to ourselves anyway, after tomorrow, because Papa and Blaise are going to Europe for a long honeymoon. Peony's traveling with them as their maid, and Genesis and her son have a little cottage out behind the big house. Aaron spends most of his time with Frankie anyway."

"You've got it all planned," Luke said, and laughed.

Her wonderful eyes twinkled, and a tendril of her soft, fair hair danced against her cheek. "In detail," she affirmed, leaning forward and whispering. "Now, since these people are busy dancing, drinking and eating cake here, why don't the three of us go home?"

Within five minutes, he'd borrowed a buggy, offered his congratulations to the bride and groom, pumping Jonah's big hand with special vigor, and settled Charity in the rig, with the baby in her lap. The big ranch house looked just the same, but was unusually quiet, since most everybody was at the wedding.

That was fine with Luke. He got down,

took his daughter from Charity, and carried her up the front walk.

"Don't expect to stay on here," he warned, opening the door for her. "I'll have our place built by spring."

Charity didn't argue, for once in her life. "All right," she said.

"I suppose there might be a few acres for sale in these parts."

"I suppose," she agreed. When had she gotten to be so docile?

They started up the stairs. "I didn't see Father Elias at the wedding."

"He's not well. Besides, it was a Protestant marriage."

"What about Montego? I didn't catch sight of him, either."

Charity flashed him a mischievous smile and took the baby, leading the way down the corridor. "He got married six months ago. Last week he finally persuaded Molly to leave her practice long enough to take a trip with him. They're in San Francisco, I think." They entered her room, which had been altered to accommodate a crib and various other baby-related items. He was careful not to glance toward the bed, though he had a sidelong impression of ruffles and lace. "Go and take your bath, Luke. I've got some mothering to do."

"What am I going to put on after I get out of the water?" he asked. He supposed he'd borrow another set of Jonah's old clothes, just until he could get to town and buy a wardrobe of his own.

Her cheeks were pink, and she did not look at him, but busied herself with changing the baby's diaper. "A towel," she replied.

He headed for the fancy bathroom.

Half an hour had passed when he got back, scrubbed and shaved and smelling of some of Jonah's bay rum. He found Charity sitting in a rocking chair next to the window, her bodice open, nursing their child at her breast. The sight was so beautiful, so simple and right, that he was stricken by it, unable to move or speak.

She had heard him, this woman of his, and turned her head. "She's almost asleep," she said, in a drowsy voice. She sighed and tilted her head back, and Luke's gaze followed the long line of her neck from just beneath her chin to her collarbone, the upper rounding of her breast, and the small, downy head that rested there.

"I love you," he said. The words came out sounding hoarse and new.

"I know," Charity replied serenely. "It was yourself you didn't love. That's what really kept you away. Tell me, when did you change your mind? What made you decide that you belonged with me after all?"

He closed the door behind him, conscious that he was naked except for the towel he wore around his middle. "I read that article— all it said was that the Barnham wedding would take place on September 17, at 2:00 P.M. If there were any other names, I honestly didn't see them. I thought you were finally marrying Montego, and I realized I had to stop it if I could." He smiled at the recollection, glad to be where he was instead of where he'd been. "I was in a dining hall in Seattle, and I'd just ordered my breakfast. Before the food got to the table, I was on my way here."

She stroked the sleeping baby's small head with a gentle hand and then modestly closed her bodice. Her voice was soft as she carried little Marietta to the crib and laid her down. "But you must have thought I'd already married Raoul. That was what you said you wanted."

He stood beside her, admiring their daughter. "I didn't know whether you had or not, and as long as that was the case, I could pretend you were waiting." He turned her to face him, touched the damp spot on the front of her elegant dress. "After I saw the article, I couldn't lie to myself anymore."

She took his hand. "Lie down beside me, Luke. Hold me."

He surprised her, as well as himself, by shaking his head. "No," he said. "Not until we're truly married. I didn't do right by you before, and I mean to make up for that."

She pouted prettily. "Does it matter what I want?"

He laughed. "Not in this case," he answered. "Now, Mrs. Shardlow—fetch me some clothes, if you will. If Jonah comes back and catches me like this, there won't be enough left of me to prop up in front of the priest."

She hesitated, then crept out, returning in a few minutes with a fancy suit of clothes, a comb, and a pair of scissors.

"Sit down," she said, gesturing toward the

same chair where she'd sat nursing their baby a little while before. "I like your hair long, but it needs trimming. If we're not going to make love, I might as well occupy myself making you presentable."

He sat. "I've got money saved," he said. "We'll buy some land of our own, build a house, raise cattle and horses." He paused for a smile. "And kids."

She was combing the tangles out of his hair, and he suspected it didn't need to hurt quite as much as it did. "You've got our future all figured out, it seems. Has it occurred to you, Mr. Shardlow, that I might have an opinion or two?"

"More like a hundred of them," he said, and flinched when she yanked out a hank of his hair. "All right. What do you want to do?"

"Just what I have been doing for the last thirteen months—looking after the Double B. We can annex your land to the ranch and build a house on the rise above Jubilee Creek. With you to help us, Papa could spend more time traveling with Blaise and I could have another baby—"

He caught hold of her hand and kissed it. "I like a woman who knows what she wants," he said.

She ran a fingertip along the underside of his jawline, up over his chin, and around the edges of his mouth. "What a happy coincidence," she teased, "that I'm *precisely* that kind of woman."

He cleared his throat. "I'd better get dressed and go find Father Elias," he said, "before I forget that I'm a gentleman."

"I'm not finished with your haircut," Charity said, and went back to snipping. "And since when are you a gentleman?"

"Since I haven't thrown you down on that bed yonder and relearned every part of your body, that's when."

She was silent. He supposed that was an occasion all on its own.

Father Elias arrived wearing his best cassock and a beatific smile. Even priests liked to be proved right, Charity thought happily, as she escorted him into the main parlor.

Blaise was there, fussing with Aaron's collar, and Jonah and Luke were closed away in the study, talking. Once in a while, Jonah's voice rose to something resembling a bellow, though Luke's remained even and calm.

"Such a happy day," Father Elias remarked, after extending his congratulations to Blaise. "Not one wedding, but two!"

"Yes," Blaise answered sweetly, "provided the afternoon's bridegroom does not murder the evening's."

The priest chuckled. "A good talking to won't do that young man any harm. He can be wrongheaded."

"Now there," Blaise said, rolling her eyes at Charity, "is an irony." They all laughed.

Presently, Jonah and Luke came out of the study, both of them looking a little flushed and ruffled.

"What did he say?" Charity took Luke aside to ask. She'd brought Marietta downstairs

378

for the ceremony, and the baby was cooing in Genesis's capable arms.

Luke answered out of the side of his mouth. "He took off a few strips of my hide, then told me if I ever did anything to hurt you or his granddaughter, he'd wear my scalp on his belt for the rest of his life. We drank to the agreement and here we are." He leaned down and kissed her forehead. "Now, let's get married. I don't think I can sustain all this nobility for very much longer."

She laughed, but there were tears in her eyes as she linked her arm through his.

"There's just one thing," Luke said, snapping his fingers.

She looked up at him, sniffled. "What?"

"That wish you promised me, a long time ago. Do you remember?"

She nodded, looking mildly puzzled.

"Well, here's my one wish, Charity," he said. The words were awkward, as though he'd gotten something wedged in his throat. "I want to live with you, love you, and look after you for the rest my life."

The smile that spread across her face was as glorious as sunshine after rain. She made a curtsey. "Your wish is granted," she replied.

Within twenty minutes, they were married, once and for all.

Their lovemaking was slow and tender that night, a sacred reunion, and when they lay still afterward, curled contentedly in each other's arms, Charity voiced the question that had been nibbling at the back of her mind ever since Luke had ridden into the churchyard that afternoon and snatched her up onto his horse like a crusading prince claiming spoils.

"What kept you away?"

He sighed, stroking her hair, which he had carefully let down from its pins almost the instant the bedroom door closed behind them. "My name," he answered, after a long time. "I didn't think it was right to saddle you with that, and all the things that go with it."

"And now?"

"Now I realize that it isn't a man's name that matters. It isn't what Trigg was, it's what *I* am. I'm going to make it mean something fine and good, for your sake and for my own. I want our sons and daughters to wear it with pride."

With one fingertip, she made an idle circle on his belly. "I love you, Luke Shardlow," she said, and she meant it with all her heart. In the long, painful months of their separation, she had learned the true meaning of loving a man.

He rolled onto his side and kissed her in a lingering, lazy way that promised much for the night ahead. "I will admit," he said, "that I am going to be a lot more comfortable with this arrangement after Jonah and Blaise have gone away on their honeymoon."

She slipped both arms around his neck and wriggled against him, delighting in his instant and powerful response. "I don't want you thinking about anything or anyone else in the world right now, but me," she murmured.

380

"Oh, lady," he groaned, "it would be hard to do that." He caught her hands together, at the wrists, and held them high over her head. Her breasts, ultra-sensitive, were arrayed before him like a feast, and she gloried in that, in being a woman, that most spectacular and blessed of all creatures. With a raspy sigh, he fell to her, and nibbled lightly at one nipple.

All the passions he had just satisfied reawakened in Charity; her back arched off the mattress. "Luke," she whispered.

He kissed her all over, from her face to her feet, until she was tossing frantically on the bed. They might have been alone in the world, just as they were alone in that room, for all the thought she gave the matter. When at last he took her, she rose to meet him, her hands roaming wildly from his hair to his shoulders to his hips, trying to take him deeper and deeper into her.

He continued to kiss her while they moved and pitched together, seeking the ecstasy that led them on, farther and farther into the fire and the light.

"Come with me, Charity," he ground out, just before they both shattered from the inside. The force of their pleasure sent them spinning, stole the breath from their lungs, and finally dropped them from the heights. They descended slowly, clinging to each other, making no sound.

They made the same journey several more times that night, and once in the morning, before bathing and hastening into their clothes to join Blaise and Jonah for breakfast downstairs. There was a mountain of trunks and bags in the entryway, and a new surrey was waiting out front to bear the bride and groom away to Spokane, where they would board a train for the east. A separate buckboard was required to convey the luggage.

Jonah looked slightly worried, which wasn't surprising, given the fact that he'd run the Double B single-handedly for most of his adult life, and was now leaving it behind in the care of his daughter and her new husband. He and Blaise would not return until spring.

While Genesis was still clearing the breakfast dishes away, Blaise was out in the yard, supervising the loading of the baggage, which was mostly hers.

"If that's what we're taking," Jonah remarked, "I hate to think what we'll be bringing back."

Charity laughed and stood on tiptoe to kiss his cheek. Baby Marietta was squirming in her arms. "Stop grumbling, Papa, and enjoy your honeymoon trip. There'll be plenty for you to do when you get back."

He smiled, sighed, and then kissed her on the forehead. "You look out for that granddaughter of mine, now," he said, in a gruff voice. "I reckon she'll be walking by the time we come home."

"I'll teach her to say 'granddaddy,'" Charity promised.

Next, Jonah pumped Luke's hand. "Keep an eye on that new foreman," he said. "I'm not quite sure about him yet. Charity picked him out."

Luke nodded gravely, though Charity knew he was fighting back that grin of his. The one that melted women at the knees and irritated men like a persistent itch. "Yes, sir," he said. "I will."

There were more farewells—Blaise wept a little at leaving her son—and finally Mr. and Mrs. Jonah Barnham got into the surrey and drove away, Jonah looking straight ahead, reins in hand, and Blaise waving a handkerchief.

Aaron was standing next to Luke, who reached out and ruffled the boy's hair. The sight made Charity's throat tighten; that gesture conveyed so much about Luke, about the kind of father he would make.

She put an arm around his waist as Aaron turned around and raced off to find Genesis's son. They were planning a day fishing at the creek.

"Do you wish we were taking a trip like that?" Luke asked, looking down into her eyes.

She shook her head. "No," she said. "I've got all I need, right here. All I could ever have asked for or wanted—you, our child, and a part in the running of this ranch."

He leaned down, kissed her, kissed the bright, fuzzy head of the little girl they'd made together. "Let's not stand here burning daylight," he said happily. "We've got work to do."